Still Waters

Still Waters

Russell Westmoreland

rustyswordspublishing

CONTENTS

CONTENTS

Why is a boat referred to as "She"?
She is slim and graceful with beautiful lines
She sits on the water, a picture to behold
When she goes out, she likes a little bit of paint
To make her spick and span
She likes to be well dressed – sails
To do her best
She likes lots of love and care
You can call her what you like
But always remember that she is a "Lady"

Hector Waldo Semaschko (1908 – 1995)

reproduced from a handwritten note

Thursday 18 April 2019 (Day 1)

It was a mother's worst nightmare; a child that should have been home two hours ago. Carla looked at her mobile. It told her what she already knew. She had rung her partner, Vinnie, six times; each time the call went unanswered. The messages she had left became increasingly urgent as her concern grew. She understood she harboured a higher level of anxiety than most people and that Vinnie was the polar opposite; cocky, confident and laid-back.

She resisted the urge to ring again. Deep down, she felt everything was alright and that Vinnie and her 11-year-old son Aiden would walk through the door at any moment and her heart rate would return to normal. She knew too that Vinnie would mock her for worrying over nothing and that she should just relax a bit. Somehow, his casual approach to everything in life increased her anxiety and she wondered if their relationship was sustainable.

Carla and Vinnie had only been together for a year, although they had known each other since primary school. Aiden was a product of her marriage to Shaun Chambers. It had been a generally happy marriage until she pined for something different. Her one night of straying outside the rules had brought the marriage to an end.

After ten minutes, Carla couldn't resist the urge any longer. She rang Vinnie's mobile. Again, it went to voice-mail and she shuddered uncontrollably as she listened to Vinnie's voice, suggesting that she leave a message. She hung up, distressed but now also angry and frustrated. There was no reason why Vinnie should not already be home with Aiden, or at least to have rung her back.

The plan for the afternoon was straight forward. Shaun was to pick Aiden up from school, drop him at Vinnie's shed then Vinnie would bring him home. There'd been some confusion because Vinnie had an afternoon meeting but that had been cleared up. Simply, they should be home.

Enough. I can't stand this any longer.

Holding her mobile in a shaking hand, she stabbed Shaun's number onto the screen.

'Hi, Carla. What can I do for you?' Shaun asked in an impersonal tone. Although they were still on speaking terms since their separation, Shaun showed his hurt every time they spoke and made no effort to hide it when they saw each other face to face. However, right now, Carla was oblivious, consumed by her own emotions.

'Shaun, did you drop Aiden at Vinnie's workshop today?'

'Of course. Why?' He hadn't meant to sound defensive but for some reason, he detected accusation in her voice.

'He's not home yet. I'm really worried, Shaun.'

'Shouldn't you be asking Vinnie?'

Carla burst into tears as she blurted, 'He's not home either and I can't reach him by phone. I've tried him six or seven times and left messages but he's not getting back to me.'

Shaun paused. *Typical bloody Vinnie. The prick is so unreliable and inconsiderate.*

'Well, what do you want me to do about it, Carla?'

'Aren't you worried?' She was exasperated. 'They are over two hours late. Don't you think there's something wrong?'

Shaun thought, *probably not*, but he couldn't be sure. 'Alright,' he said, 'how about I meet you at the shed and we'll sort it out? I'm warning you now, though, if Vinnie's just stuffing around there and hasn't bothered to think about anyone else, I'm going to have a piece of him.'

'Thanks, Shaun. You can have a go after I've had my say. Any chance you can pick me up? My car's playing up and I don't want to go out at night in it.'

Ten minutes later, Shaun stopped outside Carla's house - the one she had once shared with him. He had always believed that the fourteen years they had been married were the best years of his life and he had thought they were for Carla as well, but he had not recognised her need for something different. It still irked him that Vinnie had just strolled into a relationship with Carla after he had worked so hard at it.

He remembered how difficult those early years in Goolwa had been, trying to build his practice, working long hours and studying on weekends. Then there was the business development, trying to encourage local farmers and businessmen to move their loyalty from old Geoff Turner, who had been their accountant for decades in many cases, to a new and unproven young buck. But eventually, he made headway and they gradually switched to his practice. The referrals started an avalanche as more and more people saw that he could give them a modern way of looking after their affairs. When Geoff retired, Shaun had to employ staff and he now had a thriving business of his own.

During those tough years, Carla had suffered two miscarriages. Somehow, they had been able to pull closer together and their love for each other had grown as they shared and fought each adversity. The reward eventually came when Aiden was born. Despite all their efforts after, another pregnancy never came. They discussed IVF and even adoption but, as time went by, they simply basked in the joy of Aiden's upbringing. Until they had separated, they were in complete synchronicity in their parenting philosophies and practice.

Then, that night, that one night.

Shaun realised he was almost strangling the steering wheel as he saw Carla running toward the car. A steady drizzle had now started and he turned on the car's windscreen wipers as Carla got in.

'Let's go', Carla said, her eyes fixed straight ahead.

Shaun drove from the kerb and looked across at her. *God, she was beautiful.* He knew that Vinnie could never love her the way he did, even after "that". Her beauty was not just in her looks – the long dark, wavy hair, brooding brown eyes and lips so full he had never lost the desire to kiss them. For Shaun, more than her looks, it was, well it was just her. And it had always been her that he had wanted, still wanted.

The drive from Carla's house in Goolwa Beach to Vinnie's shed off Liverpool Road was less than five minutes, but to Carla, it seemed an hour.

She was conscious that she hadn't spoken to Shaun the whole journey. It was not that she didn't want to; she simply didn't know what to say.

Her gut was tight with fear and anxiety; she couldn't think of anything other than making sure Aiden was safe. As they approached the shed, she realised that she hadn't been concerned at all for Vinnie's safety, only Aiden's. Was that because Vinnie could always look after himself or because she didn't care for him anywhere near as much as she did for Aiden? She didn't bother to search for the answer.

As they approached the shed, they saw Vinnie's Toyota Hilux parked on the road outside the shed.

'Oh, thank God,' Carla exclaimed, 'they're still here.'

Shaun held his tongue but moments later cautioned her. 'I don't like it. If they are still here, why is the shed in darkness?'

He pulled up next to Vinnie's car and gave it scant attention before striding to the two barn doors at the end of the shed. The doors faced the road and the shed extended, long and thin toward the river. At the other end of the building was a slip used to launch boats directly onto the water. It perfectly suited Vinnie's business, buying and renovating boats for resale.

Carla was already at the doors, tugging on the heavy padlock securing them.

'Let's try the side door,' Shaun offered. As they turned the corner, Carla let out an exasperated sigh. The padlock securing this door was also locked. She tried to peer through the window but it was too smeary to make anything out in the darkness behind it. That only left the double opening doors at the top of the slipway. Carla groped in the darkness at the doors until she found the latch – locked.

'Well, obviously, they are not here.'

Carla shot a filthy look at Shaun and yelled, 'They must be, Shaun. His car is here. I want to look inside.'

'Do you have a key? Look, maybe Vinnie's car broke down and they've walked back.'

Carla was desperate for that to be true. 'But surely he could have rung.'

'Maybe his phone battery is flat.' Shaun was looking for reasons, but privately he was becoming concerned too; not for Vinnie, but Aiden.

'No, Shaun. Something is wrong. I want to look inside. I haven't got a key. We will have to break in.'

Shaun knew that Vinnie would be furious if they broke the latches without good cause. Somehow, he thought wryly, that made it easier to agree to her request.

'Wait at the side door,' he said as he turned back to the car.

Moments later he met her at the door, armed with a torch and a wheel brace.

'Hold this,' he said, handing her the torch. She shone it at the padlock.

Shaun prised the wheel brace into the latch and pulled down hard. Timber splintered as the latch separated from the door and it sprang out toward them.

Shaun gripped the wheel brace and was about to tell Carla to wait while he made sure it was safe, but she surged past him. She waved the torch until she centred it on the master light switch on the side wall.

The overhead lights clicked as they flickered into action, flooding the whole shed in a brilliant white light. Before Carla could turn, Shaun grabbed her and held her tight in his arms.

'Carla, don't. Don't look. Vinnie's ....'

Carla ripped herself from his grip and spun around. She let out an ear-piercing scream as she slid to the floor. Shaun dropped to the ground and held her. He looked at Vinnie Waters' head and upper torso poking from beneath the unbearable weight of the boat he had been working on.

'Aiden, where's Aiden,' Carla shrieked. 'Is he here?'

'Aiden ...Aiden,' Shaun yelled. No response.

He released his hold on Carla and ran to where Vinnie lay. He saw his face was a purple eruption of blood vessels surrounding a twisted mouth.

'You poor bastard,' he muttered as he briefly looked down at Vinnie, then turned and walked away.

He returned to Carla. He helped her stand and supported her as they walked around the shed, pointing the torch into all the hidden spaces; under tarpaulins, behind shelves, in the small office to the side of the shed. They saw Aiden's school bag on the old wooden desk, some of its contents strewn amongst Vinnie's mess of office papers. Carla picked up his lunch box, now empty. A muesli bar wrapper showed that he had eaten the last of its contents while he was at the shed.

She put the lunch box back on the desk and walked over to Shaun who was staring at an old and grimy desktop computer; clearly, office tidiness was not a key priority for Vinnie. Shaun clicked on the mouse, bringing the computer screen to life. They both looked at the game of Minecraft that must have kept Aiden occupied before he disappeared. Otherwise, there was nothing unusual in the office.

'I don't get it,' Shaun said as they walked from the office back into the main shed space. They had looked everywhere except under a 37-foot Tartan yacht with its keel removed, the same boat that had expelled life from Vinnie Waters.

'No, Shaun, you don't think Aiden's under there too, do you?' Carla was screaming as Shaun walked over to the boat. He dropped to his knees and then his stomach in order to be certain that the boy was not also a victim. Aiden was nowhere to be seen. Satisfied, Shaun rolled back out and rose to his knees.

'Thank God,' he said with a weak smile at Carla.

'Where is he, Shaun? Do you think he saw what happened?' Carla sobbed, tears streaming down her cheeks.

'I don't know. I hope not, but I don't know. Maybe he did and he's run off to look for help. Or maybe he's just terrified and in shock.'

'Shaun, we have to call the police. They have to find Aiden.' Her voice was shrill, leading Shaun to put his hands on her shoulders and pull her in close.

'You're right. I'll call Riley,' he whispered into her hair.

2

Thursday18 April 2019 (Day 1)

Riley O'Brien walked through the front door of his small cottage on Liverpool Road. It was no more than a run-down shack when he had bought it two years before but the location had breathtaking views across the lower River Murray to Hindmarsh Island.

At the time, it had seemed like a good idea. He had decided to commit to his hometown for the next few years, at least, and he knew it was highly unlikely the police force hierarchy would ask him to move. They had a problem in getting cops to country regions and his team had become a stable, well-respected presence in the river town. *Why break what wasn't broken?*

At the time, Riley had just been promoted to Senior Sergeant following the solving of the Amy Richards and Kyle Hooper murders. The promotion had come with a modest increase in salary. In reality, he had to credit Callum Johnston with bringing that crime to a solution but as they say, "Luck's a fortune." Indirectly, Callum had also been responsible for Riley's rented house becoming too big for his needs. Soon after the murders were solved, Riley's sister, Sally moved out of his house and in with Callum.

All these changes forced Riley to contemplate his future. His promotion stimulated him to conclude that he needed to plan the "settling down" stage of his life. He was reputedly the most eligible bachelor in town, but at that time he had no desire to strike up a lasting relationship. So, the house was a project. He figured he could renovate it in his own time, without worrying how much mess he had to live in while it all happened.

But things had changed. In two very important ways.

The first was a girl named Kate. An Adelaide girl, she had moved the 85 kilometres to Goolwa to take up a teaching post at the primary school. Unlike the local girls, she had no real interest in Riley at the outset. The pool of eligible men in Adelaide was much bigger and she'd had her share of short-term relationships, just not one that had stuck. So, when she was first introduced to Riley at a mutual friend's party, she was pleasant and friendly, but not awestruck by his good looks and local reputation. She wasn't put off by him, just not immediately attracted.

For Riley, it was different. Kate fascinated him. She was an independent, confident woman who didn't embarrass him the way the local girls did, usually through overbearing flirtation in front of a group of friends.

This was new territory for him and he found himself watching her all night, just a little apprehensive about taking it further. Finally, it was Sally who manoeuvred a conversation between them and tactfully removed herself from the threesome after a short time.

The conversation between Kate and Riley was easy.

The fact that neither was "in the market" relieved any pressure to impress. They found they had common interests in sports, Netflix binge-watching and wining and dining. They were also both keen bushwalkers. At the end of the night, they went their separate ways.

After two weeks, Riley could stand it no longer. He rang his sister, but it was Callum who picked up the phone.

'Hey, Riley, how are you going?'

'Great, Callum. How is that new kayak program that you started up?'

'You know what? I'm glad I am having another go at it. I think I'm made for working with kids who are motivated to do something a bit different.'

Riley smiled as he reflected how different a person Callum had become. Some, maybe most of it, had to do with his relationship with Sally, but Riley also knew the strain the murder investigations had put on Callum. Even when he had come to Goolwa a year or two before the murders, Callum had carried some baggage, falsely accused of having a relationship with a young student named Emma Satchin at Loxton High School.

'Anyway, is Sally around?'

'Sure. She's just come in from putting the bins out. Here she is.'

Sally chirped into the phone, 'Hey, Riley. What's up, big brother?'

'Callum's got you well trained, Sal. Taking the bins out? You never did that when you lived with me.'

'Didn't need to. You always beat me to it. Anyway, you didn't ring to ask me about our rubbish routine. Is something up?'

'No, nothing serious.' Riley's hesitancy made Sally frown with be-musement. 'I was just wondering... you remember that girl at the party, Kate? Do you have her number?'

Sally squealed. 'I knew it. I knew you would hit it off. Leave it with me.'

'Sal, I just want her number. I don't need you to...' Sally didn't let him finish the sentence.

'Too late, bro.' I'm calling her tomorrow to set something up.'

And before he knew it, Sally was gone and he knew he'd lost control.

That had been twelve months ago and the dinner that Sally organised was followed by a sequence of delightful walking, talking, dining and moviegoing engagements. Before they realised what was happening, they were an established couple and Riley's many female admirers moved onto their next target. Yet, for all that, Kate was private when it came to talking about her early life. She had told Riley that she had been estranged from her family for some years but when he tried to draw detail out of her, she shrank into a shell that he found uncharacteristic. He now simply accepted that she was the girl he knew now. The past didn't matter.

So Kate was the first change in Riley's life. The second he found harder to understand, let alone articulate.

The week in 2016 when he had worked on the murders had been the most challenging of his career. He had always maintained that he returned to his home town to serve the community he grew up in and he still believed that. But he also realised now that he was capable of more and he wanted more. That week had made him realise that Goolwa was not likely to present him with the challenges that he craved. His career would be one embroiled in car accidents, neighbourhood disputes and paperwork, not the complexity of a murder investigation. This thought made him feel guilty – who wants to get their job satisfaction from someone else's suffering at the hands of some brutal perpetrator?

That was the part that perplexed him. He was happy, yet unsettled. After buying the house to renovate and entering into a satisfying relationship with a warm, beautiful woman, he should have felt like he had everything he'd wanted. As Paul Smith had once told him, 'Success is getting what you want and wanting what you get.'

He wanted Kate; he wanted the house. Now he wanted more, but could he have it?

His train of thought was broken as he walked into the kitchen.

'Hey, babe.' Kate sprang into his arms and locked her legs around his hips, planting her delicious lips on his. Riley immediately released any thoughts of discontent and set about enjoying the part of his life he knew could not be perfected.

***

They lay in each other's arms, intoxicated by their blissful lovemaking. After a tender kiss, Riley turned toward the window.

'Well, it's dark now. I guess we should think about restoring the calories we've just burnt up.'

'Typical male', Kate laughed, 'always thinking of your stomach. I've got a lasagne all prepared. We just need to re-heat it.'

A fringe benefit, Riley thought. Kate's school day generally finished well before his, meaning that most nights he didn't have to prepare dinner and they then had several hours after dinner to relax and talk. Unless, of course, Kate had a school meeting or he was called out for an urgent matter.

Riley's mobile rang and he had the sudden feeling that tonight it would be the latter. He glanced at the screen as he picked it up.

It was his old school friend, Shaun, so perhaps dinner was safe.

'Shaun. Long time, no speak. How are you?'

Two minutes later, Riley disconnected the call and sat motionless, looking at the screen. A confused and concerned Kate broke his mesmerised expression.

'What's happened, Riley?'

'A friend of mine from way back, Vinnie Waters, has been killed in his boatshed. But it's really strange. Vinnie always seemed bulletproof. I just can't imagine him dead. The other thing is that his partner's eleven-year-old son was supposed to be with him and he's missing. I'm afraid I'm going to have to pass on dinner, sorry.'

'Don't be sorry, Riley. You do what has to be done. I'll keep your dinner for you. And look after yourself. It can't be good when it's someone you know.'

Riley quickly dressed, kissed Kate on his way to the door and tucked his cap under his arm as he hurried to his patrol car.

3

1990

Shaun and Riley were kicking around at the wharf just off the end of the main street. The winter and spring rains had long since gone and the summer sun roasted the town. The only cool places were airconditioned shops and houses and the cold waters of the River Murray. Over the summer holidays, the boys watched the mostly unfamiliar faces of tourists swarming into the town. For the first time they had taken notice of the city girls hanging out at the shops and the beach and walking the streets. Then, as quickly as it had started, the tourists returned to their normal lives and Goolwa took a deep breath. The young folk enjoyed this time of year most, reclaiming possession of their favourite river swimming spots, exploding the calm with an endless chorus of screams, laughter and splashing.

In Goolwa, a town of only two thousand or so, nearly everyone knew everyone. It meant that young kids were always within eyeshot or earshot of one or more of the town do-gooders. To seek real adventure, they sought their own private places – secluded glens on the riverbank, Goolwa Beach or at the wharf.

In a way, Shaun and Riley looked forward to the start of the up-coming school year. This would be their first year at the Victor Harbor High School, and the prospect of joining an influx of kids from other surrounding towns created a sense of expectation and curiosity. The summer lingered - long, dry and hot. Over the break, they exhausted every game they knew or invented and explored every previously un-known place around town. Now they hankered for a change.

They threw their towels on the boardwalk and sat on them in the shade of a building.

'Has your dad given you the big chat yet?' Riley said, knowing Shaun was an only child and that Shaun's mother had walked out on his father a few months earlier.

'What, the "sex" talk, you mean? Yeah, he tried. I wanted to stop him though. He went on so much it got creepy. I told him we got all the information we needed at school. What about your mum and dad?'

Riley laughed.

'No way. My mum wouldn't talk to me about it and Dad would be leaving it to Mum. I reckon I'll learn everything I need to from Adam.'

Adam was Riley's cousin, three years older. He already dated girls and had his shit together, so everyone said. Riley would follow in his shadow, which is not to say that Riley would be less visible, less confident or have his shit together any less. He carried himself with the same self-assuredness as his cousin.

'You shaving yet?' Shaun chewed on a twig he'd picked up as he asked.

'Not yet. Mum's put a razor in the bathroom cupboard for me. She labelled it with my name, for Christ's sake. I got pubes coming around my dick, though. You?'

'Yeah, I guess', Shaun lied quietly. So far, just a solitary wispy hair poked through, but he didn't want to admit it.

Riley was gifted with good emotional intelligence. He'd had a stable, loving upbringing and his parents had always encouraged open discussion in the home. He had grown up confident but empathetic; very good at sports but a team player; smart but not smug. He was popular at school not because he tried to be. He was naturally likeable.

His empathy came to the surface as he sensed Shaun recoil at the discussion of their emerging puberty.

'Can I tell you something, Shaun? You're a good mate.'

Shaun was flattered. He knew that Riley could make friends with almost anyone he wanted while he always felt that he was the kid at the back of the crowd; there but unnoticed. He looked across at Riley, who noticed his puzzled expression.

'Well, I just feel like I'm myself around you. Not like at school - all the jocks strutting around trying to show how good they are. Can you imagine what they've been doing all holidays? They'd all be trying to outdo each other, making out like they are big boys now.' He burst into a sudden bout of belly laughter.

'What?'

'I bet they even held a dick-measuring contest to prove who's the biggest man.'

Shaun joined the laughter as he imagined a congregation of testosterone-loaded teenage boys dropping their pants behind a shed on the town oval. When he regained his composure, he became serious and turned on his side to face Riley, who seemed to be staring at the solitary cloud that hung over Hindmarsh Island on the other side of the river.

'But we talk about shit. Why are we any different?'

Riley smiled with the enigmatic grin he saved for his most profound statements.

'It is different. You know why? We don't need to compare with each other. We don't care who's better; it just is what it is and we accept each other for that. It's easy. And you know what else? That's probably the one thing I'm not looking forward to when we go back to school.'

'What's that?'

'Being expected to be like them instead of just being myself, like I am now.'

'Yeah, I get that.'

Shaun didn't really get it. So, he changed the subject.

'Hey, the Landers are moving out soon.' The Landers were an elderly couple who lived next door to Shaun and his father. After living in the same house for fifty years they'd decided the time had come to move into a retirement village on the other side of town.

'Right. Do you know the people who're moving in?'

'I think there's a kid about our age. He'll be going to our school. And then there are two girls who're going to Goolwa Primary.'

'Right,' was all Riley offered. If Shaun was more aware, he may have wondered if Riley felt slightly apprehensive about the newcomer moving in so close to his friend. Riley jumped to his feet.

'Let's go for a swim.'

The boys shook off their thongs and ran across the hot boards. Riley climbed onto one of the supporting pylons and, with a banshee yell, launched himself into space. He spread his arms in a faux celebration as he crashed side-on into the water, surfacing moments later with a wide grin.

'Shit the water's cold. Come on in.'

Shaun climbed onto the pylon and copied Riley's action. He didn't quite reach the same height in his arc, but nonetheless made an equally meritorious theatre of his entry into the water.

'Aah,' he screamed as he surfaced. 'Bloody hell, my nuts are frozen.'

Riley burst into laughter. 'I believe you.'

The sun still burned with a heat that bent the air, distorting the top of the hill as they pedalled toward town. They had ridden only a few minutes before the icy chill of the river had morphed into an energy-sapping sauna-sweat.

'Let's go get a drink at Jones's deli,' Riley suggested.

Riley and Shaun rode toward the main street, shaded by the giant Norfolk Island pines that towered over them. Along the main street, the broad shop verandas gave them some further respite from the heat but they were still sweating profusely as they parked their bikes against the shop window.

Riley wiped his wet fringe from his face as he walked to the fridge inside. He selected a can of Coke and passed one to Shaun. Mrs Jones, the shopkeeper, also volunteered at the school tuck shop and saw both boys often.

'Hello, boys. Are you enjoying your holidays? High school starts in a couple of weeks.'

"Yep, we're ready, Mrs Jones.' Riley gave one of his most disarming smiles. "We'll miss you though, that's for sure, won't we Shaun?'

'Yeah, we will. Hi, Mrs Jones. Just the Coke thanks.'

'Well, you two will do well, I'm sure. Here's a little gift from me.' With a secretive wink she handed a Hubba Bubba gum to each of the boys. 'Just don't tell Mr Jones.'

'Your secret's safe with us,' Riley responded.

Pushing through the clear plastic curtain on the door, which must have accumulated fingerprints from every kid in town, Shaun nudged Riley.

'You laid that on a bit thick, didn't you?'

'Doesn't hurt, I reckon. Besides, tell me she doesn't appreciate it? Anyway, we got a Hubba Bubba out of it.'

'Yeah, I suppose.'

'Do you want to go to the oval and see what's going on over there?'

The Goolwa Oval was a lush green oasis in the middle of the parched town, meticulously cared for by the groundsman in anticipation of the cricket match next Saturday. Sure enough, there was a group of boys from their year congregated near the entrance.

Riley and Shaun spontaneously broke into unrestrained laughter, remembering their earlier conversation. The leader of the group was Chad Grey, a boy of small build but a big attitude.

'What are you two laughing about?' he asked, out of curiosity rather than hostility.

'Nothin' much,' Riley replied, 'I just said to Shaun, I'm finding it hard to walk with a stiffy.'

'You haven't got one, have you?' Chad asked. 'Oh, don't worry, I don't want to hear. Hey, want to hang out, Riley?'

'Nah. I'll catch you later.'

Riley and Shaun walked on.

'Boy, I'm hot. Let's go back to your place, Shaun.'

'Ok, but our air-conditioner's packed up, so we're still going to be hot. Shall we go to yours?'

Riley and Shaun played on the Nintendo until near dinner time. Riley's mum gave them cordial and biscuits, reminding Shaun how much he missed his own mother.

He got a phone call from her once a week, a rushed conversation that she usually terminated because she said she called STD and the call cost too much because the government didn't care about families trying to stay in touch and she really didn't have lot of money to spare after she paid her rent and city living was so much more expensive than Goolwa, blah, blah, blah. Even though he got annoyed with the consistency of her excuses, he still looked forward to every call.

As he pedalled home, the hot air burning his nostrils, he wondered if she would come back. He was sure it would help his father's moods, though he had been testy even before she left.

As Shaun arrived at the front gate to his house, he saw his father unloading the back of his ute. He owned a plumbing business and the last task of the day before he came inside was to unload the ute. Shaun had no idea what had to come out of it, but the reverse took place each morning when his dad loaded up with stuff for the next day's work.

'You just getting home now?'

'Yes, Dad. Why?'

'Did you remember you were supposed to put our dinner in the oven to heat up? And set the table. And get the washing in. That's all going to be bloody stiff as a board in this heat. Christ, Shaun, can't you do anything without being reminded every five minutes?'

This was an ongoing ritual between the two, especially since Shaun's mother, Karen, left them. Shaun understood he should be doing more to get things organised at home. His father, Glen, left early in the morning, usually around 7.00 when Shaun rose and didn't return home before 6.30 in the evening. The problem was that whatever Shaun did, he always felt that it wasn't good enough for his father. Glen always questioned him on what he learnt at school and then challenged the practicality of what he had learnt. It made Shaun wonder what his father expected from school.

Glen himself had only completed two years at high school before entering an apprenticeship. The need for practical skills remained his measuring stick and he saw no value in academic pursuits that led to a profession. After all, how many doctors, teachers, accountants or lawyers did Goolwa need? He expected Shaun to take over the plumbing business someday so he needn't get highfalutin ideas about going to university or the like.

'Sorry, I'll do it now Dad.' Shaun walked inside, satisfied with his day of freedom but feeling trapped by night.

4

Thursday 18 April 2019 (Day 1)

Riley eased the police car along the narrow lane that led down to the boatshed. There were no street lights here. Generally, no one used the lane at night, other than Vinnie if he was working late. A fine drizzle fell across the windscreen but barely enough to warrant the use of wipers even set on intermittent. A soft moon was mostly hidden behind grey clouds that floated slowly across the night sky.

Vinnie's 4x4 was parked next to the shed and alongside was Shaun's late-model BMW. The accounting business must be doing well, Riley thought. He noted the bright light illuminating through the doorway on the side of the shed, spilling onto the damp grass outside. He could hear the gentle murmuring of the river as it lapped up against the grassy banks on the side of the lane. He capped his head as he walked to the door. Entering the brightness, he immediately noted the splintered latch and heard Carla's sobbing.

'Thank Christ you're here, Riley.' Shaun was sitting next to Carla, his arm around her shoulders.

'Aiden's missing, Riley. We can't find him.' The tremor in Carla's voice told Riley her fear was real.

'Ok, let's start with Vinnie. That is probably going to help us most to find Aiden too. Don't worry, Carla. We will get a search underway and hopefully, we'll track him down very soon.' He hoped he sounded encouraging, although he wasn't sure if he believed it himself yet.

He walked over to where Vinnie lay, the lower half of his body still beneath the boat. He quickly felt for a pulse but the lack of a beat and the coolness of Vinnie's skin told him the worst. He would call for a doctor to confirm death. He glanced at the electric winch and harness used to lift boats. Someone would need to check that over.

'Have you touched anything in here?' Riley looked around quickly before turning to Shaun and Carla, who sat staring at the floor, unresponsive.

'Well?' He raised his voice and glared at Shaun.

'What? No, I mean, yes. We didn't touch anything around him but we were looking for Aiden. We moved some of the tarps and things.'

'And the door?'

'It was locked so I forced it open with a wheel brace.'

Riley thought for a moment. 'All the doors were locked?'

'Yes, that's why I broke in, Riley. You don't think I smash doors up for no reason, do you? What are you going to do about Aiden? Carla's going nuts here and frankly so am I.'

'Sorry, Shaun. Look, I just need to follow a process. At the moment, trying to get some understanding of what's happened here gives us the best chance of finding Aiden.

'I'm going to make a couple of calls and then we'll be in a position to get moving on the search for him. I need you guys to stay right there for now, ok?'

Shaun nodded sullenly and whispered to Carla, 'Are you ok?' She just nodded.

Riley stepped outside. Thankfully, the drizzle had stopped. The air was cool and crisp, with the scent of wet grass filling his nostrils. River birds settling for the night momentarily distracted him, before he composed his thoughts and pulled his phone from his pocket.

He rang Tony Cleaver, the local doctor who police relied on when they needed confirmation of death. Satisfied he would be there shortly, he punched in the next number.

It rang only once, a gruff voice interjecting. 'Smith.'

Detective Inspector Paul Smith had been assigned to the murders in Goolwa three years earlier and he and Riley had developed a mutual respect during that investigation. Smith's sometimes abrasive personality was balanced by an ability to bring out the best in people, no more so than Riley and his Sergeant, Rachel Cross.

They had both stayed in touch with him since that time and enjoyed telling each other anecdotes from their most recent conversations.

'Sir, it's Senior Sergeant Riley O'Brien here from Goolwa.'

'I know who it bloody is, Riley. We talk almost weekly and I've got your number in my contacts.'

'Sorry, sir, it's just that you answered....'

'I know. I always answer "Smith." Now, what do you want? I'm busy.'

Riley was momentarily off-put by Smith's abruptness and wondered whether he had been wise to call him. He could have gone through different channels but he knew Smith would be a good initial sounding board. He figured Smith must be under some pressure. He would normally be very receptive to a call from his favourite understudy.

'Sorry, sir.'

'Stop bloody saying sorry all the time, Riley, and get on with it.'

Riley continued, relaying the discovery of Vinnie Waters' body and the missing child, Aiden. He was partway through explaining the relationship between Shaun, Carla, Aiden and Vinnie when Smith cut him off.

'Ok, so you have a bloke who has had a shitty day and a missing kid. Get on with finding the kid. You can't do anything for the other poor sod.'

'Well, sir, it just doesn't smell right. When Shaun and Carla arrived at the shed, all the doors were locked on the outside and all the windows are locked. How does someone lock himself inside by closing all the padlocks on the outside?'

'If you're sure the kid was there, maybe he freaked out and shot through, locking the door on his way out.'

'Sir, with respect, one of the first things you said to me was not to forget my ABC. Assume nothing, believe nothing, check everything. That's all I want to do. From what I know, Aiden is a pretty shy kid. Freak out, yes, but shoot through, I don't think so.'

'Ok, well still focus on the kid at this stage until you have something more to go on. You need to be composed, Riley, and I know you can be but you're sounding a bit shaken and stirred at the moment.'

'I know, sir.' Riley dragged a sleeve across his forehead.

He was surprised that he was perspiring freely even though the night was cool. 'I'm sure you're right. I've known the victim for a long time and it has probably got to me a little.'

'Jesus, Riley. Not another case where you're personally involved. You know how careful you need to be.'

Riley sighed. "I know, sir. This is different. Vinnie and I were friends once, but that was a long time ago. I really want to check this a bit further and I'd like your help.'

'Well, I'm sorry I can't get down there. I'm just heading out the door now. I've got a two-hour drive to Loxton to look at a drug raid that didn't go as expected. The team didn't find the drugs they were looking for; just a couple of deceased, so now we have a double murder investigation as well as the drug squad all over the place.'

'Sir, obviously I'll secure the site here and get the search started for Aiden. I presume you're suggesting it's too early to call in the major crime squad, but can I at least get forensics down here to have a look?'

'Ok, good start. If you don't find the boy by early morning, I suggest you get the divers on standby. After all, you're right next to a murky, muddy river. I don't want to be the prophet of doom, but you need to consider the possibility he's in there. I'll tell you what. I'll clear the path for a forensic team on my way up to Loxton. Why don't you get young Rachel to get statements from the victim's girlfriend and her ex?'

'Right, thanks, sir. I really appreciate your help.'

Riley looked ruefully at the phone as he terminated the call. The words 'be careful what you asked for' were ringing in his ears.

Only two hours ago he had been frustrated by the lack of serious police work he was exposed to. Now he bore the full brunt of responsibility for getting to the bottom of Vinnie's death and more importantly finding a young boy probably scared out of his wits ... or drowned.

Riley turned around to find Shaun standing next to him.

'Are we going to get started looking for Aiden? Shit, Riley, who knows where he is or what's happened to him. We need to get a team looking for him.'

'I know, Shaun, but look, let's stay calm and do this methodically. Now, I need to get statements from you and Carla but...'

'Fuck the statements, if you're not going to look for Aiden, I bloody well am. I can't believe your lack of urgency,'

'Shaun, please. What I was going to say was that I have to get your statements, but first I want Sergeant Cross to take you and Carla back to your houses. Let's make sure Aiden isn't at one of them, panicking because you're not there. While you're doing that, I'll organise the search team and you can join it if you want as soon as you are done with Rachel. Is that fair enough?'

'Yes, I'm sorry. It's just that he's just a kid and no kid should have to deal with this sort of trauma. We're really worried about him.'

'Of course, you are. It's only natural, especially with what's happened to Vinnie. Listen, let me call Rachel. You need to be looking after Carla right now. Doc Cleaver will be here in a minute and we can get him to have a look at her.'

Shaun trudged back into the shed and emerged a minute later supporting Carla, who was still distraught.

'I think we'll wait in the car, Riley. She doesn't need to be with Vinnie.'

Riley ended his call with Rachel Cross as he saw headlights round the corner, a car turning off Liverpool Road onto the track. He would only have a few minutes with the doctor before he needed to brief Rachel and get the search party activated.

'Nasty business, this.' Tony Cleaver exited the car, an older model Mercedes Benz that had never had the care that its original price tag suggested it should have. The doctor was a tall, rangy man with wispy grey hair and an untidy moustache that extended below his top lip. He was known for his economy with words and strode purposefully past Riley, his medic bag in hand.

As he approached the body, he turned to Riley, pegging his nose.

'Well, he certainly cleared his bowel before he left this world, didn't he?'

Riley hadn't noticed the smell before but now its toxicity forced him to involuntarily cover his mouth with his hand.

The doctor put his bag on the ground and grasped Vinnie's wrist. He felt for a pulse. and adjusted his hold two or three times before bending down to open his bag.

'No pulse. Do we know how long he's been under here?'

'Not precisely, Tony. We know that Shaun Chambers dropped his son here sometime after school finished and before Vinnie was due to take him home. So, it could have been anytime between, say three-thirty and an hour ago, eight pm. Do you have any better idea?'

Tony Cleaver had put his stethoscope to Vinnie's chest and was listening intently.

He frowned and looked at Riley.

'What did you ask? Oh, yes, he's been here a while, going by the temperature of the body. Closer to your earlier time than the later, but not much. I'd say maybe five-thirty, six o'clock. Can we take him out, please?'

'Yes, of course, as long as the lifting equipment still works,' Riley answered. "Actually, let me just take some photos first.'

After using his phone to take photos from various angles, he put on a pair of rubber gloves, found the control for the electric lifter and tentatively tested its functionality

'Can you stand back while I lift the boat, Tony? I don't know how secure this is.'

The doctor watched as the boat slowly rose, gradually exposing the rest of Vinnie's body.

'I'll make sure this doesn't slip, Tony, if you want to pull him out. Don't put yourself under the boat just in case.'

The doctor wrapped his arms around Vinnie's arms and pulled him out a small distance, but found Vinnie's trousers snagged on something under the boat. Anxious to be further away, he applied more strength and tugged violently backwards.

He was surprised by the sudden release of the weight as the snag freed and, unable to keep his balance, he fell back with Vinnie sprawled on top of him.

'Get him off, for Christ's sake. I actually never liked him much alive and certainly don't want to be intimate with him now,' Cleaver pleaded.

Despite the macabre sight in front of him, Riley was unable to suppress a small chuckle. He quickly secured the lifting equipment and rolled Vinnie from an embarrassed doctor.

Cleaver jumped up from the floor and dusted his clothes with a great display of disgust.

'It's not bad enough I'm covered in dust and grime, but I smell like shit, his shit.'

He retrieved his stethoscope, which had flown a couple of metres away, composing himself by the time he returned to Vinnie's prostrate form. The eyes of the dead man were fixed on the roof above, sightless.

Leaning over the body, the doctor noted that the dead man's eyes showed the trauma associated with asphyxiation. The blood vessels looked like they had burst and his neck was covered in a purple-crimson blotch.

Riley leaned over and tried to read the doctor's thoughts.

'Looks pretty typical of mechanical asphyxia,' the doctor said. 'All this petechia on his face and neck is a result of the higher intravascular pressure in the upper part of his body.'

'What about the bruising on his neck?'

The doctor turned, 'Well, it might look like bruising but again it's the result of the pressure, even though it's not actually the site where the pressure was applied. The poor bugger may have initially had a chance; many crush victims do. He may have survived for a while with all this weight on him unless his ribs broke and pierced his lungs. The post-mortem will tell but I would say that he suffered for a time.'

He stood and started packing his stethoscope into his bag. Turning to leave he took a parting glance at the body. An irregularity caught his eye and he kneeled again, examining the man's temple.

'Interesting. Quite a decent knock there. Recent too, looking at the bruising.'

'It couldn't have happened, you know, when the boat fell?'

'God, no. I'd say this happened before he died. Just how that may have played into this, I don't know.'

'Doc, I've been uneasy with this whole episode. I know he's always been so cocksure of himself, but I can't imagine why he wouldn't have put blocks under the boat in case the winch failed. He's surely not that stupid. You don't think it could have been something more sinister?'

'What I will say is that I believe he died from traumatic asphyxia. As to any other aetiology; that is, whether anything else might have happened here, that's not for me to say. That will be up to the coroner. He will be looking for an autopsy, I'd say.'

As Doctor Cleaver drove away, Riley saw the flashing lights of Rachel's police car turn onto the narrow track. The cars slowed as they passed, each moving onto the grass verge to make space.

As Rachel alighted, Shaun got out of his car.

'About bloody time. Can we get going?'

Riley held his palm out to Shaun. "One minute, mate, and you'll be moving.'

He pulled Rachel aside and explained what she needed to do.

'No problems, Riley,' she said, 'As you asked, I've spoken to the local State Emergency Services co-ordinator and he should arrive with a team fairly soon. We also have a couple of officers coming over from Victor Harbor to help as well. What if Shaun wants to join the search?'

'After you've checked their houses, they need to contact his friends' parents in case he's gone to one of their houses. Then, after you have taken their statements, fine, Shaun can join the search. Just keep your eyes open for the boy as well. He could be kilometres away by now. Thanks, Rachel.'

Riley watched as an angry Shaun and a forlorn Carla trudged to the police car. As Rachel drove past him, he caught Shaun's eye for a moment. Angry just moments before, Shaun gave Riley a pleading glance. It reminded him of a time many years before when they were boys faced with a desperate situation – a time when he, Shaun and Vinnie were close friends. It was also when Riley was a rock for Shaun, the person he would rely on in good times and bad.

Although they had not been close for a long time, with Shaun's glance, Riley knew their enduring friendship had not changed and that Shaun was looking for Riley to be there for him again. And Riley would. Except, he suddenly thought, what if Shaun was implicated? Shaun had a motive; Vinnie had taken his wife. Shaun had an opportunity when he dropped Aiden off at the shed. The weapon was there all the time.

Riley stopped himself.

It couldn't be. There was no way, he told himself, that Shaun could get that angry and vengeful. And what about Aiden? There was no way Shaun would have put him at risk. Or to put Carla through this anguish. But...

Riley stood before the assembled group about to undertake the search. Leading the SES volunteers was Brian Thompson, a veteran of thirty years in managing storm damage remediation, bushfire assistance, motor vehicle accidents, and on rare occasions missing persons' searches on land and water. Brian took great pride in his team being part of a highly trained, responsive and effective emergency services agency. Alongside the sea of orange-coated SES volunteers were the two police officers who had arrived from Victor Harbor.

'Right, everyone,' Riley started, 'sorry to interrupt your evening, but I guess you're all used to that.'

There was a murmur of appreciation that Riley had acknowledged their constant call to duty, leaving home at short notice to assist in resolving someone else's emergency.

'We're looking for an eleven-year-old boy, Aiden Chambers, who, as far as we know, was last seen in this shed sometime around four o'clock this afternoon. The man who was looking after him was found deceased in there about an hour ago.'

A man at the back of the group interjected. 'That's Vinnie Waters' shed. Is he dead?'

'Not for release to anyone else at this stage, but yes it was Vinnie. Keep that to yourselves. Back to the boy. We expect that he fled the scene, but we don't know if he saw what happened or not. At this stage, we should expect that he'll be traumatised. We don't know where he would've gone, but we're checking both parents' homes. Some of you may know Shaun and Carla Chambers. They are separated, which is why we have two houses to check.

'At this stage, we should concentrate our search between here and their houses. Shaun's is on Brooking Street, central Goolwa and Carla's is on Underwood Avenue at Goolwa Beach. Do you agree with that approach, Brian?'

The veteran nodded.

'Great. Can you organise your guys? We'll search in the vicinity of the shed. It's got to be isolated until forensics have a poke around tomorrow and it makes sense for us to ensure it's kept secure. Any questions?'

'Do we know what the kid looks like? A photo or description?' The man who called out craned his head around those in the front.

Brian Thompson spun around and stared a stabbing glare at the questioner.

'How many eleven-year-old kids do you think will be out on the streets at nine o'clock at night, Derek? And if you do see any, you ask them their name. That will do it.'

There were stifled chuckles amongst the team.

The men left, a number in the SES truck and a small group on foot.

Riley and the two Victor Harbor officers walked back to the shed.

'What do you want us to do, Riley?' Craig Thompson was a nephew of Brian's, but could not have been more different. Where Brian was seasoned and hard-nosed, Craig was raw and empathetic. He related well to people. It had taken him some time to develop a harder edge as a policeman, but he was coming along nicely. Riley liked and respected him. His colleague was Oliver Townsend. Not from the district, Oliver had a private school background and it was a mystery how he had come to join the force. His father was a well-known ophthalmologist and had certainly foreshadowed a different path for his youngest son. All the privileges in the world had not bestowed on Oliver the grades needed for entry into law, which was his father's vision. Instead, he joined the police force to spite his father – close to law, but not the lucrative side.

Riley took the two men inside.

Oliver gagged at the sight and the smell of the corpse on the floor in front of him.

'Oliver, why don't you check around outside? See if there's any sign of where the boy might have gone, especially by the river. Make sure the doors are secured and taped up to preserve the scene and just keep your eyes open for anything unusual.'

'Like what?' Oliver was already heading toward the door.

'Well, Aiden was dropped here by his father after school. Now, he's not here. His school bag is inside but he may have taken something when he left. I don't know what, but look out for anything that he may have had with him.

'I also want the wheel brace that Shaun used to open the door bagged up properly so it doesn't get contaminated; the same with his torch. You'll find them out there somewhere too. Other than that, just be alert for anything.

'One more thing. I didn't want to say anything in front of the SES guys, but it looks like Vinnie copped a knock on the head before the boat fell on him. We don't know when, how or where, but if you see anything that could have been a weapon for that purpose, I want to know.'

Craig walked closer to the body. 'So, I guess we should look in here for any weapon, as well?'

'Yes, but let's not spoil any evidence for the forensics guys who will be here in the morning. We can have a cursory look, but I really want the site contained as quickly as we can. I just need to make a call and I'll be back.'

Riley walked back to his car, watching Oliver taping across the front doors to the shed. When he was out of earshot, he punched a number into his phone.

'Rachel, hey, where are you now?'

'We're just about to leave Shaun's house. Aiden wasn't there so we are heading to Carla's once they are back in the car.'

'Can they hear you now?'

'No Shaun's just locking up. Why? What's up?'

'I don't know, Rachel. I have this uneasy feeling about this whole thing. Too many unanswered questions. Listen, I just want you to watch for any strange behaviours from Shaun.

'I don't like saying this but there's a chance he could be responsible. At least, I can't dismiss it yet. Also, tell him we'll want to search his house tomorrow. He shouldn't have any objection. Let me know if there's a problem, but I'll join you as soon as I can get clear of here.'

'No worries, boss.'

Riley contemplated calling Paul Smith, mainly for reassurance. In the end, he decided Smith had his own issues. He also reminded himself that Smith's last advice had been to get on with the search for the missing boy.

Instead, he rang Brian Thompson.

'Any update, Brian?'

'Mate, we've only just left and we're being thorough. But no, nothing yet. Goolwa town is tucked away for the night and we've seen no sign of young Aiden.'

'Ok, let me know if anything comes up.'

5

1991

Shaun watched as the moving truck pulled up outside the house next door. He fidgeted as he saw moving men pull furniture from the back of the truck but there was no sign of the family that was moving in. The men started stacking furniture on the front lawn.

Earlier, his father had left the house in another of his dejected moods. Shaun had become accustomed to the wild fluctuations in Glen's behaviour over the past few months. He didn't feel insecure or in danger that his father would become violent but it had become clear that Glen resented Shaun's presence and wanted only to wallow in his own self-pity.

School would recommence next week and Shaun couldn't wait. Riley had gone to Adelaide for the last week of holidays and Shaun had nothing to do all day, other than to wait for his father to return home. After dinner they would sit together, watching television until Glen fell asleep, a half-empty glass of cheap whiskey at his side. Usually, Shaun would turn the television off, go to his bedroom and read for a while before going to sleep. Sometimes his father would still be in the chair when he got up in the morning. He would try to wake him by clattering around in the kitchen but if that didn't work, he would tap his shoulder until he stirred.

Shaun heard voices coming from the front and he raced to the window to see what was happening. He saw a man, must be the father, talking to the truck drivers. To the right was the mother of the family. She was carrying a suitcase, struggling under the weight as she tried to unlock the front door to the house. Two girls, around six and eight, loitered near the car. They didn't seem to be committed to helping with unloading and Shaun could sense a rising tension within the group.

He wondered where the son was. He had heard there was a boy, about his own age, who would be going to the same school. His question was answered when, all of a sudden, a chestnut-haired, stocky lad rounded the corner, pulled along by a massive dog.

'He's had a piss. Did a shit on the neighbour's lawn, too. Reckon they'll be dirty when they step in it,' he laughed.

'Alright, mate,' the man said, 'go and help in the house.'

Shaun watched as the boy walked up the driveway. *Surely, he wasn't his age.* This boy was huge, maybe not in height, but he had a man's body. He was still staring when the boy stopped and turned toward him. The new boy raised his arms as if making to shoot a rifle, took aim and fired off an imaginary shot. He winked at Shaun and ran to the front door.

Embarrassed, Shaun recoiled from the window. He felt stupid. The new kid had made him feel stupid. The new kid was brash, not just the rifle action and the wink, but his whole demeanour. He carried his big body with a swagger, repositioned his long fringe with an exaggerated flick and didn't even look back to see Shaun's reaction to his antic. Shaun didn't go to the window again all day. He was mortified that he might see the kid again or, more correctly, that the kid would see him and find another way to humiliate him.

The moving-in process was finished before Glen got home from work. Dinner was a hastily put-together mix of leftovers. It didn't matter to Shaun. Glen left Shaun to tidy up the dishes while he grabbed a glass and headed to the cabinet to get his whiskey bottle. He was distracted by a knock on the door. It had been a long time since they'd had guests at the house, especially since Karen had left. He expected to be greeted at the door by a salesperson or a Seventh-Day Adventist. Instead, he saw a man, a woman, a couple of cute but shy girls and a teenage boy.

'G'day, mate. The name's Colin Waters. We're your next-door neighbours and I thought we'd better come by and introduce ourselves.'

Before Glen had time to respond, the whole family had started brushing past him. Colin put a couple of long-necked bottles of West End Bitter into his arms.

'Sorry, mate, they're not as cold as they could be. Only just got the fridge up and running, but I figured you'd have a couple of cold ones you could swap them for. Anyway, let me introduce the mob. This is my wife, Marion, daughters Katherine and Amanda and this here's my wife's brother, Vincent.'

'Vinnie,' the boy corrected.

Glen regained his composure. 'Oh, right. Come in and make yourselves at home. Um, my name's Glen and my boy is Shaun. Shaun, come in here,' he called into the kitchen.

'Missus not home then?' Colin asked.

'No, she's not. I'll get some glasses. Sorry, Marion, I don't have a wine to offer you. I can do beer or whiskey.'

'Don't worry, Glen. Beer's fine.'

'Right you are. Shaun, fix up a drink for you kids, will you?'

Shaun walked over to the two young girls who stood behind the protection of their mother's flowing dress.

The mother smiled at Shaun apologetically. 'Sorry, the girls are a bit shy. They'll come out of their shell in time. Maybe a water for them please, Shaun.'

'And I'll have a Coke, if you've got one thanks, Shaun.'

He turned to find Vinnie standing right behind him, smirking and winking in the same way he had earlier in the day.

'Don't worry, I'm already out of my shell,' Vinnie continued. He held his hand to Shaun and pulled it away quickly as Shaun moved to shake it.

'Vinnie, stop being a smart arse. You're a guest in Shaun's house,' Marion rebuked.

'I'll just go and get the drinks.'

Shaun stood in the kitchen next to his father as he poured the beers.

'That kid's giving me the willies. They're a bit weird, if you ask me.'

'You're being hyper-sensitive, Shaun. You need to mature a bit and loosen up around people.'

Over the next couple of days, Colin "dropped by" in the evenings. Marion and the children stayed home, for which Colin repeatedly apologised.

'She's got to clean up after dinner, bathe the girls and get them to bed. Not to worry. You and I can still have a good chat anyway, hey Glen?'

Vinnie also never came with his father but Shaun often heard him in the evenings, skateboarding up and down the street. If he hadn't felt so intimidated by Vinnie, Shaun would probably have joined him but he could tell that Vinnie was pretty skilful and he didn't want to suffer any more ridicule at the hands of the new kid.

Instead, Shaun sat in his room, reading comics or playing his Game Boy while the men talked and drank half a carton of beers. At least Glen was now drinking less whiskey and his mood improved, although Shaun couldn't say if it was because he was drinking less or because he had a companion to replace his runaway wife.

One night, Shaun was listening in on the conversation between the two. He had wondered what Vinnie's story was; why he didn't live with his parents. Colin explained to Glen that Marion and Vinnie had both been born in Yankalilla. Marion had been an only child until her late teens when Vinnie came along as a surprise baby. Their parents were in their early fifties by then and had trouble with the newborn right up to his early toddler years. Eventually, they decided they were too old to bring up a child who was so headstrong and as Marion had now married and moved out, perhaps she could look after him for a bit. The temporary arrangement had been in place for ten years so far and there seemed no indication that it was going to change. Colin said he didn't particularly like Vinnie – the boy was headstrong even for the young married couple – but he adored Marion and wasn't going to upset her by forcing the issue.

The disclosure made Shaun feel sorry for Vinnie. With his own mother gone, he had a sense of what it was like for a parent not to want you. He tried to imagine what it would be like with neither parent wanting you. It struck him that, given the choice, Glen probably would have been happy not to have the responsibility of bringing up his son alone. Ironically, Shaun realised, Glen was most likely upset because he didn't get in first and leave Shaun with his mother.

He also realised that maybe he and Vinnie weren't that different and maybe Vinnie's behaviour was a result of his abandonment. He decided he'd give the kid another chance.

He didn't have to wait long. The following day, Vinnie knocked on the door of Shaun's house. Shaun opened up to see Vinnie looking back sheepishly at him.

'I hit my ball over the fence. Alright if I go get it?'

'I guess.' Shaun led him through the house and out the back door.

Vinnie found his ball way under a lemon tree, crawling on his belly to avoid a spike from the painful thorns poking from the lower branches. He flicked the ball out and started worming his way out from under the tree. Almost out, he lifted his head too early and felt a jab in the top of his head.

'Holy shit,' he screamed.

He pulled himself out to face Shaun, who was holding his hand over his mouth in an attempt to suppress laughter.

'What's so funny, Shaun? That fucking tree hurt. If you're not careful, I'll cut it down.'

Shaun could control himself no longer and burst into a full belly laugh. Vinnie stared at him momentarily before joining in.

'I guess that sounded pretty stupid.'

'Yeah, it did. Hey, do you want a coke or something?'

The two went inside. Shaun grabbed a couple of cans from the fridge and handed one to Vinnie. They went out and sat on the lawn under the shade of a gum tree. Shaun was still intimidated by Vinnie and looked him over as discreetly as he could, trying to assess how old he must be.

Surely, he was a couple of years older than him. He could see armpit hair through the arm holes of his singlet top and he was sure he could see chest hairs poking out the top. On top of that was his physical presence. He was probably only a couple of inches taller than Shaun but his body was like that of a man. The tops of his hairy legs were like tree trunks and his chest was full, not bony and weedy like other kids Shaun knew.

Vinnie had been watching Shaun watch him but he wasn't at all fazed by it. In fact, he relished the attention.

'I'm big for my age, aren't I? I always have been, but I'm not fat, just big.'

'How old are you?' Shaun had to know.

Vinnie was nonchalant. 'Thirteen last month. You?'

Shaun gaped. He was speechless.

'What? Don't you want to tell me?' Vinnie spat.

'Er, sorry, I, er, thought you would be older. I was thirteen in October. You're so much bigger than anyone I know.'

'Yeah, well, I know. I can't help it but it does have its advantages, getting started early, if you know what I mean.'

'No, I don't. Do you mean like with sport and things?'

Vinnie rolled onto his back and stared into the branches above.

'Nah, I don't go for sport much. I'm talking about with girls. Girls like boys that are well-developed. They expect it everywhere.' He shot another wink at Shaun. He could see that he'd lost him. He continued.

'Look. Girls mature earlier than boys, right? That's why they go for older boys. But if you're in their class at school but you look and act like an older boy, you have a head start. Get it?'

Shaun was perplexed. Yes, he'd started thinking about girls and knew that soon it would lead to deeper, more complex thoughts, but right now he felt like it was another world. He stared at Vinnie, frowning.

'But are you, like, ready for all that? You know, are you thinking about sex and that?'

'All the time. I get boners every day. But I'm not a virgin so I know what to do.'

'You what?' Shaun was embarrassed and curious. He was struggling to keep his mouth shut.

'About six months ago, my parents got this babysitter in, for me and the girls. Anyway, as soon as the girls are in bed, the babysitter, she was about seventeen or so, asks me how much I know about sex. I knew nothing but I made out I did, so we started kissing. She worked out pretty quick that I hadn't done it before so she said she'd show me.'

'And she did?'

'Yeah.' He rolled back onto his side and faced Shaun. 'It was cool.'

Shaun was speechless and had no idea where to take the conversation. He had so many questions but at the same time, he felt naïve and inferior. This kid, who was nearly two months younger than him, was so much older in so many ways.

His discomfort was broken by the sound of the back door closing. He saw his father rubbing his head as he walked toward them.

'G'day, Dad,' he called.

'Hi, Shaun. Vinnie. Good to see you boys hanging out together.' His voice was laced with anxiety, the tone flat and expressionless. 'Vinnie, I wonder if you'd mind heading home now. I've got something I need to talk to Shaun about.'

Vinnie sprang to his feet. 'No problem, Mr. Chambers.' He flashed Glen a smile and patted Shaun on the back as he passed him. He whistled as he walked toward the house, tossing his ball in the air. On the third throw, he dropped the ball.

'Bitch,' he muttered.

'He's a character.' Glen's voice was still flat and his eyes were firmly fixed on the ground in front of him. Shaun sensed something was wrong.

'What's up, Dad?'

'It's your mother, son. She's been killed in a car accident.'

6

Thursday 18 April 2019 (Day 1)

By the time Riley left the boat shed at almost ten, the wind had sprung up and the temperature had dropped a few degrees.

He drove back to the station satisfied that the crime site was secure but equally concerned about the welfare of Aiden. Despite his worst fears, he hoped the eleven-year-old was in hiding somewhere safe and sheltered. The main street was deserted as he had expected. The lights in the town's two hotels were still on but he guessed it would be only the staff cleaning up.

He stopped at the Corio Hotel first and rapped on the front door.

It took two minutes to establish that Vinnie's death and Aiden's disappearance were already well known to the hotel's patrons.

A loose tongue among one of the volunteers would have been all that was needed. On the positive side, it meant that all the patrons departing from the hotel would have had their eyes open for Aiden. The Goolwa Hotel was the same.

There had been no sightings of Aiden, but everyone knew he was missing.

Parking his car behind the Goolwa Police Station, Riley called Brian Thompson one more time, knowing that he would have already heard if there had been any new developments.

'Hi, Riley.' He sounded more upbeat than Riley thought he would have. 'Nothing yet mate, but we'll keep working the streets for a bit longer. I'm thinking I'll give the blokes another hour and then we'll call it a night if that's ok with you. Then we can be fresh again in the morning if we're needed.'

Riley wiped his brow, out of increasing frustration rather than due to sweat.

'Yes, I think that makes sense. Maybe he's holed up somewhere by now because of the weather. If that's the case, hopefully, he'll come out again in the morning. That is, if he's not in the river, God forbid.'

'I know,' the SES man said softly. 'Let's hope we don't need to go down that path. I'll call you if anything comes up.'

'Thanks, Brian. Talk later.'

The police station was small, sited on a corner near the end of the main street, but still close to the town centre. Riley walked through the door, greeted by Constable Phil Reid.

'Rachel's in the interview room with Shaun and Carla. It's good you're here, they are starting to get a bit antsy.'

'Well, it's going to get more antsy for them before it gets better, I'm afraid. Listen, can you just get Rachel to pop out to give me an update? I want to hear from her before I front Shaun.'

Rachel joined Riley in the staff room.

'Well, this has been interesting,' she said. 'These two have been at each other since we left you. We went to their houses, but no sign of Aiden there. I had a good look around and I'm convinced he hasn't returned to either of their houses.'

'So, how did they go when you were looking around?'

'Well, obviously they were keen to find him. They both looked around pretty thoroughly and called out for him. They seem genuine. Do you think it's possible Shaun didn't go to the boatshed at all and that's why Aiden's not there? Although, the way the blame's being bandied around, I can't believe it's anything other than what they've said.'

Riley smiled at her. 'I'm glad you were attentive to that. After all, we only have Shaun's word that he took Aiden to the boat shed and, of course, the fact that Aiden's school bag is there. I guess he could have planted it there and still taken Aiden. So, what was the conversation between them like?'

'Well, Shaun has no time for Vinnie. I suppose that's only natural when he'd lost his wife to him.'

'Yeah, and Vinnie and Shaun go back a lot further than that too.' He reflected quickly on their years of adolescing together and the water that had flowed under the bridge since. 'You said there had been some blaming between them. Tell me about that.'

'I guess much of it just reflected their anxiety.' Rachel paused as she tucked her shirt into her pants. 'But, when their son is missing, you would think they would try to pull together. Carla persisted with Shaun asking him if he was sure he had taken Aiden to Vinnie's and he kept on at Carla about how irresponsible Vinnie has always been.'

'I guess he has a bit of history to draw on. How did they seem about Vinnie's death? Was Carla upset?'

'I don't know, I think she was mainly concerned about Aiden. I get the feeling she might have seen Vinnie as a temporary thing and not a long-term relationship. As for Shaun, I wouldn't say he's happy Vinnie's dead, but he's certainly not shedding too many tears over him.'

'Ok, time to have a chat with them. I think we'll do it with them together to start and we can separate them after if we need. Before we go in, they haven't disturbed too much at their homes, have they? We may want forensics to have a look tomorrow.'

Rachel paused at the door, tugging on Riley's sleeve.

'Riley, are you thinking Vinnie's death was more than an accident? If not, shouldn't we be out with the search team?'

'The search team is almost finished what they can do tonight. We'll start again in the morning. As for Vinnie, I don't know, but I just feel like something's not quite right. Why, or how, did all the doors to the shed get bolted from the outside if Vinnie's dead inside? Also, Doc Cleaver noticed some bruising to Vinnie's head. It may be unrelated but maybe not.'

As soon as the door opened, Shaun leapt to his feet.

His tie, which had earlier been as neatly tied as if he was at work, was now loosened and pulled down. The top button of his shirt was open and his hair dishevelled from constantly running his fingers through it.

'Riley, we can't sit here much longer. Carla is a mess, can't you see?'

'Shut up, Shaun.' Carla's voice was calm and firm.

Disposable coffee cups and shredded tissues lay on the table in front of her. She was wringing another tissue as Riley sat opposite.

'Listen,' he said gently, 'I know this is hard on you, but please help us to help you and that will give us the best chance of finding Aiden. The search crew is packing up now and I know I said you could join them once we were done here, but to be honest, there's not really anywhere else to look until morning. It's a rough night out there, so I'm hopeful that, one way or another, Aiden is under cover.'

'What do you mean, one way or another,' Carla asked.

Shaun stood glowering in the corner of the room.

'Well, to be frank, we don't know whether he left the boat shed by himself or with someone else. Either way, let's hope he, or they, won't be out in this weather.'

'What makes you think it could be "they"?' Shaun stood over the table hands planted firmly on the edges. Riley saw anger in his glistening eyes and softened his tone further.

'Shaun, I'm not prepared to speculate based on what we do or don't know right now. At the same time, I'm not going to eliminate any possibility. I can assure you we will be doing all we can to find your son.'

'Just tell me he's going to be alright,' Shaun begged.

Rachel looked at Riley. She knew that with the long association between Riley and Shaun, their future friendship could be determined by the response to Shaun's plea. It was time for her to break the circuit.

'Shaun, Carla. At the moment, there's so much we don't know. We all hope he will turn up fine and healthy in the morning, but we don't want to be complacent about this resolving itself. So, it's really important that you work together with us. We are going to have to go over some things that will seem irrelevant and unnecessary to you, but believe me, every bit of information will be important.'

Riley saw acceptance in both their eyes. Rachel had handled this better than he could ever have hoped. He made a mental note to thank her later. It was time for the formal interview to start.

'Can we start with how the day started, Carla? Right from the beginning.'

Carla wiped her eyes with the shredded tissue as she composed herself.

'It was a normal morning. Vinnie had stayed over.' A grunt from Shaun. Carla continued, 'He got up and had his shower, while I went into the kitchen and made breakfast. I went and woke Aiden and we all sat and ate together. Then Aiden went and got dressed and brushed his teeth, Vinnie took a phone call and I packed up. Then they left. Vinnie dropped Aiden to school and then went to work.'

'So, nothing out of the ordinary, then?'

'The whole situation is out of the ordinary,' Shaun interjected. 'He shouldn't be in that house.'

'You left, remember!' Carla fired back.

'All right, you two. This isn't helping. So, that phone call Vinnie took. Is that normal early in the morning? Who was it?'

'He gets calls at night sometimes and obviously through the day at work. I don't know who the call was from. He took it in the other room and just came back saying he had to meet someone later in the day. He wanted to change the arrangement with looking after Aiden because of the meeting but that didn't work out.'

Riley checked that Rachel was making a note to check Vinnie's phone records. He didn't want any details overlooked.

'Ok, so that was the morning and as far as you know, Aiden was at school all day and Vinnie was at work, just like any other day.' Carla nodded.

Riley turned to Shaun.

'Tell me about your day, Shaun, right up to when you went to pick Aiden up from school.'

'Nothing unusual. I went into the office, worked on tax returns and had a couple of meetings with clients. Then I left the office at three and drove to the school. I gathered his schoolbag from the rack then waited outside his classroom until the siren went.'

'How was he?'

'He was fine, chirpy in fact. He was going on about how Vinnie was going to let him play Minecraft on his computer. I wasn't happy about that but he wouldn't have known.'

'Why weren't you happy?'

'He spends too much time playing computer games. I'd rather see him doing more active things outside.'

'At the boatshed?' Riley quizzed. Shaun looked down at the desk.

'Ok,' Riley continued, 'what happened when you got to the boatshed?'

'Nothing happened, that's what. I went in with Aiden, got him settled. Vinnie set up Minecraft in the office and I chided him about trying to change arrangements at the last minute. Typical, unreliable Vinnie.'

'Nothing more than that?'

'No. What are you suggesting, Riley?'

'Nothing, Shaun, just asking. Did you close the door on your way out? Lock it maybe?'

'I closed it, but I didn't lock it.'

'What did you do after you left?'

'I had meetings until six, which I'm sure you can substantiate.'

Riley took the details of the people Shaun said he'd met with. He checked his watch. 11.10.

'Ok, it's getting late and we'll need an early start tomorrow. Before we break for the night, Rachel and I want to ask you both some questions about Vinnie's and Aiden's movements, moods and so on over the last few days. We're going to separate you to do this because we want to get a perspective from each of you without influence from the other. Understand?' He looked at them both and was rewarded with blank nods.

'After we've been through that, we'll have someone drive you both home.'

'Can't you take me back to my car?' asked Shaun.

'Sorry, mate, we might want forensics to look it over.'

'What? Oh, never mind, let's just get this done.'

Rachel escorted Carla to a separate interview room.

An hour later, she joined Riley to debrief.

Carla had been forthcoming, explaining her relationship with Vinnie as one that was casual rather than committed, sexual rather than loving and convenient rather than invested. However, they got on well and largely allowed each other space to live their own lives as they wanted.

Vinnie was good with Aiden and had never shown any malice toward him.

Carla felt that Aiden was generally coping well with her separation from Shaun. His grades at school were good and he seemed to be happy most of the time with a solid circle of friends that he discussed openly with her. He had asked Carla on a regular basis whether she and Shaun would get back together but seemed accepting when she explained that there was a lot of tension between them and that it was hard to say if they could ever resolve it. She hadn't explained to Aiden the reason for the marriage break-up and didn't think she needed to.

When asked how Aiden was with his father, Carla was reticent. She told Rachel that Aiden didn't discuss his time with Shaun too much.

It was like he wanted to keep that side of his life more private and she hadn't pressed him on it, but Carla felt sure that Shaun wasn't holding back on his criticism of her and Vinnie.

Riley had a more difficult conversation with Shaun.

The two had gone back many years. They had both experienced highs and lows in life, Shaun more than Riley. Vinnie had grown up with them as well which meant that there was a history that impacted on each man's view of the others.

Shaun's breakup with Carla had destroyed a friendship as well as a marriage and Shaun's bitterness was evident in every word he uttered about Vinnie. He shed no tears for Vinnie; Riley thought the unspoken truth was that Shaun was glad he was gone and that he may have a chance to reconcile with Carla. That truth was unspoken now, but only because Shaun was distraught over Aiden's disappearance.

The dilemma for Riley was that in this case, Shaun possessed two of the critical elements that made him a prime suspect of a murder – motive and opportunity. That couldn't be true if this was just some terrible accident. But Riley did not accept the theory that Vinnie died by accident –

the locked doors, the lack of evidence of equipment failure, the bump to Vinnie's head and Aiden's disappearance all told him there was a more sinister reason for Vinnie's death. It would be easy to focus on Shaun as the key suspect, except for one thing – why would Shaun hide Aiden?

Riley shared his musings with Rachel and they came up with some possible explanations. Perhaps Aiden had seen Shaun murder Vinnie and Shaun was concealing him to avoid him revealing it to the police or perhaps Aiden had run off in fright. Out of left field, Rachel asked whether Shaun could have killed Vinnie and then Aiden to spite Carla.

Rachel urged Riley not to discount that possibility.

'Rachel, I won't,' he had said, 'but I'm not buying it either. He loved that little boy and no matter how much he hated Vinnie and maybe even Carla, I don't believe he would have laid a finger on Aiden. I'm sure we will find his alibi stands up.'

It was after one in the morning when they ran out of energy.

Riley had received a message from Paul Smith advising that the forensic team would be on-site at eight in the morning and Riley wanted to get the search resumed before then. He also had to explore the need to call in divers to search the river if Aiden wasn't located soon.

The two left the Police Station and arranged to meet again at seven.

When he got home, Riley opened the door silently, trying hard not to wake Kate. He needn't have worried; she was still up watching television.

'You shouldn't have stayed up,' he said. 'You've got work in the morning.'

'And so do you, I bet. I was worried about you, with it being an old friend and now it's so late. Can I get you a drink?'

'Yes, please. A double Scotch on ice. I don't like the look of it. His death looks like an accident but there are a few pointers that make me wonder if it could be more sinister. It doesn't look like I'm going to get a lot of outside resources with the investigation other than the forensic team so I really hope I'm not going to be out of my depth.'

Kate returned with two generous glasses. 'Well, I have every confidence in you, sweetheart. What about the missing boy?'

'No sign yet. The search party's been out but they haven't found any trace. We'll start again in the morning and I hope we find him quickly or this could get very ugly.'

Riley drained the glass with a final deep swallow clenching his teeth as the Scotch bit and warmed.

'We should get some sleep. I've got an early start.'

Kate rubbed his arm. 'I put your dinner in the fridge. I didn't think you'd want it this late.'

'Oh, I'm sorry, Kate. And the evening started so normally.'

7

1991

Shaun missed the first week of the new school year. His mother's funeral was on the Wednesday and his father didn't push him to return to school for the rest of the week.

The service was held at the funeral chapel and they buried her in the Currency Creek Cemetery. Shaun wondered why his father didn't choose cremation but supposed it was because he wanted a grave to visit. He had decided he wouldn't ever go to the grave after the burial. What was the point? She had left him so how could he get any comfort from visiting a body cold in the ground that had been so cold above ground?

Only a few people had attended; his mother's boss, although Shaun couldn't help but wonder if he was more than a boss; her sisters, Janet and Helen from Strathalbyn, and their old neighbours, the Landers. To Shaun's gratitude, Riley came with his mother.

The boss man left straight after the burial. He didn't approach Glen during the whole service, which Shaun thought was odd but, then, he wasn't really sure about funeral protocols. His aunties came and talked to him for a few minutes, expressing their sympathies and assuring him that his mother loved him dearly while, all the time, sobbing into their handkerchiefs. Shaun really just wanted the whole thing over and had trouble engaging in conversation with them. He knew they meant well but at the same time, he wondered if he would ever see them again now that his mother was gone.

Finally, they bid their farewells. Glen was in deep conversation with the Landers and the aunties gave him barely a glance before walking to Janet's Mercedes in the car park. Shaun looked around and saw Riley walking toward him. His mother stood nearby under the shade of a big leafy tree.

Riley put a hand on his shoulder.

'I'm really sorry, Shaun. I wish I'd been here for you last week.'

'Thanks. It's ok; not much you could have done really.'

'How did it happen? I mean, sorry, I don't mean to … oh, fuck, forget I asked.'

Shaun laughed nervously.

'Don't worry about it. I don't know how this stuff goes either. Anyway, Dad tells me I have to be able to talk about it. Apparently, Mum was driving home from work and lent over to get something out of her purse. She didn't see the red light and got cleaned up by a truck. They said she died instantly.'

'Are you alright? I mean, I know it's been a big shock but are you, you know, going ok?'

Shaun shuffled his feet slightly.

'Yeah, I'm alright. I'm sort of used to her not being around anyway. Now, I guess it's permanent. I don't know about Dad, though.'

'She was still your mum, mate. Anyway, if you need anything, let me know.'

Riley's mother walked up and expressed her sorrow to Shaun and repeated that Riley would be there for him if he needed. After they left,

Shaun joined his father, who had seen off the Landers and was waiting at his car.

The drive home had been silent, as had the days since. Colin Waters hadn't come in and Shaun hadn't seen Vinnie. He supposed they were giving them space.

It was a relief to be at school. Shaun felt some return to normality and although kids asked him about his mother, he was able to deflect conversations quickly. The school counsellor had pulled him out of class on his first day and offered all sorts of support. He seemed a bit miffed when Shaun declined all of them and hadn't approached him since.

In a way, it was the move into high school that created the biggest change in his life. He had to catch the school bus from Goolwa to Victor Harbor, along with all the other local kids including Riley, Vinnie and, of course, his nemesis, Chad. In the new school, they were year eights, the young kids, not the biggest kids like they had been at primary school. There were loads of kids who he didn't know in his class and year level. As well as from Victor Harbor and Goolwa, there were kids from Port Elliot, Middleton, Inman Valley and other surrounding towns. Some he knew through inter-town sport but not many. The classes were all organised differently as well. They had to switch classrooms between subjects and it was their responsibility to get organised.

He was very happy to find that he'd been placed in the same class as Riley, and Vinnie too. Luckily, Chad was in a different class so he'd only interact with him during lunch and recess breaks. Oh, and on the bus as well.

Predictably, Riley had given Shaun support as he integrated into high school and dealt with the loss of his mother. Although the change in environment was also new to Riley, he embraced the change and quickly became popular among the students, including Vinnie. Riley was there for Shaun to talk to about what he was dealing with and gave him the space to be on his own when he wanted. He seemed to understand that Shaun wasn't just dealing with the obvious changes; he was also coping with a fractious relationship with his father. The bus trips to and from school were when Shaun would confide in Riley about the strain in the house now that it was clear his mother wouldn't be returning home. Glen had become reclusive at night, back drinking whiskey heavily and short-tempered in the mornings. On weekends, he was prone to migraines, making him unapproachable much of the time.

Vinnie, on the other hand, for all his physical maturity, had never really left primary school. He was inattentive in class, playing the fool and annoying the teachers. But he did provide a different type of support to Shaun. In the evenings, he became a source of distraction, sharing stories of his childhood in Yankalilla. They were laced with boldness, daring and, Shaun often thought, improbability. At school, Vinnie had also taken a dislike to Chad. Shaun couldn't be sure whether it was because he wanted, in his own way, to shield him from Chad's jibes.

On Friday in the third week of term, the class was enduring a tedious history lesson. Their teacher was old Mister Collier, a bull of a man who always went red-faced if the class became disruptive, generally an inverse measure of the subject interest. Fable had it that after a minor infringe-ment of behaviour, Collier had chased Michael Maynard all around the classroom the previous year, toppling desks and sending books flying. It was only when a teacher, having heard the commotion, came in from the classroom next door that the fracas dissipated. It was also said that in the days before corporal punishment had been banned, he carried a special stick with which he threatened disruptive boys. It consisted of a thick branch of a rose bush, thorns intact. Around that was coiled barbed wire which was then connected to an electric plug.

For some reason, Vinnie took delight in taunting Collier and there had developed a mutual disrespect between the two. One day, Mister

Collier was talking about irrigation in ancient Egypt and noticed that Vinnie had rested his head on his arms folded neatly on top of his desk. He looked like he could be napping.

Collier glided between the desks to the back of the room, addressing the class as he walked. The whole class, other than Vinnie, realised something was about to happen; Collier rarely stepped out from behind his front desk. The teacher turned at the back of the room and started walking toward the front.

'Now, class,' he said, 'yesterday, I asked you to read chapter three of your textbook for your homework.'

By this time, he was standing directly behind Vinnie. He prodded him sharply in the ribs making him jump out of his seat in protest.

'Ouch. Why'd you do that, sir?'

'Well, Mr. Waters, we need your help to answer a question from last night's homework. Sit down.'

Vinnie sat. Collier continued.

'So, Waters, if you did your homework, which I doubt, you will know the answer. If you do not, then I shall need to set you some extra work. So, young man, the Mesopotamians and later the Egyptians used a crane-like tool to irrigate their crops by lifting water from a water source onto land. Can you tell me the name of this tool?'

'Yes, sir, I can.'

'Don't play games, Waters. Tell me its name.'

'Sir, I believe it's a shaduf.'

The class erupted.

'That's quite enough,' Collier fumed, 'Well, Vincent, maybe still waters do run deep. Waters, it looks like you picked the right day to do your homework. Keep it up and stay awake in class, for heaven's sake.'

The class was followed by the morning recess break. Vinnie, Shaun and Riley filed out of the classroom.

'How the hell did you know the answer to that, Vinnie? Don't tell me you actually did your history homework.'

'Nah, of course I didn't. I was going to and I had the book opened at the start of the chapter but I decided to play Nintendo instead. My eight-year-old niece, Kelly, started looking at the book and asked me what the thing in the picture was. I had a look at the description and it was, would you believe, a shaduf.'

'You're an arsey bugger, Vinnie,' Shaun said.

In the yard, Chad wandered past the group and made a point of nudging Shaun with his shoulder. Vinnie whipped around.

'You're a real shaduf, Chad. You know that.'

Riley and Shaun burst into laughter while Chad stared at the three of them, bewildered.

'What are you on about, Waters?' he exclaimed.

'It means you're a tool, Chad. Do your homework.' More laughter.

Chad could take no more and charged Vinnie, pushing him to the ground. He clearly hadn't calculated Vinnie's strength and found himself dragged down with him. It took Vinnie seconds to roll Chad onto his back and then to sit astride his chest. All around them, boys stood shouting 'Fight, fight!'

Teachers arrived to break up the melee and Chad and Vinnie were summarily dispatched to the principal's office.

At lunchtime, Vinnie announced that he and Chad had been given detention for the rest of the week. He was unaffected by the penalty and was his usual, ebullient self when the three boys were approached by some girls in their class. The leader of the group was a girl named Carla Ferrari. She was of Italian heritage and wore her black hair long and provocatively. Somewhat like Vinnie in her carefree nature, she tended to push the school rules to the limit, especially in relation to dress and grooming. Next to her was Debbie McLean. An attractive blonde, she was more reserved than Carla and more self-conscious in her demeanour. She turned to Vinnie.

'I liked what you did in class today, Vinnie and even better was how you shut Chad up.' She turned to Shaun. 'Don't let him get to you, Shaun. He's just a bully dickhead.'

'Yeah,' Carla added. You don't have to put up with his shit.'

Shaun didn't even realise that the girls in class took any notice of him, let alone cared about his feelings.

'Hey,' Riley chimed in, 'I'm going down the beach for a surf this afternoon. Do you guys want to come down for a swim or something?'

Carla and Debbie were enthusiastic and Vinnie quickly jumped on board. He was eyeing Debbie with interest, buoyed by her flattery toward him.

Shaun hesitated. 'I'm not sure, Riley. I wouldn't mind a surf but I'd have to ride my bike so I don't know how I'd get the board there.'

Vinnie scoffed. 'I'm not going for a surf. Can't be bothered and I'm not the athletic type; I couldn't run out of sight on a dark night. I don't mind a sun bake though.' He winked at the girls.

Debbie giggled.

Riley brought the conversation back to the issue at hand. 'Not a problem, Shauno. My dad's taking me down with my board so I'll pick you up on the way. May as well give you a lift too, Vinnie, if you want. What about you girls?'

Carla shook her head, her long black hair swinging across her shoulder. 'No, we're good. We both live within walking distance.' Two other girls in the group, Jemma and Lisa, also said they would be there.

Shaun didn't take his eyes off Carla. He'd known her all through primary school but he looked at her through different eyes, like she was the most beautiful creature he'd ever seen.

That afternoon became one of many that the schoolmates spent together. For the rest of summer, Friday afternoons were regularly at the beach. Riley, Shaun and occasionally one or more of the girls surfed while Vinnie played the field on the sand. He moved his attentions effortlessly between all of the girls, as though he was ready to connect with any or all of them at any time.

Shaun was enchanted by Carla but he held his feelings in check. He saw her as unattainable. She was vivacious and outgoing as well as attractive; surely more interested in Riley or Vinnie or one of the other class boys than in him. For her part, Carla didn't show any special interest in Shaun. She tantalised all the boys equally but didn't allow herself to fall under Vinnie's spell. She realised that she had much more power than Vinnie and he knew it too. He tended to work harder on the easier targets, regularly taking one of them for a walk in the sandhills.

Summer drifted into autumn and then winter. School days became a repetitive grind, students eagerly looking forward to the next holidays. The friendships forged in the early part of the year grew stronger among the core group. Riley, Vinnie, Shaun, Carla and Debbie were rarely separated. Jemma and Lisa eventually fell away from the group, tainted by Vinnie's wavering attention. They were succeeded by other girls who came and went. Vinnie was doing all he could to educate the young women in matters of physical attraction but made little effort to maintain respect in other ways.

Carla and Debbie were less easily influenced. Carla, in particular, kept Vinnie at arm's length. It was like she let him savour her deliciousness by letting him read the menu but never allowing him a taste.

Saturday mornings during winter were usually dedicated to sports. Riley and Shaun played football on the Goolwa Oval or at one of the neighbouring towns. Carla, Debbie and some of the other girls played netball. For Vinnie, it was a time to sleep in.

At other times, whoever was available would meet in the main street and ride their bikes to any one of the places where they could hang out for a few hours. Sometimes it would be on the oval or at the rotunda next to the Corio Hotel. If somewhere more discreet was required, they would head to one of their secret places along the river. Even though they were public areas, some privacy could be found among the overhanging trees fringing the water.

It was on a winter's day that Shaun and Carla had met up in town. Riley had gone to Adelaide to play in a league-representative football match and Debbie had gone away with her family for the weekend. Vinnie was sleeping in longer than normal. Carla suggested going to one of the secret places so they could have a smoke. Smoking was of no interest to Shaun, he hated the smell, but there was no way he would give up a chance to talk to Carla on his own.

The afternoon was just another way to spend the day for Carla. She enjoyed Shaun's company but she really thrived when she could be the centre of attraction in a bigger group. For Shaun, it was special. He soaked up every word that Carla spoke, every body movement she made and even the smell of her permeated his senses over the cigarette she smoked.

At home, Shaun had found a way to survive. Glen was still moody. Colin had resumed his evening visits and the pair would drink well into the night. Shaun had asked Vinnie about Colin and Marion's relationship; whether Colin's drinking and absence from home impacted on the family. Vinnie was unfazed. He knew that Marion was bitterly unhappy but Colin was affable at home; they never fought and when Marion expressed her disquiet, Colin would wash over it professing his undying love for her.

Even though he realised that it wasn't perfect, Shaun envied the Waters' household. At least they had a workable arrangement where everyone was happy; well, maybe except for Marion. Shaun and Glen barely spoke. More than ever, Shaun felt like he was unwanted, that his father tolerated his presence out of obligation rather than love. When they did speak, Glen would usually pick fault with Shaun's academic achievements, A's in five out of seven subjects. Glen criticised the focus of schooling. He believed Shaun should be learning more practical skills, such as carpentry or metalworking rather than Mathematics, English and Science. More than once, he told Shaun that "he couldn't cut butter with a hot knife."

On the other hand, Glen regarded Vinnie as the son he really wanted. It wasn't that Vinnie had shown any prowess in "cutting butter." In fact, Vinnie wouldn't even have put in an effort. But Vinnie had the power of influence. He was charming, cheeky and confident. He talked the talk.

Shaun had become accustomed to Glen's mood swings and eventually found patterns that he could predict. During the week, he would shut himself in his bedroom while Glen drank with Colin and on Saturdays, when Glen always suffered from migraines, Shaun spent the day out and about as much as possible. By Saturday night, Glen was recovering from his migraine and was energised and engaging. He and Shaun would usually walk into town and grab a pizza and a video. It was one of Shaun's favourite times. Sundays could be anything. Some days Glen would suggest they go for a drive, others he would be sullen and morose, shutting himself in his shed and catching up on work. Those days, he would ignore Shaun, who drifted into town to meet up with whoever was around.

It was on such a Sunday in November that Shaun ran into Vinnie at the front of his house. They rode to the usual haunts, finding none of the gang. Behind the Corio Hotel stood huge Norfolk Island pines edging a lawned reserve and playground. Shaun and Vinnie arrived to find Chad and a couple of his mates lounging around on the playground equipment.

'Well, look who's here,' said Chad, 'it's the scarecrow and the lion. Where's tin man.'

'What are you on about, Chad?' Vinnie jumped off his bike to front him.

'Ever seen the Wizard of Oz? Shaun's just like the lion. Gutless. You're the scarecrow, mate. No brains.'

Shaun was off his bike now as well. 'You talk rubbish, Chad. You would have no idea.'

'Is that right,' Chad retorted. 'Let's see how brave you are then, Shaun. How about you climb up to the first branch of that tree.' He pointed at the closest Norfolk Island pine. The bottom branch was at least three metres off the ground. To get to it would mean scaling the trunk and gripping the rough bark with hands and legs like a koala.

Vinnie walked up to him until their chests were touching. 'You're so tough, Chad. Shaun will do it but only if you do it first. Come on, show us how it's done.'

Chad jumped up and brushed past Vinnie, dropping his shoulder into his chest.

'I've done this heaps before,' he boasted as he planted his first grip.

It took him five minutes but eventually, Chad clambered onto the limb and stood upright, staring down at the group below.

'There. Easy. Your turn now, Mr. Lion.'

Shaun approached the tree.

Chad called down to him. 'What, you got no brains either? I need to get down before you come up, idiot.'

He crouched on the limb to grip the trunk to start his descent but before he got a grip his foot slipped and he dropped to the ground at Shaun's feet.

The group looked down at Chad, twisted and motionless, eyes closed.

'Move back, boys.' The voice behind was a man in his fifties walking his dog as the drama unfolded. He handed the leash to Shaun. 'Hold this.'

He knelt over Chad and checked his pulse and breathing. Both were regular. He was about to put him into the coma position when Chad began to stir. The boy's eyes opened and he stared back at the man leaning over him.

'I can't move my legs.'

An ambulance came to collect Chad and after a few minutes took him away. The next day, Chad wasn't at school. Some days later, the news filtered through that he had broken his spine and was unlikely to walk again.

Even though Shaun knew that the accident wasn't his fault, he blamed himself for letting Chad do the challenge first. He wasn't helped by Glen's response when he related the event and its unfortunate consequence to him.

'Well, at least Chad had the guts to have a go.'

8

Friday19 April 2019 (Day 2)

Riley was up, showered and dressed by six. He would have liked to have gone for his customary five-kilometre run, but his mind was pre-occupied with Vinnie's death and Aiden's disappearance. He couldn't help but wonder if there was a chance that Shaun could have been responsible in some way for what had happened. After all, he had both the opportunity and the motive. Riley couldn't reconcile that thought with the Shaun he had known since primary school - someone who was introverted rather than outgoing, measured rather than spontaneous and certainly gentle, not violent. Additionally, Riley couldn't explain how or why Shaun would orchestrate Aiden's disappearance. He and Carla had a strained relationship, but they had always been as one when it came to Aiden's care and upbringing. There was no logical reason why Shaun would have a need to hide his son away, let alone harm him in some more sinister way. Still, perhaps he needed to question Shaun further.

Riley's sleep had been fitful and, although he had woken feeling like he had been trampled by bulls, the coffee he'd just poured wakened his body and settled his nerves for the day ahead. Even so, he couldn't slow the urge to get to the station as he gulped it down.

Kate stirred when he put the coffee he had made her on the bed-side table.

'I'm off now, babe.' He sat on the bed and gently brushed the hair from her face. He loved her half-awake look in the mornings. It was a stark contrast to how he woke, alert and ready for activity, but ruggedly untidy.

'Thanks, Riley. Are you ok? You didn't sleep well, did you?' She wasn't accustomed to him being unsettled during sleep. Usually, he slept like a bear, softly snoring.

'I'm fine. Just preoccupied with this case, I guess. I'll be right once I get going. Unfortunately, I don't know what time I'll be home tonight.'

'That's ok, just take care.'

Riley lent over and kissed her gently on the forehead.

He eased the door closed as he left, Kate's soft breaths telling him that she had already drifted back to sleep.

He'd call her later.

The main street was empty as he drove into the police station car park. The Goolwa station was not attended 24 hours a day, seven days a week unless circumstances demanded and Riley wondered if those circumstances now existed. He was the first to arrive and he fumbled with his key in the lock as he attempted to answer his ringing mobile. It was DI Paul Smith.

'Morning, sir. Just bear with me while I disarm the alarm system.'

'Good. You're at work then.' Smith was short on pleasantries. 'Any developments since we spoke last night?'

'Not, really. The search team wasn't able to locate the missing boy but we'll be starting up again this morning. I'm still unsure about the Vinnie Waters' death, though. The doctor who attended last night identified an injury that may not be consistent with the accident that we thought happened. I'm expecting the coroner down here sometime this morning and you mentioned forensics will be down by 8.00.'

'Yes, I spoke to Shelley Harrison a few minutes ago. You'll remember her from the murders a couple of years ago. She and her team will be down with you at around 7.00. You're lucky, you have a good one with her. Listen, she's a bit stretched on resources at the moment so you're going to have to throw in some help for her. Whatever you do though don't let them get under her feet.'

Riley remembered Shelley as being very effective and he was happy to have someone he'd worked with before.

'Sir, that's great. Thanks for your support on this. I know it might end up being a non-event as far as a crime is concerned but I would feel uncomfortable if we didn't explore all possibilities.'

'That's what makes you a good cop, Riley. One day you might want to think about joining my team as a detective. Now, is the site secure?' Smith knew the answer but had to ask.

'Yes, sir.' Riley expected the question and allowed himself a brief smile when it came.

'Good. Now, as I mentioned last night, I'm balls-deep in this situation in Loxton; otherwise, I'd come down for a look as well, but I'm afraid that's not going to happen. Not for the next few days, anyway. Look, you're more than ready for this, O'Brien, but you have my number if you need it. Hopefully, as you said, it could all be a non-event.'

As Riley ended the call, he heard Rachel Cross opening the station door. She was talking to someone.

Moments later she entered the room and marched up to Riley.

'Look who I found,' she said beaming. 'It's Shelley.'

'Hey, Riley, it's been a while.'

'Hi, Shelley. Great to see you again. Where's your team?'

Shelley looked at him, a little embarrassed.

'I'm it, I'm afraid. A couple of investigators are on leave and now with the double homicide in Loxton, we didn't have anyone else to spare on this one, which frankly, was sold to us as a probable accident.' She gave a small shrug. 'Sorry.'

'Did you talk with DI Smith?'

'Yes. Look, don't blame him for this case being downgraded. He pushed pretty hard, based on his confidence in you, Riley, but at the end of the day, the powers that be made the call that there wasn't enough to treat your case as a homicide ... yet.'

Riley grimaced, exasperated. 'What about the missing boy?'

'Riley, he's just that – a missing boy. That calls for a search team, not a criminal investigation.'

'Fine!' Riley stormed out of the room, heading for the front door. 'I've got a search to get organised.'

'Riley, wait. Listen, take me to the shed and show me around. At least let's do what we can with what we have. If I find anything, I promise I'll push to get more resources.'

The drive to the shed was silent. Riley and Rachel led the way, with Shelley following in her station wagon packed with her equipment.

As they approached the shed, they noticed Brian Thompson and his team assembled under the shade of a large tree.

It wasn't yet eight o'clock and the day was already warm, a vivid yellow sun burning through the brilliant blue sky. It was going to be a hot one.

Closer to the shed was a large white van. Riley recognised the van as one used by the coroner's office. The sole occupant was alighting the vehicle, a tall gaunt man dressed in a black suit, white shirt and black tie. His shiny black shoes completed his undertaker's appearance.

Riley turned to Rachel.

'Can you get Brian and his team started? He knows what to do, God knows he's done it plenty of times before. Just make sure they cover all the tracks they did last night, maybe something will be visible in daylight. We also need them to look for any signs along the riverbank, in case poor Aiden's ended up in the river. Oh, and if Shaun turns up, he can assist with the search but always accompanied by someone.'

'You're treating him as a suspect, then?'

'I have to, Rachel, even though it's not certain we have a crime yet.'

'Ok, no worries, Riley. Do you want me to go with them?'

'No. I'll get Phil to do that. You and I'll need to be doing more investigative work on Vinnie's death, I think.'

Shelley joined Riley and they walked toward the shed where the gaunt man was waiting.

'John Lovell,' Shelley said. 'Strange dude, but very good.'

'Are you ok if we get him organised first?'

'Sure, why don't you brief us at the same time.'

John Lovell stepped forward with hand outstretched.

'Hi, John,' Riley said. 'Shelley gave me your name. I'm Senior Sergeant Riley O'Brien.' He wasn't surprised that the man's handshake was clammy.

'Ms Harrison, good to see you again. Well, Senior Sergeant, let's see what we have here.'

The three walked to the shed door where Craig Thompson, one of the two police officers assisting from Victor Harbor, was standing.

Riley grasped him on the shoulder. 'Craig, you must be exhausted after being here all night. Thanks for looking after the site for us. Why don't you and Oliver go home and get some sleep.'

'No problems, Riley. Happy to help. We'll head off shortly, but we can come back later in the day if you want us. Our station head has cleared it if you need us.

'Oliver has something important to show you too when you have a minute. He's behind the shed.' He nodded toward Shelley and John Lovell. 'You two might be interested as well.'

'Thanks, mate. We'll check with him now.'

Lovell was unimpressed, wanting to get started on the tasks covered in his position description but followed Riley and Shelley, regardless.

'Senior Sergeant O'Brien.'

Riley looked to where Oliver was waving.

'What have you got, Oliver?'

The young policeman was standing knee-deep in the reeds that lined the river. With his gloved hand, he pointed to a plastic sheet on the grass. On it lay a large adjustable wrench.

'This could be our weapon,' he called.

'It could,' Shelley replied, 'Bag it up carefully so that we can check it for any traces of skin, blood or maybe fingerprints. Good work, Oliver.'

'Can we look at the body now, please? I need to get back to Adelaide as soon as I can.' Lovell was not to be side-tracked from his key purpose.

It was dark inside the shed, the glass panes in the roof covered in a layer of black grime accumulated over the years. The steam-powered Cockle Train and Oscar W paddle steamer maintained a fine layer of soot over the buildings closest to the river.

Riley flicked the light switch, using the end of his ballpoint pen to avoid contaminating any fingerprints.

'So, who has been in here since the death?' Shelley asked.

'Well, apart from us, Shaun and Carla Chambers, who found the body. They could have touched almost anything in here. The two police you met outside have been in here, but they know better than to interfere with an incident scene and then there's the doctor, Tony Cleaver. He confirmed the death.'

'Was he under the boat when you got here, Riley? If so, who pulled him out from underneath?'

'Yes, he was. The Doc pulled him out. I used the winch control pad over there.' He pointed to the dangling switch.

'And it functioned as normal?' Lovell asked through needled eyes.

'No problem. There didn't seem to be anything abnormal in the mechanism at all.'

'Peculiar. And what did the good doctor suggest caused this man to stop living?'

Riley relayed the doctor's opinion that the cause of death was mechanical asphyxia and explained as best he could in his own words, the indicators the doctor had identified, including the purple-crimson blotching of his skin.

'Yes, so it would seem on first appearances. Did he make comment about this?' Lovell pointed to the wound on the victim's temple.

'He thought it was inconsistent with the crush injury and most likely before he died, due to the bruising, I think.'

'Yes, I concur with your doctor, although let's see what the autopsy shows before jumping to conclusions, shall we? I'm not prepared to say at this stage that you have a murder here, Senior Sergeant, but I will suggest you don't close the door on that possibility. In any event, I would like photographs of that wrench your man found out there and in due course Ms Harrison can you provide me with a mould? I'd like to check it against the dent in this man's head but I presume you will want to extract fingerprints, DNA and the like first.'

'Absolutely, I'll prioritise it,' Shelley responded and winked at Riley.

'Well, let me get to work so I can get this fellow into the van and you can get on with your job.'

Shelley and Riley moved away from Lovell.

'I told you he was good, even if he is a bit quirky.'

Riley smiled. 'I don't mind quirky as long as he helps us clean this up. Do you want me to show you around or shall I leave you to it?'

'I'm sure you have plenty to do, Riley, so leave me to it. One question, though. I notice the door was forced open. Why was that?'

'Shaun used a wheel brace to break the lock so they could get in. We have the brace put aside for you plus the torch that Shaun used. The strange thing is, all the doors were locked on the outside which is why they had to break in. How does a man lock himself in from the outside and then suffer this terrible accident?'

'The boy? I mean, could he have locked it on his way out?'

'Maybe, I don't know. And we won't know until we find him.'

'It's odd and I can see why you are wanting this looked at closer. Leave me to it.'

'Um, Shelley, if this is a murder, we obviously have to start thinking about who the killer might be. At this stage, I have only one lead and a couple of possibilities.'

'Let me have them.'

'Ok. Shaun Chambers had the opportunity and motive. I find it hard to accept for a number of reasons but if that wrench shows any link to Shaun, I will be focussing on him as number one. However, what would he have done with the boy, and why? My second option is that somehow Aiden did something. Maybe it was an accident caused by Aiden and he got frightened and ran off. But then how does the wrench fit in, if at all and how did Vinnie get the hit on his temple?'

'Could the boy have seen Shaun kill Vinnie and run off? It would explain your first scenario.'

'Maybe. Anyway, I just wanted to suggest that as Shaun may become our key person of interest, it would be worthwhile putting your forensic nose over his car. It's been parked outside since last night.'

Riley stepped outside and immediately noticed the increase in temperature. He shaded his eyes as he searched for Rachel. She was nowhere to be seen, but he realised the best place to be in this heat if you couldn't be indoors was inside an air-conditioned car. As he approached the car, he saw Rachel in the driver's seat, talking with Carla, seated alongside.

He opened the rear door and sat inside.

'Am I interrupting?'

'No,' Rachel replied. 'Shaun is with the search team and it was too hot to stay outside. I was just about to give Carla a lift home.'

'I don't know why I'm even here, Riley, but when Shaun said he was coming down to join the search, I just felt like I needed to be nearby. You know, just in case. But now I'm here, I feel useless.'

'Sure. Let's go and maybe we can have a bit more of a chat, Carla.'

They arrived at her house, a two-storey contemporary style, built high on Underwood Avenue with windows facing the sea to take advantage of views of the beach that curved around to Middleton, Port Elliot and Victor Harbor. As they left the car, they could hear the waves crashing on the beach.

A perfect day for a surf, Riley mused.

Carla unlocked the front door and led the two officers inside.

As Riley had expected, the house was themed for beachside living, with casual furniture and wooden floors. Paintings adorned the walls with images of the beach, surf and boats. An illuminated tank in a corner held tropical fish, iridescent in the sunlight that streamed through large windows and a skylight in the roof. Shaun and Carla had built the house only two years ago, planned as a dream family home but now the residence of only one of them and their missing son.

Carla saw Riley look at the tank.

'Shaun's idea. He thought it would be good for Aiden to have an interest other than computer games. He was right, I suppose, but guess who gets the job of feeding them and cleaning the tank?' The comment seemed odd given the circumstances.

'I can imagine. Can we have a look around, especially in Aiden's room? It's a long shot but we may get a lead on his whereabouts.'

'Of course,' she exclaimed, 'what are you looking for?' They started up the stairs to Aiden's room.

'It's more likely what's missing, anything he might have taken with him. Or maybe a note or an address that tells us where he could have gone.'

'You think he's run away? God, I hope you're right, Riley. I just want to get him back.'

Aiden's bedroom looked like a typical boy's room.

His bed was unmade but clean. A few toys, stuffed animals and a Nerf gun, lay on the top. His wardrobe door was open, showing shelves of clothes laid out neatly and on the top was a bike helmet and a soccer ball. In the corner of the room was a small study desk laden with open books, pencils and other stationery. The books partly obscured a photo frame at the back of the desk. Riley picked it up and looked at a photo showing Shaun, Carla and Aiden smiling broadly at the camera. In front of them was a birthday cake with candles forming the number eleven. The photo had been taken on Aiden's birthday and nothing in the photo suggested there was any abnormal tension between them. It was unclear whether Vinnie was there; perhaps on the other side of the camera.

'Let's work on the theory that he's run away for a minute. If that's the case, he may have been spooked by what happened to Vinnie; he may well be in shock. Can you think of where he might have gone, maybe someone like a friend that he would have run to?'

'You think I haven't already played that out in my mind? I've rung all his friends' parents. No one's heard from Aiden since school. My parents are in Adelaide and he'd have no way of going there. The only other place

I think he would have gone would be Shaun's. His place is much closer to the shed, but he obviously didn't go there.'

Rachel had been going through the drawers in the small study desk and looked across at Riley. Their eyes met but words were unnecessary to signal what each was thinking.

What if Aiden did go back to Shaun's? Then what?

'Do you notice anything missing that should be here, Carla?'

'Well, his school bag would normally be in the corner there if he was home, but that's still at the shed, isn't it?'

'It is,' Riley said. 'Anything else? Was he wearing anything other than his school uniform?'

'Um. Oh, he has a leather wristband he sometimes wears. It would be on his bedside cupboard if he wasn't wearing it. It's not here so he must have it with him.'

'Ok, are we set to go, Rachel?' She nodded and they went downstairs to the kitchen area.

'Carla, before we leave you, I just want to ask you a couple of other questions. Just take a seat.' Riley motioned to the chairs at the kitchen table. He sat opposite her while Rachel continued to browse in the kitchen and living area. 'Did you notice anything unusual with Vinnie's behaviour or movements in recent times?'

'What do you mean? What could anything else have to do with this dreadful mess?'

'I just need to consider all possibilities,' Riley said gently, 'I know this is difficult for you but we need to prepare as comprehensive a review as possible.'

'Well, you know Vinnie, Riley. He's always so laid back but also on the go all the time. I can't get a read on him most of the time; you just have to take each day as it comes. Now that you mention it though, I've been thinking about the phone call he got yesterday morning.'

'What about it?'

Carla leant her elbow on the table and put her hand to her cheek, contemplating. 'I don't know. After the call, suddenly everything seemed urgent and he didn't want to look after Aiden after school because of who he was meeting. He got annoyed with Aiden because he was taking too long to get ready, but you know what kids are like, time doesn't mean as much to them. Anyway, Vinnie seemed tense and uptight and he's never really like that.'

'Who was the call from?'

'I don't know. I guess it was to do with work. He wouldn't get any other calls at that time of the day and he never tells me much about his work anyway.'

Riley wrote in his notebook. They needed to speed up the check on Vinnie's phone records to see who he spoke to.

He peered up at Carla who looked distant as though trying to work out what to cook for dinner.

'Ok, what about Shaun? How has he been lately? With you, with Aiden, with Vinnie?'

Carla snapped out of her daze and searched Riley's face for understanding.

'What has Shaun to do with anything?'

'Well, as far as we know, he was the last person to see Vinnie alive and possibly the last to see Aiden before he went missing.'

'You can't think Shaun's done anything.' She laughed, not because she found it humorous but because it was ridiculous. 'You can't be serious. Shaun is one of the gentlest people I know. Yes, he disliked Vinnie and he probably hates me, but he has justifiable reasons for that, as you well know; or, at least I assume you do.'

'But if you think Shaun is vengeful enough to harm Vinnie or Aiden, you're crazy. He loves that little boy. And you, Riley, you're his friend from way back. You couldn't possibly...'

'Carla, Carla. Steady up. Sorry if I'm asking painful questions but it's what I have to do.' He reached for her hand but she jerked it away and glared at him.

'Look,' he continued, 'it doesn't matter what I think or how long I have known Shaun or Vinnie or even you. At this stage, I need to gather as much information as I can about what's happened in the last 24 hours, so we can be sure about how Vinnie died and where we can find Aiden.'

Carla was not appeased and stood; eyes fixed on Riley.

'Well, why don't you get on with it then? Get out of my house and find Aiden.'

As Rachel drove them back to the police station, Riley sat quietly, concerned that he could be too close to the people involved in this investigation and wondering if, contrary to Paul Smith's opinion, he was up to the demands of it. He had reservations before but nothing as intense as he felt now.

'Well, she really gave it to you, didn't she?'

Riley looked across to see Rachel staring at him.

'Watch the road,' he snapped. A minute later, 'Sorry, I guess it did get to me.'

'Don't worry about it. I've had worse. Look, she's upset and she's having to think about possibilities she doesn't want to face; horrible things about her son, her ex-husband and her lover.'

'Yeah, well, we need to find Aiden soon or it will only get worse.'

He reached for his phone and punched a number. A couple of minutes later he confirmed with Brian Thompson that there had been no sighting of Aiden or indeed any trace of him.

Riley knew he would have already heard if there had been. Good news, bad news he supposed – at least there was no evidence that Aiden was not alive. Brian had told him that his team had explored the routes they covered the night before and had also investigated parks and open spaces near the shed and around the town centre. He was now joining Phil Reid who was searching the riverbanks for any indication that Aiden may have slipped into the river.

Riley didn't really want to pursue that thought but decided that he should arrange for divers to search in the water, at least around the shed.

He called another number.

'Phil, Riley. How is the search going there?'

Phil responded. 'Well, it's as hot as buggery, today, but the good news is we haven't found any sign that Aiden has gone into the river.'

'Ok, good. Listen, Brian and his team are going to join the guys you have there. Can you leave them to it? I need you to do something else for me. I know it's only been a few hours, but can you see if you can get Craig Thompson and Oliver Townsend from Victor Harbor to help you? Hopefully, they've had a bit of rest.

'I'd like you to do a doorknock of the houses and any businesses around Vinnie's shed and near the lane that goes down to it. I want to get a feel if he had any visitors to the shed yesterday. Someone could have seen something. Is Shaun with the search team?'

'No. He was with us but decided to go home in case Aiden showed up there.'

Rachel pulled the car into the police station car park.

'What are you thinking, Riley?'

'I don't know yet and maybe I'm overreacting but what if whoever unsettled Vinnie yesterday morning followed up with a meeting later on at the shed?'

'That sounds like it's worth checking. What do we do next?'

'Well, let's go and have another chat with Shaun.'

They found Shaun sitting under the rear porch of his bungalow on Brooking Street. The house was old and in need of some updating, not in keeping with the position Shaun held in the town. He sat on a chair, a beer in his hand and half a dozen empties on the table.

'Welcome to my shit-hole.'

'Do you think this is a good idea?' Riley motioned at the empty bottles.

'Can't think of a better one. My son is missing, or worse, a bloke I used to love and now despise has just been murdered and my ex-wife won't talk to me. Doesn't sound like a great day, does it?'

'You're jumping to conclusions, Shaun. We don't know that Vinnie has been murdered. What makes you think he has?'

'Because you have been asking Carla questions that suggest I did something to Vinnie and then abducted my own kid. Now she's thinking I have something to hide and won't talk to me. What the fuck, Riley?'

'Shaun, you know we have to ask the hard questions. We need to eliminate the obvious so we can focus on other possibilities. Listen, why don't you show us around your place so we can see if there's anything that might point to where Aiden has gone.'

'And, so you can see if I'm hiding him here, right? Well, you go your hardest because he's not here.' Shaun's voice was raised.

'If you like,' replied Riley. He motioned to Rachel to start looking through rooms and pulled up a chair opposite Shaun. 'How's it working out at this place?'

'Like I said, it's a shit hole. I just took the first place I could find on a weekly rent. I figured sooner or later Carla would get sick of Vinnie and want me to come back home, but that hasn't happened.'

'So, do you think you two are done? What was Carla's relationship with Vinnie like?'

'Are we done? With what's going on now, how would I have any fucking idea whether we're done? I still think Carla would have eventually wanted more substance in a relationship than Vinnie would give her but does that mean we would get back together? I really don't know but I do know I still love her and she's the mother of my child, for Christ's sake.'

Riley had never seen Shaun so emotional, even through the loss of his parents, years before. Could he kill Vinnie? Riley couldn't believe it was possible. He got Shaun to go over again the events of the previous afternoon from picking Aiden up from school to dropping him at the shed and afterwards returning to the shed to find Vinnie dead and Aiden missing.

His explanation was fully consistent with his earlier statement.

'Shaun, what do you know about Vinnie's business?'

Shaun laughed bitterly. 'What does anyone know about his business? He kept it pretty close to his chest other than when he wanted to gloat about how well he was doing. He was like the duck swimming; most of what kept him moving was going on under the surface.'

Of course, Riley knew that Vinnie was a wheeler and dealer and had harboured suspicions that not all his activities were legal, but he hadn't had any reason to investigate further.

'When you dropped Aiden off at the shed, did you see anyone else there or was there any indication Vinnie was expecting someone?'

Shaun looked at him quizzically. 'Like who?'

'I don't know. Vinnie took a phone call yesterday morning that seemed to upset him. We don't know who it was from, but we will find out. I'm just wondering if you saw anything that indicated he was expecting someone.'

'No, nothing. And anyway, what's that got to do with Aiden's disappearance? Do you think someone came in and took him? If bloody Vinnie's shonky business deals have resulted in Aiden getting hurt, I'll fucking ...' Shaun suddenly realised the futility of finishing the sentence and buried his face in his hands.

'Okay. Listen, we are just fact-finding at the moment. I can't say what has or hasn't happened to Aiden and we won't know if Vinnie's death was foul play until we get the post-mortem results. But, look,' Riley placed his hand on Shaun's shoulder, 'the best thing you can do at this time is to stand alongside Carla and support each other through this.'

Shaun nodded as Rachel emerged from the house, shaking her head at Riley.

'One last question, Shaun. Do you know where Aiden would be likely to go if he was scared? You know, maybe he freaked out and ran off.'

Shaun was defeated and murmured, 'I'm sure he would have come back here, or maybe he would have walked all the way to Carla's but I doubt it.'

'Ok. We are going now, but do what I said, alright?'

They walked back to the car to the sound of Shaun sobbing.

By the time, they were back at the station most of the day had passed and they were no closer to understanding what had happened to Aiden or how Vinnie had met his fate.

Riley reminded Rachel to have Vinnie's phone records checked.

He still had the feeling that the call Vinnie had taken in the morning could be connected. In the meantime, he stood in front of a whiteboard and drew a line down the centre. On the left, he wrote what they knew and on the right was a much longer list detailing what had to be done and what they still needed to find out. He examined this list and mentally prioritised those he could control.

First on the list was to arrange the dive team. Tomorrow, he would interview the boy's teacher, even though it would be Saturday and not a school day. He was also hopeful of meeting with some of Aiden's school friends. By the time he had that completed, he hoped he would have the results of the autopsy on Vinnie's body, at least some preliminary results from the forensics team, details on the mystery phone call and anything that arose from the doorknocks being undertaken by Phil and his team.

After disconnecting his call to Adelaide, Riley placed a call to Brian Thompson.

'Sorry, mate, still no sign of Aiden. It's like he's disappeared into thin air. I don't know where we can look next.'

'Ok, thanks, Brian. I have the divers coming in to start a search in the river starting tomorrow. I seriously hope that Aiden doesn't turn up there but until we get a new lead, we don't have any clear idea where to continue the land search. Can you just come in tomorrow and mark on a map all the areas you've searched so far?'

Riley felt dispirited. They had no leads at all on where Aiden could be, with the only remaining activity potentially leading to an answer that no one wanted. He drove home to find Kate marking school homework.

'Hi, sweetheart,' she called as Riley came through the front door, 'how has your day been?'

'Well, not great. I don't feel like we've made much progress on Vinnie's death or in finding Aiden. Hey, what do you know about him at school?'

Kate handed Riley a glass of red wine. 'Here, you need this. I haven't had much to do with him. I've never had him in my class, but from what I know he's a lovely little boy. He's a bit quiet and reserved, never any trouble in class. The whole school community is so shocked. It was very surreal all day.'

'Well, it will be more real tomorrow. I'll need to talk to his teachers and friends.'

'Ok, but now you need some downtime. Why don't you sit down and relax while I finish getting dinner?'

Kate returned a few minutes later to find Riley asleep on the sofa.

9

1991

The first year of high school came and went. Riley and Shaun both achieved good marks in their end-of-year assessments. While Riley's parents congratulated him on his grades and praised his efforts, Glen took only a cursory look at Shaun's before consigning the report to a drawer in his office.

Vinnie's grades and the teachers' reports were not as favourable and his class teacher had warned that if he didn't improve his effort next year, they would consider holding him back. That didn't worry Vinnie in the slightest. As he told Shaun, he only intended to stay at school until he was legally able to leave, so what did it matter if he spent a year repeating? His plan was to head north or west as soon as he turned fifteen and get a job on a cattle or sheep station.

When the summer holidays started, any concerns the boys had about grades or future careers were put to one side. The six-week break was going to be all about relaxing and having fun. Even the girls would not be a distraction. Carla's parents were taking her and her siblings to Italy to meet a family she'd heard about but never met, while Debbie was heading to Yorke Peninsula where her family had a beach shack. Riley had asked her what was wrong with Goolwa Beach and Debbie had to explain that her father liked the fishing from Point Turton much better, so they all had to tag along.

Colin and Marion invited Glen and Shaun to join them for Christmas lunch. His aunties, Janet and Helen, had invited them to Strathalbyn too but Glen said he couldn't imagine anything worse than having to spend the day with "those two old biddies."

Their lunch was filling and packed with joy. Regardless of any other issues, Marion and Colin knew how to hold a family do. The day for Shaun had started sorrowfully as he reflected on the Christmases before, when his mum had been around. She had always put in a big effort for Christmas, decorating the house weeks beforehand and putting on a feast for lunch. It reinforced just how much he missed her.

After lunch, Glen and Shaun returned home. Glen was a bit the worse for wear but his intoxication had, for once, put him into a good mood. They sat in the lounge room and relaxed.

'Dad,' Shaun asked, 'do you reckon we could go away for a couple of days? You're not that busy with work, are you?'

Glen contemplated for a moment. He topped up his beer glass before responding.

'Yeah, why not? What say we go down to the river mouth and camp for a couple of nights? We can go fishing and swimming. Take the kayaks and head into the Coorong a bit. Yeah, we could.'

Glen mused on the thought. They had done a lot of camping when Shaun was younger, maybe six or seven. Karen was happy in those days. They would eat the fish they'd caught and listen to music by the campfire at night until drunk and happy. Then they'd fall into the tent, giggling. Sometimes, they'd make love, taking care not to wake Shaun just a few feet away on the other side of the tent.

Glen slapped his hand on the arm of his couch.

'Yeah, let's do it. Next weekend. We can head down on Friday and come home on Tuesday, in time for New Year's Eve. Hey, why don't you ask a couple of your mates? What about Vinnie?'

'Dad, does that mean Colin will come too?' Shaun was worried that Glen's enthusiasm was buoyed by the prospect of a couple of days drinking solidly with Colin. His voice gave away his disappointment.

'No, no, son. Colin's working this weekend so he couldn't come anyway. No, just me and you and your mates. Who else do you want to bring?'

Friday morning came around. The back of the Hilux and the trailer were almost packed. Even though the trip was only for a couple of nights, both were filled to the brim with kayaks, fishing gear, tents, sleeping bags, cooking equipment, a packed esky and timber for a fire.

Vinnie had arrived early and helped pack the car. Riley turned up with his sleeping bag and backpack and they were ready to go. It was only going to be a short drive, a little more than half an hour along the beach, but it may as well have been to a different country. Shaun hopped into the front of the Hilux next to Glen, and Vinnie and Riley sat in the back. They headed off and by the time they got to Beach Road, the anticipation had the boys chattering with excitement.

'Hey, Dad, can we put some music on?' Shaun asked. He hadn't felt this relaxed with his father for a long time; probably since before his mother had left.

'Sure, son. Just let me navigate through the entrance to the beach.' Glen had already set his tyre pressures for soft sand driving. He pulled to a stop before engaging the four-wheel drive and turning off the bitumen. The first part of the drive was the worst. Once on the beach, it wasn't so bad but many vehicles got bogged either just starting or just finishing their beach drive. A few minutes later, they were on the beach, heading east toward the river mouth.

'Ok, how about that music?' Glen turned on the radio. Bon Jovi's Blaze of Glory had just started.

'Man, I love this song!' screamed Vinnie from the back seat. 'Turn it up.'

Shaun leant across and turned the dial. He shot a sideways glance at Glen to make sure he wasn't going to react badly. The chorus began and the boys lowered their windows and joined in.

Riley and Vinnie had their heads out their windows, singing at the cars parked on the beach as they passed. Friendly waves came from bikini-clad women and men in their budgie smugglers. Shaun looked across at his father. He was grinning.

They arrived at the mouth to find that at least twenty other cars were already parked there.

'Shit, that's a pain.' Glen hit his steering wheel.

Shaun looked around. 'Looks like they're mostly day visitors. Maybe they'll all go by nightfall.'

'Let's hope so, son. I don't fancy pitching our tent in the middle of this lot.'

Glen drove the car around the point so that they faced Hindmarsh Island. Across the water, they could see several houses along Sugars Beach. He found a spot that was reasonably set away from other cars and pulled up. The trailer and car were unpacked in no time and Glen set up an awning against the car so that they at least had some shade before the tent was erected.

By late afternoon, only a couple of cars were still on the beach, the closest about fifty metres away. Shaun, Riley and Vinnie set up the tent while Glen organised a fire pit and set up the cooking equipment. They had been out in kayaks earlier in the day and with the rising tide had caught four decent-sized mulloway. As dusk set in, Glen started the fire;

even in summer, it could get cool at night. He waved off the last of the other cars at the point and sat next to the fire with a glass of whiskey.

The boys were mucking about on the sandhill and he had no desire to call them back to disrupt his solitude. As he sat, he let his mind wander. He'd had a good Christmas and he felt re-connected with his son. Maybe if he'd tried harder with Karen, the family would still be together. *Who was he kidding? She would have left anyway. Her fucking boss or should he say fucking her boss?* So, she just went, living the life she wanted without any regard for her husband. And leaving him to look after their son, the son she had spoiled. *"Are you alright, Shaunie?"* She never let him learn things the hard way, always mollycoddled him. *No wonder he's grown up soft as butter.*

Glen knew he was talking himself down but he couldn't stop it. He didn't know why it happened. He just got these dark moods and no matter how much he told himself to snap out of it, he couldn't. He could put on a different face when he was working or having a drink with Colin but it was still there, hiding in the background. And Shaun … he couldn't put it away when he was with Shaun. The boy just frustrated him. He knew it was Karen he was angry with but it was Shaun that was in front of him, day after day.

He had finished his third whiskey by the time the boys came back. Shaun could sense the difference in his father already. He didn't want the boys, but especially Riley, to see his father blow up so he decided to tread carefully around him. He helped Glen cook the mulloway, while Vinnie and Riley set the picnic table and dished up some salad. The boys drank water with their dinner. Glen had another whiskey.

Shaun suggested to Glen that he sit by the campfire while the boys cleaned up. Glen poured another whiskey and walked down to the shoreline.

'Is your dad ok?' Riley asked.

'Yeah, he just gets a bit down sometimes. Especially with mum not around anymore. Hey, maybe let's go for a walk along the beach for a bit.'

Shaun called out to Glen. 'Dad, we're just going for a walk along the beach, ok?'

Glen stood facing the water and without turning, lifted an arm to wave.

The boys strolled through the shallows, the water reflecting the yellow and blue-grey sky of the setting sun's half-light. The silhouettes of the boys and the sandhills behind were the only contrast to the moody stillness of the water.

'I've never seen your dad like this, Shaun. Is he like it very often?'

'I s'pose,' Shaun muttered. He was a bit embarrassed at the turn of the conversation. 'It's been hard for him, you know.'

Vinnie chimed in. 'I've seen him in some stinking moods, Riley. It's not fair on Shaun. Someone should punch his lights out one day.'

Riley was surprised. He knew Shaun had his challenges with his mother gone but never appreciated how hard it had been.

'So, what do you do when he's like this, Shaun?'

'Just give him some space, I guess. He'll be bad for the rest of the night but he could be fine tomorrow.'

It was after ten, darkness taken hold, when the boys returned. Glen was sitting in one of the foldup chairs. The empty whiskey bottle lay on its side next to the chair.

'What's wrong?' Glen mumbled. Shaun was bent over, holding his wrist.

'He fell in a hole and sprained his wrist,' Vinnie said. 'It must be painful.'

'Get over it, Shaun. It can't be that bad.'

'It hurts, Dad,' Shaun blubbered.

'Let me look at it then.' Shaun walked to Glen, who grabbed the wrist and squeezed it. Shaun yelped. 'It's not that bad, Shaun. Stop being such a baby.'

'I'm not, but you made it worse.'

Glen erupted. 'Look, I'm sick of your fucking drama, Shaun. Why can't you grow up a bit like these boys? You're carrying on like a two-year-old.'

Shaun was overcome with a mixture of shame and embarrassment. *Was he really a baby? What did his friends think?*

He ran down to the water.

'Come back, Shaun. Stop being such a sook. You're showing your mates just how big a baby you are.' Glen let out a mocking laugh.

Despite the pain, Shaun grabbed a kayak and paddle and waded into the water.

'Shaun, don't mate. It's dark on the water and dangerous.' Riley ran down after him.

'Oh, fuck. I bet the little idiot hasn't put on his buoyancy vest.' Glen got out of his chair and walked to the waterline. 'Shaun, come back. Now.'

They couldn't see him in the darkness. Glen grabbed one of the other kayaks and took it to the water. 'You two, stay here. I mean it.'

'Mr. Chambers, I don't think you should ...'

'Quiet, Riley. I don't care what you think. You just stay here.'

Shaun paddled out a hundred metres or so and allowed his boat to drift. He was embarrassed beyond comprehension and he could see no way that his friends would ever respect him again. Either he was a sooky baby or his father was a drunken bully. Either way, he didn't know how he could face them again. He heard his father calling to him but he knew he couldn't see him.

He paddled further. He wasn't ready to go back yet. He headed toward the river mouth and stopped again to drift. He wept as he tried to work out what to do. He felt the falling tide pull his boat further toward the mouth and decided to turn back. The pull was too strong and he couldn't turn the kayak. The wind had sprung up whipping the surface into angry swirls. His father was still calling out, closer now.

Shaun didn't reply and just tried to hold his boat in the same position. He heard his father paddling near and saw him a short way off. Glen spotted him at the same time and turned to paddle toward him.

'Stay there, you fucking little fool. What the fuck do you think you're doing? Honestly, Shaun, you are the most useless fucking waste of space.'

As he finished his tirade, Glen pulled alongside Shaun. He reached across to grab his son's boat. Shaun was still angry, upset and miserable.

'Go away,' he screamed and thrust his paddle at Glen's chest. Although his kayak was a relatively stable design, the push was enough to unbalance his heavily intoxicated father and he struggled to keep himself upright. Slapping his paddle on the water, he found himself trapped in a whirlpool. He thrashed to pull himself out of it but a wave caught him side-on and he capsized. Shaun watched as Glen tried to grab his kayak but it had drifted out of reach.

'Shaun, give me a hand.' Glen's voice was desperate. Shaun didn't move. He couldn't. He was frozen in the moment, watching his father flail in the choppy waters. The waters frothed and eddied then Glen wasn't there.

Shaun watched Glen's kayak float away. He waited for Glen to reappear. He didn't. He'd let his father drown; he had watched it happen.

He was still sitting in his kayak, paddling backwards to stop it from going closer to the mouth, when he heard Riley's voice.

'Over here, Riley,' he responded.

Riley drew alongside. 'Where's your dad?'

'Gone,' was all Shaun could say.

Riley saw Glen's kayak twisting in the eddy. 'Where is he, Shaun? Where?' he shouted.

'I don't know. He just disappeared.'

Riley paddled around the area desperately looking for any sign of Glen. He returned to where Shaun sat, staring at the cold, dark water around him.

'C'mon, mate. Let's get back.'

They paddled slowly back to their campsite, exhausted from fighting the pull of the tide. Vinnie ran to them as they pulled into shore.

'Grab a blanket, Vinnie. He's in shock, I reckon.' Riley grabbed Shaun around the shoulders and led him to a folding chair next to the fire. Vinnie wrapped the blanket around his shoulders.

'What happened? Where's Glen?'

'I think he's drowned. He must have fallen out of his boat. We couldn't find him.' Riley said.

'You mean you couldn't find him, Riley. I let him drown. I just watched him disappear. Oh, fuck.' Shaun hunched over his knees and threw up onto the sand.

'Shaun, there's nothing you could have done. It was rough out there.'

'He asked me for help and I just watched him. I didn't care that he was drowning.'

Riley knelt alongside him, carefully avoiding the vomit. 'You don't mean that, Shaun.'

Shaun said nothing. Riley stood and pulled Vinnie away, nearer one of the tents.

'We have to get help. I'm going to paddle to one of the shacks over on Sugars Beach and get them to call the police. Can you stay and look after him?'

'Yeah, sure. What about what he said, about not doing anything? Is that true?'

Riley led him back to Shaun.

'Mate, I'm going to get help. I'm sure they'll organise a search. Maybe your dad was able to swim to the beach on the other side of the channel.'

Shaun kept his head down but nodded. Riley turned Shaun's head to face him. 'Shaun, you can't tell anyone what you just told us, ok. It was just a terrible accident alright, nothing you could have done.'

'But ...'

'No but. What you said is just between us. No one else needs to know. Alright, I'm going now. You just rest.'

Riley walked down to his kayak, followed by Vinnie.

'Be careful, Riley. Don't make it two missing people.'

Riley paddled into the darkness. When Vinnie could see him no longer, he went to Glen's tent and pulled out an unopened whiskey bottle. He cracked the seal and took a deep swig. He pulled up a chair next to Shaun and passed him the bottle.

***

Midnight passed. Shaun hadn't spoken for ages and Vinnie didn't know what to do. He had taken three or four swigs from the bottle – he couldn't remember – and was starting to feel fuzzy. Shaun had refused the bottle and had just sat there shivering for about half an hour before he became catatonic.

Suddenly, Vinnie saw a light bobbing in the distance and shortly after heard an engine throbbing. He ran down to the shore and called out 'Over here,' even though he knew they could probably see the fire which he had kept alive with fresh logs.

Riley and an old man jumped from the boat. Vinnie thought the man looked about sixty, a solid man with white whiskers. He wore fishing overalls over a checked flannelette shirt and rubber boots.

'This the lad, then?' he asked, pointing at Shaun.

'Yeah,' said Vinnie, 'but he's, like, out of it.'

'Shock,' said the man. He leant over Shaun and took his pipe from his mouth. Shaun seemed to take in the strong, sweet tobacco smell and turned to look at the man. 'You all right, son?'

Shaun looked at him blankly. The man picked up the whiskey bottle lying next to Shaun's chair and glared at Vinnie.

'How much of this has he had? Not good for shock.'

'No, nothing. I had it, not him.'

'Good.' He turned to Shaun. 'You'll be right, lad. Help is on its way.'

Riley ran to them puffing. 'There's a police car not far away, I saw the lights flashing.'

The 4WD patrol car arrived and left its motor running, headlights pointed at the group. Two officers got out. The driver was a big, solid man with an enormous belly. He was obviously the senior of the two. The other policeman was tall and lean. He followed in his senior's footsteps.

'Jack.' The senior nodded at the old man.

'Evenin', Gordon. Bad business here.'

'What have the boys told you, Jack?'

Jack pointed his pipe at Shaun.

'This lad's father went out in a kayak, apparently. Hasn't come back in.'

'Have you had a look for him?' the younger officer asked.

'Don't be daft, son. He went toward the mouth and I'm not taking my boat there in these conditions.'

'That's ok, Jack,' Gordon said. 'I wouldn't either.' He turned to the boys. 'Alright boys, let's get you back to Goolwa and you can tell me exactly what's happened.'

'What about my dad?' Everyone turned to Shaun. His voice was low and weak and no one had expected it. 'Are you just going to leave him out there?'

Gordon spoke quietly to Shaun. 'We can't do anything tonight, on, it's too dangerous. Don't worry, we'll get a search out at first light in the morning.'

The young constable chipped in. 'If it's too dangerous now, what will be different in the morning? The wind might pick up more.'

'Well, Constable, we'll use someone who knows these waters better than anyone.'

Jack took a deep draw on his pipe. 'Yep, you need Hector for this one.'

10

1991

Sergeant Gordon Cook strolled down to the water's edge. Moored a few metres away from the wharf was a low-sitting boat of around twelve metres. He looked up at the sky, cloudless and bright. The wind had dropped away overnight and he was hopeful the old man would be able to wrap up the search for Glen Chambers sooner rather than later.

It was always a nasty business when someone drowned in the river but it was even worse when their family witnessed it. Today a thirteen-year-old boy had been traumatised.

He was puffing by the time he stood next to the boat. He knew he needed to get a bit fitter, shed a few kilos; but he liked a beer after work and he wasn't asked to exert too much physical energy so he'd let himself go a bit.

'You there, Hector?' he called into the open hatch of the Fairy Queen.

The old man poked his head out. 'Sergeant Cook. What brings you down here this morning?'

'I'm afraid it's nothing pleasant, Hector. I'm hoping you can give us a hand.'

'Someone drownded, I'm guessing,' Hector said as he stepped onto the deck.

Gordon Cook smiled wryly. Hector always used the word "drownded" and Gordon still had no idea whether it was a deliberate mispronunciation or not. He assumed it was because, although Hector's education was limited, he was an articulate man.

Hector was dressed in his usual kit; a long-sleeved shirt rolled to the elbows under braces holding up his trousers. As usual, his hat was perched on his head; Gordon couldn't remember ever seeing him without it. He held a roll-your-own cigarette in a holder between his index and middle finger and wagged it as he spoke.

'I'm afraid so,' Gordon responded, 'down near the mouth. With the wind last night, I'm not sure where the body could have gone.'

Hector grimaced. 'Not just the wind, Gordon. The tide was a strong one last night, too. Could have taken him out to sea. What time?'

'We think around eleven, a bit after.'

'Close to the turn of the tide then. Might be lucky and he's stayed inside. You want me to have a look?'

Gordon was relieved. If anyone could find Glen, it was Hector.

'Let's get started then, can we? I'm going to Zimmermann's this afternoon for a cuppa.'

Gordon knew that Hector's routine on a Saturday afternoon was to catch up with his pals, Eldon Zimmermann and his wife, Mary. A glass or two of red wine for Eldon, a white for Mary and a cup of tea for Hector. All with the sharing of tales. And Hector had tales.

The old man was of Czechoslovakian heritage but had been raised in Murray Bridge during the great depression. He'd bought the Fairy Queen in 1938 and worked along the river constructing and maintaining infrastructure. After, he settled at Milang on Lake Alexandrina where he became a successful fisherman and earned the title "the old man of the lake." He was also known to have travelled to the southeast of the state to hunt foxes on farmer's properties and to have shot rats for the bounty along the banks of the river.

The construction of the barrages in the river system restricted the flow of salt water from the sea into the river. Hector had to relocate his boat to Goolwa, closer to the sea, to be able to continue fishing.

Gordon didn't know Hector well. He'd called on him a couple of times to help search for drowned bodies and had quickly come to respect the old man's knowledge. Many in the town regarded him as a recluse; it was probably truer that he just never made a fuss and was selective in his choice of friends, with whom he socialised often.

Although the breeze was lighter than the night before, it was enough to take the heat out of the day as they made their way to the barrages. The old boat was slow but steady. Hector steered from the helm at the stern and kept a keen eye on river traffic ahead. Gordon watched him as his cheeks grew rosier in the breeze. Hector wasn't a big man, or heavy set, but the life on the river had instilled a tough resilience and a strong character.

'It's a sad case, this one,' Gordon explained to Hector. 'The bloke's young lad watched him go under. They were out canoeing when the father got into trouble; God knows why at that hour.'

'Locals, are they?'

'Yeah. The bloke had taken his son and two of the boys' mates on a camping trip to the mouth. They all live in Goolwa.'

'How old were the boys?'

'About thirteen. Why?'

'I've been having some trouble with some kids throwing rocks onto the roof of my boat. Pretty bloomin' annoying, I can tell you. Hope it wasn't them.'

'I don't know, Hector.'

'One thing I dislike more than those kids, though.'

'Oh. What's that?'

Hector pulled his cigarette holder from his mouth and pointed. 'Pelicans,' was all he said.

Gordon assumed it was because they robbed some of Hector's catch.

Ahead they could see the houses of Sugars Beach. Gordon raised his binoculars and pivoted around toward the river mouth. The sandy shore stretched back to the sandhills behind and he could see the police four-wheel drive parked near the campsite that Glen had set up the previous night. Gordon had asked a couple of his officers to return this morning to see if Glen's kayak had washed up and to wait for him and Hector to arrive. He was pleased to see that they were already there.

As they approached, one of the officers waved and after a short exchange, established that they hadn't sighted the missing kayak. Alongside the officer stood a boy, shielding his eyes against the sun as he watched the Fairy Queen. Gordon had asked Vinnie to accompany the officers should they require any clarification about what had happened; where Shaun and Glen had set out from in their kayaks and in what direction.

Hector steered the Fairy Queen away from shore and toward the river mouth.

'That the boy whose father drownded?' he asked.

'No. That was one of his mates that camped with him. You know him?'

'Only that he's one of the little ratbags that stones my boat.'

'What are you thinking, Hector? About the body, I mean.' Gordon asked.

'If the kayak hasn't drifted back toward the campsite, it's either gone out the mouth or further east, away from the campsite. If we find the kayak, that will indicate which way the body might have drifted. What I reckon is that with the turn of the tide, the kayak and the body will have come back away from the mouth and the wind had then pushed them away from the camp toward the Coorong.'

Minutes later, they had crossed the mouth. The current was known to be treacherous in the area at times and there was no one better than Hector at reading it. On this occasion, his expertise wasn't needed but Gordon was nonetheless happy to get onto the other side.

'The kayak will float easier than a body and probably catch the wind better, so I think it will be further along than the body. On the other hand, 'said Hector, 'the kayak will be easier to spot. What colour was it?'

'Yellow.'

'Then let's look for a yellow kayak. As long as it had the proper flotation, it won't have sunk.'

It took thirty minutes but eventually, Gordon spotted a flash of yellow on the bank of the Coorong. They had travelled a little more than two kilometres from the camp. Hector steered the Fairy Queen close to the bank so that Gordon could jump out. A brief inspection showed nothing unusual. The kayak had taken on a little water and the paddle had drifted off separately but otherwise, it was in good condition.

Hector threw Gordon a rope which he attached to the carry handle of the kayak. After Gordon had scrambled back on board, Hector turned the boat back toward the mouth, trailing the kayak behind.

They travelled back slowly, winding from bank to bank to provide the best visibility of either side as well as the middle of the channel. Gordon sat on the foredeck with his binoculars raised and after twenty minutes raised his hand to Hector.

'Over there,' he pointed, 'there's something floating.'

Hector changed course. His theory had been correct. As the Fairy Queen eased alongside, they grabbed the body and hoisted it aboard.

'Looks like this is your man, Gordon.'

'I certainly hope this is him, Hector. Listen, if you drop me back with my officers, you can feel free to head back to Goolwa. And thanks, mate.'

Gordon watched as his officers loaded the body bag into the rear of the police 4x4. He turned to watch the Fairy Queen motoring slowly back toward the barrages. He hoped he never needed to call on Hector's assistance again but he was relieved that the old man would be there to help if he did.

He walked to where Vinnie was standing.

'Come on, son. Let's get you home.'

11

Saturday 20 April 2019 (Day 3)

Riley was gone before Kate woke. He was on the road before almost anyone in Goolwa was awake.

While he had fallen asleep on the sofa, fatigued mentally more than physically, he found himself unable to sleep once they had gone to bed.

The only car he passed on the way to the station was driven by the newsagent, starting his morning run of deliveries. He wasn't sure what more he could be doing about the investigation this early in the morning but that wasn't why he had decided to get moving. During one of his waking moments, he remembered that the Goolwa Wooden Boat Festival was to be held the following weekend. It was an event that attracted thousands of tourists to the town to look over hundreds of wooden boats and to partake in all the associated festivities. As the town's most senior police officer, his responsibility was to review the strategic and operating plans put together by the festival's committee and assess any police resourcing that was required.

Riley was grateful that the event had been run for several years and had developed sound practices over the years to ensure the safety of all the attendees but he also knew that no one could be complacent.

As a licensed venue, there was always likely to be some over-indulgence in alcohol, leading to inappropriate behaviours at many levels. The combination of alcohol consumption and water-based activities was a further risk factor that necessitated all the emergency services taking an interest in the festival. And, of course, the usual lost children, lost property, traffic and personal injury issues.

He had just finished going over the plans and confirming that the necessary police resources had been booked when he felt an urgent need for coffee and food. He walked out the front door of the station and almost bumped into Marty Hunt. Marty was the leader of the dive team assigned to the search for Aiden. Highly experienced, he had dredged the murky waters of the Murray River on too many occasions and it had never become any easier. The coldness, lack of visibility and the risks of getting snagged on some unseen object made his job one of the most dangerous in the police force. However, the squad operated, as expected, with a high level of teamwork, each member with a focus on looking after their colleagues and with a resolve to get the job done despite the inherent discomfort resulting from the tough conditions and the risks.

Marty had assisted Riley on several occasions before when people had gone missing in the river. Sometimes it was a swimmer who had over-estimated their ability to deal with the tricky river currents, sometimes a fisher who had fallen from their boat without a buoyancy vest and on occasion a drunk who had wandered off from a party and fallen off a slippery bank to their demise. The children were the worst. A few months earlier, Marty and his team had dragged the body of a toddler from the river a few kilometres upstream from Goolwa. Although they were successful in completing their assignment, success for Marty's team rarely brought pleasure. More often, it was the beginning of a period of misery for someone's family and loved ones.

Despite this, Marty was a good-humoured cop, lean and pleasant-faced. He could provide a calming influence, even after emerging muddy, cold and wet from a dive. His first need was always for a piping hot, sweet black tea accompanied by a Scotch Finger biscuit and his team never failed to have it ready for him.

Riley pulled up short, in front of Marty, but still had to put his hand to Marty's chest to prevent a full-frontal collision.

'Oh, Marty, I wasn't expecting you blokes for a little while yet.'

'Well, we wanted to get started early. The forecast is for a northerly wind later on. That's going to chop the water up a bit so we'd like to be done before then.'

'Makes sense. Hey, we'll be doing our briefing in fifteen minutes or so if you want to sit in on it. I understand if you want to get moving though.'

'Yeah, I will, Riley. I just wanted to let you know we were here. The guys are setting up down by the boat shed. We know that area pretty well after fishing a fellow out of there a couple of years ago, so unless there's something more we need to know, we'll get on with it.'

'No, nothing else, Marty, and I hope you don't find the young lad down there. As I mentioned, though, we may also have a homicide associated with the boy's disappearance, so if you find anything else that looks like it's been recently dumped there, we'd like to have a look at it.'

'No worries, mate. I'll give you a call if we have anything before you come down.'

Fifteen minutes later, Riley was back in the temporary incident room they had set up. His team were all present; Rachel Cross, Phil Reid and the two young constables he'd been able to second from Victor Harbor - Oliver Townsend and Craig Thompson.

Riley stood in front of the whiteboard and addressed the team.

'Ok, everyone. Here's how I see what we have so far. Vinnie Waters was killed, apparently crushed under the weight of a boat he was working on. There are a couple of things that make this look like it was more than an accident, but nothing that proves it. Firstly, there's the fact that the boy he was looking after, 11-year-old Aiden Chambers, has gone missing from the boat shed. We'll come back to Aiden shortly. Secondly, Doc Cleaver identified what looked like a separate injury to Vinnie's head, one that occurred before the boat fell on him.

'Finally, there is the wrench that Oliver fished out of the river. It doesn't look to have been there long and there is no obvious reason why it should be there unless someone wanted to hide it.'

Phil Reid queried, 'So, it's possibly the weapon used to knock Vinnie out?'

'Possibly, Phil, although I reiterate, we don't have any proof. Hopefully, the post-mortem and the forensics will give us a clearer picture. I hope to have something from both of them later today. In the meantime, we've been following up on some other leads, which I'll come to in a minute. Now, you might be wondering why I'm focussing on Vinnie's death first, rather than Aiden's disappearance. The reason, and I might be wrong, is that I am strongly of the view that the boy is missing because of Vinnie's death, however that happened.'

There were murmurs of agreement around the room.

'Brian Thompson, with some of you, has had his guys almost turn the town upside down looking for Aiden. No sign of him anywhere. Brian is coming in this morning to mark up the search areas on the map so at least we know where they *have* looked. Rachel and I have spoken extensively with his parents and we are convinced they can offer us no more than they already have. To be blunt, we have run out of leads. Right now, we have a dive team about to search the river and, hopefully, that will come up empty. I am planning to interview some of Aiden's teachers and friends today if I can track them down, to see if they can shed any light on where he might be. I also suspect we will need some media liaison later on as well. Remember, no one talks to them unless they are authorised to.

'So, back to Vinnie's death, which, as I said, I think is key to this. We know that Vinnie received a phone call Thursday that unsettled him. We don't know if that's connected to his death, but we need to check it out. Rachel, how did you go with his phone records?'

Rachel leaned forward. 'Riley, this isn't what you want to hear, but he didn't get a phone call until after 10.00 am on the day he died.'

'But Carla was definite she heard him take a call and his demeanour changed straight after.'

'I'm sorry,' she said, 'but there's no record. Could he have had a second phone?'

'Messenger.' It was from Oliver Townsend. All eyes in the room turned to him.

'Facebook Messenger,' he expanded. 'If you don't want a call traced, you could make it using Facebook Messenger. It's done using the internet rather than the mobile phone network, so there's no trace of it in your phone records. I hear a lot of conversations people don't want to be recorded are done this way now. There are other apps too but I can't say I know them.'

'Would there be any trace of the call?' Riley asked.

'Unless he deleted it, there should be a record of it on his Messenger app. If he wiped that, I don't know. We would have to get an IT nerd onto it.'

Riley looked at Rachel. 'We have his mobile phone. Can you check that out as soon as you can?' She nodded.

Phil Reid could hold back no longer.

'Riley, I know you are questioning whether there was a follow-up to that call. I guess you're wondering if someone might have paid Vinnie a visit at the boatshed. Well, we had just one thing that came out of our door knock yesterday. We spoke to a Mr. Symes who lives near the boatshed. His wife, Anna called back a few minutes ago. She'd been away, in Adelaide, and just got home this morning. The point is, she remembers that while she was out walking her dog Thursday afternoon, she noticed two cars parked there. One presumably was Vinnie's but two people got out of the other car, a Blue Holden Commodore.'

Riley felt a growing excitement. This could be the lead they needed.

'Did she get registration details, even the model?'

'No,' Phil replied, 'she didn't think much of it, but she thought it was maybe early 2000s. I can go back with photos of the different models of Commodore to see if we can refine it.'

'Yes, do that. What about the two people? Could she give a description?'

Phil flicked open his notebook. 'She said one was a big, burly bloke. Probably 190 centimetres tall and maybe 120 kilograms, dark hair, leather jacket and jeans. The other one was smaller. She thought maybe 160 to 165 centimetres tall and light build. He had fairer hair. She couldn't remember what he was wearing. She said he could have even been a lad.'

'Ok, we need to identify them. Anyone know of someone local that fits the descriptions and with previous records?'

He was met with shaking heads.

Duties were assigned and it was agreed to reconvene once the forensic and post-mortem results were available. At last, Riley felt that he had something to follow and yet he was no closer to finding Aiden.

Phil Reid and Rachel Cross were investigating their leads, so Riley grabbed Oliver Townsend and Craig Thompson and headed to the boatshed. He was keen to see how the divers were progressing and to make sure that they had the necessary security around their operations.

He was pleased to see that Marty had planned well ahead and two non-diver constables were managing the tape barriers to keep on-lookers at a distance. Riley noted that amongst the small but interested crowd was Shaun Chambers. He wasn't surprised when Shaun strode to the police car as it pulled to a stop on the green verge next to the tape.

Riley turned to Oliver.

'Just make sure the divers have got everything they need, will you? I'll be over shortly for an update but I'd better talk with Shaun first. Craig, you stay with me.'

Riley wasn't expecting any trouble from Shaun but wanted to be cautious. He held his hand to his eyes to protect against the glare of the morning sun as he turned to Shaun.

'Word travels fast, Shaun.'

'Yeah, well I have friends who live nearby and they kept me informed. It's a shame you didn't.' Shaun did not attempt to mute his accusatory tone.

'Shaun, do you really think you want to be here if these guys do find Aiden in there? It won't be nice.'

'So, you do think he's drowned?' The defiance was gone and his eyes were pleading for hope.

'I hope not, Shaun, but you know, we have to explore all possibilities. We haven't found him anywhere else so we have to exclude this option as confidently as we can.'

'I don't know what to do, Riley, but I need to be here in case. It's so hard, everyone here, watching. Sympathising.'

Riley put a hand to his shoulder. His old friend was nearly broken.

'Listen, why don't you come and sit under the tent? You'll be the first to know. Is Carla coming down?'

'I don't think so. She's not saying much.'

Riley led Shaun to the tent the divers had established where they kept spare equipment and any evidence they needed to tag. He sat him down on a chair, and then walked down to the river bank.

Marty and a colleague were pulling themselves out of the muddy silt onto the bank. They were donned in full wetsuits and scuba gear.

'Christ, it's cold in there,' Marty exclaimed as Riley gave him a helping hand up the bank. Oliver arrived from the tent with a thermos and two cups. He poured one for each of the divers.

Marty nodded thanks to Oliver and looked up at the young constable.

'Thanks, Buddy. Any chance you could fetch the packet of biscuits from the tent?'

Riley sat on the bank next to him, watching the second pair of divers enter the water. The wind was just starting to rise, but if they were lucky, they would still get a couple more hours in before the swell called an end to diving for the day.

'Anything of interest?'

Marty sipped on the hot, black tea. 'Not yet. It's pretty murky so we are mainly relying on feel. We've only covered a small area so far and because it's so cold we are rotating pretty quickly.'

'I don't envy you. I need to do some interviews, so I'll drop back in an hour or so but let me know if anything comes up, will you?'

Marty gave him a nod and a thumbs up. After checking again on Shaun, Riley and Craig returned to the police car. About to get in, Riley's phone rang. He tossed the keys to Craig and walked around to the passenger side as he answered.

'Hi, Rachel. What have you got?'

'Well, Oliver was on the money with the phone call. It wasn't on the phone network; it was a call through an app called Chatterley which works much the same as Messenger. Vinnie received a call at 8.05 on the morning he died, lasting for 39 seconds.'

'Do we know who it was from?'

'The name shown is A Narchist, but I can't see anyone in his contacts with that name. It looks like the only other call he had from this Narchist was over twelve months ago.'

'Can you see if we can trace who this person is? I admit I have no idea how.'

'Already onto it. I have the tech guys in Adelaide looking to see if they can track it. Apparently, they may be able to come up with an IP address for the device the call was made on, but they warned that it might not get us any closer to knowing who has that device. There's every chance it's a burner phone.'

'Can you even get a burner phone in Australia? I thought you had to provide ID to get a SIM so that it can be traced.'

'That's true, but apparently, people bring them in from overseas and then hook them into a wi-fi network or VPN so that they're untraceable. The guys say they can probably also find an email address or mobile phone number used to set up the Facebook account but again they suggest that's going to be a dead end.'

'OK, thanks. Rachel. Stick with it. At least we can confirm that Vinnie got a call and the fact it was an unusual one, maybe unexpected, makes it of continued interest to us.'

Riley ended the call and looked across at Craig.

Riley had expected him to start driving but he was looking blank-faced back at him.

'Oh, sorry, Craig you need to know where we are going, don't you?'

He fished a folded paper from his pocket and read the address to Craig. They arrived at the home of Aiden's class teacher a few minutes later. The discussion with her yielded nothing they had not already known; that Aiden was a quiet, well-behaved boy with few friends, all of whom checked against the list that Carla Chambers had given them.

The teacher was aware of the family situation and knew both Shaun and Vinnie from the times they had picked Aiden up from school. She wasn't aware of any conflict in the home and Aiden seemed reasonably well-adjusted to the change in the family structure.

As they left the teacher's house, Riley was relieved to see that the wind had softened into a mild breeze. The wind shift that was predicted to bring stronger winds from the north had not yet arrived, which was good news for the divers.

He was deep in thought when his phone again rang. Jolted, he looked at the screen and saw it was Ray Dennis, the pathologist undertaking the autopsy on Vinnie Waters. He knew that Paul Smith regarded him highly.

'Senior Sergeant O'Brien? It's Ray Dennis from the Coroner's office.'

'Yes, good to hear from you. I've heard a lot about you from DI Smith.'

'Likewise, I'm sure,' Dennis replied, 'I guess you're keen to hear the result of the autopsy on Vincent John Waters?'

It had been a long time since Riley had heard him called Vincent; perhaps way back in his teens when Marion or Colin had addressed him in a serious tone.

Doctor Dennis confirmed the cause of death presumed by Tony Cleaver; mechanical asphyxia caused by the crushing weight of the boat.

His ribs had not broken and his lungs had not been ruptured, which had meant that it had taken some time for Vinnie to die. He also explained to Riley how the crush had forced increased intravascular pressure in the upper part of his body causing blood vessels to burst in his eyes, what he had called a subconjunctival haemorrhage, and on his face.

'You're aware also, Senior Sergeant, of the significant injury on his temple?'

'Yes, our local doctor believes that it was inflicted before he died. Is that right?'

'It is. But the thing that you will find of real interest, is that we have matched the indentation to his skull with the wrench that your man fished out of the river. I will let the forensics people elaborate, but the fact that Mr Waters' hair and other DNA was found on the wrench indicates that this was certainly the weapon that caused the head wound.'

'But didn't kill him?'

'No, the boat was the weapon that killed him.'

Riley thought momentarily before conjecturing.

'You described the boat as a "weapon." You believe someone killed Vinnie Waters.'

'Yes, I do. Here's my reasoning. The wound that was inflicted on Mr Waters' head was delivered in a round arm action from the right and behind him. It was most likely a right-handed person, possibly using both hands to hold the wrench. It was also either someone who was shorter than the victim or was at least positioned lower than him.'

'So that would have disabled him. Then he was dragged under the boat, which was lowered onto him.'

'That's my hypothesis. We have also identified bruising on his wrists that indicate he may have been dragged by them to the locus of his death. Regrettably, there are no scratches or other DNA evidence on his body to indicate who that might have been. The other compelling fact that again forensics will pass on to you, is that the lifting mechanism appears to be in perfect working order. There is no suggestion that it had failed and we are certain that Mr Waters did not operate the control from the position where he was found. Ergo, someone else lowered it onto him.'

'Thank you, Doctor Dennis. I had felt that Vinnie's death didn't make sense and this just confirms it.'

'Happy to help, and make it Ray next time. I'll get my formal preliminary report to you in the next day or so, but in the meantime, I presume you will be wanting to speak with Forensics. No doubt Shelley Harrison will call you shortly.'

'Well, Craig,' Riley said, 'that was a call that's changed the game. I think we need to get back to the station and reset. First, though, let's call past the boatshed. I reckon they will be nearly ready to pack up for the day.'

Riley didn't know whether to feel upset, relieved or vindicated that his intuition had been proven correct. On one hand, it made more sense to him, knowing Vinnie as he had.

It also gave him hope that Aiden was alive. On the other hand, it wasn't pleasant to hear that a one-time friend had been murdered; he felt like an unfortunate accident could be accepted so much easier. It was also disturbing to him that if Aiden was still alive, he could most likely be in grave danger. Far from investigating potentially two accidents, it was clear he was probably looking at two crimes; the murder of Vinnie Waters and the abduction of Aiden Chambers.

They arrived at the boatshed to see a significantly smaller group of people watching the dive activities. While it was obvious that the team was in the middle of packing up for the day, most bystanders had simply got bored and dissipated into their normal routines. Shaun, however, was still in the tent, watching and waiting. Carla was with him leaning into him for support. Riley was encouraged that they had been able to team together to manage the stress they were going through.

Oliver greeted Riley and confirmed that the dives had not yielded anything pertinent to the investigation and, thankfully, not the body of an eleven-year-old boy. Riley sat with Shaun and Carla.

'So, no news is good news at the moment,' Shaun said flatly.

'Well, certainly from this site. But we may have a couple of leads to work on.'

Carla and Shaun lent forward. This was the first time they had heard news that had given them any hope. He relayed to them the findings of the post-mortem and the sighting of the Blue Commodore at the boatshed around the time that Vinnie had been killed. He also told them that they were following through on the call that Vinnie had received that morning and urged Carla to search her memory for any other details of the call. Finally, Riley questioned Shaun whether he had sighted the Blue Commodore when he had dropped Aiden at the boatshed. He hadn't.

Riley suggested they go home as there was nothing further that they would learn from the scene and promised to keep them updated.

He watched them walk solemnly away, Shaun's arms around Carla's shoulders.

Marty Hunt walked up to him, pulling his wetsuit sleeves down around his shoulders.

'It must be hard for them, but at least there's a chance the boy is still alive.'

'I know.'

Riley invited Marty and his team to join them back at the station for the afternoon briefing, but Marty declined. In his view, there was nothing further his team could offer in the absence of a more definitive lead on the potential location of Aiden's body or other vital evidence. Nonetheless, he offered that Riley could call on them again if anything arose.

Riley and Oliver returned to the station. Riley was keen to get the briefing underway but wanted to get the forensics results from Shelley Harrison first. He was relieved when she answered his call on the third ring.

'Riley, hi. I was just about to call you. Should have been earlier but, you know, too much to do, not enough people. Sorry, anyway, I'm rambling. I guess you want to know about Vinnie Waters?'

'You got it. I spoke to Ray Dennis earlier, so I'm hoping you can fill in some gaps for us.'

'I reckon I can, a bit at least. You probably heard from Ray, we have a match of the DNA and hair on the wrench to that belonging to Mr Waters. Superficially, at least, that means that the wrench was the weapon used to disable Mr. Waters, but not kill him. By the way, we've also matched the skull indentation with the wrench, so we're very confident that this was what he was hit with.'

'Ray also said that the blow was most likely delivered by a right-handed person who was lower than Vinnie.'

'Yes, my feeling is that it was someone a few inches shorter than him and probably using both hands.'

Riley asked the question that had played on his mind since hearing Ray Dennis's report. 'Could the wrench have been swung by an eleven-year-old boy?'

'In my opinion, it's possible but unlikely. It's a pretty significant piece of equipment, weighing in at nearly five kilograms, 4.7 to be more precise. Look, I won't say it couldn't have been the boy, particularly in light of other evidence.'

'Oh, yeah, what's that?'

'Well. We didn't get any useful fingerprints off the wrench. We did lift prints from the door. We picked up three or four sets that we are trying to identify. At present, we have matches for Vinnie Waters, to be expected, and for Shaun Chambers. We know Shaun was there, so that doesn't mean much. At least one of the other prints is for a smaller hand, possibly a woman or child. There's no match to Carla Chambers, so perhaps they're Aiden's. We've also picked some up in the office that look like a child's and we think that they are Aiden's but they don't match those on the door. We won't know which are his until we get some that we know are Aiden's prints to compare. We've organised with Carla to get them tomorrow.'

'What about the control for the electric winch?'

'Ok, that gets interesting. Again, we have Vinnie Waters' prints, plus a couple of others. Again, a small print, a woman's or a child's. They match those on the door but not those in the office.

'The other prints on there are adult but not viable for identification. If we just stay on the fingerprints, we picked up several others in the shed from different locations. At this stage, we have positively identified some as belonging to Vinnie Waters, Shaun Chambers and Carla Chambers. We have around five other sets that we are trying to match against our databases but get this, three of the unidentified sets are from small hands. One matches those in the office and one matches the ones on the door, but the third set we can't identify anywhere else. So, in summary, we have three sets of fingerprints that are small enough to be a child's or a small adult. One of them is probably Aiden's, but we don't know about the others.'

Riley was becoming confused. 'So, we know we have Vinnie's prints which we would expect. We know we have Shaun's and Carla's but nothing that incriminates them in any way.'

'Not yet, at least,' Shelley confirmed.

'And,' Riley continued, 'there are several other sets yet to be identified and some of those appear to belong to different people, is that right?'

'Well, children, say teen or pre-teen, or women, or a man with small hands. Or some combination of the three. Is it possible Aiden had a friend at the shed?'

'Not on the day in question, as far as we know.'

'Well, all these prints are pretty fresh, so I think you 're looking at people who were in the shed on that day.'

'Man, Shelley, your investigations have raised more questions than answers. Was there anything else from the forensics, so far?'

Shelley sighed. 'Nothing you don't know already.

'We know that Shaun and Carla had handled the tyre lever and the torch when they forced the door and we can confirm that the door was indeed locked from the outside. We went through Aiden's school bag and nothing came out of that, but we can say that the computer he was playing Minecraft on had an automatic timeout after ten minutes and it timed out at 5.33 on the day in question. In other words, you can assume that Aiden, or someone, was still using it at 5.23.'

After the call with Shelley, Riley convened his team for a briefing to update them on the findings of the post-mortem and the forensics investigations. The consensus was that they were now dealing with a murder investigation as well as a missing person. Riley only hoped it wasn't a double murder.

The fatigue of the team was becoming evident. Working on a murder case was a new experience for most of them and they'd had only limited support during the investigation so far. Riley instructed them to take Sunday morning off. They could re-group in the afternoon with the search team if no new leads came up. He also decided that his first call in the morning had to be to Paul Smith, not only to bring him up to date with their findings but to appeal for additional resources.

12

1992 -1995

Compared to Shaun's mother's funeral, Glen's was a big affair. Most of his customers attended as did the many friends he had accumulated in a lifetime at Goolwa.

With the crossover into the new year, the service was delayed until the second week in January. Initially, Shaun's Aunt Janet had wanted to take him to her house in Strathalbyn but Shaun hadn't been keen. He had lost both parents in the space of a year and couldn't bear the thought of being separated from his friends as well. Aunt Janet had never been in a situation like this before and decided that she would stay with Shaun in Glen's house until he was ready to move.

In the early hours following Glen's drowning, the boys were given a full medical examination to assess the level of trauma they had experienced. Of course, the main concern was for Shaun and it took a couple of hours for him to become communicative. He was the last to be interviewed.

Riley and Vinnie held to the script they had agreed. They explained that the day had been normal, a perfect start to their planned adventure. This was later corroborated by other witnesses who had been at the beach during the day. The boys related how they had gone exploring in the sandhills and came back to a depressed and subdued Glen. After they had gone for a walk, they returned to find Glen drunk and abusive toward Shaun. They explained how Shaun had taken off in his kayak and that Glen had followed him, probably not the best thing to do in his state. They said that Glen must have gone too close to the mouth and been sucked in. Nothing was said about Shaun watching his father as he struggled to stay afloat. As far as they were concerned, Shaun hadn't seen Glen after he left the beach.

By the time Sergeant Gordon Cook eventually interviewed Shaun, it was after three in the morning. Everyone was tired and the sergeant was as gentle as he could have been. Shaun was unable to explain what happened in any detail and made no mention of watching his father as he drowned.

Vinnie had gone home with his parents earlier. At Riley's request, his parents waited until Shaun's interview was finished and suggested that Shaun stay with them until alternative arrangements were in place.

In the days that followed, Shaun and Riley talked about what had happened and agreed they would keep to the story as they had told it. Shaun couldn't imagine what people would think of a boy who watched his father die in front of him, no matter how abusive his father may have been. And, Shaun thought, his father hadn't really been abusive; he'd just struggled with the same issues as he had. Glen had dealt with it differently though; he'd found refuge in a bottle and had lost connection with his son.

Riley and Shaun called Vinnie one evening and in a hushed conversation confirmed the pact to keep their secret.

Shaun's Aunt Janet cut short her summer holiday in Victoria and arrived in Goolwa three days after Glen's drowning. Although Shaun would have preferred to stay with Riley's family, he knew that wasn't a long-term solution. After some discussion, Janet agreed that he could stay in Goolwa a bit longer and she would look after him in Glen's house. She accompanied him to the police station for another interview. Gordon Cook told them that the post-mortem had come through, confirming that Glen had died by drowning and that his blood alcohol level was a contributing factor. Simply, the sergeant said, once Glen took to the kayak, it was an accident waiting to happen. He told them that the coroner would make a report but that in his view it would be labelled as accidental death through misadventure. As far as he was concerned, his investigation was complete.

After Glen's funeral, Janet insisted that Shaun move to her house at Strathalbyn, about thirty-five kilometres from Goolwa. Shaun wasn't happy to move but he knew that there was no alternative. His farewell to Riley was the hardest. The day before the move, he cycled to Riley's house and broke down. Shameful tears rolled down his cheeks.

'I don't want to go to Strath, Riley. All my friends are here, especially you.' He felt he was embarrassing himself. Maybe he was the baby his father accused him of being.

Riley put his arm around him. 'Shaun, we will still be able to catch up. Maybe your aunt will let you still play footy for Goolwa. That way you'll still see us all. And if that doesn't work out, I'll get Mum to take me to Strath some weekends. Anyway, you'll be right. You'll make new friends at school and you already know some of the kids who play footy there.'

'I know. But you're my best friend. I don't want to make new friends.'

Shaun saw Vinnie on the morning of the move. Their parting was more matter-of-fact. Shaun put that down to Vinnie having moved from Yankalilla only a year before, so for him, it wasn't a big deal.

'So, what's happening with the house?' Vinnie asked.

'I don't know. Aunt Janet said something about wills and probate and stuff that I don't understand. I think it'll get sold.'

'So, you'll be a rich man, Shaun.'

'Rich? I don't think so. I'll be living with my auntie away from all my friends. I don't call that rich.'

'Don't worry about it, Shaun. Strath's a bigger town than Goolwa. There'd be heaps of kids our age. Anyway, take care. I gotta go help Dad in the back garden. Drop in when you're in Goolwa, yeah?'

And with that, Vinnie had moved on.

Aunt Janet's husband, Malcolm, had died a few years before. He was a farmer and when he died, she had kept the property. She leased out most of the farmland and kept a block for her own use, comprising the main house and a few hectares that stretched down to the River Angas. Shaun had always enjoyed coming to her house, exploring along the riverbank, sometimes trying to catch small fish and yabbies. But that was a visit. Now, he was going to live here.

He still loved the block but it was a few kilometres from town, so he wasn't going to be able to just jump on his bike to visit friends. He'd have to spend weekends getting bored around the house.

The house itself was large and cold. It had been built in the 1920s and had floors that squeaked and a roof that creaked with even the slightest wind. On the positive side, it never got hot in summer, protected by solid brick walls and surrounded by a generous verandah. Shaun had fond memories of sitting on the west-facing verandah with his mother, watching the pink sky, waiting for a burning sun to drop behind the gum trees.

Now, he just had dread. Years of isolation. Did he love his aunt? He hadn't really thought about it. She'd always just been there. Janet and Helen had both been fairly close to Shaun's mum; they were on the phone with each other all the time. Neither of them liked Glen much and the feeling had been mutual so it was unusual for them to come to Goolwa if Glen was around. Glen hadn't been to Strathalbyn for years.

Janet was old as far as Shaun was concerned. She was fifty, about six years older than Karen, but she acted much older. She was dowdy, conservative and quite strict as far as child behaviour went. With no children of her own - Helen didn't have any either - Janet had no understanding and little tolerance of the peculiarities of young people. She did, however, have a sense of duty and Shaun suspected that Janet was almost grateful that Glen was no longer on the scene so that she could raise her sister's child the way she thought he should be raised.

A week after the move, Janet took Shaun to the high school to enrol him for the new year. He acted as enthusiastically as he could and, on the way back to the farm, he broached the subject of playing football at Goolwa instead of Strathalbyn.

'So, what does that entail, Shaun? I'm not sure it's practical.' She winced as she drove the Mercedes at a snail's pace.

'Well, there'd be training at Goolwa on Tuesday and Thursday nights between five and six pm. And then the home games are at Goolwa every second week. Away games are in other towns like Willunga, Langhorne Creek and Victor Harbor.'

'That's a lot of travel, Shaun, and I don't like driving at night; too many kangaroos. I think training could be a problem.'

Shaun didn't know how to argue against her logic. He knew she wouldn't drive at night.

'Why don't you just play for Strathalbyn?' she continued, 'I'm sure I could arrange for a neighbour to bring you home after training and I suppose I can manage Saturdays.'

As the year progressed, Shaun settled well into school and while he resented the isolation at the farm every afternoon, he busied himself with his homework. His grades were exemplary. In winter, he took up football, donning the Strathalbyn Roosters guernsey and becoming mates with other boys in the team.

Riley, however, remained his best friend and visited Shaun every second week. Riley's mother would find an excuse to shop in Strathalbyn and leave Riley at the farm with Shaun for two to three hours. Janet welcomed Riley's visits. She was conscious of Shaun's isolation and she approved of Riley. He was a good-mannered boy who had a sensible head. She wouldn't say the same for Vinnie, who only came to the farm once. He was brash and sly, she thought. All he was interested in was trying to find someone with a trail bike so that they could tear around the block.

Shaun and Riley came across each other on the football field a couple of times during the season. Riley was an accomplished player and spent most of his time on the ball, while Shaun was a serviceable defender. The games between the Goolwa Port Elliot Magpies and the Strathalbyn Roosters were generally close affairs in their grade. In their second contest of the year, Shaun was surprised to find Riley with the ball right in front of him. He made a desperate lunge and was able to pull Riley to the ground, earning a "holding the ball" free.

The next day, Riley came to visit Shaun. They took themselves down to the river and sat under the shade of a large gum tree.

'Good game yesterday,' Riley said. 'We were lucky to win.'

'Three points. I thought Strath was going to win it at the end.'

'That was a good tackle you laid on me.'

'Lucky, more like. I saw Chad at the game yesterday. How's he doing?'

'He's ok, I think. He comes to most games and to training. Just helps out where he can but it must be tough in that wheelchair.'

'Yeah. Poor bugger. Hey, are you still hanging out with Vinnie much?'

Riley leant back on his elbows. 'Oh, still at school, I guess. Not so much outside school. It's different since you left.'

'How?'

'I dunno. I think you were the glue that held the group together. Even the girls don't hang out much anymore.'

Every time Riley visited, Shaun got an update on what was happening in Goolwa. As the high school years progressed, Riley's visits became less frequent. They were still good friends and sometimes talked on the phone, but weekends got too busy and study demands became more intense.

At the end of 1994, Vinnie left Goolwa. He had found high school difficult, mainly due to problems with concentration and distraction. He was able to focus more readily on the girls in his class rather than on the teacher out the front. Following poor school reports and a few minor skirmishes with the law outside school, Colin eventually relented to his repeated requests and allowed him to leave school. Vinnie followed through on his dream and made his way north, working as a station hand on a cattle station east of Coober Pedy. At 24,000 square kilometres, Anna Creek was the largest station in the world, a perfect place for a strong boy to make his mark.

At the start of the next year, Riley and Shaun were in year twelve, working toward their SACE certificates. They met up once, at a careers evening in Strathalbyn, where a progression of speakers reinforced the need for them to study hard and to make the most of their opportunities. That, they said, would be the foundation for a successful career.

Shaun was hoping for good enough scores to get into university, although what he studied would depend on the scores he achieved. Riley had set his mind on joining the police force. He had sent in his application mid-way through the year, when he was still seventeen. By the end of the year, he would be eighteen and eligible to join as a cadet.

It was a stern, grey-haired man at the careers event that searched their souls.

'Students,' he had said, with a penetrating seriousness, 'Some of you may come from a family where expectations are so high, you may feel you cannot possibly succeed. Others of you will come from a family where the expectations are so low, you can't possibly fail.

'My advice to you is to set your own expectations – realistic, achievable but challenging expectations. Only in that way will you meet your greatest potential and lead a happy, fulfilling life.'

When Shaun asked Riley what he thought his family's expectations were, he just smiled and shrugged.

'I dunno. I guess they just want me to be happy whichever way I go but I reckon they're fine with me becoming a cop. What about you?'

'I dunno either. We've never discussed it. I guess as the guy said, I'll have to work it out for myself.'

A lot of water had flowed under the bridge. Boys who'd had a glorious year of discovery had drifted apart. Boys were becoming men, focussing on where they were going, not where they'd been. At that time, they had no thought as to how or when they would meet again.

Sunday 21 April 2019 (Day 4)

Riley woke to the smell of eggs and bacon cooking in the kitchen. He rolled over and wiped his eyes. For a moment he was disconnected from the case that had preoccupied him over the past few days. His sleep had again been fitful, punctuated with long periods of reflection and speculation.

In his mind, he had dissected the facts of the case as he now knew them and had tried to thread them together to weave plausible scenarios that explained what had happened to Vinnie and Aiden. He wasn't comforted by the fact that he now knew that Vinnie had been murdered and that his death wasn't a tragic accident.

However, it did give him one element of certainty in a case that was still riddled with questions that could not be answered, the biggest one of which was what had happened to Aiden.

He didn't believe that Aiden had been responsible for Vinnie's death. While it was possible that the boy had fled the scene in shock, he doubted it. It seemed far more likely that whoever was responsible for Vinnie's death was also responsible for Aiden's disappearance. But that seemed to open up a whole raft of questions he was no closer to answering. Why would someone kill Vinnie? There was no obvious motive. Why wasn't Aiden at the shed? Had he been abducted or murdered? Riley contemplated possible reasons. He had dismissed the likelihood that Shaun was responsible, either as revenge against Vinnie and Carla or in a bid to seize custody of Aiden. Apart from the fact that it was inconsistent with Shaun's personality, the scenario made no sense when Aiden was still missing.

In the early hours of the morning, his thinking pulled back from the question of why and returned to the known facts. Vinnie had been murdered sometime between when Shaun had dropped Aiden at the boatshed, say 3.30, and when his body was discovered by Shaun and Carla at around 7.00. Aiden had gone missing in the same space of time. The doors to the shed had been locked from the outside, most likely by Vinnie's killer. Vinnie had been disabled by a blow to the head delivered using a heavy wrench by a person likely shorter than him. His death had been caused by the crush of the boat lowered onto him. At this stage, fingerprints had not identified anyone other than Vinnie, Carla and Shaun, but it was clear that others had been in the shed.

Riley had reflected on the internet phone call from A. Narchist. The call had disturbed Vinnie, but more mysterious was that the use of Chatterley seemed to have been an effort to hide the caller's identity and perhaps even that the call had been made. Finally, there was the blue Commodore that had been sighted near the boatshed. Who were the two people who had alighted from the car and did they go into the boatshed? Was one of them Narchist? What business did they have with Vinnie and could they have killed him? Could they have taken Aiden?

Riley slowly replayed his night logic as he wakened but soon became frustrated as he confronted the multitude of questions he couldn't answer. He was sure that he needed to identify A. Narchist and establish whether there was a link between whoever that was, the blue Commodore and Vinnie.

He crawled out of bed and dressed in jeans and a tee shirt that he'd thrown onto a chest of drawers on his last day off. *When was that? Monday, Tuesday?* Kate was standing at the table as he walked into the kitchen. She was dishing up breakfast of bacon, eggs and toast. Mugs of black coffee were already steaming on the table.

'Hello, sleepy bones,' she said, 'I was just about to come and wake you.'

'Hi, what time is it?'

'9.30. You were sound asleep when I got up so I thought I'd let you go. Are you going into work today?'

'I have to. I should have been up and about by now, but I feel like I worked on the case all night.'

They sat at the table and ate breakfast. Kate watched Riley's face as he continued to process facts and theories, even as he ate.

'I'm going to catch up with Sally today. We might even head to the movies, so don't worry about me. You just make sure you look after yourself, Riley.'

He snapped out of his trance and took their plates to the sink. 'Thanks, Kate. I'll catch up with you later in the day, I promise.'

A hot shower enlivened him and he dressed into his uniform, remembering he wanted to call Paul Smith as a priority. He kissed Kate as he walked through the front door but hadn't reached his car before his phone rang.

'O'Brien? Paul Smith here'

'Oh, sir. I was going to ring you with an update shortly.'

'Well, don't bother telling me now. Can you meet me at the station in fifteen minutes?'

Riley was gob-smacked. Smith was in Goolwa. Perhaps he was going to take the case away from him, which wouldn't surprise him.

His underlying concern that he wasn't covering all avenues, plus the lack of progress in finding Aiden, made him believe that maybe someone with more experience was needed. He was surprised that Smith had decided to get involved, given he was dealing with a double homicide in Loxton and also that he wasn't aware that Vinnie's death was now confirmed as murder, not an unfortunate accident. Then again, maybe he had talked with Shelley Harrison or Ray Dennis. A wave of relief washed over him, knowing that he would have a highly experienced detective leading the case.

He found Smith in the interview room, seated with a young woman who he could tell was a police officer in plain clothes. She looked up briefly as Riley entered the room before casting her eyes back to her phone. Riley figured she was around her mid-thirties. Her hair was dark, cut short and wispy. Dressed smartly, she had attractive features that were accented by minimal makeup. Her demeanour indicated that she didn't need to use her looks as a weapon in her work.

Smith rose to greet Riley and shook his hand.

'Senior Sergeant O'Brien, it's been too long.'

Riley was surprised by Smith's unusual turn of formality, something he hadn't experienced before. Smith must have realised that he had caught him off-guard and stepped forward with a broad grin. He grasped Riley around the shoulders and embraced him.

'Riley, good to see you again.' Stepping back, he waved to the woman who had remained seated. 'This is Detective Sergeant Cassandra Callaghan, but you can call her Cassie.'

Cassie put her phone on the desk and stood with her hand outstretched. Riley took her hand but felt no warmth and saw none in her eyes.

'Pleased to meet you, Cassie, and welcome to Goolwa.'

'Good to meet you too, Senior Sergeant … O'Brien.'

'Riley, please.'

'DI Smith talks very highly of you. Goolwa is very lucky to have someone of your talent.'

Riley felt no sincerity in her voice and, if anything, suspected she was having a jibe at him and Goolwa. He held her eyes, blue and cool, silently assessing. Smith broke the impasse.

'Take a seat. I wanted to have a chat with you before we talk to the team more generally. You can also give me your take on what's happening with your case.'

'Sir, it's good to have you here. I'm surprised you can spare the time with us with the situation in Loxton, but don't get me wrong, I'm grateful.'

'Yes, well, there have been developments in Loxton and it's no coincidence that we are down here now.'

Riley was puzzled. 'Sir?'

'As you know, we are investigating a double homicide in Loxton. It didn't take us long to assess the killings as executions. Both victims were shot in the back of the head while kneeling.'

'Drug-related?'

'That appears to be the case. The victims were a husband and wife. We don't know the wife's involvement, but we believe the husband was knee-deep in running a meth lab and the distribution network in the Riverland.

We also have reason to believe that your victim was associated with this operation, although we are still establishing the details of what that association was.'

Riley was stunned but regained his composure quickly. 'Sir, you know that we have now determined that Vinnie Waters' death was not an accident? Both the post-mortem and the forensics point to him also having been murdered.'

'Yes, I spoke to Ray Dennis earlier. And you can now appreciate why we are here.'

'Yes, sir. I have to say that I feel like I've been blind-sided if Vinnie has been involved in drugs. I mean, it wouldn't surprise me that he has dabbled, as a user or even a low-level dealer, but deep enough to get himself murdered? That, I'm having trouble with.'

Cassie interjected. 'Well, O'Brien, that's the trouble with being too close to people involved in an investigation.' Smith had obviously told her that Riley was, once at least, good friends with Vinnie.

She continued, 'Anyway, at this stage we don't have all the information we need, so that's why we are here to help.'

Riley caught the wry turning of the corners of her mouth and the touch of snideness in her voice.

Riley turned to Smith. 'So, you're taking over this case, sir. Not that it's a problem. You will have our help all the way.'

'Ok, let's talk about case management now that Cassie has raised it. We are not going to take over your case. I want you to keep doing what you're doing.' Riley noted Cassie slightly roll her eyes. 'I am going to oversee both cases, yours and the one in Loxton. What we need to do is see if there's a link between the two, which we strongly suspect, and then potentially not only solve three murders but also disable a major drug operation. So, tell me what you have concerning Vinnie Waters to date.'

Riley outlined the procedural progress that had been made, including the outcome of the post-mortem and the forensic investigation.

He detailed the interviews that he had undertaken with Shaun and Carla Chambers and the search for Aiden. Smith questioned him about the blue Commodore that had been parked near the boatshed on the day of Vinnie's death and the description of its two occupants. He finished his briefing with the mysterious telephone call Vinnie had received on the morning of his death.

'Sir, I believe that call may be the key to Vinnie's death. The fact that the caller used the Chatterley app to minimise the chance of any tracing seems odd unless there was a reason that they wanted to be secretive. We're trying to trace it but the techs suggest it may not be possible.'

'Burner phone, probably,' Cassie said.

'Yes, that's what the techs are saying. The only clue we have is that Vinnie's phone shows the caller to be a person called A. Narchist if that is, in fact, his real name.'

The sudden silence sucked all the air out of the room.

Smith and Cassie looked at each other and Riley immediately knew something had changed.

It was Smith that broke the silence. 'Riley, that's not a person. A. Narchist is probably code for Anarchist. That's the name of the bikie gang that we believe is running the drug operation. Now, most people think that bikie gangs are defunct with the Outlaw Motorcycle Gang legislation. It's also true that they no longer have headquarters like they used to and they no longer wear their colours in big groups which has reduced the risk of public confrontations. However, in many ways, they have just changed their *modus operandi*. Much of their communication now is electronic and amongst smaller numbers. That's made it harder for us to conduct surveillance and understand the scope of their membership and activities. But make no mistake, they are still running illegal operations.'

Riley whistled under his breath. The case had taken a dramatic twist in the past half hour.

The thoughts in his mind were a jumble. He looked at Smith, who was scratching notes onto a pad.

'What do you want us to do now, sir?'

'I want to brief your team as soon as possible. I know it's Sunday and some of them are probably having the day off but can you call them all in? We need to try to get a better handle on who the two characters in the car were, see if we can tie them to the Anarchists, plus match any of the forensic evidence to known criminals.'

'Sir, before we do that, there is also the matter of Aiden, the missing boy. I have felt that his disappearance was a result of Vinnie's death. Is it possible that the Anarchists abducted him, or worse? And, if so, why? Maybe because he was a witness?' Riley's stomach turned at the thought of his next conversation with Carla and Shaun.

'Those are questions we still need to answer, Riley. Clearly, we need to keep looking for the boy, but there's not much doubt that it's connected to the murder.'

'Sir, if you don't mind me saying, you said that your murder was an execution. Are you thinking that Vinnie Waters' death was also an execution murder?'

'That's what Detective Sergeant Callaghan here believes. What do you think?'

Riley regretted asking his question. He knew that his answer to Smith would now put him further at odds with Cassie. He chose his words carefully and made sure he maintained eye contact with Cassie as well as Smith.

'Sir, with respect, I don't think Vinnie Waters' death is consistent with an execution. Why wouldn't they have shot him in the back of the head rather than drop a boat on him? Furthermore, why did they need to beat him on the head with a wrench first? I think it's more likely that Vinnie's death was the result of a conflict at the time rather than something pre-planned.'

Smith eyed him carefully, but it was clear that he had contemplated this alternative scenario as well. 'Well, time will tell but at this stage, we should keep our minds open. One thing I haven't told you yet, Riley, is a further coincidence between the cases.

We also have a missing person from the Loxton killings. The 18-year-old daughter of the victims, Emma Satchin, hasn't been seen since they were killed. We're looking for her too but we hold grave fears for her safety.'

'Emma Satchin? You remember her, don't you, Sir?'

Cassie Callaghan looked dumbly from Riley to Smith as the realisation hit the Detective Inspector.

'Forget briefing your team for now. Cassie, book us into the motel and I'll catch you soon. Let's go, Riley.'

14

1996 – 2000

Riley

From the night of Glen's drowning, Riley was fascinated by the role that the police played in the community. Before that date his exposure had been limited, seeing officers driving around the town, occasionally at the bakery or fast-food shop ordering a meal or at the Christmas pageant and street fair.

Even during the pressure of the interviews on that December night and the days that followed, Riley was drawn to the processes but, more importantly, the personal interactions that were involved in police work. He watched Gordon Cook closely. He submitted to the authority that the sergeant's position carried and he felt the respect that the man earnt. At the same time, he witnessed the empathy and compassion that he gave to Shaun.

By the time he left school, Riley understood that police work was more than a job – it was a job that had to be done – it was a commitment. It was a service to the community that required enforcement and support in equal measures. He knew that there were bad cops, even bent cops. He'd seen enough crime shows on television to see that some cops were no better than the criminals they were trying to apprehend. He knew that others, while not bent, didn't earn respect because they leant too heavily on their delegated authority and lacked emotional connection with their community.

Riley could see himself as a good cop. He knew he could connect with the people in his community and he also believed he could learn how to use his vested authority assertively when needed.

The Fort Largs Police Academy was based nearly twenty kilometres northwest of Adelaide, nestled alongside the placid Largs Bay beach. Riley took up the accommodation in the barracks with another young recruit, Robert Baker, from the Mallee town of Coonalpyn. Riley had always been fit and a good athlete. Robert had worked on his father's wheat and sheep farm before applying to join the force. He wasn't the athlete that Riley was, but he was as strong as a bull even though he was lithe in stature.

The two melded from the outset. They drove each other to maintain fitness, running the sandy beach between the academy and Semaphore, usually finishing a run with a gruelling session on the "Torture Track." The track was a circuit up and down a series of steep sandhills, named because of the pain it imposed on runners' legs and the oxygen it stole from their lungs. Their wind-down was a two-kilometre swim in the academy's outside pool.

Days at the academy were largely classroom-based, learning aspects of law, policy and procedure. Riley didn't mind this; he had always been a good student and adapted well. Outside the classroom, they were trained in control and restraint techniques, including handcuff use, self-defence and more physical conditioning. At the end of their twelve-month cadet training period, Riley and Robert graduated with high credentials.

'Well, Riley, mate. I guess this is where we part ways for a while. We must stay in touch, hey.'

Robert got his posting to a large station at the southern end of Adelaide's metropolitan area. It was a growth area with a high proportion of young families accompanied by a high proportion of youth unemployment. With that would come youth crime; Robert was certain to cut his teeth dealing with offenders not much younger than he was. Robert had no intention of returning to Coonalpyn unless he was made to. He saw his future as a city cop and was happy to learn his trade in a new environment.

Riley, on the other hand, was keen to get back to Goolwa. He wanted to serve his community, the one that he knew and loved so well. If he was disappointed with his posting, he didn't tell anyone. He understood that he would need to earn his way to the position he wanted and he would do what was asked without complaint. Unlike Robert's posting, Riley's was to an old suburb – old by any definition. Port Adelaide had been the main port for South Australia located not far from where the first settlers had landed at a muddy swamp called Port Misery.

While much of the inbound shipping now berthed at Outer Harbour, a few kilometres away, the "Port" as it was known was still the centre of trade; the base of the chandlers, customs brokers, stevedores and so on. The many hotels in the Port were founded when the inner harbour was flourishing and most hadn't shut down when the trade declined. Some of the pubs fostered other activities including prostitution, fencing of stolen goods and assault. Riley was hand-picked for his posting. A tough, old-school station that would prepare a young cop for almost anything; but the young cop needed to be mentally and emotionally capable of getting through it.

During his time at the Port as a probationary constable, Riley boarded with a retired couple who had befriended his parents. He played football for Port District for a couple of years on weekends until a chance meeting with Shaun Chambers saw him transfer to the Adelaide University team where they shared a Division 1 premiership in 1999.

Although he enjoyed his time in the Port, Riley really wanted to get back to the country, preferably his hometown of Goolwa. He managed to get home to see his parents and sister, Sally, a few times a year but not often enough. When a posting at Murray Bridge came up, he applied without a second thought. It was still an hour's drive to Goolwa but it was a stepping stone and would give him valuable experience in country policing.

***

Vinnie

One year into his time at Anna Creek Station, Vinnie had learned a lot. The strong, brash boy had been transformed into a stronger, hardened and smarter man. If he thought he would have been able to use his disarming smile and brash charm to make his way, he was wrong. In one sense, at least.

The men who worked at Anna Creek Station were hard-working, tough characters who had learnt their own lessons and were not inclined to let a kid turn up and get an easy ride. Some of the men had come for adventure, some had come to lose themselves or to become invisible. One man had no hesitation in letting Vinnie know that he had gone out bush to escape prosecution for the murder of his neighbour, who had made the mistake of being caught in the wrong bed. Others had tried their hand at opal mining in Coober Pedy without success but didn't want to return to the city or even a town anywhere near a city.

Vinnie's Irish heritage had done him no favours and for months his skin was like a roasted tomato, exposed for hours to the blazing sun. Over time, it morphed into a deep tan, although it was accompanied by deep creases around his eyes. His hair had always been a dark reddish brown, worn with a fringe that swept across his eyes. Good looks, with his broad shoulders, drew the attention of the female kitchen-hands and on his days off, Vinnie practised his smile and charms on them.

There wasn't a wide choice but it didn't worry Vinnie. There was enough variety to keep life interesting, especially with the girls who were from overseas getting a real taste of Australia, working in the outback - girls from England, South Africa, Poland, Germany and Asia. His favourites were the Swedes; they were less constrained by moralistic upbringing and looking for the full experience.

In time, Vinnie had picked up many new skills. He never regretted leaving school early; now he could handle horses and cattle, he could drive a four-wheel drive anywhere, ride a motorbike where a car couldn't go and could fix an engine on any vehicle on the station.

From Vinnie's perspective, everything had worked out pretty well. For the station management, they weren't so sure. Vinnie was a satisfactory worker, although he didn't always follow directions, which frustrated them. He also had a problem with some of the men, who couldn't get past his brash, backhand comments. More than once, Vinnie had been enticed into a scuffle in the mess hall. On the last occasion, his adversary had needed to be flown to Port Augusta for treatment for a broken jaw.

After two years, Vinnie was on his last chance with management. Not that they had told him it was his last chance; they would just send him packing if he transgressed again. Unfortunately, Vinnie didn't read the tea leaves.

It was common, during school or university term breaks, for an influx of young people to come to the station for a week or two. They were the children of the station's management and this was often the only time they would see their parents and enjoy a welcome break from their boarding school.

One such girl was Narelle Stone. Her parents had left Brisbane for an outback adventure four years earlier and took short-term assignments on the station while they travelled. They fell so much in love with the lifestyle they decided to stay on the station and packed Narelle off to boarding school. In her final year of high school, the seventeen-year-old came to Anna Creek Station for what she hoped would be the last time. The following year she would be at university and her parents could go to hell if they thought she would come back to this hole in the middle of nowhere. She'd get a part-time job and let them pay her fees and accommodation but she would be free.

For some reason, Narelle and Vinnie hadn't taken much notice of each other before. This visit, however, Narelle had her eyes open; she was a woman now and she was ready to flex her independence. She watched Vinnie working in the yard and when he stopped for a break, she walked toward him. He was perched on the top rail of the yard fence, his shirt caked with dust and perspiration.

Narelle rested her elbows on the fence next to Vinnie. She looked up at his face. She was entranced by the tanned skin, the lines around his eyes and the little dimples in his cheeks.

'Looks like hot work out there.'

Vinnie took off his Akubra and wiped his brow with the sleeve of his shirt, He flicked his fringe back. Narelle's lips parted.

'Yeah, you could say that,' he answered. 'Haven't seen you here before.'

'I'm the assistant manager's daughter. I've been here a few times before. My name's Narelle. Who are you?'

Vinnie eyed her up and down. *Been here before? How have I not noticed you, sweetheart?* He swung his legs over the rail and jumped down on her side of the fence.

'I'm Vinnie. Pleased to meet you, Narelle.' He wiped his hands on his dirty trousers and extended his right hand to her. Narelle took his hand and shook it. She laughed.

'What's up?' Vinnie asked.

'Your hands are so calloused. I should have expected it, I'm sorry.'

Over the course of the next few days, Vinnie took every opportunity during his off-duty time to search out Narelle. She didn't want to look like she was playing hard to get so she made herself easy to find. Not in the most obvious place, but not too hard either. By the time Vinnie found her, he was hungry.

One night they found themselves alone for the first time, walking under a clear, star-filled sky. The day had been warm but a cool breeze wafted between the outbuildings. Vinnie had showered and dressed in clean jeans and a collared white shirt. To Narelle, he looked completely different to the dusty station hand who she idly chatted with during the day.

They found themselves away from the homestead and next to the shed where the farm vehicles were stored. Narelle leaned against the corrugated wall of the shed and allowed Vinnie to rest his hands on the wall, one on each side of her head. She reached up to brush his fringe from his eyes, smiled and placed her hands each side of his face. He brought his head closer, waiting for her to lift her chin. She didn't take long and brought his face to hers until their lips met.

Vinnie took her hand and led her into the shed. He'd not brought a girl here before but he relished the challenge of being innovative. He guided her onto a seat of one of the quad bikes and parted her knees.

On their way back to the homestead, Vinnie took Narelle's hand.

'That was your first time, wasn't it?'

'How did you know?'

'I just did. No regrets?'

'No. Should I have?'

'Nah. You should have fun on holidays, right?'

Vinnie went to his sleeping quarters, worried. He'd enjoyed the chase, savoured her body. He knew he wasn't making any commitments but he was now worried that Narelle might have expectations. It was one of the few times he'd worried about one of his conquests.

The next morning, Vinnie was summoned to the station manager's office. The station manager was there, and so was his assistant, Narelle's father. Vinnie looked at Narelle's father first. He was red-faced, clearly unhappy.

'Pack your things, Waters,' the manager said. 'You're finished here. We'll deposit what you're owed in the bank by the end of the week.'

Vinnie made to protest.

'Shut the fuck up, Vinnie.' Narelle's father was shouting. 'I didn't bring my daughter here to be messed up by someone like you.'

'Alright, Tom.' The manager raised a hand. He turned to Vinnie. 'Narelle told Tom what happened last night. Did you know she's only seventeen? You took advantage of a young girl, a virgin at that. She's scared shitless she could be pregnant. You can take your cock somewhere else. It's not wanted here. Go.'

Vinnie packed his things and returned to Goolwa. He didn't intend to stay long; just enough time to catch up with his family and then he would head off, perhaps west. On his return, however, he learned that his sister, Marion, was sick. She'd been diagnosed with breast cancer and Colin begged him to stay longer while she went through treatment.

With mixed emotions, Vinnie stayed and even though he'd returned from Anna Creek Station with a bag full of cash, he took a job as a motor mechanic in a local garage. He applied the skills he'd picked up on the station and settled into the job quickly. After only a couple of weeks, he started to notice one man coming into the workshop but always with a different car. Vinnie was never allowed to work on his cars and eventually, his curiosity got the better of him. After the man had dropped a car in one day, Vinnie approached the owner of the business.

Bill Bedford was a gruff man, not given to small talk. He seemed to perpetually wear a scowl on his stubbled jowls. The only time he came into the workshop was when this man brought in a car when Bill would give hushed orders to one of the other mechanics before returning to his office. These cars would always be taken to a separate workshop and not seen again.

'Hey, Bill,' Vinnie asked. 'what's the deal with the cars that bloke brings in?' He knew he was sticking his nose where it wasn't wanted. But he smelled opportunity and if it was, he wanted part of it.

'None of your business, Waters. You just worry about the jobs you're given. And, a word of warning, don't go making it anyone else's business either.'

Vinnie let it go but he decided he would wait and watch until the opportunity could be turned to his advantage. He didn't need to wait long. A few weeks later, two police officers arrived with a warrant and the mechanic who usually worked on the mysterious cars was taken away. Bill was red-faced and sweaty.

'What's wrong, boss?' he asked Bill.

'Fucking idiot's been caught with a shed full of stolen goods. Left me in the lurch. Christ.'

'Anything I can help with, Bill? I know something on the left-hand side of legal is going on with the cars that are coming in. I'm very discrete and you know my work on cars is good.'

Vinnie began working on the stranger's cars the following week. Whenever the man, who Vinnie later learned was called Barry "Shifty" Coleman, arrived with a new car, Bill let him know what "re-purposing" was required. Vinnie took it into the other workshop where it was locked away from prying eyes.

A few days later, the car would be returned to Shifty with a new colour, new plates and accessories it didn't have before. What Shifty did with the cars, Vinnie never asked. As long as he got his bonus cheque, he didn't need to ask questions.

***

Shaun

The University of Adelaide was a new world for Shaun. He was a stranger amongst strangers. Unlike high school, very few students knew each other when they started. When Shaun had moved to Strathalbyn, he already knew a few of the kids through inter-town sports. Those he didn't know were already part of a group of like-minded kids; he just had to find the group he fitted in with best. At university, everyone started out as an individual. Collective groups had yet to be formed. It was perhaps the loneliest time of his life.

He'd found a flat to live in near the city. The money that he had received from Glen's estate had been sitting in a bank account for years and provided enough for him to furnish the flat and buy a decent second-hand car as well as pay for his course fees and books. He found a job working nights at a local pizza joint which gave him enough to pay his way week to week.

He breezed through his Bachelor of Commerce and considered the option of taking the Honours degree once he graduated. His aunts came to the graduation ceremony and proudly took photos of him in front of the prestigious Bonython Hall. No one in their family had ever gone to university before and they congratulated themselves on the fine job they'd done in getting Shaun through the troublesome teens.

And, Shaun had to acknowledge, they had. He was grateful for all that they had done, especially Aunt Janet. Despite their imploring, he told them he wouldn't be returning to Strathalbyn. He wanted to build an accounting career in Adelaide. The aunts went home, proud but sad. They wanted nothing but happiness for Shaun and couldn't bring themselves to tell Shaun that Janet had recently been diagnosed with a terminal illness.

After deciding to stay in Adelaide, Shaun needed a job. Initially, he had his mind set on a career with one of the Big Four accounting firms. A solid career that could one day lead to a partnership opportunity. A telephone call with Riley changed his mind.

'I had an interview with Deloitte last week and I have one with PwC next week,' Shaun had told him.

'Well, good on you, mate,' Riley had said down the phone. He was sincere in his congratulations, wanting his old friend to get a well-deserved chance. 'Somehow, I didn't have you figured for city life in a suit and tie.'

'Why, what did you expect?' Shaun had countered in an offended tone.

'Don't get me wrong. It sounds like a great career. I'm sure you'll do well but I just thought you'd go down a different path. Don't worry about it.'

'No, tell me. What path?'

'I don't know. I guess I assumed, rightly or wrongly, that you'd go back to Strath and work closer to your roots.'

Shaun was piqued. 'You have obviously forgotten what my roots were, Riley. Not too much worked out that well for me in Goolwa and I don't know that Strath was ever home for me.'

'So, you're locked into working in a chartered accounting firm, then?' There seemed to be a reason for Riley's question; Shaun's curiosity was aroused.

'It seems a logical place to go. Why do you ask?'

'Oh, I was just wondering. I don't know if you'd be interested, but I saw an internal staff notice the other day. The police are looking to recruit cadet forensic accountants. Is that something you'd be interested in?'

Shaun didn't respond immediately. He hadn't really given it any thought. He'd always seen the choice as being between a chartered accounting firm and a big firm in commerce. Between those two, he imagined chartered accounting would offer more variety in his work. Criminal forensics had always intrigued him but, he wondered, was there a career for an accountant in it.

'You there, Shaun?'

'Yeah. How can I find out about it?'

Shaun went to the interview with PwC but couldn't get his mind off the opportunity to work with the police. He applied through the designated channels for the police cadetship. The week after, he was offered a position with both Deloitte and PwC. He hadn't heard back from SA Police but in the end, decided to take a risk and declined both the jobs he'd been offered.

After a nervous couple of weeks, wondering if he'd made a career-destroying decision before it had even started, he heard back; he had an interview. Two months later came the confirmation he'd been waiting for. He would become a crime buster.

That deserved a celebration. A group of university friends was drinking at a bar called Inferno on Hindley Street. The music was loud and the crowd was in good spirits. Shaun went to the bar to buy the next round of drinks. He heard a shriek and then an outburst of laughter and turned toward the group at the end of the bar. He couldn't believe who he saw. Carla Ferrari was drinking with a group of girls; it looked like they'd been hitting the piss for a while.

Carla caught Shaun's eye and waved. She walked over to him and gave him a hug.

'Carla. I haven't seen you for years. God, you look great.'

'Thanks, Shaun. You look good too.' There was a slight slur in her voice. 'Hey, I'm busy now but give me a call. Maybe we can catch up.' She fumbled in her bag and pulled out a biro. She scrawled a number on the back of Shaun's hand, before walking unsteadily back to her group.

Shaun took the drinks back to his table but couldn't stop watching Carla. One by one, her friends started drifting off until Carla sat at the bar chatting to some guy who'd seen an opportunity to hit on her. Even though he knew it was none of his business, Shaun stared. *This guy couldn't be her type.* He looked smooth and sharp; no, it was sleazy.

He had trouble maintaining focus on the lively conversation of his friends. He was worried about Carla. *This guy is trouble.* Garth, one of his friends, tapped him.

'What's up, mate? This is meant to be your celebration.'

Shaun nodded toward Carla. 'I'm worried about her.'

'You know her?'

Shaun didn't answer. He stared as Carla wobbled unsteadily before sliding down the bar. The man with her grabbed her around the shoulders and started walking, almost dragging her toward the door.

Shaun stood in front of him.

'I'll take care of her, mate,' he said.

'The fuck you will. She's with me, Pal. Piss off.' He stabbed his finger at Shaun's chest.

'She's not with you. She didn't come with you and she's not leaving with you. I'm a friend of hers. I'll look after her.'

The man glowered but didn't speak. Shaun noticed that his friends had made a circle around the three. It was clear he had numbers on his side. The man pushed Carla at Shaun and stormed off. Shaun grabbed Carla, barely keeping her from falling to the floor.

'Thanks, guys. Hey, can someone give me a hand to get to my car?'

Garth took one side of Carla and with Shaun on the other, they manoeuvred her outside and into Shaun's car.

'So where do you know her from, Shaun?'

'Carla? We were at school together, a long time ago. I have no idea where she lives though.'

'You'll have to take her back to your place. I'll give you a hand and get a taxi home.'

Carla woke the next morning with a pounding head. She had no idea where she was. She knew she was in a strange bed but had no idea whose. She thought she'd slept alone; the state of the bed seemed to suggest no one else had been in it with her.

She called out. 'Hello.' *Oh, my fucking head.*

She heard footsteps. Shaun came into the bedroom with a glass of Berocca.

'Well, thank God for that. You've woken.'

'Shaun. How did...'

'You were drinking with a guy last night. Do you remember?'

'Vaguely. I know I'd had a bit to drink but, seriously, I just suddenly lost it. I can't remember anything.'

'I reckon he spiked your drink. He was an arsehole. How are you feeling?'

'Like shit. Oh, fuck, I'm supposed to be going home to Goolwa this morning...'

Shaun smiled at her. 'That's ok. I don't expect you to stay here any longer than you need. I just wanted to make sure you are ok.'

'No, I don't mean that, Shaun. I'm so grateful. Thank you. But I did promise Mum I'd go home this weekend. She worries about me in the city so I have to go home just to keep the peace.'

'That's ok, I understand. What do you want me to do? Take you home now?'

'I don't think I could drive. I still feel half out of it. Would you come to Goolwa with me? It'd be fun. We can talk about old times.'

It was the last thing Shaun wanted to talk about but he couldn't resist the chance to spend a day with Carla.

15

Sunday 21 April 2019 (Day 4)

Late afternoon on a Sunday was one of Callum Johnston's favourite times. Weekends were dedicated to catching up with friends at a local pub, wine bar or restaurant or otherwise maintaining his physical fitness by kayaking, swimming or running.

By Sunday morning, these activities had run their course and while he enjoyed every moment of them, there was no substitute for what came on Sunday afternoon, regardless of the season.

Callum and Sally had developed the habit of ensuring that this was *their* time. It was time when they made sure they talked – about anything; real problems, future plans, local gossip. The breadth and seriousness of the topics were generally dependent on the amount of red wine they had consumed.

As it happened, this Sunday afternoon was punctuated by a sudden change in weather and heavy showers had made the prospect of staying indoors even more appealing. A bowl of curry accompanied their first bottle of red and their conversation so far had been focussed on whether and when they should start planning a wedding.

The second bottle would likely see them transition into a discussion as to whether they were ready to start a family.

That discussion would be entirely unrelated to the first and it would be Callum who would be arguing the case for the affirmative. After topping their glasses and emptying the first bottle, Callum headed to their spare room where they stored their wines. As he walked down the hall, there was a knock on the front door.

'I'll get it,' Sally called after him.

She opened the door to the sight of a young woman, bedraggled and soaking wet. Her damp clothes hung off her and her pale face was framed by long, lank hair, strands stuck to her cheeks and forehead. Sally didn't know her and guessed her age as being late teens.

'Can I help you?'

'Is Mr. Johnston, I mean Callum, at home?' The girl's voice was weak and she shivered as she stood in the cold. Sally was confused but was concerned for the girl.

'Come in, come in. You look freezing. What's your name? I'll let Callum know you're here.'

Callum returned, bottle in hand.

'Emma, what the...? What are you doing here?'

Sally pulled a throw rug from the sofa and draped it around Emma's shoulders.

'Mr. Johnston, I'm so sorry for all the trouble I caused you. I've got nowhere else I can go. I'm so sorry.'

Callum held her around the shoulders, something he'd never have imagined he could do after the damage she had done in Loxton four years earlier.

'It's ok, Emma, that's all in the past. But something's obviously got you really distressed now. Tell us what's going on.'

Sally now knew that this was Emma Satchin who had falsely accused Callum, at the time her kayak coach, of having sex with her. She knew she should have felt anger but instead all she had was pity for this poor girl. She guided her to a couch and sat her down.

'Callum, why don't you get Emma a cup of tea while she warms up?'

Emma sat quietly while Callum was gone, looking down at her feet and trembling. Sally sat next to Emma and took her hand. She could now see that she was probably twenty years old, a young adult, but in her current distressed state, she was more like a very vulnerable teenager. Callum returned and handed Emma a cup.

Emma took a sip of her tea and looked up.

She told them that she had been studying in her bedroom on Wednesday night. Her parents were doing bookwork for their tyre retailing franchise in the shed on the adjoining block at the back of the house. At around nine, Emma had gone to the shed to see if her parents wanted a cup of tea or coffee but as she approached the shed from the side, she heard unfamiliar voices. She looked through the side window to see two men standing over her parents who were knelt on the floor. Her mother was looking up at one of the men, crying and pleading, while her father was silent looking at the floor in front of him. One of the men stood behind them, a pistol aimed at the back of her father's head.

The man in front of them was talking but Emma couldn't work out what he was saying. She thought he may have asked her father a question. Greg Satchin had looked up at the man and shook his head and in response, the man had slapped him with a vicious backhand sending him tumbling to the floor. The man behind lifted him back onto his knees. Greg Satchin turned to his wife and Emma thought he had mouthed 'I'm sorry.'

The man in front nodded and the other fired one shot into the back of Greg Satchin's head. He fell sideways, blood immediately pooling beneath him. Pat Satchin had released a short scream before she too was felled by a shot. The two men simply turned and walked out. Emma had stood frozen at the window, hand over her mouth, disbelieving what she had seen. She waited until she heard the car pull away then ran to the front of the shed. She saw the car turn the corner of the street.

Under the street light, she got a good look at the car but wasn't able, and didn't have the presence of mind, to get the registration number. She hesitantly stepped into the shed and what she saw only confirmed what she already knew.

Both her parents were dead.

Emma described her terror and her fear that the men would return for her or go to the house so she had panicked and run down to the river.

Her father had a speedboat moored at a jetty there and she had climbed under the tarpaulin and hidden for the night.

Early in the morning she left the boat and decided to get as far from Loxton as she could. She had suspected for a time that her father had been involved in some activities that were, at best shady, and at worst, illegal. What transpired the night before had confirmed it and she had seen enough television crime to fear that bad cops could even be involved. She didn't want to take the risk of calling the police and exposing the fact that she had seen the murders take place.

'So, I hit the road, just walking at first, but then I realised I wouldn't get far, so I started hitchhiking. I got to Adelaide later that day; that was Thursday, I think.

'I hadn't eaten all day and didn't have any money. I shoplifted some food from a convenience store in the city and slept rough for a couple of nights with some teenage runaway kids.

'Anyway, they were starting to get really weird with me so I decided I had to move on. I couldn't think of what to do or where to go. Then I remembered reading an article about you, Mr. Johnston.

'About how you helped solve a murder here in Goolwa, so I thought if anyone could help me, you could.

'I hitchhiked down here and asked around about you. It didn't take long to find out which street you lived in and then a neighbour pointed me to your house. I'm so sorry but I had nowhere else to go.'

Callum knelt in front of her. He looked at Sally. She had tears streaming down her cheeks.

'Emma, it's ok. We'll make sure we take care of you but you must go to the police. They need to know what you saw.'

'No, no. Please don't. You don't know who might be involved.'

Sally wiped her tears with the back of her hand. She spoke quietly and slowly, looking deeply into Emma's eyes.

'Emma, my brother Riley is the local sergeant here at the police station. I can vouch for him absolutely and he will make sure you are not compromised. Please at least talk with him.'

'I don't know. I am so scared and I don't know what to do.'

'I'll tell you what,' Sally said, 'how about you have a hot shower and warm up. I'll get some fresh clothes for you. I think you'll just about fit into some of mine. Then we'll talk about it once you come back. How about that?'

Emma nodded and rose from the chair. As Sally walked her down the hall to the bathroom, she looked back at Callum. He simply gave her a thumbs-up and smiled.

A few minutes later, Sally returned and hugged Callum.

'That poor girl. She seems so sweet. I can't believe she did that awful thing to you.'

'Yeah, well, I guess people make some bad decisions. Doesn't necessarily make them bad people.'

They were interrupted by another knock on the door.

Callum rose.

'Be careful, Cal. Don't open it to someone you don't know in case they followed Emma.'

Callum looked through the peephole and when he saw who it was, opened the door.

Paul Smith and Riley O'Brien came in. It was Smith who spoke first.

'Evening, Callum. It's been a long time. I'm sorry about last time but fortunately, it all worked out.'

'It's all done with now and you were only doing your job, which is why I assume you're here now.'

Smith nodded. 'It is. Have you by any chance had a visitor recently?'

'If you mean Emma Satchin, the answer is "yes". She arrived about half an hour ago, pretty upset. She's been in the weather for a couple of days, so she's just having a shower now. She won't be long.'

Sally went to Riley and kissed him on the cheek.

'So, this is about her parents?'

'Yes. What has she told you so far?'

Callum looked at Sally before replying.

'I think you'd better hear it straight from her. Be aware, though, that she fears police might be involved. She wasn't keen on us contacting you.'

By the time Emma walked into the room, Sally had organised tea and coffee for everyone and she had toasted a sandwich for Emma.

Emma glared at Callum when she saw the uniformed police officer and the detective.

'I said I didn't want to talk to the police. We were going to discuss it after I had my shower and you've gone and done it anyway.' She fell into a chair and sobbed hysterically. Sally tried to sit with her and put her arms around her shoulders but Emma pushed her away.

Smith stood.

'Emma, I know you might feel like you've been betrayed, but that's not how it is. We've been looking for you since Thursday. We got a report a few minutes ago from the person who gave you a lift to Goolwa. They'd responded to a public service announcement and once we knew you were in Goolwa, we had a reasonable idea of where you might go. Callum and Sally didn't call us. We just turned up.'

Emma glanced at Callum. She looked broken.

Callum turned to Smith.

'Detective Inspector, Emma is concerned for her safety and, to be honest, I can't blame her after what she's been through. Now, presumably, not many people will know she's come to Goolwa; just the person who gave her a ride and the police. I presume it's only the people in this room who would know that she's come to this house. If that's the case, she is perfectly safe as long as we keep it tight-lipped and she stays here until you find the killers. Do you agree?'

Smith rubbed his chin.

'Well, at the moment, that's it. I agree that the safest place for Emma to be is here,' he shifted his gaze to her, 'and we'll make sure that we limit the number of people who know your whereabouts to as few as possible and only the people working out of the Goolwa station.'

Emma nodded as Smith continued. 'The thing is, Emma, that you may be the only person who knows what happened to your parents and therefore our best chance of finding the killers. So, we need to know everything you know. Before you tell us, though, I want you to know that we're also investigating a murder here in Goolwa, that happened the night after your parents were killed. The deaths may or may not be related but we do believe that the victims all knew each other and that's a coincidence that we can't ignore. So, how about you munch down that sandwich and then you can tell us what happened.'

Once Emma had finished her sandwich, Sally and Callum grabbed their unopened bottle of wine and retreated to the kitchen so that the police could talk to Emma in private.

Emma was much more composed now and recounted the same details to Smith and Riley as she had earlier. The officers allowed her to complete her narrative, with Riley taking copious notes before Smith followed up with questions.

'Thank you, Emma. Now, can I just clarify a couple of things? You said you saw the two men who were in the shed. Can you describe them?'

'There was one who was really big, maybe a hundred and eighty to a hundred and ninety centimetres, and he was very solid too. I don't know weights but he was lots bigger than you.'

Smith turned to Riley. 'I'm one eighty-five and one twenty-five kilograms, so let's say he's one-thirty plus, for the sake of our record. What about the smaller bloke, Emma?'

'He was sort of the opposite. He was small. I guess he would have only been maybe one sixty centimetres and he was built a bit like my mum so maybe sixty kilos.'

'You're doing really well, Emma. Did either of them have any other distinguishing features like facial hair, scars, tattoos, strange movements and so on.'

'It was pretty hard to see the detail, but the big man had a shaved head and a long beard, sort of reddish in colour. I didn't notice any tattoos but he wore long sleeves.

The smaller man had long dark hair in, like, a mullet. I couldn't be sure but his face looked a bit pockmarked, like acne scars. I can't remember anything else.'

Smith smiled at her. 'You've done better than most people. Tomorrow, we'll bring around some pictures of people who might fit your descriptions, to see if you can identify them if that's ok. Otherwise, we'll arrange to bring an artist in to do an Identikit. Are you ok with that?'

Emma nodded, a little unsure.

Smith reassured her.

'Emma, we believe a motorbike gang is involved and it's pretty likely that with your description we will know exactly who we're looking for. You mentioned a car that left the shed. Did you see it?'

'Yes, it went under a street light. I know cars pretty well because I see all types in Dad's tyre shop. It was a dark Commodore, a VX Executive, early 2000's. Sorry, it was too dark to get the colour or the rego.'

'Is there anything more you can add? Don't worry if you can't. You've been very helpful and will help a lot in catching these guys. Just let us know if you think of anything you might have overlooked. Now, I have one last question and then I'll leave you to it. Do you know or did you hear of someone called Vinnie Waters?'

Emma thought momentarily before answering.

'There was this guy, Vinnie, that had dinner at our place. It was probably twelve months ago. Dad said he was a business associate from out of town. He had dinner with us and was still drinking with Dad when I went to bed. He was a really friendly guy, although he was almost flirty with me, which was a bit creepy. The next morning, Dad mentioned that Vinnie had to sleep on his boat because it was so late. Why, who is he?'

'Vinnie Waters was the man who was murdered in Goolwa. We're still investigating whether his connection with your father has any relevance to the killings. Now, Emma, tomorrow, we will arrange for you to look at those photos as we discussed and we'll need to get a statement from you. We'll also arrange a counsellor to call in on you.'

Emma nodded with a greater assuredness than she had shown earlier.

'I feel safe here and if you'll let me stay here out of the way, I'll do whatever you need.'

Callum and Sally accompanied Smith and Riley as they left the house. Sally patted Riley on the arm.

'We'll look after her. Looks like she's going to need it.'

On the drive back to the police station, Smith leant back in the passenger seat.

'Well, O'Brien, we might just have got the big break we were looking for. I'm glad we came down. Oh, and don't worry about Cassie. She's a good cop, a lot like you, but she takes a while to warm to people. And for people to warm to her.'

'I bet, sir. I still don't entirely buy the connection with the murders and now that Emma's turned up, with Aiden still missing, there's one similarity that's gone out the window.'

'You're right about that. Now, Cassie should have booked us into the motel by now, so I reckon you can drop me straight there and we'll pick up in the morning. I suggest you go home and get some rest too, ready for tomorrow. Have you got yourself a woman, yet? Or should I be politically correct and ask if you have a partner yet?'

Riley laughed.

'Political correctness is not something I would expect from you, sir. But yes, I do have a partner, a very lovely lady called Kate.'

'Ok, well you spend some quality time with lovely Kate and I'll see you in the morning.'

16

2001

Riley

Murray Bridge was in many ways what Riley had expected and yet it was what he hadn't expected that taught him the most. Colleagues had scoffed when he had applied for the posting there. Even his boss had pulled him aside and advised him against the move.

'Mate,' he'd said, wrapping his arms around him, 'I don't want to lose you here. You're a good lad and I think you're going to be a fine copper. If you go to Murray Bridge, well, let's face it, it doesn't have the action of the city. I'm talking professionally as well as personally. I can tell you that people get lost in the system once they go bush. Not literally, but it's like they're stuck in some sort of black hole.'

'How do you mean?' Riley asked.

'Riley, you go to the country and, after a while, no one notices you. If you want to climb the ladder, you have to be noticed. The other thing is that it's hard to get back to the city from the country. There are not enough young cops who will want to take your place, so it's easier for the brass to leave you there. That's my opinion and I might be wrong, but I've seen too many good, young cops go to the country and not come back.'

Riley felt otherwise. For him, working in the city was impersonal. It was harder to be part of your community, more difficult to relate to people you'd never met before. In Goolwa, he knew nearly everyone and nearly everyone knew him. He figured that young cops didn't leave the country because they got satisfaction from working in a small community. This was what he looked for in Murray Bridge as well and one day he'd make it back to Goolwa.

In reality, it wasn't that easy. It took time to get to know people and the ones he got to know first were those that got into trouble. It seemed to him that he was exposed to less of the friendly types he knew in Goolwa; the families, the retirees, the weekenders. Instead, particularly on night shift, he found his "acquaintances" were troubled youth and hardened criminals. Some of them were generational criminals.

One area where he excelled from the start was dealing with the gangs of youths that had taken it upon themselves to disrupt the town at night. Riley was set in his mind from the outset that, regardless of the preconceptions of his colleagues, including his seniors, he would make his judgements based on his own experiences.

It was an approach that worked well for him. He understood that he alone couldn't solve community problems that were driven by poverty, racism or long-term unemployment. But he could still be constructive and supportive where he could and use enforcement when it was necessary. The youth gangs came to respect him and began to share their issues with him. They still got in trouble but, in Riley, they found someone who would treat them fairly and with genuine concern. He developed the skill of resolving issues without being overbearing and throwing his authority around.

He had living proof one night when he heard a knock on the door of the house he rented. At the door was a kid he'd come across a few times, one of the tough young nuts in town called Billy Rigney. He was mixed up in a gang that made a nuisance of themselves, getting drunk, smashing shop windows and abusing innocent citizens. Some of the kids from the gang had been arrested and gone to court for vehicle theft and house-breaking but so far Billy had not committed any serious infringement, or at least hadn't been caught for one.

Riley had been on duty one night and was called to a laneway where a group of youths had been hanging out. The anonymous caller said that the youths appeared to be attempting to break into a warehouse. When Riley and his partner arrived the group scattered, leaving Billy stuck on a first-floor window ledge. After they'd helped him down, Riley sat Billy down and questioned him about what the gang had been doing. He learnt a lot about Billy's home circumstances and understood that the boy was a product of his environment. Despite his partner's protesta-tions, Riley let the boy go with a caution and advice that he and his gang should tone down their behaviour. Riley had seen Billy on the streets since then but hadn't seen him cross the line.

Riley showed his surprise when he saw Billy at his door, largely because he had no idea how he would have found out where he lived. He wondered how many other gang members knew.

'Billy, what's up?'

Billy looked over his shoulder. It was obvious he didn't want to be seen at a cop's house. Riley ushered him inside.

'Er, Mr. O'Brien, I sort of need a favour. See, my brother, Wayne, he's thirteen and he's goin' to get himself in trouble.'

'How?'

'Him and his mates. They're goin' over the top, ya know. Not like my mates; we know the boundaries.'

Riley raised his eyebrows.

'No, we do, Mr. O'Brien. We're real careful now.'

'Ok, tell me about Wayne.'

'They've got into trouble with this other mob. They had a bit of a brawl the other night and now they're talkin' about burning down this bloke's 'ouse. I was wondering if you could, you know, talk to him before it gets out of hand.'

Billy told Riley what he knew about the planned attack. Riley sent Billy home with a promise he'd do what he could. A couple of days later, Riley found Wayne and his friends hanging out at the basketball courts. He hinted enough to them to let them know that the police were all over their plans and that, apart from the real danger of personal harm, they all risked a custodial sentence when they were caught. Eventually, Riley was able to organise a meeting between the two gangs and some sort of truce was agreed between them.

After time, Riley found himself part of the Murray Bridge community. He played football and cricket in the local teams and was known to the locals in pubs around town. Despite this, Riley was keen to get back onto the Fleurieu Peninsula. He went home to Goolwa for family birthdays, Christmas and the occasional weekend but he really pined to become part of the community he'd grown up in. He also realised that he'd missed a big part of his sister Sally's teen years. She'd been a child of thirteen when he left to go to the academy and was now nineteen, a young woman. He patiently waited for the opportunity to arise.

***

Vinnie

Repurposing cars had been lucrative for Vinnie and, he imagined, far more lucrative for Bill Bedford and Shifty Coleman. Together with the money he'd brought back from Anna Creek Station, he was building a decent nest egg. His plan was at some point to leave Bill's employ and set up his own garage, not necessarily in competition. While he earnt good money with Bill, Vinnie could see that he was vulnerable, at the bottom of the food chain. That meant he was probably disposable if the proverbial hit the fan.

The twist did come, but not how he expected. The office phone rang one morning. Bill wasn't in, so Vinnie picked up the call.

'Hello, is that Vinnie?' A woman's voice, distressed. He was surprised; he rarely spoke to customers and this was the first time he'd ever answered this phone.

'Yeah, this is Vinnie. Who's this?'

'You don't know me. I'm Rita, Bill's wife. Bill's had a bad heart attack. He's going to be out of action for a while. He's just gone off in the ambulance but he told me to specifically ring you and ask you to look after the garage while he's off. He said to say that Barry would be in later today and you would know what that meant.'

'Oh, shit, I'm sorry, Rita. Yeah, yeah. I'll look after things, for sure.'

Vinnie looked after things with Barry "Shifty" Coleman that day and for a few days after that. He found the man's demeanour the same as his appearance – like a weasel. Despite that, he took Shifty's cars and started work on them as if Bill was there. What he didn't know was what happened when Shifty picked them up. He searched through Bill's paperwork for invoices that would give him a clue how much Shifty was charged for services performed but there was nothing. Vinnie correctly surmised that the absence of paperwork meant two things. Firstly, there was no paper trail of the dodgy business that they were doing on the cars and, secondly, payment was always in cash.

Bill was still in hospital when Shifty arrived to pick up two cars that had been finished. Shifty walked up and down the cars, inspecting the paintwork closely, searching for any sign that the previous paint hadn't been fully covered. Then he lifted the bonnet and checked the VIN plates.

'Good job, young Vincent.' A cigarette hung loosely from his lips as he spoke. 'Congratulations. I thought things might go downhill without Bill here. When's the big man back?'

'I'm not sure. He's pretty crook. Listen, what's the payment arrangement for this work?'

'Well, son,' Shifty eyed him through a stream of smoke, 'I don't reckon that's any of your business. I'll be working it out with Bill when he comes back.'

Vinnie moved a little closer to Shifty, keeping his eyes fixed on his.

'Ok, but see I have my instructions not to do any more work on your cars until you pay for these.' Vinnie hadn't discussed this with Bill or Rita; in fact, he doubted that Rita even knew the extent of Bill's dealings with Shifty. He figured, though, that Shifty was in no position either to check Bill's instructions or to hold back payment if he wanted more work done.

The weasel-like man paused, then wiggled a finger at Vinnie. He released a silly laugh and then pulled a wad of notes from his pocket. He handed it to Vinnie, turned on his heels and walked out.

It was more money than Vinnie had ever held in his life. Inside Bill's office, he counted the notes. Twenty thousand dollars. The cars he'd been working on he knew were good but there was no way that he'd added that much value to them. He realised what a good business model Bill had set up and hungered for a share.

That evening, Vinnie drove to Bill's house to hand over the cash and to see what extra bonus he might receive. The door opened to a distraught Rita.

'He's gone, Vinnie. Died this afternoon,' she sobbed.

Vinnie comforted her for a while, his mind processing what this meant for Bill's business – all aspects of it.

'Why don't you let me get you a cup of tea, Rita,' he offered. 'You've had a lot to deal with today.' Vinnie took himself to the kitchen and put the kettle on. He pulled out the wad of notes and counted off ten thousand dollars. The rest he shoved back into his pocket.

He set the cup of tea down for Rita.

'Rita, I was going through Bill's paperwork today. I checked the safe for any banking and I came across this.' He showed her the wad of notes. 'I guess Bill meant to bank it but never got around to it. I was going to ask him if he wanted me to do it tomorrow, but I'm thinking rather than put it through the bank, why don't you just take it? I'm sure you could use it now to tide you over and, well, no sense in paying tax on it, is there?'

'Oh, Vincent, thank you. Bill handled all our money. He just gave me my housekeeping every week. I was worried about how I'd get by.'

'Don't you worry, love. That'll keep you going for a while until we can get it all sorted. I'll look after the business until you can get a buyer. Jeez, if I was smart, I'd look at buying it myself.'

A month later, Vinnie was the owner of the workshop. He'd paid Rita a fair price for the business based on the value of what went through the books. The cash business with Shifty, he picked up free of charge, along with nearly fifty thousand dollars in cash that Bill had stashed in his safe.

Vinnie continued doing work for Shifty Coleman, building a sizeable cash reserve. When Shifty came to him one day complaining about the arrangement he had with his car reseller, Vinnie was happy to oblige and bought a used car outlet. His business and cash reserves were growing exponentially.

***

Shaun

The day after Shaun saved Carla from herself wasn't as bad as he had feared. Because of a roaring hangover, Carla had no desire to go down memory lane with him and he was relieved about that. When they arrived back in Goolwa, Carla's parents greeted him warmly. While they remembered him vaguely as a twelve-year-old, they didn't really know him and certainly recalled nothing about his family background and the reason he'd left Goolwa. For them, they were just delighted to see their daughter in the company of such a fine young man.

During high school, Carla had learnt to enjoy a wild adolescence filled with drunken parties, sexual experimentation and the occasional joint. She was a challenge for her parents who tried to impose a strict, traditional Italian discipline but they just couldn't rein her in. Her behaviours didn't improve while she was training as a nurse and she lived life at the same pace as the car that shared her name – Ferrari.

Suddenly, she had brought home Shaun Chambers, a calm and stable young man who had studied to become an accountant and now worked for the police. While not Italian, they imagined and took comfort that here was a boy who might be able to tame their daughter.

Shaun was flattered by Carla's parents' attentions; Carla was mortified but not enough to protest.

On their return to Adelaide, it was actually Carla who suggested they catch up again. Shaun wasn't sure if it was out of a sense of gratitude or obligation but he was excited by the chance to stay connected to this girl that he'd "loved" forever. Carla found that she enjoyed Shaun's company and, while the times she spent with him were quieter and more restrained, she was the happiest she'd been since moving to Adelaide. She would never be able to explain why.

Shaun thrived in his cadetship in the police force. He loved the work; he had a great boss who was enthusiastic about training him in forensic accounting and he'd been assigned his first big case to run. It involved investigating a travel agent who'd been accused of syphoning payments from his clients to fund a gambling habit.

The case was due to go to trial in April. Shaun had finalised his evidence and was eagerly but nervously looking forward to presenting it in court. The Crown Prosecutor had briefed him, testing him for any potential weaknesses in his evidence and he had come through creditably. He was disappointed to hear at the last minute that the accused had, in the face of all the disclosures, decided to plead guilty. Naturally, Shaun was delighted that his work had led to a successful outcome and his boss had passed on hearty congratulations and praise. He couldn't help but also feel a bit disappointed that he wouldn't get the courtroom experience. Still, he told himself, there would be plenty more opportunities.

Those opportunities evaporated a month later when Shaun received a phone call from his Aunt Helen. He'd just got home after a night at the movies with Carla.

'Shaun, love,' Aunt Helen had said, 'I don't want to worry you but your Aunt Janet has not been well of late. She has cancer and it's developed quite quickly. She's in the hospital for a few days. I know she would love it if you could visit her sometime soon.'

'Of course. I'll come down tomorrow.' His diary was relatively clear and he knew he'd have no problem swinging leave for a day or two.

When he arrived at the hospital in Strathalbyn, he was shocked to see how much Aunt Janet had deteriorated. Her cancer had caused her to lose a lot of weight and she seemed to have aged ten years since he last saw her three months earlier. The prognosis wasn't good. Her doctor gave her a few months to live, at best, and then only with significant ongoing care. He suggested that Janet be homed in an aged care facility that could provide palliative care when the time came.

'I really don't want to go into one of those places,' she said. 'If I'm going to die, I want to spend what time I have at home, somewhere that I can feel comfortable.'

'I'll come and look after you, dear,' Aunt Helen had said, 'although I'm not as strong as I used to be. I don't know how long, you know, I, um, will be able ...'

'No, that's not fair on you, Aunt Helen. We don't want you wearing yourself out. I can take some leave from work, probably up to twelve months. It's the least I can do after all the years you looked after me, Aunt Janet.'

Within a week, Shaun was back in Strathalbyn. His boss had been more than happy to grant Shaun leave without pay and wished him well. Caring for Janet was much more difficult than he could have imagined. A few weeks after her release from hospital, she lost much of her mobility. Fortunately, Shaun had been able to do some work from home, helping out a local chartered accountant, Geoff Turner, a long-time friend of Janet's who had heard about Shaun's return.

For the most part, however, he was stuck at Aunt Janet's home. Every now and then, Helen would care for her for a few hours, especially when Carla came by. Their relationship had faltered; Carla always needing to get to Goolwa to see her family and Shaun anxious to get back to his aunt.

Aunt Janet died in September. At the end, she went peacefully in her sleep. Shaun decided to stay in Strathalbyn a bit longer to sort out her affairs. He still had plenty of leave available from the police force and there was a lot of work to do before his aunt's property could go on the market. He was gob-smacked that she had left her entire estate to him even though he knew she had no living relatives other than Aunt Helen and him.

'Your Aunt Janet and I discussed this some time ago, Shaun,' Aunt Helen had explained. 'I certainly don't need her money and she always felt a need to make sure you were well provided for. She loved you dearly, you know.'

Shaun never returned to his job in Adelaide. By the time he had wrapped up the estate, Carla had decided to move back to Goolwa. She'd landed a nursing job at Victor Harbor and saw the opportunity to be nearer to her family and Shaun; a chance to settle down. Far from the wild girl she'd been, she now wanted more than anything to be with Shaun. He was a little bemused; he'd always thought he'd go back to the city, to the job he loved and to the girl he loved. Carla hadn't asked him about his career plans and assumed he wanted to settle back into country life.

He wasn't upset by the change. He enjoyed working with Geoff and could see the potential to build his own profile in the region. What he wasn't comfortable with was the prospect of moving back to Goolwa, if that was what Carla was thinking and expecting.

17

Monday 22 April 2019 (Day 5)

Riley and Kate rose early. He talked her into going for a run at 5.30. It was still dark when they set off and the air was mild.

Kate had been surprised that Paul Smith had come to take over the case and felt miffed on Riley's behalf at the inference that he was not handling the case well. By the time Riley explained the connection to the Loxton murders and that he would still be running the Goolwa case, in particular the search for Aiden Chambers, she was mollified. Having heard about Smith from Riley before, she was keen to meet his mentor and suggested that Riley invite him for dinner one evening.

This forced Riley to talk about Cassie Callaghan and his tentative early relationship with her. He explained that it would be difficult to invite Smith for dinner and not Cassie as they were both staying at the same motel.

The dawn was breaking as they ran toward home. A steamy mist breathed over the river, filtering the sun's rays. The unseen paddling of a pelican's feet was the only thing that wrinkled the mirrored surface of the water.

'I still think you should invite DI Smith to dinner and, if Cassie has to come as well, perhaps that would help your relationship. How does Wednesday night sound? I have teacher-parent meetings tomorrow night and tonight might be too short notice. What do you think?'

'Well, who knows? The case might be wrapped up by then, but somehow, I doubt it. The other thing is, you know how these things go. We might end up following a lead on Wednesday afternoon that we can't leave. I wouldn't want your dinner to spoil.'

Kate looked at him. 'No problem, I'll cook something that can be kept for the next night, like, say, a pasta.' She lightly punched him on the arm. 'C'mon. It'll be fun and I want to meet this Mr. Smith and see if he's really the dinosaur you say he is.'

'Hey, I didn't say he was a dinosaur. Just that some people might think he is because he's an old-style cop. For all that, he does try to see things from a more contemporary point of view. Anyway, I'll see if he and Cassie are ok with Wednesday night.'

Riley also mentioned to Kate that Callum and Sally were taking care of Emma, refreshing her about the full back story. He impressed on her the need for secrecy about Emma's whereabouts but at the same time suggested they may need to be available to provide support to Callum and Sally if needed.

He had initially been reluctant to say anything but at the same time, he knew that Kate and Sally spoke almost daily and it was inevitable that the arrangement would be disclosed. He knew he could rely on Kate to keep a lid on it and that she would be more than willing to help as required.

After breakfast, they left for their respective workplaces and before Riley had started his car, his phone rang. It was Shaun Chambers, sounding frustrated.

'Riley, what's happening? Has there been any news of Aiden? I've got Carla with me and she's beside herself. Surely, you can tell us something.'

Riley was surprised that Shaun and Carla were together so early in the morning. Did that mean they might have spent the night together, maybe reconciled? He dismissed the thought.

'Shaun, I'm sorry I can't give you any news on Aiden specifically. We've searched Goolwa thoroughly, we've released an appeal through the media and every cop in the state is keeping an eye out for him but at this stage, we haven't had any sightings.'

'So, is that it? What's next?'

'All of that is continuing, Shaun. As well as that, we're still investigating Vinnie's death. We strongly believe that if we can find out what happened to Vinnie, we can use that to find Aiden.'

'So, Vinnie wasn't an accident?'

'We have information now that confirms he was murdered. I can't go into details but we now have some tangible leads we're following.'

'Riley, you're telling me nothing. What have you got? It's fine for you but this is our child who's missing. We deserve to know what's going on.'

'I'm sorry, Shaun, but I can't tell you anymore. I'll stay in touch.'

Riley waited for Shaun to respond but he had already hung up. The burden hung over Riley like a winter's cloud. He just hoped that like a winter's cloud, there would be relief when the storm broke.

He walked into the police station just after seven. As the planned briefing the previous day had been postponed when Emma suddenly turned up, he took fifteen minutes to update Rachel on the status of the case.

Smith and Cassie Callaghan entered the station just as they were wrapping up. Rachel was unable to contain her excitement and rushed to Smith, embracing him warmly.

'I'm so sorry, sir. That's not very professional, I know, but it's great to see you again.'

Cassie Callaghan looked on, bewildered. She had not imagined the dour DI Smith having such a relationship out in the boondocks.

'Well, you too, Cross. Sergeant Cross now, isn't it? Congratulations on your promotion. Well deserved, I'm sure.'

'Well, I'm sure your good word for me helped too. Thank you so much, sir.'

DI Smith introduced Rachel and Cassie.

'OK, let's get started. Just before you kick off though, O'Brien, I should bring you up to speed on what we think the scenario is at a high level. I didn't get the chance to go through this last night.

'So, Cassie and I are here in Goolwa because of a connection we believe exists between the deaths of Greg and Pat Satchin in Loxton and Vinnie Waters here in Goolwa. Despite initial indications, Waters' death is now not considered an accident but a murder. Why do we believe they are connected?

'Well, firstly, the Loxton murders occurred on Wednesday evening, Waters on Thursday. Of itself, that doesn't mean much but we do know that the Satchins and Waters did business together. We also now have a witness, Emma Satchin, who states that Waters has visited them at the Satchin home. We established that Greg Satchin was running some sort of drug operation out of his businesses in Loxton. We don't know the full scope yet and the drug squad is looking into that right now. Greg Satchin had a tyre retailing business but we also know he'd commenced a used boat outlet in the last two years, hence the business relationship with Vinnie Waters.

'Our thinking is that Satchin was running a drug distribution network out of Loxton and we suspect he also had a lab situated on a property out of town. We strongly believe an outlawed bikie gang known as the Anarchists are knee-deep in this shit.

'Thanks to some good work here, we know that Vinnie Waters has had contact with the Anarchists, most recently on the day he was killed. Coincidentally, a car and two persons with matching descriptions were sighted on the days of the murders in both locations. You can see we have something to go on. So, the question is, what was Vinnie's role in the network? He hadn't been on the radar up until his death but he certainly is now.

'My guess is that he was either running drugs on the Fleurieu Peninsula or he was part of the money laundering side of the operation, maybe both.

'Anyway, the reason I'm here is to oversee the operations of both murder investigations; the one here and the one in Loxton. I also need to make sure we're coordinating our findings with the drug squad. Senior Sergeant O'Brien will continue to run the murder case here.'

Nods around the room indicated that everyone understood the lines of command.

Smith continued. 'The one thing I need to get started is a forensic examination of Vinnie Waters' accounting records. I want to find the link between him and the Satchins, which it appears, may also be related to his death. I'm guessing you don't have any forensic accounting expertise in your team and, at this stage, all other available resources are working through the books in Loxton, so I've got to see what I can rustle up.'

While Smith had been talking, Riley had given some thought as to the distribution of duties for the day. He'd expected that Smith was going to take over the case and was caught short by his continued responsibility. It wasn't that he didn't want to make the most of this opportunity.

He was more concerned about botching up the investigation. On the one hand, therefore, he was glad to have the Detective Inspector on-site as a guiding hand but he also knew that Smith would be watching and assessing him even more closely. He was also acutely aware that they had made no headway at all in the search for Aiden Chambers.

Smith handed over to Riley.

'Ok, well sir, while you get that started, I want to follow up on the identification of the fingerprints that were found in the boatshed.

'Also, I need to check with Constable Reid to see whether Anna Symes was able to provide a vehicle identification for the Blue Commodore seen outside the boatshed. Hopefully, it will match the vehicle seen by Emma Satchin in Loxton.

'Now that we have descriptions of the two men at both sites that seem to be consistent, it seems reasonable that they could be the same people. Knowing who they are is critical at this stage. Rachel and Cassie, I'd like you to put together a set of photos that match the descriptions provided by Anna Symes and Emma Satchin. Let's see if you can get one of them to provide a positive identification.'

Cassie piped in. 'I'll give Brad from the Morpheus Task Force a call. He should be able to give us a full list of all the known Anarchist members through AGICC.'

'What's that?' Rachel asked.

Cassie smiled at her. 'The Australian Gangs Intelligence Coordination Centre.' Cassie looked pleased she had scored a superiority point over Rachel. She wouldn't have realised that it didn't bother Rachel in the slightest.

Riley turned to Smith. 'Sir, given the turn of events, I think we should undertake a search of Vinnie Waters' house to see if there's any sign of his connection with the drug operation. The boatshed was turned upside down but we haven't needed to search his house until now. If he has been moving drugs or money, you would expect there to be some evidence somewhere. He also has interests in some businesses here and in nearby towns. They should be checked as well.'

Smith nodded his agreement. 'Maybe you and I can do that later this morning. Will we need warrants?'

'I doubt it, sir. Vinnie's not going to object and unless the staff are involved in something, I don't think they'll mind.'

Riley wrapped up the meeting. Cassie and Rachel left the room, chatting as they made their plans.

The two looked like they would work well together.

Riley turned to Smith.

'Sir, I know we need to crack onto this, but I wonder if I might buy you a coffee and bounce an idea off you.'

They walked to the café a couple of hundred metres down the road and bought takeaways. Riley didn't want to discuss his idea in a packed café. The sun was beaming and a cool, light breeze kept the temperature at a pleasant level.

Riley led the way to the lake between the main street and the football oval. They sat in the shade of a covered gazebo overlooking the water.

'You know, O'Brien, I never did bring my wife down for that excellent breakfast at that little café. I said I would three years ago and I still haven't done it. Sometimes, I swear I'm a prick of a husband.'

'I'm sure Mrs. Smith wouldn't say that, sir.'

Smith burst into laughter, sputtering coffee in his path.

'Yes, she bloody would. Anyway, tell me about your idea.'

'Sir, as I've said to you before, I don't buy the theory that Vinnie's death is the same as the Satchins. They were executed. Vinnie's was made to look like an accident. Why would the Anarchists do that if they meant to kill him? Surely, they would execute him with a bullet to the head too if they were trying to make a statement. So, while I agree that the two cases are linked, I think they are very different. I don't think Vinnie's death was premeditated. I think that something went wrong and Vinnie was killed on the spur of the moment.

'There's another thing. With Emma's reappearance, safe and sound, what does that mean for Aiden's disappearance? At first, that seemed to be a common thread between here and Loxton, but it's not any more.

'Why would the Anarchists take an eleven-year-old boy? Surely not for ransom. That's not part of their game and not the reason they were at the boatshed. Plus, there hasn't been any contact for ransom.

'You have to think that the only reason they would take him would be if he witnessed the murder. They could have killed Aiden then, in the boatshed, but they didn't. Was it because they couldn't bring themselves to kill a child? If that's the case, then what have they done with him since?'

Smith stood and walked to the railing surrounding the gazebo and stared out over the water. When he turned, he smiled at Riley.

'I accept everything that you've put forward. It's a well-thought-out summation. But you said you had an idea to discuss. I'm thinking that wasn't the idea and that there's more to come.'

'Well, yes there is, sir. If we accept that the Anarchists are responsible for what's happened, then that clears Shaun Chambers of suspicion. We've also checked his alibi that he was engaged in meetings in the period that Vinnie was killed and it checks out. I'd like to suggest we use Shaun to undertake the forensic accounting of Vinnie's books. He's an experienced and competent accountant and used to work in forensics in SAPOL in his early career. He knows the local businesses well and has a huge motivation to help us resolve this. He also knows a little bit about how Vinnie worked; I don't mean specifically with the drugs but his overall business practices.'

Smith rubbed his chin. 'I don't like it, Riley. He's too close, too emotionally involved.'

'Sir, with respect, we don't have any alternative resources that are capable of this work and you said yourself that this is critical to solving the murders and the drug operations. It's also critical to finding Aiden.'

'OK, do it. But make sure he's properly briefed and knows to keep his mouth shut. And I want someone to watch what he's doing every second.'

'Will do. I can get Constable Oliver Townsend to sit by his side. He's bright and won't miss a thing.'

Smith made to leave but Riley remained seated.

'Something else, O'Brien?'

'Well, yes, sir. We, that is Kate and I, were wondering if you and Cassie would like to join us for dinner on Wednesday evening. I'd probably see if Rachel wants to come as well. That is, if you are ok mixing work with pleasure, sir.'

Smith beamed. 'Well now. I'd be delighted to spend an evening with you and your lady. And, yes, get Cross along too. But, O'Brien, if you call me "sir" on Wednesday night, I'll cuff your ears, understood?'

With that, he strode off back to the station and it took Riley a few paces to catch him. By the time they returned, Cassie and Rachel had left.

Riley left Smith, who wanted to check on the progress with the Loxton investigation, and found Constable Phil Reid in the kitchen making himself a coffee. Phil's meeting with Anna Symes had failed to confirm that the blue Commodore parked outside the boatshed was the same VX model that Emma had seen in Loxton. She had only identified that the car was a Commodore because of its badging but beyond that her ability to tell one car from another was limited. It was a setback, but only a minor one. The fact that the cars may have been the same was purely corroborating a theory and they would have to rely on much stronger evidence to prove that the same men were involved in both incidents.

At the back of Riley's mind over the past few days had been the up-coming Wooden Boat Festival. It was now Monday and the festival was due to start on Friday. He was satisfied that the organisers had their plan well-sorted and he had already requested some uniformed support from Adelaide.

Nonetheless, he worried that with all the other activity, he may have missed something. He decided that it was time for him to ask Phil Reid to step up.

Ten minutes later, he had briefed Reid and handed over the folder with all the details. While he retained overall responsibility, he trusted Phil to take care of the detail and to bother him with problems on an as-required basis.

18

2003

The sun beat down on the Goolwa main street, reflecting heat onto the footpaths and the adjoining shop fronts. The street was generously laden with shade-giving trees but on a forty-two-degree Celsius day, nothing could prevent the town's lethargy. At the Goolwa Hotel, smokers were usually banished to the outside tables to feed their habit. Today, even they stayed resolutely in the air-conditioned comfort.

Not that there were many inside. Even though it was the peak of the season, most holidaymakers had decided to stay in their cooled caravans or beachside shacks, playing cards or watching television.

Those who ventured outdoors were at the beach or the river, swimming, surfing or skiing in the cool waters.

The hotel front bar was occupied mainly by the regular punters; the die-hards who came in every Saturday to share a pint and a punt on the horses. The weather did not hamper a habit fostered over many years, even though they left the pub most days with lighter wallets than they had when they walked in. Conversation between the die-hards was subdued; only entered into between races and when eyes were not transfixed on a racing guide or the bottom of a half-empty pint glass.

No one paid any attention to the three young men sitting on their own at a table at the other end of the bar, well away from the plethora of screens dedicated to the punters.

'Well, here we are. The three amigos.' The tone of Vinnie's voice was friendly, although tinged with sarcasm. 'What's it been? Ten years?'

'At least eleven,' Riley corrected. 'A lot of water under the bridge since then.' The latter comment was intended to remind Vinnie that the last time the three had been together, the circumstances had been challenging and the secret between the boys still lingered like a dark cloud. It was perhaps the secret that had been the catalyst to reconnect after such a long time apart and with the different paths that each had taken, their lives were now bound only by that secret.

Since his return from Anna Creek, Vinnie had expanded his business interests, both the legal and illegal ventures. His cash work for Shifty Coleman continued to be lucrative and he'd invested in real estate around town.

He mixed with the people he admired and respected, working his contacts through the local Rotary Club, the golf club and the Goolwa Regatta Yacht Club. All the same, he knew he was not one of them; his business practices alienated him, even though most had no knowledge of what really happened at the repair shop and used car lot. While they tolerated his involvement with Rotary, mainly because of his generous donations, they murmured their reservations about the brash, young would-be if he could-be in the corridors.

Over the past few months, Shaun realised it was time to put the tragedy of his past life in Goolwa behind him. He knew that Carla would not want to move from Goolwa again and, if his future was to be with her, he would need to move closer to her. He was certain that was what he wanted. And so, he had returned a few months earlier, using his inheritance from Aunt Janet to start his own practice and to buy a house.

Like Vinnie, Shaun knew the importance of networking and had also joined the local Rotary. Unlike Vinnie, Shaun's professionalism and gentle manner immediately resonated with the town's business leaders.

Naturally, Shaun's and Vinnie's paths had crossed and, although they conversed freely, it was clear that the fire had gone out on their past friendship and that they had followed very different paths. All that was left was the secret they shared.

A couple of weeks earlier, Shaun had pulled Vinnie aside after a Rotary lunch.

'So, did you know that Riley has been posted back to Goolwa?'

Vinnie lifted his eyebrows in curiosity. 'Riley O'Brien? He's a copper now, isn't he?'

'Yeah. He's been in Murray Bridge for a year or so and he's coming back. Apparently, they had an urgent need to fill a vacancy here and they decided to pull him out to fill it.'

Vinnie immediately recognised the value of having a friend in the police force, although he knew that the relationship had lapsed over the last ten years. At best, they were now former friends, but that could change if he worked on it.

'Right, then we need to catch up, the three of us. It's been too long and now that we're all back in the same town we should talk about old times.'

Shaun was mortified. 'I don't think we need to go back over all that.'

'Nah, that's not what I mean. I'm talking about the good times. We were such good mates; we have to reconnect. The other stuff, well, let's leave that where it belongs; just between us and not to be spoken about.'

'I don't know, mate. I'm not sure if Riley would be keen.'

'Do you have his number?'

'Yes, but ....'

Vinnie was firm. 'No "but". Just ring him. If he doesn't want to and you don't want to, then we'll let it pass but I don't know how we can live in the same town without running into each other.'

Shaun knew that Vinnie was right about that. He also realised that the two could run into each other in circumstances that were more official than friendly, given the rumours about Vinnie's business activities.

'Ok. I'll call him and see what he says.'

Shaun had rung him.

Riley had been less than enthusiastic about the catch-up; he knew enough about Vinnie to want to keep clear of him but eventually, Shaun had used the same argument that Vinnie had. They simply could not ignore each other in a town the size of Goolwa.

And now here they were – three amigos in the bar but certainly not peas in a pod. The uncomfortable feeling when they first met was eased once beers were in their hands and they each recounted what they had been doing over the past few years. While Shaun and Riley had stayed in touch through phone calls, these had been short and infrequent and more out of a sense of duty than a strong need for friendship.

Soon the discussion was brought to the present.

Vinnie led, 'So, Shaun, does Riley know that you and Carla are getting pretty serious?'

Shaun blushed. He hadn't openly discussed his developing relationship and had certainly not talked about it with Riley. He couldn't explain why, but it was probably because of the association with the period of his life that the three boys had shared but was now largely buried. He had no idea how Vinnie knew about it but wasn't surprised.

'Carla Ferrari from school?'

Riley was surprised but genuinely happy for Shaun. 'Wow, she was a bit of a wild one. No offence, but I didn't think you would be the one to tame her.'

Shaun was a bit miffed and simply responded, 'We've all changed, Riley. Carla and I included.'

'Yeah, sorry mate, it's just that, you know, she played really hard, even after high school.'

Riley felt remorseful about embarrassing Shaun and quickly changed the subject. 'So, Vinnie, what about you? Any love interest in your life?'

Vinnie rose to the occasion and spread his arms. 'Well, you know, mate, in Goolwa it doesn't take long to play the field and I might have played it a bit hard.'

'Oh, a string of broken hearts?' Riley quipped.

'Maybe, but I am hoping to put down some solid roots with someone; she just doesn't know it yet.'

'Anyone we know?'.

'Well, yes actually. I'm pretty keen on Debbie McLean. She's a vet nurse now and I've taken my dog in a few times. We've chatted, but I've got a bit of work to get it to the next stage.'

'Oh, Debbie. A bit ambitious for you, Vinnie. She's probably above your batting average, but good luck.'

Unsurprisingly, the conversation was loosening further after a few beers, although Shaun had shrunk back following the discussion around Carla. Vinnie sensed his mood change and looked to lighten the talk

'Yeah, we'll see. I like my chances. But let me tell you a story. It's true, I swear. You'll like this one, Shaun.'

'Oh, yeah, I can imagine.'

'No, you can't. Trust me.'

Vinnie now had the attention of both men.

He leant his elbows on the table, beer in one hand. He glanced from Shaun to Riley before starting with the deliberation of a politician's maiden speech.

'Okay, so you know that I lived with my sister, Marion, and her husband, Colin, and they had two kids. I was their uncle.'

The others nodded.

'Right. Well, I'd always suspected that there was something fishy. Like, I never understood why I couldn't live with our parents – Marion's and mine. So, I always wondered if maybe I was really Marion's kid; after all, she was so much older than me.'

Shaun remembered Marion and recalled she was a fair bit older. 'So how much older than you was she?' he asked.

'Like, seventeen years.' The others pursed their lips; it seemed feasible.

'Anyway, Marion got sick a couple of years back; cancer, terminal.'

'Sorry, Vinnie, I didn't know,' Riley interjected.

'Yeah, shit happens. Anyway, she's on her death bed and Colin says to her that she should come clean to me that she's really my mum.'

The others' eyes widened.

'Then Colin says to her that she should tell me who my real dad is because apparently, all this happened before she met Colin. Even he didn't know who my father was. Marion resisted saying anything about it until just before she died. And, finally, she does. She tells Colin but says he can only tell me after she's gone.'

'So, he did tell you?' Shaun asked, his concern about Carla now despatched to the sidelines.

'Yes, he did. It goes back to when our parents and Marion were living in Yankalilla. In the last year of high school, Marion had hooked up with this guy from Myponga, Wayne Hargreaves.'

'I know Wayne,' said Shaun, 'or, at least, I know of him. His son was one of my clients for a while.'

'Yeah, well Wayne's dead now, but your former client is my half-brother.'

'Wow, that's so bizarre and you had no idea?'

'Not until Colin told me. So, he tells me about Marion and Wayne and then says that Wayne had five more kids after he got married. So now, I have all these brothers and sisters I didn't know about. When Colin tells me, I can't handle it and I just say to him "Oh no. That's fucking awful.". And Colin says "Don't worry, son, I'll still be your dad. And Wayne's not a bad bloke." By this stage, I've lost it. I'm still trying to process it but eventually, I say to Colin, "No, you don't get it. I've shagged my fucking sister." See, only a couple of months before Marion died, I had a one-night stand with Louise, the oldest Hargreaves kid – my bloody half-sister.'

Riley and Shaun sat silent for a few seconds before bursting into laughter. Vinnie joined in and soon the intensity of their joviality brought them to tears. Even the hardened punters at the other end of the bar turned away from their TV screens and racing guides.

'Does she know? Louise, I mean,' asked Riley.

'Well, I'm not going to tell her, am I? Her brothers, our brothers, would probably kill me.' The three erupted into uncontrolled laughter again.

All of a sudden, it seemed like the clock had been turned back eleven years and close friendships had been miraculously restored.

The trio spent the rest of the afternoon reliving old times, but only the good ones.

The secret that they had vowed to protect all those years ago was unspoken. At five, they left the hotel, bonded again and intent on moving forward as the mates they were. Even the ulterior motives that Vinnie had harboured no longer seemed important.

19

Monday 22 April 2019 (Day 5)

Riley knew the day was getting away from him. He had wanted to follow up with Shelley Anderson concerning the fingerprints much earlier. He also wanted to start Shaun on the forensic accounting as well as getting out to Vinnie Waters' house.

When he finally rang Shelley, he was put on hold while she attended to another call. He waited five minutes before she answered, just as Paul Smith came into the incident room.

'Hi Shelley, it's Riley O'Brien here.' Smith motioned for him to put her on loudspeaker.

'Hi Riley,' Shelley responded, 'I've just got off the phone with the team in Loxton. I have some good news. Their site was much cleaner than yours and we didn't get much in the way of prints to work with from them. The one set we did get, though, we've been able to match to one that we lifted from the door at the boatshed.'

Riley looked up at Smith. 'So, Shelley, you're saying that we can put the same person at both locations?'

'Two people actually. We have Vinnie Waters' prints at Loxton. The other person, we've been able to match is on our database and, surprise, surprise, he is a known member of the Anarchists Motorcycle Gang.'

'Just tell us, Shelley, who is he?' Smith was getting impatient.

'His name is Tony Fantis. His last known address was in Adelaide. The team in Loxton will be calling you shortly, sir, to discuss a warrant for his arrest.'

'Good, what else have you got?'

'Ok, the small prints we talked about that we lifted in Waters' office that we suspected belonged to Aiden Chambers. We've now been able to confirm a match with some we got from his bedroom.

'Lastly, there's the other prints we got from the boatshed that we hadn't identified. There were two sets from a small hand we knew didn't match those in the office; that is Aiden's. The other sets were on the door to the boatshed and also on the winch. Now I know you would love for us to have been able to tell you who those belonged to, but I'm sorry, we have no match on the database.'

After finishing the call to Shelley, they called Mick Martin who was leading the team in Loxton. Mick was an old-style detective cast from the same mould as Paul Smith.

Riley didn't know him well but knew that he'd worked along-side Smith for many years, without progressing through the ranks as Smith had.

Martin didn't curry favour because of his criticism of the hierarchy in the police department. That didn't make him a bad detective, just an unpopular one in some quarters.

Mick answered the call on the second ring. Paul Smith led the discussion.

'Mick, I have Senior Sergeant Riley O'Brien here from the Goolwa station. We've just talked with Shelley Anderson and she's updated us on the fingerprint situation at both locations. Have you got anything further at your end?'

'No, mate. We think we should get a warrant for Tony Fantis' arrest to see what he has to say for himself. We'll also do a deeper search of the Satchin house, but I'm not expecting anything there. Our thinking is there is another site where all the drug handling is done, but at this stage, we don't know where that is. The drugs boys are running that side of it.'

'Ok, no sign of the murder weapon yet?'

'No, mate, but forensics have run the ballistics tests on the bullets and shells we recovered, so we know what we're looking for. I'll email you the details. No sign of the Satchin girl yet, either, but we still have an alert out on her.'

'Oh, shit, sorry Mick, I should have told you. We've located the girl. She's safe and in good hands. Do me a favour and cancel that alert on her, will you?'

'Sure, but where is she?'

Smith shot a look at Riley.

'No offence, Mick, but we need to keep a tight lid on her whereabouts. She could still be in danger. She's already confirmed the car model and we're hoping she'll be able to identify the two men who were seen at both sites. With any luck, she'll pick out Fantis.'

There was silence from the Loxton end of the line before Mick let out a sigh. He seemed put out by Smith's secrecy.

'Alright, what do you think about the warrant?'

'Well, we know Fantis is a member of the Anarchists, so there's a good chance the second man will be as well. Let's get the warrant on Fantis plus a search warrant on any of his known premises. But I don't want you to act on them yet. Let's see if we can nail them both rather than have the second bloke do a bolter.'

'Very well, sir.'

Riley noted the change in formality from Mick. Paul Smith did as well, leaning into the speakerphone.

'Mick, don't get your knickers in a knot. This isn't about a lack of trust. We've just undertaken to look after Emma until it's clear she's safe, alright?'

'Sure, Paul. I'll talk to you later.'

Once the call was disconnected, Smith turned to Riley.

'Bloody detectives can be precious sometimes, O'Brien. Don't ever get like that if you head down that path.'

Cassie Callaghan and Rachel Cross burst into the incident room. They both appeared pleased with themselves. Riley noted that Rachel had obviously hit it off better with Cassie than he had. He could have been annoyed but instead was pleased for Rachel; it was an important part of her development to be able to work in different teams.

'How did you go with Emma? Was she ok with you two turning up?' Smith asked.

'Yeah, she was fine,' Cassie said. She motioned to her left. 'Rachel's a natural at putting someone at ease. Emma was able to identify one person with confidence. The big man, she thinks, was a bloke called Tony Fantis. He has priors for aggravated assault and drug offences. He's also a member of the Anarchists.'

'Ok, that's good, because we just learnt that we have his fingerprints at the boatshed and also at Loxton. What about the other one?' Riley asked.

For a moment, Riley thought Cassie resented him asking the question instead of Paul Smith, her immediate superior. She must have recalled Smith's clarification that Riley was in charge of the Goolwa investigation.

'Emma wasn't sure. Unfortunately, we just had a headshot of the known Anarchists and some were pretty fuzzy. However, she did think that the other could have been a bloke called Damien Hargreaves. His description matches the one Emma has put into her statement. He's quite distinctive being so small, so we're confident she's picked him correctly.'

'We might need more than that in due course, but it's a good start.'

Rachel gave Cassie a little nudge. Cassie smiled at her and said, 'Go on, you tell them.'

Rachel looked to Riley and Smith. 'Would it help if we told you that he has a VX blue Commodore registered in his name?'

Smith clapped his hands together and looked to Riley.

Usually, he would be itching to push hard on further clarification and organising next steps. For now, he was happy to let his protégé take the lead.

He would, of course, jump in if he felt all the necessary bases were not being covered.

Riley checked his notes. 'This Damien Hargreaves. Does he have a record? If so, we can check for a fingerprint match.'

'I'm afraid not. Not yet, anyway. We have the rego for the car, though, so we can get an alert out for that if you want.'

'Before you do that, let's get a warrant for his arrest and let the team in Loxton know. Hopefully, we can get lucky and pick them up together. Once we have Hargreaves under arrest, we can get fingerprints for a match. We should also get a warrant for his home. Do you have his address?'

Rachel was beaming. 'He lives in Yankalilla; a bit closer to our patch.'

Riley turned to Smith, who had been watching with interest.

'Sir, would you mind accelerating the warrants and letting the guys in Loxton know where we're up to?'

Smith smiled approvingly.

'Very happy to, Senior Sergeant. If you like, I'll also coordinate a team in Adelaide to search Fantis' house and arrest him if he's there. What do you want to do about Yankalilla?'

Riley wanted to reward Rachel and Cassie for their good work, but he also wanted to make sure they would be safe.

'Let's say we can get the warrants today. I think we should coordinate with Adelaide so that we do the searches of both Fantis' and Hargreaves' houses at the same time, say first thing tomorrow morning.

'That will probably also give the best chance of catching them at home. I'd like your advice on this, sir, but I suggest Cassie and Rachel lead the search on Hargreaves' house. They can take Constables Thompson and Reid and I wonder if you'd like to accompany them.'

'Me, take a back seat? Unlikely, O'Brien, but I'll give it a crack.' Smith was enjoying watching his team take responsibility but still making sure he was engaged. He suddenly felt old but gratified. He could see that his transition to retirement was going to work well if every case could be conducted like this one. Maybe he would be able to take Mrs. Smith on that long overseas holiday sooner than he thought.

Riley smiled and turned to Cassie and Rachel. 'Just so you're aware of my movements, we're going to use Shaun Chambers to do some forensic accounting on Vinnie Waters' books. We're looking for any commercial arrangements between him and Greg Satchin or the Anarchists. I need to brief him in the morning and I want Ollie Townsend sitting alongside Shaun to ensure we have an appropriate level of supervision.'

Eyebrows were raised, particularly by Cassie and Rachel.

Smith was aware from the earlier discussion with Riley and observed the concern of the other two.

'Ladies,' he said, addressing Cassie and Rachel, 'I'm sure you have some doubts about using a member of the public for this work, but frankly, we have little choice. I know he's close to the case, but we've eliminated Shaun as a suspect and, let's face it, he has a lot of skin in the game when it comes to solving this case. Remember, his son is still missing and we have absolutely no clue where to look. So, I think Riley has made the right call on this and the sooner we get him started the better.'

'Thanks, sir. Let's all remember, too, that there is a chance that Aiden Chambers is being held at one of the premises we are going to search. We don't know it or even suspect it at this stage but let's be extra careful just in case.'

Riley looked to the Detective Inspector.

'I guess we should coordinate with the CIB Tactical Response Group for backup and also get the illicit drugs team involved. I'm sure you have all the contacts there. Could I ask you to streamline their input? I'd really like to get to Vinnie's house and see what we can uncover there.'

The team disbanded and Riley collected Phil Reid on his way out to Vinnie's. The day was bright and the town was quiet, basking in the late afternoon sunshine. The two men donned their sunglasses as they headed to the police car.

As Phil was driving, Riley looked across at him. He'd developed nicely over the past couple of years and had been running the station operations while the rest of the team had been tied up on the investigation over the past week.

Riley looked at the wide scar on Phil's forehead, a legacy of the night he had been slashed by a spade in the Currency Creek Cemetery. Phil had recovered over time and it had taken a few months for both the physical and mental scars to heal sufficiently for him to return to duty.

'I don't even notice it now much, sir.'

'Sorry, Phil, I didn't think it was that obvious that I was looking.'

The constable laughed.

'It's no big deal, honestly. In fact, believe it or not, it gives girls a reason to talk to me. They're curious how I got it and when I tell them, my stocks only go up.'

'Well, good on you, Phil. Still would have been better if it hadn't happened, but I guess we can't undo it now.' Riley had always felt some guilt about exposing Phil to that danger three years ago but was gratified that the young man had coped so well with the trauma.

'I've been meaning to check with you, Phil. How are the arrangements for the Wooden Boat Festival this weekend?'

'All under control, sir. Resources are booked and I'll meet with the organising committee later in the week to confirm arrangements.'

Vinnie's house was on Hindmarsh Island. A two-storey, waterfront property, the front lawn was neatly manicured, a stark contrast to the empty blocks on either side that featured hardy weeds growing out of compacted sand. Once promised as an idyllic lifestyle location, the island's development had been slowed by the Global Financial Crisis and the estate was a mixture of homes like Vinnie's and empty blocks.

Riley took a key from his pocket, extracted from Vinnie's personal belongings after his death. He opened the front door and stepped into a large open hallway. The house had a large living area at the front that extended through to the back of the house. Folding glass doors over-looked a small lawned area sloping down to the marina. A small private pontoon ran from the lawn, capable of mooring a boat but presently unoccupied.

The living area was immaculately clean; Vinnie must have had a cleaner. Only an empty upturned glass sat draining on the kitchen sink.

Phil Reid whistled. 'Obviously, things were going pretty well for him before they went really pear-shaped.'

Riley had never been to Vinnie's house before and nodded in agree-ment. 'Must be good money in boat repairs and cafes. Or something else, maybe. That's what we're here to find out.'

The two poked around the whole of the ground level and found nothing that was of interest. Upstairs were three bedrooms and two bathrooms, one an ensuite attached to the main bedroom overlooking the marina.

Phil started in the spare bedrooms, while Riley went into the master. The bed was pulled up but not properly made. The cleaner had probably not been since Vinnie's death. Riley made a note to track them down.

He worked his way through Vinnie's cupboards and drawers, finding nothing with any relevance to the case. Inside his walk-in robe, two suitcases were stored on a high shelf. Riley pulled them down. One was light and when he opened it, he was not surprised to find it empty.

The second suitcase was heavy. The catch was jammed and for a moment, Riley thought it was locked. When he prised it open, he found it stacked with photo albums, each varying in shape, size and colour. They'd been accumulated over years, but someone, most likely Vinnie's ex-wife Debbie, had painstakingly organised and labelled them. There were albums that pre-dated their marriage and Riley noted some that went back to the time when he, Shaun and Vinnie had been closest of friends.

If he'd had more time, Riley would have liked to have looked at them more closely but he was interrupted by Phil's call from the second bathroom. He hastily re-packed the suitcase and replaced it on the shelf.

He found Phil halfway inside the vanity unit, under the sink.

'There's a panel down here, like a false wall. Look, this space is not as deep as the benchtop. I reckon there's a secret storage space behind.'

Phil pulled an Allen key from a bunch of assorted tools on his belt and undid the four retaining screws. He removed the panel and whistled.

'Riley, you have to see this.' He crawled out to allow Riley to get a closer look. The cavity was filled with plastic zip-loc bags, each stuffed with notes.

'Holy crap. Well done, Phil. Let's get some photos and then bag this lot up. I think we may have uncovered an interesting connection to the Anarchists here.'

After the cash was logged and stored securely in the station safe, Riley drove home and changed. Twenty minutes later, he joined Paul Smith at the Goolwa Hotel where he was "de-briefing" with Rachel and Cassie.

'Sit down, Riley. A beer?'

'Thanks, sir.'

'Paul when we're off-duty. These girls have learnt that already, haven't you girls?'

'Yes, Paul,' they sang in harmony.

Smith returned with a fresh round of beers. 'Well, we're ready for the bust tomorrow. Let's hope our friends are home and we find something interesting.'

Riley gave him a cheeky smile. 'If you're lucky. You'll find something as interesting as Phil found at Vinnie's house.'

The others leaned in. Smith threw his arms apart. 'Well?'

'He discovered a hidden cavity, stuffed with cash.'

'How much?' Rachel was excited. She'd never been this close to a big case before.

'Over sixty. Thousand, that is.'

'Ha-ha.' Now Smith was excited. 'I can't wait for tomorrow!'

20

2005

Business for Vinnie was going better than he had expected. The workshop was performing as well as it ever had and Shifty kept a steady supply of cars. The used car lot was the cream on the cake. It meant that Vinnie could pay Shifty an agreed price for a stolen car, then set his own price for resale. The advantage of having that control was that he could afford to sell the re-purposed cars at better value by averaging his margins across his legitimate stock. Vinnie's Motors became known as the place to go for well-priced, quality vehicles.

With business success came more cash. It became a problem for Vinnie to avoid disclosing his true wealth. He figured the best way to deal with the problem was to engage in more legitimate businesses that dealt in cash so that he could absorb his surpluses into them. He eyed off a pizza shop in Strathalbyn followed by a fast-food business in Goolwa. He extended their offerings and re-badged them as *Cafetopia*, offering eat-in dining as well as takeaway. Cash takings skyrocketed, supplemented of course by Vinnie's other business. The staff in the shops could not believe what a good businessman Vinnie Waters was. He largely left them alone and gave them all a good pay rise to promote stability and reduce staff turnover. He even took some of the admin load away from them, handling the daily banking himself.

The only person who didn't rate Vinnie as a boss was Chad Grey. Chad had been employed in the Goolwa shop ever since school. Limited opportunities were available to him in a wheelchair and he'd been grateful for the chance to learn a trade when it was offered to him by the gentle old couple who owned the business. When Vinnie bought the business, it all changed. If Chad thought that their school day feud was behind them, he was wrong.

'I'm sorry, Chad,' Vinnie had said, 'but I'm afraid I'm going to have to let you go. This business needs to be run more efficiently and I need to cut staff numbers. Frankly, you don't have the same output as the other staff so you are the one to go.'

'Vinnie,' Chad had argued, 'you've just given everyone a pay rise. Their wages are now way above anyone else in town. Even as far as Victor Harbor, I reckon. How does it make sense to pay them more, then get rid of me?'

'That's why I'm successful at business, Chad. See, I know the value of contented staff. They'll give more back; much more than carrying someone who doesn't pull his weight.'

Chad knew that the real reason had nothing to do with economics but there was nothing he could say. Even though the other staff sympathised with him, they wouldn't risk the generosity that they had received.

Everything considered, things were working out for Vinnie. With his ever-increasing wealth, he built a reputation around the town as a go-getter. It didn't impress everyone; some of the older heads around town wondered how the brash young man had grown so quickly; how he had made a small fortune much quicker than they had ever been able to. There were rumours. Surely, he must be doing something shonky to be getting where he was so quickly. But the rumours were just that. There was no evidence of wrongdoing and Vinnie's staff would have nothing of it; he was simply a shrewd bloke who knew how to treat his people.

His personal life was also satisfying. He ate at the best restaurants but could also have a beer in the front bar. He dressed sharply for work and would be the centre of attention at the various charity events he attended. That was where he had finally won over Debbie McLean.

A ball at the function centre on the river had been organised to support cancer research. The man at the centre of organising the ball had lost his wife to breast cancer earlier in the year and he'd been delighted when Vinnie donated five thousand dollars to the fundraiser. It was an act of generosity that was talked about around town and Vinnie's stocks continued to rise.

Vinnie arrived at the ball, parking out front in a Porsche 911 and dressed in a formal black suit. The contrast to the more subdued dress of the good people of Goolwa was unmissable and he drew the gaze of men and women alike as he walked around greeting people.

He hadn't arrived with a partner. He never really had time to find a woman who appealed to him; looks were everything. It suited him to be able to work the room without worrying about a partner, building new contacts and sustaining existing ones; identifying people who could be of use sometime later. Right now, he was bored. He'd ended up talking with the owner of one of the dress shops in a nearby town, a droll woman who had the mistaken belief that she knew fashion from farts. She'd obviously picked the most garish item from her stock to wear to the ball. He felt like telling her there was a reason why the piece hadn't sold. Instead, he listened to her moaning about the difficulty of specialty retailing on the Fleurieu Peninsula; the lack of customers in winter, the costs of power, GST, the high rent of her premises, blah, blah....

There was only one reason he had persisted with the woman. He had been watching Shaun Chambers and his delightful partner, Carla with fascination. It was more correct to say he'd been watching Carla. She was still as beautiful as ever and looked even more glamorous than he'd ever seen her before in a tight-fitting long dress and high heels. It reminded him of the fascination he'd had for her at school, knowing that she'd always been out of reach for him. *Carla and Debbie. Now, where was Debbie?* He'd expected her to have come tonight; she was, after all, a good friend of the dead woman in whose name the ball had been organised. One reason why he'd donated five thousand to the cause was so that he could make an impression on Debbie. Where Carla was unattainable, Vinnie always believed he had a chance with Debbie. When all was said and done, he was a practical man. If he couldn't have Carla, he'd take the next best with a lot less effort and, really, Debbie wasn't far behind Carla in the looks department.

As if on cue, Debbie sidled alongside Carla. Vinnie waited for Debbie to kiss cheeks with Carla and then Shaun before breaking off from the dress shop owner.

'Please excuse me, I need to move on,' he said to her, 'but look, if business is so fucking tough, why don't you just get out and stop whingeing?'

'I beg your pardon?' The woman stood gaping as Vinnie strode away from her toward Debbie.

She wore a shimmering red dress that showed a lot of leg and a generous amount of cleavage. Bright red lipstick and immaculate makeup complemented her dress and the mass of curls in her blonde hair. Vinnie was mesmerised as he stood behind her; *not far behind Carla at all.* He tapped her shoulder gently.

'Debbie, how are you? It's been a while.'

Debbie spun around, smiling. 'Vinnie. It's nice to see you. Is it true that you donated five grand tonight?'

'Well, yes, but it was nothing really. I mean we have to look after our community, don't we?'

'Don't be modest, now. It was very generous of you.'

Shaun nudged Vinnie in the ribs. 'Yes, it was very generous, Vinnie. You have the town talking.'

Vinnie continued to feign modesty and found himself penetrating Debbie's defences. When the formal speeches were given, it was only proper that Vinnie's generous donation was mentioned and acknowledged with an enthusiastic round of applause. Debbie grasped his hand and squeezed. She let her hand rest in his until the speeches were completed.

'So business is good, Vinnie?' Shaun asked.

'It is. You wouldn't have thought that a lad off a cattle station would make a good businessman, but there you are. I must have learnt something. In fact, Shaun, it's going so well that I wondered if you have any clients that might be wanting to sell. I'm in the market for more investment.'

Debbie giggled and looked into his eyes, clearly impressed.

'Anything in particular you want? I mean type of business.'

'Nah, just as long as it's got potential to make money. There's a certain dress shop I reckon I can get cheap.' He nodded toward the woman he'd been talking to earlier.

Shaun laughed. 'I don't reckon she'll sell. She's loaded and the shop is just a hobby for her. You didn't get sucked in by her whining, did you?'

Vinnie felt his ego deflate a little. 'Alright, we need a drink. I'll be back soon, gorgeous,' he murmured to Debbie and headed to the bar.

Carla grabbed her friend by the elbow.

'You're not seriously interested in him, are you?'

'I might be. He's changed, don't you think? He seems more together, you know. He's successful, generous ...'

'He hasn't changed. He's the same cocky smart-arse he was at school,' Carla rebuffed.

'Carla's right,' Shaun added. 'Be careful, Deb. There are rumours that Vinnie's not the good guy he comes across as.'

'Who says?' Debbie defended.

Shaun shrugged. 'It's just talk. But, you know, where there's smoke, there's fire.'

'I can't believe you listen to gossip, Shaun.' Debbie was getting excited, surprising even herself. 'Anyway, you might have to get used to it. I think I like him. I might even bring him along to your wedding.'

Vinnie returned with their drinks. 'So, did I miss any exciting chat?'

Debbie grabbed his hand. 'Come on, let's dance.'

A few months later, Vinnie did accompany Debbie to Shaun and Carla's wedding, much to their disdain. Riley was Shaun's best man and, although he knew already that Vinnie had finally got his girl, he was surprised at how easily they got on. Debbie doted on Vinnie and he returned the affection.

'Do you reckon it will last?' Riley asked Shaun.

Shaun swallowed a mouthful of food before answering.

'Haven't you heard? They're engaged. Getting married in a couple of months.'

'Wow. Moving quick, aren't they?'

'Deb's pregnant. I think they're both pretty happy about it though.'

21

Tuesday 23 April 2019 (Day 6)

The raids on Fantis' house in Adelaide and Hargreaves' in Yankalilla were scheduled to take place simultaneously at seven am. Riley was up early. He wanted to see the team off from Goolwa. The drive to Yankalilla was forty-five minutes and, allowing for time to rendezvous with the Tactical Response Group, the set-off time was six.

There was a buzz of excitement as the team booked out their weapons and ammunition, donned their safety vests and ensured the paperwork was all in order.

The Goolwa team allocated for the raid were Paul Smith, Cassie Callaghan, Rachel Cross, Phil Reid and Craig Thompson, seconded from Victor Harbor. Riley watched the two cars leave. At that moment he felt pangs of envy. He wished he was with them but accepted that getting Shaun started was an important, if mundane, step in securing the convictions they were looking for.

Shaun was not due to arrive at the station until nine, so Riley decided the best use of his time until then was to prepare breakfast for Kate, who, he was sure, would still be sleeping. He arrived home to find exactly the opposite; Kate was showered and dressed, munching on a piece of toast while she tidied the kitchen sink.

'Riley, what are you doing back? I thought you'd gone to work.'

'I had but I'd decided to do something nice for you seeing I've hardly been here the last few days. I was going to get you breakfast in bed but you've beaten me to it.'

Kate pinched his cheeks. 'Oh, you sweet man. Did you forget I told you last night that I had an early meeting? Oh, aren't we a good pair, just ships passing in the night lately?'

Riley shrugged. He loved this girl and wanted to spend as much time with her as he could but it just wasn't possible right now. He recalled how only days ago he wanted more from his job. Now he had it and the pendulum had swung to the other side. Still, he knew this was temporary and their lives would return to normal once the investigation was complete.

Kate grabbed her handbag and pecked him on the cheek. 'Don't forget. I'll be home late tonight but I guess you will be too. That's ok, we'll catch up tomorrow night for a few hours.'

Riley looked at her inquisitively.

'Oh, Riley, remember we've got Paul Smith and the other detective, Cassie is it, coming for dinner? Rachel's coming, too, isn't she?'

The expression on his face gave away his lapse of memory but he replied quickly to try to hide it.

'Yeah, yeah, of course. I don't think you'll separate Rachel and Cassie anytime soon. They're getting on like a house on fire.'

Riley placed a couple of slices of bread into the toaster as Kate slipped out the door. He still had one slice clenched between his teeth as he got back into his car and drove to Sally and Callum's house.

It was still early and he half expected to get them out of bed. Instead, he was greeted at the door by a cheery Sally.

'Hey, Riley, come in.'

They walked through to the kitchen where Callum and Emma were deep in discussion.

Callum turned to Riley and smiled.

'You're timing is perfect. Emma was just wondering what was going to happen with her parents; the funeral and all. Can you help?'

Emma looked up, no longer the frightened girl who had arrived at Sally and Callum's house; instead, she looked secure and confident.

'I just want to know if I should be planning anything. All our relatives will want to know what's happening, with them and with me. No one even knows where I am.'

Riley pulled up a chair next to her.

'Well, as you know, there is still an investigation into their murders, so the coroner will want to keep them until he's satisfied that he can write a report that is complete and accurate. He's not likely to release their bodies for a while yet.

'As for your disappearance, I'm sure your relatives and friends are very concerned but as you know we need to keep your whereabouts secret for your own safety. What I can tell you is that things are starting to move along quickly and we're hopeful of a major breakthrough soon, like in the next couple of days.'

Emma locked her eyes onto his.

'What? What's happening?'

'Sorry, Emma, I can't say any more than that at present but we're trying to resolve what's happened to your mum and dad as soon as we can.'

Riley's phone rang and he glanced at it to see Paul Smith was calling. He stood and put his hand on Emma's shoulder.

'I've got to take this but I'll update you as soon as I can.'

Before she could respond, Riley was on his way out the door. Outside he spoke for the first time.

'Sir, how did it go?'

'Well, not entirely what we hoped for, Riley. Hargreaves wasn't at his home and neither was Fantis. According to their wives, both have been at home just a few hours each since the murders in Loxton. They're obviously holed up somewhere, so that's our next challenge; find out where they are. So obviously, no sign of Aiden either.

'On the good news front, we recovered some firearms at both premises, so we'll be able to check the ballistics against those at the scene in Loxton. We also recovered small quantities of drugs and a bit of cash.

'They've thrown a bit of a spanner in the works though. We found the number plates that belong on Damien Hargreaves' car at his house. It looks like they switched the plates to make it harder for us to track them.'

Riley caught the disappointment in Smith's voice. They were now confident they were on the track of the killers but it seemed like they were no closer to arresting them. And, the assurance he had given Emma now seemed optimistic. To top it off, he had no good news to pass on to Shaun as he had hoped he would.

He arrived at the station and still had time to kill. Before Shaun arrived, he reviewed the rosters for the next few days. Aside from the Wooden Boat Festival, there was ANZAC Day in two days. The day began with a dawn service at six am, but it was what came afterwards that required police resources. Around the town, there would be barbeques, two-up games and parties commemorating Australia's proudest day. Police could be inundated with a variety of drink-related issues, potentially a blue or two at the pub and, most likely, drink driving.

Riley was grateful that additional resources for the day would be supplied from Adelaide and that some of his team may be able to get some well-earned rest on the public holiday.

Oliver arrived in time for Riley to brief him before Shaun arrived. He was miffed because he hadn't been invited to participate in the raid but was also thrilled to play an important role in the building of forensic evidence to resolve the case.

'So, Shaun Chambers, he is a mate of yours, Riley?'

'Well, we go back a long way, Oliver, way back to school days. We haven't had a lot to do with each other lately but all the same, I have to regard him as a friend. But the thing is, my relationship with him can't be seen to have any bearing on his assistance with going over the books. Shaun was also well known to our victim, Vinnie; not close, but the three of us were friends a long time ago. That's why I need you to sit at his elbow, understanding every transaction he looks at. You need to ask a question any time you don't understand. Make sure everything is logged and we will have a de-brief with DI Smith at the end of each day.'

Shaun arrived as scheduled and sat with Riley and Oliver in the interview room. Vinnie's computer sat on the desk in front of him and a mound of files perched precariously on a chair in the corner of the room.

'Thanks for asking me to help, Riley. Anything I can do that will help work out what's happened to Aiden, I'm happy to do. I can't stand sitting around waiting. So, what have you got?'

Riley waved a hand to a chair that sat to the side of the desk. It was piled with books and files that had been taken from Vinnie's boatshed.

'As far as we know, he kept all his records there but of course, we can't be sure. These are books for the café businesses as well as the boatshed, bank statements, the works.'

Shaun gave them a cursory glance. 'What about his personal accounts? Did he have an accountant?'

'We haven't found anything else in any of his premises, so what you have is it. As far as we can tell he used an accountant in Adelaide, a bloke called Gavin Trower, but we are not expecting much cooperation from him.'

'Why is that?'

'Trower is a known associate of a bikie gang.'

Shaun looked at Riley wide-eyed. 'What the hell was Vinnie involved in?'

'Trower is also a lawyer and looks after all the legal side of the bikie gang's financial affairs and probably some of the illegal stuff too. As far as the outside world knows, he runs everything entirely by the book. However, I'm told by the guys in Adelaide he resists any request to disclose information unless it's backed up by a warrant. We need something to put in front of a magistrate that is compelling enough to get that warrant.'

Shaun lifted his hands to his forehead. 'Do the bikies have Aiden, Riley?' He lifted his eyes to meet Riley's.

'The truth is that we don't know, Shaun. What I can tell you is that we raided two houses this morning but we didn't find the bikies or Aiden there. Nor any evidence he had been there.'

'Who are these bikies?'

'They are from an outlaw gang known as the Anarchists. There are two men, in particular, we're looking for; a bloke from Adelaide called Tony Fantis and another from Yankalilla. Damien Hargreaves.'

Shaun sniggered. 'Bloody Damien Hargreaves. Now, there's a piece of work.'

Oliver had been listening quietly to this point but was unable to restrain himself. 'You know him?'

'I did, years ago. I used to look after his tax for a while. He got greedy and wanted to hide away money he'd earnt so he didn't have to pay tax on it. What he wanted was blatantly illegal and I refused to help him so we parted ways. I had no regrets about that, maybe until now. If he's holding Aiden, I'd rather be with him than against him.'

'What else do you know about him?' asked Oliver.

'Not much. But he has a reputation as a sadistic, vicious trouble-maker. What he lacks in size, he makes up for with his choice of weapons – knuckledusters, razors, guns, you name it. I only know that third hand but it wouldn't surprise me if it was true.'

Riley saw beads of sweat building on Shaun's brow. It was obvious that he was worried about Aiden's safety, even more than he had been before he arrived at the police station.

Shaun suddenly jerked upright. 'Riley, do you remember that story Vinnie told us years ago? You know, how he found out he'd had sex with his half-sister?'

Oliver couldn't suppress a laugh, drawing a piercing glare from Shaun. Riley looked at him blankly.

'Remember, Riley. Vinnie found out that his biological father was Wayne Hargreaves but that was after he'd had a one-night stand with Wayne's daughter, Louise.'

Riley was confused. 'So?'

'So, the last thing Vinnie said when he told us that story was that Louise's brothers, one of them is Damien, would kill him if they ever found out. You don't think that's why they killed Vinnie, do you?'

'A lot of water's gone under the bridge since then, Shaun. I can't imag-ine Damien would care about that nearly twenty years later. We think it's more likely drug-related, but look, we should log it for follow-up.'

Riley was concerned that Shaun had become distracted. The last thing the case needed was an ineffective person driving the forensic examination of Vinnie's records.

'Shaun, I know you're worried about Damien Hargreaves but you need to leave him to us. Right now, you can be more helpful by find-ing the links between Vinnie and the Satchins in Loxton and with the Anarchist motorcycle gang. Are you ready to get started?'

Riley regarded Shaun as one of the most level-headed and logical people that he knew and he hoped that appealing to his sense of reason would sharpen his focus. He wasn't disappointed.

'Yeah, of course, Riley. Sorry, it's really hard not knowing where Aiden is and whether he's safe or not, maybe even dead. I'm trying to look after Carla, but she's a mess. She wants answers I can't give her and as much as I want to blame her for getting involved with Vinnie and causing all this, I can't. I still love her too much. Anyway, let's get started.'

Shaun shook himself and stared into the computer screen in front of him.

'Let's start with the computer. You have the password?'

'Sorry, no,' Riley replied, 'we could have it sent to Adelaide for the tech guys to crack but I wonder if we can have a try first.'

Shaun scratched his chin. 'You know what? I think you're right. If I know Vinnie, he wouldn't be that diligent with passwords and would pick something he would easily memorise. Let's try the obvious ones first.'

After a few minutes, they had worked their way through password, password1, 123456, 987654, abcde, qwerty and variations of these. All without success.

While Shaun and Oliver considered other options, Riley made them each a coffee. He returned to see that the screen was still stuck on the login page.

'Have you tried something that would be more personal to Vinnie, like say his birthday?' he offered.

'Yeah, we've done that. Let's try Debbie and DebbieM.'

Oliver looked quizzically at Shaun.

'Vinnie's ex-wife. By the way, Riley, has anyone been in touch with her about Vinnie? She should be told.'

Riley shrugged. 'We've been trying to track her down but with no luck. You know she hasn't been back here in years and there's no evidence from Vinnie's phone that he's had any contact at all with her for a long time.'

Shaun tried variations of Debbie's name in the password. Still, he couldn't open the screen.

'One more option, then I'm out of ideas. You know what I'm thinking, don't you Riley?'

'Jeremy?'

Oliver threw his hands up. 'Who? Or What?'

Shaun typed as he said, 'Vinnie's son. He died.'

The computer responded with a message indicating an incorrect password.

The three looked at the screen desperately, as if that might will it to change. Suddenly, Shaun typed a series of numbers into the dialogue box. The screen came to life with Vinnie's home screen.

'What did you type in?' Oliver asked.

'The date that Jeremy died. It's the sort of thing that Vinnie would want to remember so what better than using it every day?'

'Well done, Shaun,' said Riley. He stood awkwardly looking at the screen, his silence suddenly drawing Shaun's attention.

'Was there something else, Riley?'

Riley had already decided that he needed to provide Shaun with a deeper briefing, including the detail of the murders in Loxton, the disappearance of Emma Satchin and her refuge now in Goolwa. He'd contemplated whether this was a breach of the undertaking that he'd given Emma but, at the end of the day, Shaun was now working with the police. What Riley was less certain about was whether the gory details would panic Shaun and render him less effective.

After he'd finished, Shaun let out a sharp breath. 'Well, thanks for taking me into your confidence, Riley. I have to say that it scares the shit out of me where this is going but I promise you it will only make me work harder.'

Riley nodded at him. 'Good. Shall I leave you to it? Let me know if you find anything.'

22

Tuesday 23 April 2019 (Day 6)

It was late morning when Smith and the team returned from Yankalilla. There was a mixture of excitement and disappointment as they de-briefed. On one hand, the expectation that they would arrest the suspects had not been fulfilled. No one was disappointed that they hadn't needed to use their weapons or rely on their vests, but they had hoped that they would have confronted Fantis and Hargreaves.

Despite the setback, there was a buzz amongst the team, knowing they were on the right path and that it was a matter of when, not if, they would get a break.

Smith was the one person who was restrained in his optimism. As a long-serving cop, he was always confident that they would bring the perpetrators to justice; and that was just a matter of time. He had also been around long enough to know that a bust often didn't go to plan.; it was just one step in the process that needed to be followed and, if it didn't bring results, more perseverance was needed.

The thing that was playing on his mind most was that a little boy was still missing. His hope from the bust was that they would have located and freed Aiden; reunited a family. That hadn't happened and Smith knew that every day that passed reduced the likelihood they would find Aiden safe and well. To make it worse, he was in no doubt that Fantis and Hargreaves, wherever they were, had been alerted that the police were onto them.

He pulled Riley aside and shared his concerns about Aiden with him.

'I'm starting to wonder, O'Brien, whether we were right to bring Shaun Chambers in to help us. When we thought we were going to open this up today, it was probably ok but now we have to tell the poor sod that we're no closer to finding his son.'

'I've already told him we had no success with the raids. Right now, we're no worse off than we were yesterday and Shaun came in without knowing we were about to make arrests.'

'That's true, but now he does know. I think we'd better go and have a chat. Before we do, however, there's one other thing playing on my mind.'

'Sir?' Riley was quizzical.

'These guys were very careful at the Loxton site. They wanted to make a statement by making the murders an execution. But they left the site very clean. Even though it would be obvious to blind Freddy that there were drugs and, by association, bikies involved. Next, they come to Goolwa, kill a bloke in an entirely different way and try to make it look like an accident. Then they leave fingerprints and abduct a kid. That doesn't make sense, does it?'

'No, it doesn't. That's why I wonder ...'

Smith interjected '... if they didn't mean to kill Vinnie Waters? I'm starting to come to that point of view as well. So then, what the hell happened?'

Riley shrugged

'One thing I'm sure of,' Smith continued, 'is that bikie gangs don't like leaving sixty grand unaccounted for, assuming Waters was involved in laundering money for them. And there could be more money plus drugs still uncovered. If there is, where is it? Not in his workshop or his house. Did Vinnie have other premises somewhere?'

'The cafes?'

'I'd be surprised, Riley. Too many people around. But let's check them out. Also, let's keep an eye on his house. I'd say there's a chance that Fantis and Hargreaves might come looking for it.'

'Sir, does that give us another problem? Emma Satchin is in Goolwa. Is there any chance they'll come looking for her?'

'Well, the media has broadcast that she's missing but I don't see how the Anarchists would know she's here. She'll be safe as long as she keeps her head down at Callum's house until we sort this all out.'

Riley nodded.

'I'll organise the surveillance on Vinnie's house, just in case. There's something that's been bothering me too. Remember that Emma told us that Vinnie had to sleep on his boat the night he went to Loxton?'

'So what?'

'Well, why by boat? He could have driven there a lot quicker. But, if Vinnie was involved in drug-running, wouldn't travelling by river be a lot less visible than by road? Boats probably have a lot more storage space, especially concealed spaces, than a vehicle.'

'The search of the shed didn't turn up any drugs, but what if he'd moved them on. Maybe he stores them somewhere else once he gets to Goolwa or off-loads them onto a distributor.' Smith was beginning to buy into the possibility but immediately checked himself.

'We don't have any evidence that suggests that Waters was involved in drug-running but I agree we should check it out. I'll ask the drug team to send someone down with dogs to see if they can sniff anything out in the shed. And that boat in the shed. In the meantime, let's go and talk to Shaun Chambers.'

Shaun and Oliver were hunched over a folder, peering at entries on a page and then cross-referencing them on the computer screen. They were unaware that Smith and Riley were standing behind them until Smith gave an announcing cough into his hand.

Smith was surprised when he looked at Shaun. He'd expected to see a man broken by the stress of a situation over which he had no control. Everything he had been told about him was that he was introverted and mild-mannered, likely to buckle rather than assert.

Instead, in Shaun's eyes, he saw a steely resolve. A resolve that was focused on using the skills he had to assist the investigation, despite the deep-seated fears he held for Aiden's safety.

'Mr. Chambers.'

'Shaun, please. You are DI Smith, I gather.'

'Yes. Let me say how much we appreciate your assistance with this.' Smith waved his hands around the files littering the small room. 'I'm sure I wouldn't know where to start, but that's why you're here isn't it?'

'Yes, it is. Do you have any news on Aiden?'

'No, I'm sorry. I understand you're aware that we executed some warrants this morning but that we fell short of arresting the people we're after.' Shaun nodded.

'Well, Shaun, I want to reassure you that we are continuing to do everything we can to find these men and with them, hopefully, your son. However, I have to caution you that these are dangerous men. We believe they're deeply involved in the drug trade and are responsible for several murders.'

'Are you trying to tell me that you think Aiden may already be dead, Detective Inspector? Don't you think that I've already considered that?' Shaun lowered his voice. 'Regardless, I want to find the truth. What was Vinnie involved in that led to my son's abduction?'

'I'm sorry, Shaun. I just felt you needed to be aware of the possible outcomes. There seems no logical reason for these men to have abducted Aiden, even if he was a witness to Vinnie Waters' murder. That's my biggest unknown at the moment. Why would they take Aiden?'

'I understand. I'm sorry for my outburst, but believe me, I am a realist. Now, do you want to know what we've found?'

Smith and Riley looked at each other, surprised.

'You have something already?'

'Well, it's not definite. More of a suspicion at the moment based on irregularities.'

'What sort of irregularities?'

'Ok, we've been looking at the café businesses. Now Vinnie does all the bookwork for them. He collects the cash every couple of days and banks it. Staff handle credit card transactions and the ordering of ingredients, but Vinnie handles all the cash - the cash they receive and the payment of wages. Now, that's ok but it means that he is, or was, the only person who saw what the business was really doing. The thing is that the bankings are very high for this type of business, or alternatively the expenses are very low for the turnover of the business.'

Smith nodded.

Riley put his hands on his hips. 'I don't get it,' he said.

Oliver interjected.

'What it means is that there was probably money being banked into the café's bank account that came from other sources.' He looked up at Riley's still blank face. 'Like drug money.'

'So, he was laundering through the café?'

'It looks like it,' said Shaun. 'We were just about to check the owner-ship of the cafes but I'm guessing that they're in the name of a trust and through some complicated structures, eventually the beneficial owner-ship will go back to the Anarchists.'

Smith tapped Shaun on the shoulder. 'Great work, you two. How do we prove it?'

'Let us keep working through it but, at some point, it will be worth talking to the staff to see how much they reckon they're taking in cash compared to what's being banked. Oliver was going to do that this afternoon if you have no objections.'

'Not at all,' said Riley, 'get onto it. Sir, I think we should leave these two to it.'

'Agree, Senior Sergeant.' Smith pulled Riley aside as they left the room. 'They're making good progress in there, Riley. You have your plans for now, so I'm going to head back to Adelaide tonight. Mick's back in Adelaide now so I'll catch up with him tomorrow to get an update on the Loxton side of things.'

'No problem. Somehow, I don't think we'll wrap this one up while you're away. Not like last time.'

Smith smiled as he recalled the sudden conclusion to their investigation three years earlier. He hadn't been put out at all by the fact that he hadn't been there at the action end.

'Somehow, I think you're right about that. Anyway, I won't be gone that long. I haven't forgotten about dinner tomorrow night.' He patted Riley on the shoulder and headed toward the station door. At the last moment, he turned.

'How's the ANZAC Service here, Riley? My father served in the Second World War and I try to attend a service if I can.'

'We have a very active RSL down here, sir, and they take ANZAC Day very seriously, especially the Dawn Service. We get an excellent turn-out from the community. Umm, it's normal for the senior police officer from the station here to lay a wreath at the service. I'd be honoured if you would share that duty with me, sir.'

'I'd be delighted to, O'Brien. I'll see you tomorrow.' Riley almost sensed an emotional tremor in Smith's voice. He smiled as he saw the DI pass through the door without another word.

Riley spent the rest of the afternoon organising rosters and ensuring the arrangements for ANZAC Day were all in place. He had been concerned about who he could allocate to the surveillance of Vinnie Water's house. He was pleasantly surprised as he went through the rosters with Phil Reid that the young constable put himself forward for the graveyard shift. Riley assured him that he would relieve him as soon as he could in the morning.

He remembered that Kate had parent-teacher meetings in the evening, so he headed to Sally and Callum's house. He needed to give Emma an update on the breakthrough he had mentioned to her in the morning.

The day was still warm when he arrived at the house. A sprinkler was watering the front lawn. It had been dry and it was unusual to still be watering gardens at the back end of Autumn. As he walked down the driveway, avoiding the overspray of the sprinkler, he heard laughter coming from the back of the house. Bypassing the front door, he walked down the side of the house and found Callum, Sally and Emma sitting on the back verandah drinking beers. Riley walked up the three steps and took a seat with them, removing his cap in the process.

'Ah, the cap coming off must mean that you're off duty,' said Sally giving a knowing wink to Callum. Her eyes followed Callum as he lifted himself from his chair and walked to the refrigerator in the corner.

Callum pulled a beer from the shelf and twisted the cap off. 'Anyone else?' Sally and Emma shook their heads. Riley took the beer from Callum and nodded his thanks.

'Is this a social visit, Riley?' Callum asked as he dropped back into his chair.

'Yes and no, I guess. I've got a beer and I'm visiting my sister and her partner, so yes, it's social. But I did also want to pass some news on to Emma.'

'You want us to leave?' asked Sally, although she gave no indication of going.

'No, no. In fact, you should probably hear this as well.' Riley looked at Emma, who was staring at him in anticipation. 'This morning, our officers raided two homes, one in Adelaide and one in Yankalilla. Those homes belonged to the men you described, who we believe are responsible for the death of your parents and also Vinnie Waters, here in Goolwa.'

Emma sat quietly, her eyes not leaving Riley as he continued.

'We weren't successful in apprehending them, but we did gather evidence that we think is useful. We don't know where they are. We think they're together and we're continuing to look for them.' He paused for a moment and glimpsed briefly at Sally and Callum. 'I think it's possible, but it's only possible, that they've come to Goolwa or will come to Goolwa to follow up on some missing business.'

'What sort of business?' Callum asked.

'Drugs, money or both.'

'Or me?' Emma's eyes showed her despair.

'I don't think so, Emma. They know you're missing. It's been all over the media. But they don't know that you saw them and could identify them. '

'Maybe now that you have raided their homes, they know someone has identified them and they've put two and two together.' Emma grabbed Sally's hand.

Riley spoke calmly. 'They don't know you've come to Goolwa and they certainly have no way of knowing you're here. The important thing is that you stay here and keep out of sight. If you do that, I'm sure you'll be safe. If it helps, I'll make sure that we have patrols coming past at regular intervals. Ok?'

Emma nodded unconvincingly.

Callum walked Riley back to his car. 'You're confident she's not in danger, aren't you?'

Riley opened the car door. 'I am, as long as she stays here undercover. As I said, they have no way of knowing she's here and it's even unlikely they know what she's told us. If anything, by coming to Goolwa, they're exposing themselves. Don't worry, Callum, I wouldn't do anything to put Emma in danger, let alone Sally and you. Just keep her under wraps, ok?'

Riley drove off with an uneasy feeling. He believed everything he had told them, but yet he couldn't relax until he knew the bikies were in custody.

23

2006

Debbie McLean married Vinnie Waters in March. It almost didn't happen. Vinnie held his buck's party at a hotel in Adelaide. It was a raucous affair mainly with people he associated with, rather than friends. Vinnie had few friends but many acquaintances, split into two groups. The first were those who were as carefree and reckless as he was in life; enterprising, if unorthodox, traders and businessmen. The second group were the successful men that he aspired to be like. They were generally more conservative and mindful of their reputations; alert to the need to be respected in all aspects of their lives, not just their business practices. These men were either not invited by Vinnie, who was smart enough to understand their values, or else they politely declined. Shaun fell into this second group but he felt obligated to attend due to his long-time friendship with Vinnie. Carla had unsuccessfully tried to convince Shaun that the relationship he had with Vinnie now was irrelevant compared to the one they'd had fifteen years before. Riley had been more fortunate. He'd been rostered on for the night and had been relieved that the party would be in the city well away from his official duties in Goolwa.

The night was what Vinnie wanted and what Shaun had expected. A few beers over a meal, followed by many more at a nearby bar. The lads became rowdier as the night progressed with a near incident involving another group of drunken revellers. The matter was resolved when some-one in Vinnie's group suggested they'd rather head to a strip joint and watch bare-breasted women gyrate than fight a bunch of ugly punks. The suggestion was met with resounding agreement and the group, or at least most, headed toward Hindley Street. Shaun looked at his watch. It was nearly midnight and he'd had enough. He made his excuses to Vinnie, somewhat to the ridicule of some of the others, but left and headed back to the hotel they'd all booked into for the night.

He'd barely walked a hundred metres when his mobile rang.

'Shaun, it's me.' Carla sounded anxious.

'Hi babe, what's up?'

'Are you still with Vinnie? It's important.'

'I've just left them. Why?'

'It's Debbie. She's in hospital in Victor Harbor. She's lost the baby. We've been trying to get Vinnie but he's not answering his phone.'

'No, he said he didn't want to be disturbed and left his phone at the hotel. I'll track him down.' He disconnected the call and turned to follow Vinnie to the strip club.

He paid the ridiculous cover charge and was immediately set upon by a woman in a skimpy dress and an excessive amount of makeup. He convinced her he didn't want a drink and scanned the club for Vinnie and the group. He found them on the side of the room, gaping at a dancer on stage.

'Vinnie,' he yelled above the music. 'I need to talk to you. Can we go to the toilets?'

'I thought you'd gone home, Shauny boy,' one of the more drunken men shouted. 'Couldn't stay away from the fun, hey?'

Another piped in, 'Sounds more like he's trying to hit on our bachelor.'

There was mocking laughter all around, including from Vinnie.

'Mate, it's important. Come on, please,' Shaun persisted.

Vinnie grabbed one of the others, Nick Sullivan, a big lad with beer dripping from his beard. 'You'd better come with me, Sully. Protect me from Shaun if he comes on too strong.' Laughter erupted from the group again as Vinnie and Sully stumbled after Shaun toward the toilet.

In the relative quiet, Shaun explained the phone call he'd got from Carla.

'Oh, fuck. Talk about spoiling my big night,' he spat out. 'What does she want me to do? I can't get back tonight.'

'At least ring her, mate. She's been trying to get you and she could do with some comforting. I'll take you back first thing in the morning. I haven't had too much to drink.'

'I haven't got my phone.'

'Use mine. But you'd better look after yourself, Vinnie. You want to be in reasonable shape when you get back.'

Sully had been quiet to that point but put himself between Vinnie and Shaun. 'Fuck that. This is your buck's night, mate. You deserve to have a big night; you're going to be tied down enough once you get the ring on your finger.'

'Sully, stay out of it,' Shaun said. 'This is more important.'

Vinnie looked blankly at them both. Sully held Vinnie's cheeks and brought his face close. 'You can't do anything tonight, Vinnie. She's in the fuckin' hospital. The fuckin' nurses are looking after her. What the fuck can you do?' He spread his arms to show he'd rested his case.

'Vinnie,' Shaun started. Before he uttered another word, Sully swung his fist into Shaun's face, sending him crashing to the floor.

'I'll see you in the morning, Shaun,' Vinnie said as he followed Sully back to the club. As Shaun recovered, one of the bouncers noticed the blood streaming from Shaun's face. Assuming he'd been in some sort of altercation, he escorted Shaun from the premises and warned him not to come back.

Shaun decided not to tell Carla or Debbie about what had happened. Instead, he told them that he'd been unable to find Vinnie, thinking it would be kinder for Debbie not to know the truth. He did drive a hung-over Vinnie to the hospital the next morning. Hardly a word was spoken during the trip of just over an hour, but when Shaun dropped Vinnie at the hospital entrance, he could hold back no longer.

'What happened last night was bullshit, Vinnie. Sully is an arsehole and so are you. Debbie deserves to be treated better than that so you'd better pull your head in.'

The wedding was a more sombre affair. Debbie looked pale and sad. She'd been angry with Vinnie for leaving his phone behind at the buck's night. She told him she'd never felt so miserable and alone. Vinnie hadn't told her the full truth about what had happened and he'd taken her rebuke on the chin, promising to be a more considerate husband.

And he was. He showered her with attention and love. And gifts ... flowers, jewellery, clothes, anything she wanted. Despite Vinnie's protestations that she should take longer to rest, she returned to the veterinary practice and immersed herself in her work. Once he was satisfied that he'd redeemed himself, Vinnie also threw himself back into his work.

Later in 2006, Vinnie was presented with a business opportunity he couldn't resist. He was looking over the previous month's results for the used car yard and workshop. The legitimate part of his business was not performing as well as it should have but he wasn't worried. The less legal activities ensured that his wealth was growing.

He looked out the window of his office and saw two men approaching the showroom door. He thought he recognised one but couldn't be sure. Entering the showroom, he noticed the men peering through the window of a Ford Mustang.

'Very nice car there, gentlemen. 2004 GT model, low kilometres. Is that the sort of car you'd be interested in?'

The two men stood and turned. Vinnie took in a sharp breath. The smaller man he recognised as Damien Hargreaves, his half-brother. The other man was tall and big, with a shaven head and a boxer's ears.

'Hello, Vincent. A car's not what we're here for, as it happens.' Hargreaves wore a sly grin, a sneer that drew his lips sideways and up. 'I've been wanting to meet you for a long time, Brother. Did you know that Vincent here is my brother, Tony? Do we look much alike?'

The big man towered over Hargreaves by a full head and half his chest.

'Looks nothin' like you.' Tony was obviously a man of few words.

Vinnie suspected he spoke with his hands more than his voice. He decided he should play dumb until he knew what they wanted.

'Sorry, I'm at a disadvantage. I don't know your name but I'm guessing you're one of Wayne Hargreaves' boys.'

'Perceptive, Vince. I'm Damien and, yes, like you, Wayne's my dad. Just like my sister, Louise. You remember Louise, don't you, Vince?'

Vinnie was perplexed by his tone which was familiar and threatening at the same time.

'Look, about Louise ...'

Hargreaves laughed.

'Now don't get your knickers in a knot. I don't give a stuff about you and Louise. She said you were a pretty ordinary root and she's moved on. No, Vince, we have a business proposition for you.

'See, we've noticed that you have a nice little setup here. Very nice for a town like Goolwa. Nice enough for you to be living the good life, buying more businesses, driving flash cars. So, we started wondering how that could be but then we heard some rumours. It all fell into place when we talked to an associate of yours. Good old Barry Coleman. Very helpful, he was.'

Vinnie shifted uneasily on his feet. He didn't like where this was heading. The big man, Tony, started walking around the showroom, ostensibly looking at cars but Vinnie felt unsettled by his roaming and constantly looked around to see his whereabouts.

'Oh, don't worry about Tony,' Hargreaves said. 'He's always restless.'

Vinnie didn't feel any more reassured. Hargreaves continued.

'Now, Vince, after our chat with Shifty, we can see that you are a sharp businessman with an eye for an easy dollar. So, we, that is my associates and me, think we would like to do business with you; come to an arrangement. Oh, you think we mean extortion, don't you? Relax, Vincent. No, we have something mutually beneficial in mind. See, we have certain products that we need a distribution network for and you are the man we want for our business on the Fleurieu Peninsula.'

Hargreaves explained that his "associates" were, in fact, the newly created Anarchists motorcycle gang and his products were illicit drugs. They were produced and warehoused near Loxton. They wanted Vinnie to collect parcels from their contact in Loxton and then distribute them to the street dealers between Strathalbyn and Victor Harbor, with potential for more growth. They also wanted Vinnie to use his cafes to launder the proceeds of sales.

To do this, Vinnie would sell his cafe business into a trust which would be run by him. The beneficiaries would include Vinnie and the Anarchists through a complex web of companies and trusts that he didn't need to worry about. To achieve the volumes they required, more cafes would be needed and Vinnie was tasked with this as a priority.

'Now, you're probably wondering how you're going to find time for this, Vincent, what with this little operation here. Here's the thing. You have to sell it. We can't be exposed to the risk that at some stage the law is going to wise up to what you're doing here. So, it's got to go.'

Before Vinnie could protest, Hargreaves raised his hand.

'We've already lined up a buyer. Shifty takes over next week and he's going to pay you well for it. With our help, of course. Anyway, how do you feel about boats?'

Hargreaves explained that the Anarchists, through a separate corporate structure, had already acquired a disused boatshed on the river. This would become the centre of Vinnie's operation, the front being the refurbishment and repair of watercraft. Vinnie would also need to purchase a boat, one suitable for travelling to Loxton to pick up stock. The Anarchists were convinced that movement along the river would draw less attention and provide more security than by road.

'Just one more thing, Vince. You have to understand that this is non-negotiable, yeah?' Vinnie felt Tony's breath behind him. It was clear he had no choice but to join the Anarchists' business venture. Not that he minded. He'd become bored with the car business and had been wanting a new challenge. Here it was, brought to him on a silver platter.

It took Vinnie some time to convince Debbie that his new venture would set them up for life, without, of course, explaining the true nature of the business. She didn't understand the need to sell the car yard and workshop but, in the end, relied on Vinnie's proven business nous.

24

Wednesday 24 April 2019 (Day 7)

Riley woke at 5.00 am, Kate breathing gently next to him. She had been later than he had expected the previous night and he had gone to bed before she got home. She had gone out for a few drinks with her teacher colleagues after the parent interviews were finished.

She wasn't drunk but she was talkative as she readied for bed. She had needed to unload her frustration on Riley after an evening of being harangued, by parents and teachers alike, for news of the investigation into Aiden's disappearance. News broadcasts over the past couple of days had finally connected the Loxton and Goolwa murders. The disappearance of a young woman in Loxton and Aiden Chambers in Goolwa was now also linked. An unease had started to creep into the community. If one young child could go missing, what did that mean for their children?

Riley had feared a community reaction and slept restlessly, wondering what more he could be doing.

He slipped out of bed and dressed in warm running clothes. While the Autumn days were still warm, the lack of cloud cover overnight resulted in icy cold mornings. He set off along the river, troubled by the continued inability to find Aiden. He wasn't worried about Vinnie's murder as much. There was nothing that could be done for Vinnie, but there must be something that could be done for Aiden. But what?

The fog that hung over the river matched his mood. He smiled wryly at the thought that the fog would lift during the morning; there was no certainty that his mood would.

He returned home to the smell of scrambled eggs and cooked toast. Kate was in the kitchen, buttering the toast.

'Oh, perfect timing. I thought you'd be home about now. Sit down and have breakfast before your shower.'

He did as she instructed, watching as she dished up. Kate sat opposite him and cleared her throat.

'Listen, sorry about last night. I didn't mean to dump on you but I'd had them at me all night. I know you're doing all you can, Riley.'

'But is it enough, Kate? I wish we could just find Aiden. I don't care so much about Vinnie's murder and the drug dealing, but that little boy ... I mean, that other stuff is important and I've been relying on solving Vinnie's murder to find Aiden. What if I'm wrong; what if I've taken the wrong path? A little boy could be dead.'

'Do you have a choice, Riley? What could you do differently?'

'That's the point. I don't know and I still feel like I'm right. It just doesn't feel good and I'm not used to that.'

'Then you just keep doing what you think is right. I reckon the Detective Inspector would be pretty impressed.' She gave him an encouraging if weak, smile.

'I do enjoy working with him. He went back to Adelaide overnight but he'll be back for dinner and I think he's looking forward to that. But you do know ...'

'That things can change. Yes, I know, Riley. I get it and if things do change that will be fine, especially if it means finding Aiden, right?'

He kissed her and headed to the bathroom. Fifteen minutes later he was in his car, driving to Vinnie's house. He pulled up next to Phil, who was dressed in plain clothes and wrapped in a blanket.

'Bit cold there, Phil?'

'Bloody freezing, but nothing a hot shower won't fix. Nothing happened last night. No sign of anyone after about ten o'clock.'

'Ok, mate. You go home and have a good day. I'll be here for a couple of hours and then Craig Townsend's coming to relieve me. We'll work out where to go from there later in the day.'

Riley had dressed in plain clothes. There was no point being there if he was going to advertise his presence. He started to wonder if this was a futile exercise; it was not much more than a hunch that the bikies would show up to retrieve their missing money.

He unfolded the newspaper he had bought on his way. He looked cautiously at the front page, anticipating more media speculation about the murders and the disappearance of two young people. He was not surprised. The headline simply said "DRUG WAR?" but it was the subhead underneath that Riley was most troubled about: "Concerns for missing youths".

The growing connection between the murders, the missing youths and the drug trade was going to escalate community fears and increase the pressure on police. Smith would be feeling the heat from headquarters, nothing was more certain.

At least, Riley thought, they knew where Emma was and that she was safe. That couldn't be shared with the media yet and that meant the speculation would continue.

He checked his watch and scanned the street one more time before calling the station. Oliver Townsend answered. Good, he and Shaun were already back into the audit.

'Oliver, it's Riley. I wanted to follow up on your conversations with the staff at Vinnie's cafés.'

'Hi, Riley. Shaun and I are just kicking off again. I managed to get to two of the cafes yesterday and it turned out to be pretty interesting. I asked them how much they could remember putting in the cash bags after they balanced the till. They had a good handle in rough terms on the amounts for the last week or so and what they would generally expect each day of the week. Needless to say, the amounts actually being banked were much higher.'

'So that confirms the theory that you and Shaun had.'

'It does. I also checked what they're holding onto at the moment. Vinnie did the banking the day before he died so they had six days of takings that hadn't been banked. It backs up what they're telling us. The amounts Vinnie was banking were about four times the amount the staff had taken in cash. It doesn't distort the overall revenue as much because of the amount of credit card business they do, but it still affects the ratio of costs as Shaun was saying.'

Riley grimaced. 'What about the trust arrangements? Any news there?'

'That's going to take a bit longer to unwind. I'm sure we're onto something though.'

Riley's phone buzzed with another call coming through – Callum Johnston.

'Gotta go, Oliver. I've got another call.' He hung up and took the call from Callum.

'Riley, we've got a problem. Emma's gone missing.'

'What, missing? Tell me what's happened.'

'Sally and I went off to work as normal this morning. Emma seemed fine, just a bit quiet. I just dropped back home to pick something up and she's not here.'

'What about her belongings, are they gone as well?'

'She didn't have much but they're gone too. I wonder if she got spooked last night.'

Riley wiped his brow. 'Yes, maybe. Ok, let's work on the basis that she's left by her own choice. I'll get patrol cars out on the lookout for her. Any thoughts on where she might go?'

'No. I reckon she'd be trying to get away from Goolwa but I'm sure she'd avoid public transport. So, she'd have to steal a car or a bike or maybe hitchhike. I can't see her returning to my place so I'm going to hit the road to look for her as well.'

'OK, but take care. Keep in touch.'

Riley started his car and radioed the station as he turned onto the main road. By the time he reached the bridge to the mainland, he had deployed Rachel to the shopping centre and Craig to the Victor Harbor Road. He would take the road out of town heading to Adelaide, which he thought would be the most likely direction Emma would take. That choice was wrong.

***

Emma had hung about in her father's workshop since she was a child. The men who worked for her father knew cars and some had used their knowledge for extra-curricular activities. Trading in stolen cars could be a lucrative business and experts in the trade not only knew how to steal cars; they also knew which cars presented the least risk. A car that was easy to steal, very common and in demand in the market was the target. "Keep it simple and don't get fancy" had been their credo.

Ricky was one of these men but not much more than a boy. He had learned the trade well. He was also very keen on the boss's daughter and boasted to her how he could find a car and drive off in it in less than two minutes. Emma, at the time an impressionable teenager, flirted with Ricky and fed his ego. She asked him to show her how to steal a car. One

Saturday afternoon, he took her to the shopping centre and taught her. Not satisfied with being shown, Emma wanted to do it for real.

Ricky had scoffed at her but stood watch as she unlocked and hot-wired a Ford Fiesta. Adrenalin fired, they took the car into the back roads of Loxton and sacrificed Emma's virginity in the back seat. Afterwards, they walked to the main road and hitchhiked back to Loxton. Ricky was caught undertaking a careless theft a couple of weeks later and dropped out of Emma's life. She soon forgot Ricky, but not the new skill he had taught her.

Leaving Sally and Callum's house, Emma walked to the Goolwa Shopping Centre. She was terrified at the prospect of falling into the hands of bikies who wanted to silence her testimony against them. She respected Sally and Callum and was grateful for the shelter they had given her. She even liked the cops and, strangely, even the older guy who talked to her like he was her father.

But she had to get away. She'd decided not to go too far; she had no-where to stay in Adelaide and certainly couldn't risk going back to Loxton. Her plan was simple. Anyone looking for her would assume that she would get as far away as possible but she reasoned she just needed to go to a place where she could hide on her own, a place no one knew about.

Her grandparents had owned a beach house in Middleton and had left it to Emma's mother after her grandmother had passed away a few months earlier. The estate was still being wound up and Emma knew it would be empty. Hopefully, there would still be at least some canned food there. She wished she'd thought of this place before resorting to looking up Callum Johnston.

***

Rachel arrived at the shopping centre to find a small group discussing and gesticulating in various directions. Before she had parked the patrol car, she had a man standing at her door. The first thing Rachel noted about him was his balding head with wispy grey hair floating in the breeze. He stepped back as she opened her door.

'My car's gone,' he said in an authoritative, no-nonsense tone.

'Ok, sir. Let's get off the roadway shall we and I'll get some details from you.'

The small group of onlookers followed them to the entry of the centre. As people exited through the self-opening doors, they either cast an interested eye at proceedings or joined the growing throng.

Rachel kept her focus on the elderly gentleman who now had his wife at his side. She was a bigger woman and held her hands on her hips, watching closely to ensure that her husband provided the correct details.

The pair provided their names, address, the details of their car and its last known location. They had been in the supermarket for only twenty minutes. Rachel turned to the on-lookers, now a group that effectively blocked the doors to the shopping centre.

'Ok, everyone, unless you witnessed something relevant to the disappearance of Mr. Kelly's vehicle, can you please move on? There's nothing more to see here.'

A small man hung back as the crowd dispersed and eventually made his way to Rachel.

'Excuse me, officer. I may have seen something,' the man offered.

'Oh, hello, Jeffrey,' Rachel knew the man well. He had been the mechanic who had serviced her car when she had first moved to Goolwa. 'No need for formality, here. Call me Rachel. Now, what did you see, Jeffrey?'

'Well, Rachel, when I first got here, I parked my car just over there. A girl was standing near the Fiesta that apparently belongs to these people. I didn't know it wasn't her car, of course. I waited for a minute because I thought she might have locked her keys in the car or something and I may have been able to help her.'

Rachel remembered that Jeffery had always been happy to provide extra attention to a young lady, although she had no reason to believe that he had overstepped the boundaries of propriety.

'Next thing,' Jeffery continued, 'she'd opened the car door and hopped inside. Anyway, I had no reason to offer my assistance. The last thing I saw of her, she was driving out of the car park.'

'That's really helpful, Jeffery. Did you see which way she turned when she drove out of the car park?'

He shook his head. Rachel quickly got a description of the girl and, satisfied it closely matched Emma, strode to her patrol car.

'Hey, what about my car?' the owner yelled after her.

'Onto it, Mr. Kelly. We'll be in touch.'

As she unlocked her car, Rachel turned back to see the man being sharply rebuked by his wife. She reported in on the radio advising the details of the theft, including a description of the car and reporting the match of the thief's description to Emma Satchin.

'Ok,' Riley responded, 'it looks like we know the car we're looking for. Craig, hold your position on the Victor Harbor Road, I'll stay on the Adelaide Road. We just have to hope she hasn't already slipped through. Rachel, can you touch base with patrols in Victor Harbor and Strathalbyn? If she's gone through Mount Compass or Ashbourne or out on one of the other roads, we'll need to get more patrols involved. I'll be in touch if we don't see her in the next few minutes.'

Ten minutes had elapsed and Riley was on the cusp of widening the search when Craig radioed in.

'I've got her, Riley. She's just turned off the main road at Middleton, heading toward the beach. You want me to stop her?'

Riley breathed a sigh of relief. 'No, mate. Just follow her at a distance. She doesn't know you and may freak out, even though you're a cop. I'll join you as soon as I can. Just keep me appraised of your position.'

He sat in his car for a moment, contemplating his next move, before calling Callum on his mobile.

'Callum, we've located Emma. She's stolen a car and driven to Middleton. At the moment we're just trailing her but I think it'd be helpful if you could be there to talk to her when we approach her.'

'On my way,' Callum replied.

Craig was parked outside a house that overlooked the beach. An offshore breeze modelled clean, well-formed wave breaks and a dozen surfers were taking advantage of the ideal conditions. A pang of envy settled on Craig and he returned his attention to the house three doors along where the green Fiesta was now parked. *Silly girl should have parked the car in the shed if she wanted to stay undetected.*

Riley pulled up behind him and joined Craig in the patrol car. Moments later, Callum arrived and the three walked to the front of the house. Riley motioned for Craig to keep an eye on the front while he and Callum walked around the side to the back door.

Riley quietly tested the knob; it was unlocked. As he entered the house he called out.

'Emma, it's Senior Sergeant O'Brien. I've got Callum here with me.'

'Emma, it's ok. We're here to help,' Callum called out.

'I'm in the bedroom.'

They walked through to find Emma seated on the bed. She looked beaten. 'I'm sorry. I know I panicked but I'm scared and I thought I would be safer here.'

'How on earth did you get in?' Riley asked.

'This was my grandparent's house. They always kept a key hidden out the back.'

Riley spoke gently. 'But you stole a car that can be traced, and sooner or later you'll need to go out for food. Come back to Callum and Sally's. You'll be safest there and at least we will know where you are.'

'I'm sorry. About the car too. I guess I'm in big trouble for that now?'

'Well, let's not worry about that. We'll get it back to its rightful owners. I'm sure they'll be very grateful to get it back and won't want to take it further.'

Callum walked over and took her hand. 'Come on.'

After making arrangements to transport the Fiesta back to Goolwa, Riley drove back to Vinnie's house. He was frustrated. He had been wasting his time watching Vinnie's house on a presumption that it would give them their next big break. Meanwhile, Emma was traumatised by the threat of the bikies to the point where she had lost faith in the safety of police protection. He wondered if she was right. What would it mean if the bikies were able to trace her? What would it mean for her? For Sally and Callum?

The street on Hindmarsh Island was quiet. It usually was. Those who lived on the island were mostly at work while the holiday homes were empty much of the year. The summer crowds had retreated to the city after the Easter break and wouldn't return in numbers until spring.

He pulled up outside Vinnie's house and immediately felt apprehensive. The front door was open. Riley scanned the street; there were no other parked vehicles. Nonetheless, he knew he should exercise caution and radioed for backup. Rachel arrived in a patrol car ten minutes later.

They approached the house with their weapons drawn. On entering the house, it was apparent that someone had broken in while Riley was searching for Emma. The living room at the front of the house had been ransacked. Furniture was overturned and the contents of drawers were strewn over the floor.

They moved cautiously, listening for any sound of movement from the other rooms. As they entered each room, the condition was the same. Satisfied that they were alone, they secured their weapons and took a closer look at the mayhem.

Riley headed upstairs to the cupboard where he and Phil two days before had found the stash of money hidden. The burglars had failed to locate the secret cavity which meant they didn't know where to look for whatever they were seeking; money or drugs.

'Ok, let's get forensics to have a look at this. Somehow, I think we know what we're going to find if anything. Damien Hargreaves and Tony Fantis have been here and didn't find what they were looking for. So, where they go next is the big question.'

Rachel nodded. 'Of course, now we know they're in the area. Maybe it's time we had some luck.'

'Let's hope so,' Riley said as they locked the door on their way out.

25

Wednesday 24 April 2019 (Day 7)

When he arrived at the station, Riley found two police officers and a dog waiting for him. They were the officers from the drug squad, arranged by Paul Smith to check Vinnie's boat shed. Cassie was chatting with them and offered to take them to the boatshed on Riley's behalf. He was grateful for her intervention; he was keen to touch base with Smith on the day's developments.

The Detective Inspector was in his car when Riley rang.

'Good afternoon, O'Brien. A busy day, I hear.'

'How did you know, sir?' Riley was, not for the first time, amazed at the DI's ability to stay at the front of the information bank.

'I spoke to Cassie when the drug lads showed up. They're underway by now, I guess. What happened at Vinnie Waters' house?'

'I feel a bit stupid, sir. I got called away to assist with the search for Emma Satchin and while I was gone Fantis and Hargreaves must have broken in.'

'You made the right choice, O'Brien. The girl could have been in danger and finding her should have been the priority. So, what did you find out about their break-in?'

'Not much. They obviously didn't find the cash because it wasn't there. We've suspended surveillance on the house; not much point now. We've got forensics organised to collect any evidence and we're also doing a door knock to see if any neighbours saw anything but I don't hold much hope. Are you on your way back now?'

'I am. I have a dinner to go to tonight. It's still on, right?'

'Yes, sir, but I wonder, should we put it off now that we know Hargreaves and Fantis are in town?'

'Definitely not. We all need a bit of time off and if we have an alert out for those two, there's not much more we can do. I'll be there in an hour. Listen, will you tell Cassie not to wait for me. I'll get myself settled at the motel and walk around to your house.'

'No worries. Anything else?'

'No, I mean, yes. One more thing. I've asked Mick Martin to join us down in Goolwa tomorrow. He can't do much more in Loxton, but I reckon he can focus on working with the drugs team from the Goolwa perspective.'

'Ok, sir. I'll see you at my house tonight.'

Riley glanced at his watch. He wanted to check on a couple of aspects of the investigation before he headed home.

His first stop was to check on the audit Shaun and Oliver were undertaking. Shaun was poring over several sheets of paper spread across the desk, while Oliver stood at a whiteboard, marker in hand. The whiteboard was filled with squares interlinked by arrows. A square on the left side of the board contained Vinnie's name while one on the right was labelled only with a question mark. From Vinnie's square, arrows fanned out to various business names which then pointed to other entities, company structures and trust names.

'How is it coming along?' Riley asked.

'We're getting there.' Oliver pointed at a link to a square that contained "Gavin Trower", the name of the accountant associated with the Anarchists bikie gang. 'See this? We now have a link that shows Gavin Trower was not only Vinnie's accountant. He was also a director and company secretary for one of the companies that was a trustee for Vinnie's café businesses.'

'That's good, right?'

'Well,' said Shaun, 'it gives us a link but we need to keep pushing it this way.' He pointed to the right side of the board. 'Until we do that, we don't have a definite link of Vinnie to the bikies; in terms of a money flow, that is.'

Riley stared at the board. He was thankful he'd called Shaun in on the audit. He was utterly bamboozled by the complexity of the diagram in front of him and he suspected Oliver was holding on only with Shaun's tutelage. His concentration was broken by Shaun's voice.

'What? Sorry, Shaun, I was trying to make sense of this. What did you say?'

Shaun was terse. 'I asked if you had any developments on Aiden. Remember, my son who's been missing for a week?'

'Yes, sorry Shaun. Well, I can tell you that I think we are getting closer.' He saw Shaun's eyebrows lift as if to say "here we go again." Riley knew it was only a matter of time before he lost Shaun's confidence and, maybe his trust. He didn't want that to happen but he knew he also had to be honest with his old friend.

'Look, you know we just missed the two suspects when we undertook the raids. Well, we just missed them again today.' Riley relayed to Shaun the surveillance of Vinnie's house and the break-in while he was redeployed searching for Emma.

He was surprised that Shaun was sympathetic.

'I guess I can't blame the girl for being spooked. These are dangerous guys and she's already lost her parents. And, Riley, I understand why you had to join the search for her. I'd want you to do the same if you had a lead on Aiden.'

'Thanks, mate. Look, at some point, these blokes are going to make a mistake and we'll get them. And I can only keep reassuring you that the end game in all this is to make sure we find Aiden, alive and safe.'

Riley left them to their contemplation and headed to Vinnie's boat-shed. He was keen to see whether the dog had discovered anything in the shed. The afternoon was starting to drift into a cooler evening. He imagined that with the clear skies, the night would be a chilly one.

He pulled onto the track leading to the shed and saw the dog handler encouraging the German Shepherd into the back of a station wagon. He was relieved that he'd arrived just in time. At the same time, he suspected that, if they'd finished already, there had been nothing to find.

Cassie was in deep conversation with the other officer at the door to the shed. They were adhering new crime scene tape across the door as he approached them.

'You'll want to hear this, Riley,' Cassie said.

'Oh, really? What's up?'

The officer turned to Riley.

'The shed was clean. Nothing at all.'

Riley shrugged. 'Not sure that is what I wanted to hear.' He looked at the officer apprehensively.

'The shed was clean,' the officer continued, 'but the boat was another matter. It had several secret compartments, most of which yielded nothing. But, above the keel, which you know had been removed, there's a good-sized compartment that has obviously been used to store drugs. Poor old Thunder,' he motioned to the dog in the car, 'nearly went off his tree.'

'So, what do you make of that?' Riley asked.

'I'd say that Vinnie Waters used the boat to transport drugs from Loxton to Goolwa. It would make sense. There's a lot less traffic on the river, reducing the risk of interception. And, even if he was stopped and searched, the only way the drugs would be exposed would be by removing the keel, which you can't do while the boat is in the water.'

'So, what next?'

'We'll turn this over to the drug team. They will investigate further, work out what the drugs were and compare the samples with those found in Loxton. As far as your murder investigation is concerned, I understand Mick Martin will be coordinating between us but I think you can conclude that Vinnie Waters was up to his balls in the drug trade. Maybe, just like the Satchins in Loxton, he did enough to upset the Anarchists to make them want him out of their operation.'

The two officers and their dog left, leaving Riley and Cassie to finish securing the yard. He passed the message from Paul Smith on to her. She laughed.

'Ha-ha. I wasn't going to wait for him. Rachel and I are having a couple of bevvies at her house while we get ready. We'll see you and DI Smith at your place.'

Riley laughed, grateful that Cassie no longer seemed to regard him as a competitor and that she had made such a strong connection with Rachel.

As they parted, she called after him, 'You know, I really see why you don't want to leave this place. I'd move down here given a chance.'

***

Riley called into the drive-through bottle shop at the hotel on his way home. He grabbed a carton of beer and one of cider and spent longer than he needed selecting a couple of bottles of red and white wine.

Happy with his selections, he drove home and unloaded his purchases. Kate was busy setting the table, a spicy aroma drifting from the kitchen.

'The curry is coming along nicely and I just need to cook the rice once they arrive. I didn't know whether to do pappadums or roti, so we have both.' She was excited. It was rare for her to entertain Riley's work colleagues and she wanted to impress them for his sake.

They had the chance to sit and de-brief on their respective days before a knock on the door signalled the arrival of Cassie and Rachel. Riley opened the door and was gob-smacked. He didn't know what to expect from Cassie but he was surprised at how striking Rachel looked out of uniform. Both girls had shed their police officer facades and replaced them with softer, more feminine appearances.

'Don't stand there gawking, Riley. Let them in before they die of thirst,' Kate yelled from inside. The girls laughed and stepped past him. Rachel didn't wait for Riley to introduce Cassie to Kate and before he had composed himself the three were chatting freely at the kitchen bench.

'Hey, Senior Sergeant,' Rachel called to him, 'how about that drink? We're dying here.'

There were peals of laughter and Riley excused himself, keenly awaiting support from Paul Smith.

***

Paul Smith left the Goolwa Motel and set out on the walk to Liverpool Road. He felt good, despite the pressure he was feeling to wrap up this case. He knew that he had a good team and that they were making progress. *If we can just get these two pricks in custody and find the young lad, all the pressure will fall away.*

He should walk more, he knew that. His fitness was nowhere near what it had been when he joined the force. Too many meat pies, burgers and other fast foods. His doctor had warned him to improve his diet and get some exercise if he wanted to enjoy his retirement. Now instead of fast food, he knew every Thai and Vietnamese restaurant in Adelaide. While he tried to take the healthy options, his favourite lunch was Banh Mi with roasted pork filling. He convinced himself that the carbohydrates in the Banh Mi roll weren't too unhealthy and certainly better than his fast-food meals of the past.

He was licking his lips with the thought of a homemade dinner as he walked along the footpath opposite the Goolwa Hotel. He glanced over, contemplating dropping in for a beer before he got to Riley's house. Old habits die hard for an old cop.

He noticed two men walking through the front door of the pub; one small in frame, the other much heavier set. He had seen the photos and immediately recognised them – Tony Fantis and Damian Hargreaves. He would have that beer after all.

***

Tony Fantis lifted the two pints from the bar and walked to where Damien Hargreaves sat. On the screens behind them, races were broadcast from venues across the country. Only a couple of punters stood watching.

'So, where the fuck is the money, Tony? The bastard must have it stashed somewhere.'

'Beats me, mate. Hopefully, Graham can help us.'

Graham was their local dealer. Vinnie delivered product to Graham and he had his own network that he kept well away from Vinnie. That's what Vinnie wanted; to keep away from the front line of the business.

Damien gave a cursory glance at the man who walked through the front door. He watched as he ordered a beer, then sat at a table on his own on the other side of the room.

He was distracted when a third man sat at their table.

'Graham, how are you, mate?'

'How am I? I'm fucked, that's how I am. My supply chain is gone and I got customers wanting product. What the fuck happened to Vinnie?'

'Don't worry about Vinnie, Graham. Shit happens. Right now, we want to restore the supply chain so you can keep your customers happy, ok?'

Graham nodded but then shook his head. 'How are you going to do that now with fuckin' Satchin gone as well? What are you bastards doing?'

Damien looked him in the eye.

'Settle down, Graham. You're going to have to pick up some of the slack. We're putting new arrangements in place in the Riverland. Not Loxton, that's finished. In a week or two, we'll be ready but we need you to take over the transport of the product. There won't be a middleman anymore.'

'Ok, ok.' Graham was getting interested. He'd taken time to get into the business and he now saw an opportunity opening up for him.

'There's one thing we need from you first, Graham.'

'What's that?' Graham asked cautiously.

Hargreaves leant forward and lowered his voice.

'Vinnie had a lot of our money, Graham. Several hundred thousand dollars. We don't think he would've been so stupid as to leave it in the boatshed and we know it's not in his house.' He glanced up at Graham's confused expression. 'We've checked,' he added.

'What we need to know from you is where Vinnie kept the money. Don't be thinking you can go collect it because we'll be watching, Graham. But, if you can tell us where it is, you'll be rewarded appropriately, do you follow?'

'Yeah, yeah, I follow, mate, but I don't know, honest. I mean, he never told me and I never asked, you know.'

'Think about it, Graham. Did he talk about anywhere other than his house or the boatshed? And don't say the cafes. There's no way he'd be keeping a stash in them.'

'I dunno, mate, honest. I'd tell you if I knew, I would. Wait up. Yeah, hey listen, he used to talk about this boat he had. Said he bought it a few years ago but he never got the chance to get out in it. But, mate, honestly, I don't know nothin' else about it and that's a fact.'

Hargreaves lifted his eyes. He had been watching the other patrons. It was a lesson he had learnt early in life and his vigilance had helped him avoid being apprehended on many occasions. Right now, he was worried about the big bloke sitting on his own. Could be a cop. He watched the man pull his phone from his jacket and hold it upright on the table. I reckon that fucker's taking photos of us.

He turned back to Graham and smiled.

'That's alright, mate. You just keep thinking about it and tell us if you remember anything. I need you to do something else, first.' He slipped a set of car keys across the table.

'Take these. There's a white Ford station wagon parked in the first park out the back. I need you to go to the boot and take out the crow-bar. Go past the car park and wait behind the fence. We'll be following you in a couple of minutes and I reckon there'll be a bloke coming after us. When we pass you, you pass the crowbar to Tony. Tony, if this bloke follows, give him a good smack in the guts, will you? But don't kill the bastard. I want to talk to him.'

***

Paul Smith watched as the third man rose and left the table. Hargreaves had passed something to him just before his sudden exit but he hadn't been able to see what it was.

He checked the images on his screen. He had been able to get a clear shot of Hargreaves and Fantis, but it was the third man he wanted to identify. He zoomed in. It wasn't perfect but it would have to do. He sent the two best images to Riley O'Brien and then hit the call button. As he looked up, he noticed Hargreaves and Fantis leaving their seats, without finishing their pints. Shit!

Smith hung up the call before it connected and watched the two men leave by the rear door. He hastily dashed to the door to see them walking through the car park. He re-dialled the call to Riley, watching Hargreaves and Fantis. He needed to see the direction they drove off to have any chance of apprehending them. His call went to Riley's message bank.

'O'Brien, I don't know what you're doing right now but drop whatever it is and get to the Goolwa Hotel. Hargreaves and Fantis are just leaving. I'll pursue them on foot as long as I can but if they have a car, I'll have no chance.'

He sucked in a deep breath as he stepped up his pace in the car park. They didn't get into a car, instead walking behind a fence into the park behind. He lost sight of them as they rounded the corner, fifty metres ahead. He burst into a run, safely out of their view for a short time. Bloody hell, I'm out of condition.

He rounded the fence at what, for him, was top speed. It was fast enough that he didn't see the steel bar coming at his midriff. He certainly felt it, though, and collapsed to the ground gasping for breath in a foetal position.

As he rolled onto his back, he heard a voice.

'Alright, Graham, you can piss off now. Car keys, mate. And stay low 'til we're back in touch.'

Smith saw two men standing over him. Fantis was holding the crowbar menacingly in front of his face. Damien Hargreaves stepped into a kneeling position alongside him. He nodded to Fantis who slammed the crowbar into Smith's stomach again.

Smith's body tightened as he tried to suck in air. He felt like he was about to pass out.

'So, what are you then? A copper? Let's have look at his wallet, shall we?'

Fantis dug into Smith's coat pocket and handed the contents to Hargreaves.

'Here we are. Look, Tony, we have the pleasure of Detective Inspector Paul Smith in our company. Why are you following us, Mr. Smith?'

Smith attempted to lift himself onto his hands and knees only to be pushed back onto the dirt. He laughed.

'How about drug trafficking and murder for a start? We have warrants out on you two and it's just a matter of time before you're in custody. Then there are the abduction charges; worse if anything happens to that little boy.'

Hargreaves shot a look at Fantis.

'I think the inspector's got us confused with someone else, Tony. Why don't you help him clear his head a bit?'

'Why don't you just shit in your hands and clap, Hargreaves?'

Fantis swung the bar into Smith's head and followed it up with a sharp kick to his groin. The policeman groaned, lifting his hands first to his head then to his crotch. Fantis again smashed the crowbar into Smith's head. His hands fell limp as he lay unconscious. Hargreaves lifted his leg and stomped on Smith's chest.

'I think that's enough. Let's get rid of this.' Hargreaves picked Smith's phone from the ground. 'We don't need those photos to be seen again.'

***

Riley was passing a drink to Kate when his phone rang. He fished it out of his pocket and saw Paul Smith's name come up. He pressed the answer button but the call had gone.

'What's up?' Rachel asked.

'I just got a call from the DI but he hung up.'

'Oh,' Cassie laughed. 'He's pocket dialled you. He's always doing that. He shouldn't be trusted with anything more technologically advanced than a bottle opener, that man.'

Riley laughed with the others but dialled Smith's number anyway.

'Now, he's engaged.'

'Ok, that means he rang you instead of his wife, Riley. How does it feel to be number one on his call list?'

More laughter. Seconds later, Riley heard the ding of a message arriving. He looked at his phone to see a notification that he had a voice-mail message. Unable to hear above the cacophony of female hilarity, he stepped into another room.

Moments later, he rushed back to them.

'Ok, Rachel and Cassie. Put your drinks down; we've got to go.' He looked at Kate with apologetic eyes. 'I'm sorry, Kate. DI Smith has seen the guys we are after and he's chasing them on foot. We need to go and support him.'

'Go, go!' Kate pushed him toward the door. 'The curry will wait until you're back but just be careful; all of you.'

Riley, Rachel and Cassie jumped into his car and he reversed onto the road at speed.

'Call the station for backup,' he barked. Suddenly sober, Cassie grabbed her phone and dialled.

They arrived at the Goolwa Hotel car park less than two minutes later and jumped out. There was no sign of anything out of the ordinary.

'Help. Over here,' a voice screamed from the adjoining park. They ran around the fence just as Phil Reid pulled up in a patrol car. In front of them, they saw an elderly woman holding a dog leash with a small terrier straining at the end. She was crouched over a prone figure on the dirt path and moved aside as the three rushed toward her.

'He was like this when I found him a few moments ago,' she said distressed. 'He doesn't look too good, does he?'

Cassie pulled out her phone to call an ambulance. Riley moved Smith into the recovery position while Rachel felt at his wrist. She looked at Riley.

'He's got a pulse but it's very weak.'

Riley walked to the woman who had retired to a park bench and clasped her dog in her lap.

'Did you see the men who did this, ma'am?'

'No, I'm sorry, it was just him. I did see a car leave the hotel in a big hurry, though. It was a white station wagon, a Ford, I think.'

Riley called Phil Reid across.

'Put out an alert for a white station wagon, probably a Ford. I'll send you a photo of the three men that were most likely in the car.'

The woman interjected. 'There were only two men in the car. One was a big man and the other was smaller.'

Phil raced back to the patrol car, while Riley returned to Smith. He hadn't paid attention before but he now saw a huge dent in the side of his head and blood oozing from his ears.

'Doesn't look good, Riley,' Rachel stammered. 'He's not responding.' She flashed her phone torch across his eyes as she held his eyelids open.

Cassie guided the ambulance from the road while Phil secured the area from onlookers. After Smith was assessed and loaded into the ambulance, Riley approached the paramedics.

'What do you think? He's our Detective Inspector.'

'Too early to say how much trouble he's in, mate. It's difficult to say as we can't assess all of his injuries here. We'll know more once we get him to the emergency department. I think you can assume he won't be back on the job for a while.'

'Flinders or Royal Adelaide Hospital? So that we can let his wife know.'

'We've called for MedStar assistance; they may fly him to the RAH once they've stabilised him.'

Riley pulled Cassie aside.

'Cassie, I hate to do this to you, but do you know the DI's wife?'

'Yes, pretty well. She'll be devastated; she's always been worried something like this would happen. Do you want me to call her?'

'Would you? I don't like putting this on you, but she'd probably prefer to hear from someone she knows.'

Riley left Cassie to make the call and beckoned Rachel. They walked into the hotel and made their way to the front bar.

Jeff, the barman, approached Riley.

'What'll you have, Riley?'

'Sorry, Jeff, nothing this time. I just wanted to ask you a couple of questions.'

'You're on duty, then?'

'Not exactly, but there's been an incident at the back of the pub we're investigating. Did you notice these three in here earlier, say an hour ago?'

'Sure. They were sitting over there.' Jeff pointed to the table that Smith had been watching. 'The bloke in the middle, with his back to the camera, is Graham Cole. He's a local but I don't know the other two. Who took the photo?'

'That was Detective Inspector Smith. We have a warrant for the other two men, Damien Hargreaves and Tony Fantis. They are bikie gang associates and we think they are responsible for the assault out the back. What do you know about Graham Cole?'

Jeff shook, his head. 'Not much I'm afraid. Rumour is that he deals in drugs but I can promise you it's not going on in this hotel, mate. I can't see Graham being on the dishing out side of an assault. He strikes me as a bit of a weasel.'

'Do you know where we would find him, Jeff?'

'Sorry, Riley, no. He's in here most nights for one or two pints but he's a loner. Doesn't really talk to anyone much. So, who copped the beating? Was it the bloke that was sitting over there?' He pointed to the table where Smith had sat. 'Big, solid bloke ... had copper written all over him.'

'Yes, but I'd prefer for you to keep that to yourself for now.' Riley handed Jeff a business card. 'Don't go asking questions but if anyone happens to mention where we can find Graham Cole ring me on my mobile number on the card.'

Jeff nodded. 'One place you might see him, Riley, is at the ANZAC service tomorrow. Graham's a Vietnam veteran, or at least he says he is.'

26

2015

Debbie and Vinnie welcomed Jeremy into the world in 2009. The only disappointment with his birth was that due to complications from her previous miscarriage and Jeremy's delivery, the doctors told her she would never give birth again.

They had argued over his name; Vinnie wanted something more masculine and Australian. He tried to convince Debbie that Jeremy was a name that English aristocrats gave their thin-lipped, poncy sons who would never need to get their hands dirty. Debbie laughed it off and stuck to her guns, eventually wearing Vinnie's resistance away.

Jeremy was a healthy baby and grew into a normal young boy, active and lively. Vinnie's concerns that his name would predetermine his future soon dissipated but he still found it difficult to say the boy's name in the circles in which he moved without being on the receiving end of some wisecrack. He started to call him "Jerry", which both Debbie and Jeremy hated.

At the end of the day, Vinnie didn't really care. He was preoccupied with his growing business and spent very limited time with the boy. He'd only really agreed to have the kid because he was still infatuated with

Debbie and she really wanted a child. He was an inconvenience, but he did give Vinnie legitimacy as a successful family man as well as a business entrepreneur.

The *Cafetopia* franchise had expanded over the years with a dozen outlets spread across the Fleurieu Peninsula. It needed to in order to process the funds that were being generated by his other activities. Once each week, Vinnie would pick up the takings from each outlet and "rework" the banking to include the extra cash that needed to be washed. On one other day each week, he would motor a boat to Loxton, ostensibly to pick up spare parts for his boat repair workshop and to negotiate the purchase of new boats for resale. Typically, he returned with a handful of parts but several kilograms of other substances hidden in the various secret compartments on his boat. The rest of the week, Vinnie kept himself busy at the boatshed, never taking on more work than he could commit to. He did little of the drug distribution there, preferring to meet in open spaces that he would change often.

The arrangements were working out well. His associates in Adelaide kept a low profile as long as the money kept flowing into the trust bank accounts. Damien Hargreaves and Tony Fantis dropped into the shed at irregular intervals to see how Vinnie was going and to reassure him that they would continue to leave him in peace as long as he continued to grow his network and the cash flows.

The only time Vinnie was troubled was when Gavin Trower came for an annual "audit". He would spend a full day looking over the business activities, reconciling them to the proceeds that he saw banked. He interrogated staff, mostly ignorant of the full scope of the activities and asked Vinnie questions that analysed his retail activities with his dealers and his wholesale transactions with the Satchins. Hargreaves and Fantis were never far away, ready to lay a heavy hand if anything was out of order. The audit day would generally end with a thinly veiled warning from

Trower that left Vinnie in no doubt that he was a disposable commodity if the Anarchists saw no value in him.

The rest of the time Vinnie was the relaxed, casual character he'd always been. He was easy-going with his staff, flippant when they came to him with issues, most of which he'd handball straight to the supervisor of whichever outlet was involved. The staff could never get over how someone so laid back could be so successful in business but they spoke well of him and improved his reputation in each town.

His peers in business regarded him as an enigma. He was irritating, brash and offensive in his dealings with them but he could also turn on the charm when circumstances required it. He didn't seem to work that hard and yet his businesses all did well and his staff spoke up for him. And then there were the rumours.

Vinnie built Debbie her dream house on Hindmarsh Island, giving her a generous budget to choose the best furnishings and artwork. She'd stopped working as a veterinary nurse when Jeremy was born, partly at Vinnie's insistence but she'd also been happy to be a full-time homemaker.

Every couple of weeks, Debbie would catch up with Carla. They'd drink coffee or a glass of wine while Jeremy and Aiden, the elder by a few months, played in the park. Sometimes they would try to arrange a dinner date as a foursome with Shaun and Vinnie. For some reason, it never worked out. It seemed like the boys had fallen out but neither would say so; they just seemed to have drifted apart.

One of the reasons was Vinnie's continued association with Nick Sullivan. Shaun had never been a fan of Sully's and the buck's night had cemented his disdain for him. He'd been disappointed with Vinnie's actions that night but he was even more concerned at his lack of awareness of Sully's negative influence. To add to his feeling, Shaun became aware that Sully was one of the town's drug dealers; not that it was stated openly but there'd been enough hearsay for Shaun to believe it was true. He'd even contemplated passing it on to Riley but he knew he had no concrete evidence. What Shaun didn't know was that Sully was also a user and that he was dealing drugs supplied by Vinnie.

Business had been good for Sully as well as Vinnie and, notwithstanding his habit, he drove a late model V8 and high-powered speedboats.

One Sunday, he dropped by Vinnie and Debbie's house. Debbie had learnt to tolerate Sully, but only just.

'G'day, Deb darlin'.' Sully wrapped his arms around her from behind and kissed her on the neck. She shrugged off his grip and glared at him.

'Vinnie's out the back,' she said tersely.

Sully shrugged his shoulders. 'Wrong time of the month, eh love.' He walked out the back door before Debbie had the chance to retort.

Vinnie was watering potted plants under the verandah, watching Jeremy kicking a soccer ball against the house wall.

'Sully, how are you, mate?'

'Doin' the domestic duties, I see, Vinnie. Let me drag you away for a while. Picked up the new boat yesterday; thought we might go for a spin.'

'Can't, mate. I've got to watch the kid. Deb's going out for a bit with Carla.'

'Bring him with us. He'll enjoy a bit of excitement. I've got lifejackets.'

Debbie was less than happy about the plan and told Vinnie so.

'I don't think he's ready for that. If you must go,' she scowled at Vinnie, 'I'll take him with me, even though you did promise you'd watch him.'

'And I will. He'll be right, Deb. He's six years old now, not a baby anymore.'

'Alright then,' she relented, 'but make sure you watch him.'

The sun was bright as they arrived at the ramp. Once the boat was in the water, Vinnie sat Jeremy at the back of the boat.

'Where's the lifejacket, Sully? I'll put it on Jeremy before we head out.'

Sully fossicked in a storage space at the front of the boat and eventually threw a vest back to Vinnie.

'Mate, this is an adult vest. Haven't you got a kids' size?'

'Doesn't look like it. That'll do, though. You're starting to worry like your missus,' Sully mocked.

A stiff breeze whipped up small waves on the river but nothing the boat couldn't comfortably handle. Sully took the boat under the Hindmarsh Island Bridge and turned.

'Let's amp her up a bit.'

Vinnie went to the back of the boat and sat alongside Jeremy. The lifejacket enveloped the boy but at least provided some protection against the cool wind as Sully pushed the boat across the top of the waves. He pulled it up as they approached the jet ski area near the barrages.

'You want to have a go? Come on, she rides beautifully.'

Vinnie made his way to the front and took the wheel. He glanced back at Jeremy. The boy looked miserable.

'Cheer up, mate. We'll just do a bit more then we'll head back. OK?'

Jeremy nodded meekly. A jet skier surged past on their right, sending a spray of water into the air.

'See if you can catch him,' Sully said.

Vinnie pulled back on the throttle and the boat lurched forward, following in the wake of the jet ski.

They were within fifty metres of it when its rider veered left in the path of Sully's boat. There was no danger of hitting the jet ski but Vinnie took the boat at speed into the waves it created. The boat's bow lifted sharply and crashed down with a loud clap.

'Woo hoo!' Sully shouted as the boat flew onward. 'That was amazing.'

Vinnie raised his hand to high-five. He looked around at Jeremy. He'd gone.

'Fuck, fuck, fuck.'

He slowed the boat and turned it sharply back to the direction they'd come, then accelerated. They could have travelled only a few dozen metres since they hit the wave. The wake of the jet ski had dissipated so Vinnie had to estimate where Jeremy must have fallen from the boat.

'Over there,' Sully pointed. The orange lifejacket was bobbing a few metres from shore. Vinnie turned toward it but his heart sank as he saw that Jeremy was not in it. They searched frantically for the boy along the shoreline; he was nowhere to be seen.

An hour later, one of the five boats that had joined the search lifted Jeremy's body from the river. One of its crew worked on him until they got back to the boat ramp where an ambulance waited. Fifteen minutes later the paramedic called it.

The funeral service was held at the end of the following week. It was a short affair through which Debbie sobbed inconsolably. She seemed distant, not even allowing Vinnie to wrap his arms around her.

After, the mourners returned to Carla and Shaun's house. The women and some of the men drank tea and ate cake in a room hung with grief and sorrow. Shaun served them while Carla did her best to comfort Debbie. She'd sent her son, Aiden, to her parents for the day. A child's wake wasn't a place for a boy almost the same age.

Vinnie and his friends were in his pool room; some played pool, while others chatted idly. Condensation sat on beer glasses, dripping tears of guilt. This was a wake for men who were incapable of expressing emotion; or empathy for those who were suffering.

27

Thursday 25 April 2019 (Day 8)

The alarm went off at 5.00. Riley got out of bed and stumbled toward the bathroom in the dark. His mind was still a blur from the previous night, numbed by the sight of Paul Smith clinging to life on the dirt path and frustrated by their inability to find Fantis and Hargreaves. The two bikies had gone to ground and the patrols alerted in the region had been unable to sight them or their car.

They hadn't found an address for Graham Cole in any of their databases. By the time they had returned to Riley's house, Kate had fallen asleep in front of the television. She woke as they came in and hurriedly re-heated the curry. Cassie and Rachel stayed for a quick bowl before heading off.

Riley stared into the mirror as he shaved. The dawn service commenced at 6.00 and he would lay a wreath before the conclusion at around 6.45. Most of the service would be conducted in the dark and, with several hundred people in attendance, it would be difficult to identify Graham Cole until the end. Cassie and Rachel had insisted on being there, in plain clothes, to help. As they had told Riley, they were entitled to participate in ANZAC Day on their day off and, if they happened to identify a person of interest, it was their duty to assist.

In truth, he was grateful for their support. The on-duty officers would also be close by if required. He figured that Cole may not be aware that he had been identified the previous evening and may not even be aware of the brutality of the assault on Paul Smith, so it was certainly possible that he would carry on life as normal.

He turned the shower on full and hot. He closed his eyes as the stream ran over his head and opened them to find Kate opening the door to join him. She put her arms around his neck and kissed him warmly on the lips.

'I love you, Riley, you know that. And I'm here for you, no matter how hard it gets, OK?'

They burst into laughter at the unintended double entendre.

'Come on. We'd better get going.' Kate giggled.

'You're coming to the service?'

'Of course. I always go. But don't worry, I won't get in the way. I'll stand with Sally and Callum.'

The ANZAC Service was conducted with the sombreness and reflection as the day warranted. Riley laid his wreath on behalf of the South Australian Police and as the night sky transformed to grey dawn the darkness lifted and he eventually spotted Rachel and Cassie carefully moving around the perimeter of the crowd.

As the formalities wound up, Riley walked to where Kate stood with Sally and Callum, scanning as he walked for any sign of Graham Cole. He had almost reached them when Cassie grabbed his elbow. She nodded at a group near the door leading into the RSL building.

Ladies were serving hot black coffee to the crowd, another lacing the coffee with rum for those that wanted it. In the queue, waiting his turn, was Graham. Directly behind him stood Rachel. He would be going nowhere without them following.

Graham took his coffee, having requested an extra shot of rum and moved away from the building. Rachel left the queue without a coffee and took up a position only a couple of metres away. Riley and Cassie circled the crowd until they were behind Graham.

Riley nudged Graham gently on the arm.

'We'd like you to join us at the station for a chat, Mr. Cole.'

Graham was taken aback but reacted quickly for a man of his age. He threw the coffee cup at Riley and bounded forward looking for a gap in the crowd. He only made two steps before he tripped on Rachel's outstretched leg. Before he realised it, he was face down with a mouthful of grass and his arms pinned behind his back.

Riley followed the patrol car to the station, accompanied by Rachel and Cassie. Although he tried to convince them to take the rest of the day off, they insisted on being with him while he interviewed Graham Cole. He wondered how he had been so mistaken in his first impression of Cassie. She was fitting into the team well, even without the guiding presence of her boss. Cassie interrupted his musings.

'I don't suppose you've heard anything more about the boss's condition, Riley?'

'No, it's probably a bit early.' He glanced at his watch. 7.25. 'Let's make a call before we chat with our friend.'

Rachel jumped out of Riley's car and joined Phil Reid who was assisting Graham Cole out of the patrol car.

'Let's put Mr. Cole in the holding cell. The Senior Sergeant will join us shortly.'

Graham protested his innocence as they guided him inside. If he expected a sympathetic ear, he was disappointed. Firm hands and no response to his complaints was all he got.

Riley and Cassie took up one of the meeting rooms, where they called Mick Martin on speakerphone.

'Mate, I can't tell you too much more than you probably already know. He was in the operating theatre until late last night. He's got some significant head injuries but they don't know the full scope yet. A couple of broken ribs, a punctured lung and a fractured cheekbone plus whatever damage he's got to the brain. Bastards did a job on him.'

Cassie interjected, 'How's Kathy?' She turned to Riley, whispering 'the DI's wife.'

'She's devastated as you can imagine. Her sister is with her, so she's in good hands. I'm dropping out to see her this morning and then I'll head down to Goolwa. I'll see you early afternoon.'

Riley leaned into the phone.

'Mick, we've been able to detain an associate of Hargreaves and Fantis. He was with them last night but we don't know yet if he was involved in the assault. Do you want us to wait for you before we interview him?'

'God, no. That was quick. Good work. Get started on him; the sooner you get something from him, the better our chances of picking up the other two.'

***

A forlorn Graham Cole sat at a small desk opposite Rachel Cross. Phil Reid stood in front of the door and moved aside as Riley entered.

'Thanks, Constable. Sergeant Callaghan is making some coffees if you wouldn't mind helping her. I don't believe you finished your last coffee, Mr. Cole. Can we get you a replacement? Unfortunately, we can't offer you a shot of rum in this one.'

Cole scowled at him. 'Just tell me why I'm here, arsehole, and let me get the fuck out of here.'

Riley smiled and took a seat opposite him. 'I'll take that as a "no". Thank you, Constable.' He opened his folder and turned to their detainee.

He looked at a man who was as miserable a man as he had ever seen. The lines on his unshaven face revealed a life that had been trademarked by trauma since he'd been a child. Riley knew that Graham was a Vietnam vet and he was only too aware of the PTSD issues faced by men like him; nightmares, fear of sudden loud noises and respite found at the bottom of a bottle or a needle in the arm. What Riley didn't know about was the abuse that Graham had suffered as a child. Physical abuse at the hands of a perpetually drunk, too often violent, father; sexual abuse from a scout-master; emotional abuse from a mother who had taken one too many beatings. And nowhere to turn, no one to help. By fourteen, Graham had found companionship in a local gang; by sixteen he had stolen his first car. At eighteen, he was an alcoholic and a drug user. It was then that he attempted and failed an armed robbery. That had earned him a two-year jail sentence and a whole series of new life experiences. He registered for the army on his release, looking for a new start. What he got was the horror and pain that Vietnam offered thousands of young men.

At sixty-five, Graham was broken beyond repair. Goolwa had offered an escape from years of homelessness and despair. When he first arrived ten years ago, he found he could live modestly in the town on welfare payments and still put a little aside each fortnight. Just as his life looked like it could turn around, he found himself sitting in the bar next to Damien Hargreaves. The little man offered him a job, paid in cash. All he had to do was peddle the drugs, which a man named Vinnie would supply him. There was a solid market and plenty of quiet places around town where he could conduct business discreetly. The problem was that Damien Hargreaves also encouraged Graham to test the products. His savings soon evaporated and he found he had to sell product just to sustain his own habit.

He was shaking as he lifted his head. The copper was looking at him like he was some kind of animal. *Well, he can just get fucked.*

'Let's get some formalities out of the way, just so we get to know you.' Riley nodded to Rachel to start the recording.

A few minutes later, Cassie brought coffees in for Riley and Rachel, bringing a pause to the routine questions that had been put to Cole. He looked agitated as the officers carefully tested the heat of their drinks. Cassie excused herself and left, casting a scornful glance at him as she passed.

Cole exploded. 'Listen, will youse dickheads get on with it? I've got things to do today. It's not right that you pull a vet in on ANZAC Day for no reason. No bloody respect for them that served the country.'

'All right, Graham. Why don't you settle down? You want to know why you are here. OK. Let's start with possession of drugs for sale. We have it on good authority that you do a bit of dealing. You want to tell us about that?'

'You got no proof of that. I got none on me and you ain't searched me 'ouse. Who dobbed on me? Whoever it was, they're lyin'. You got nothin' to hold me on.'

Rachel coughed and rubbed her leg. 'Then there is the matter of Resist Arrest, Mr. Cole. I think I'm going to have quite a bruise where you kicked me.'

'Kicked you? What the fuck are you on about? You tripped me, you ...'

'Now, now, Graham. Be careful what you say. We wouldn't want to add obscene language charges, would we? Let's see if we can clear this up. Tell us about Damien Hargreaves and Tony Fantis.'

'What about them?' Graham shrank back into his seat, increasingly wary as to where the discussion was headed.

'Well,' Riley said, 'you haven't denied that you know them and you would also know that they are members of the outlawed Anarchist Motorcycle Gang. We know that they're very involved in drug distribution so if you have an association with them that's something we're interested in.'

'Wait a minute. Yeah, I know of them but I ain't got nothin' to do with them with drugs and the like. I probably only met them once, maybe twice. Through common acquaintances, sort of.'

'Ok, here's the thing, Graham. We know you met them last night at the Goolwa Hotel.' Riley pulled out his phone and opened up the image that Paul Smith had sent to him shortly before his beating. 'See, that looks like you there, doesn't it? And the other two; well, you know who they are.'

'That photo's the back of someone's head. Could be anyone, but it's not me.'

'You have a short memory, Graham. We have a witness, a reliable one, who says that this is you in the photo. Now, let's stop playing games. Let's put the drug dealing to one side. We're not going to forget about it but there's something a lot more serious you need to tell us about.'

Beads of sweat erupted on Graham's face. 'What? I ain't involved in nothin' more serious.'

'What about a vicious assault on a police officer, Graham?'

'Or murder?' Rachel added.

'Murder, what are you talking about? And I didn't know that bloke was a copper.'

'Tell us what happened with that bloke, Graham.'

He wrung his hands and sat shaking. 'Can I have some water?'

Graham described the meeting with Hargreaves and Fantis and the instruction he had received to wait with the crowbar behind the fence.

'So, let's get it clear, Graham. You didn't hit the victim?'

'No, I swear. They made me leave after they hit him. I did what they said. I just pissed off and didn't look back.'

'Alright. We can come back to that later, but at the moment you are an accessory to a very serious assault charge. How bad that is for you will depend on how much you cooperate with us from here. Understand?'

Graham nodded solemnly. 'They will fucking kill me,' he muttered.

'Ok, Graham, let's move on. What was your relationship with Vinnie Waters? Now, don't bullshit me because we already know a lot. You can treat this as a test as to how much we think you're cooperating with us. If you don't tell us what we already know, you are in deep shit. Do you understand?'

'Yeah, I fucking understand. You're tellin' me you got me by the balls. I'm fucked whichever way I go.'

'Your problem, mate. Now, answer the question. What was your relationship with Vinnie?'

'I bought some stuff from him, that's all.'

Riley stood. 'Not good enough, Graham. What kind of stuff and what did you do with it?'

'Aw, fuck, fuck, fuck!' Graham put his head in his hands. 'Alright, it was weed, Tina and a bit of Harry.'

'Ok, so for the recording you are talking about what?'

Graham exhaled with a loud sigh. 'Marijuana, crystal meth and heroin. Hey, I thought you weren't going to slam me with the drugs.'

'That's right, Graham. If you cooperate fully, it will be taken into account. I can tell you that drug dealing isn't the main reason you're here. Now, tell us about the arrangement with Vinnie Waters.'

'Listen, I didn't touch that copper, so if this ain't about the drugs, what are you on about?'

'One more time, Graham. What was the arrangement with Vinnie Waters?'

Graham slumped further into his chair.

'Waters sold me the drugs an' I sold them around town.'

'Ok, that's a start. Where did Vinnie get the drugs from?'

Graham started twitching. He wiped his hand across his face before he answered.

'I dunno, exactly. He used to go to Loxton to pick them up and then he'd let me know when he got a delivery.'

'Who were his contacts in Loxton?'

'Are you fucking kidding me? You know who it was. It was them two that got put down.'

'The Satchins?'

'Yeah, that's them but I didn't know nothin' about them. Vinnie done that all on his own.'

Riley sat down and looked Graham in the eye.

'Graham, you're doing better now. Just keep telling us the truth, alright? Ok, then. So, Vinnie picked up the drugs from the Satchins in Loxton. Then he drove them back to Goolwa and stored them where?'

Graham burst into laughter.

'I thought youse coppers knew stuff. Youse don't know shit.'

Riley looked at Rachel. She looked confused, but then interjected.

'When the Senior Sergeant said "drove" he was talking about Vinnie's boat. Is that where he stored them, Graham?'

Riley looked in wonderment at Rachel. She had remembered from the case notes that Emma had told them about Vinnie sleeping on his boat at her parents' house. He turned back to see Graham open-mouthed.

'Yeah, alright. He used to go upriver in one of his boats, pick up the gear and come back to Goolwa. He stored the stuff on a boat he moored somewhere else.'

'Are you telling us there's a second boat? What did it look like?'

'You tell me, copper. I've never seen it. We always did our transactions somewhere remote.'

Riley now understood they needed to find the second boat but he doubted that Graham could help them. It was clear that Vinnie kept it well away from potential partners and enemies.

He excused himself and Rachel from the meeting room. They stood in the corridor as he spoke to her in a low voice.

'Hey, can you ask Cassie to help with something? There's obviously another boat involved. Can you ask her to check with registration for any boats Vinnie has ever owned, either in his name or the business?'

'Onto it, Riley. Have you considered too that maybe Emma could help with a name or a description?'

Riley brushed past a quizzical Constable Reid and resumed his seat opposite an even more quizzical Graham Cole.

'Ok, Graham. What about Vinnie's death? What happened there?'

'Honestly, I dunno. I hear it was an accident but after the Satchins I dunno. Maybe he upset the wrong people.'

'Like the Anarchists?'

'I dunno. Honest. You don't ask them blokes questions.'

'So why did you meet with them last night, Graham?'

Graham sat silently, looking down at the table.

Riley lifted Graham's chin.

'Graham, this is important. We believe these two are responsible for the murders of Greg and Patricia Satchin as well as Vinnie Waters. We can't do anything to help them. But', he stared at Graham with steel eyes, 'what worries us most is that we believe they've kidnapped an eleven-year-old boy. If you have any moral compass, you'll help us save that kid. If you don't help us, and we find out you could have, we will take you down in any way we can.'

'Kid? I don't know anything about a kid. They wanted to know where Vinnie kept the cash that he was laundering for them. They said he had a few hundred thousand dollars of their money.'

'So, you told them about the other boat?'

'Of course, I fucking did.'

Riley looked up to the ceiling. They now had a race with the Anarchists to find Vinnie's second boat. He decided that for now at least, Graham was of no further use to them. The fact that Graham did not know about Aiden's abduction was concerning to him. Potentially, Hargreaves and Fantis could have already killed Aiden and disposed of his body. In that case, there would have been no reason for them to discuss the boy with Graham. Maybe there was no reason to discuss him with Graham anyway. The fewer people that knew about what they had done with or to Aiden, whatever it was, the less chance that information could be leaked.

'Alright, Graham, here's what's going to happen. We have four hours that we can hold you without charging you.' Riley looked at his watch, more for emphasis than because he didn't know the time. 'We have two hours to go before we reach that time. I am going to hold you here for your own safety.'

He paused to make sure Graham understood the full implication of what he had said. It would not be in police or Graham's interest for him to run into the Anarchists. It must have sunk in because he now sat shaking uncontrollably, not even raising his eyes when Rachel re-entered the room.

'So, before that four-hour period expires, I'm going to have you charged with Resist Arrest and Trafficking a Controlled Drug, which you have admitted to. Once those charges are laid you will be required to sit before a magistrate, probably this afternoon, where you can apply for bail if you wish. We won't oppose bail but I strongly suggest you think carefully about whether it makes sense for you to be released at this stage. Understand?'

Graham nodded glumly.

After Constable Reid removed Graham Cole from the interview room, Riley and Rachel joined Cassie.

Cassie grabbed a piece of paper from her desk. 'Okay, I have a couple of boats that have been registered in Vinnie's name but none in the company name. Most have been small affairs, nothing that would be suitable for the sort of business he's been doing in Loxton.

'The last boat he had was a ski boat that he sold a couple of years ago. The boat in the shed had been registered in the name of a Jordan Brown. I've spoken to him and he says Vinnie bought it from him a few months ago. So, what's next?'

Riley turned to Rachel.

'Rachel, can you pull together all the material we have so far? It would be good to have something for DS Martin to read when he gets here if Cassie and I aren't around.'

'Why? Where will you be?'

'We're going to see Emma Satchin. Hopefully, as you suggested, she can give us a better description of the boat that she saw Vinnie Waters take to Loxton. Timing-wise, it was obviously before the one that's in the shed. As I see it, there are two unsolved murders in Loxton and one here in Goolwa, there is the kidnap and possible murder of a young boy and at the bottom of it seems to be this drug business. That boat has now become critical in sorting all this out and we need to find it before the Anarchists do.'

Rachel and Cassie nodded.

'Right, boss,' Rachel piped, 'what else do you want me to do? Looks like our day off is up in smoke, so I may as well do something useful here.'

'Great, thanks. Listen, could you get Graham Cole's charge sheet prepared and see if we can get a magistrate organised for this afternoon? Firstly, though, can you get in touch with Shaun Chambers and see if he can meet me here in an hour? Obviously, you can't tell him too much about where we are at. He'll certainly press you for an update. Just tell him to get here and I'll update him then. See if Oliver's available too.'

28

Thursday 25 April 2019 (Day 8)

Riley and Cassie headed out the back door of the station into the car park. Riley was still in uniform while Cassie was in the off-duty clothes she had worn to the dawn service. Many of the returned servicemen would by now have caught the bus into Adelaide to take part in the traditional ANZAC Day march while the rest of the town commemorated in other ways. So far, the day had been quiet for the law enforcers. Riley remembered when he was a boy and his father's best mate was the town copper. ANZAC Days for the police were typified by fights in the pub over a two-up game or ugly domestic violence driven by a belly full of beer.

They arrived at Callum and Sally's house to find Sally pruning a bush in the front yard. Just twelve months ago, that was something Riley couldn't have imagined her doing.

'I don't believe it,' he joked at her, 'you've found a green thumb. Or are you trying to kill it?'

'Very funny, Riley.' She wiped a strand of hair from her forehead as she squinted into the sun. She looked from Riley to Cassie, bemused by her brother in uniform and Cassie in plain clothes. 'Is this official or social?'

'Official, I'm afraid. But I wouldn't mind dropping around with Kate a bit later on if that's okay. We haven't spent a lot of time together lately, have we?'

'Whose fault is that, then?' Sally nudged him. 'So, who do you want today?'

'Is Emma around?'

'She's with Callum, watching the footy. I don't know why; Collingwood is belting the Bombers.'

They walked inside to find Callum and Emma with their eyes glued to the TV. The game didn't look one-sided.

Callum turned to Riley.

'Just a sec, mate. The game's almost over. Essendon is finishing like a runaway train and there's only four points in it.'

Riley sat next to Callum and took in the tension of the game. Cassie looked at Sally and shrugged.

'Boys and their football! I don't get it,' she exclaimed.

Emma looked up indignantly. 'It's not just for boys, you know.'

Cassie was relieved that the siren sounded and the game was over.

'Beer?' Callum asked.

'Thanks, Callum, maybe later. We just wanted to check something with Emma.'

Emma stood and suddenly looked anxious.

'It's okay, Emma,' Cassie interjected, 'we just need to follow up on something you told us before.'

'That's right,' Riley continued. 'We feel like we're closing in on the suspects, but we need to know something you may be able to tell us. Is that okay?'

'Of course, what is it?' Her uncertainty was obvious.

'You remember how you told the Detective Inspector and me about the night that Vinnie Waters stayed overnight at Loxton - in his boat?'

'Yes, of course. Why?'

'Well, we now believe that boat is crucial to the investigation. We need to know if you can tell us any more about it. Its name would be great if you can remember.'

'Oh, Riley, I have no idea what its name was. I didn't take a lot of notice of it, but it was like a motor cruiser, maybe ten or twelve metres long. Dad was pretty rapt in it. He said if he ever bought a wooden boat, that's what he would want. He told us what the brand was. Is that what it's called; a brand?'

'Ok, I don't know. What brand did he say it was?'

Emma was silent for a moment, trying to recall the name.

'I can't remember. It was like a Swedish name or something. I remember going to IKEA and seeing all these names of their furniture and they reminded me of the name he called the boat.'

'Halvorsen?' Callum offered.

'Yes, I think that's it,' Emma said excitedly.

Riley looked at Callum. 'How did you know that?'

'Oh, there's always a few of them here for the Wooden Boat Festival. Wouldn't mind one myself.'

'Ok, that's brilliant. Emma. If by chance the name of the boat does come back to you, make sure you let us know please.'

Emma smiled weakly. She loved being with Sally and Callum but she was also still grieving her parents. She felt guilty that her presence in Goolwa had been kept a secret which meant that her extended family and her friends were still in the dark about what had happened to her. Riley picked up on her growing solemnness and walked closer to her.

'Emma, this will be over soon, I promise. Then you'll be able to come out of the dark, go back to Loxton or wherever you choose.'

Although the tone of her voice still held her anxiety, her smile was more relaxed.

'There's nothing for me in Loxton now. I think I'd like to stay in Goolwa.' She looked at Sally. 'Maybe with you guys a bit longer?'

Riley and Cassie left the three to discuss future potential options for Emma. They arrived back at the police station and Riley was pleased to see Shaun's car parked out front.

They walked through the station door and were immediately confronted by Shaun. That wasn't a surprise to them but Carla hanging off his arm was.

'What's happened, Riley? Has something come up about Aiden?'

The look on her face was clear. She expected news that could be either the best or the worst she could imagine. They were both smartly dressed and Carla looked most like her normal self since Aiden had gone missing. For all that, the lines on her face portrayed the underlying tension she felt now, with the expectation of a major development.

Riley chose his words carefully.

'Hi, Carla. Look, I didn't expect you to come along with Shaun today. Right now, I really can't give you any news about Aiden that would either give you comfort or cause you dismay. All I can say is that we know who we're looking for and we have a lead on where we can find them but we can't be sure whether they have Aiden.'

Shaun had stood back until this point. He was as concerned by the call from the police as Carla was. He was less inclined to let his emotion show. His life had been punctuated with tragedy, sadness and disappointment. Recent developments had followed the pattern; Aiden going missing, the failed attempt by the police to apprehend the bikies and his former friend Vinnie's drug-related crimes. He spoke now, quietly.

'Riley, why are we here if you have nothing to tell us? Carla and I were using today to try to get some sense in our lives; just for one day, we wanted to rest on each other to deal with things. You understand that calling us in has shattered that.'

'I'm sorry about that, Shaun and Carla, I am. I didn't know what plans you had made but, honestly, even if I did, we would have called you in, Shaun. We need your help. Urgently.'

Riley outlined the outcomes of Paul Smith's attack and the arrest of Graham Cole, leading to the revelation that Vinnie's boat was key to the investigation. He also told Shaun that from their discussion with Emma Satchin, they believed that the type of boat they were looking for was a wooden-hulled Halvorsen.

'Do you think they have Aiden on the boat?' Shaun asked.

'I'm not saying that. What we know is that the bikies will have a very keen interest in that boat. It's crucial in their drug business somehow and we know they're looking for it. We need to find the boat to find them and we need to find them to find Aiden.'

Shaun saw the connection but was still unsure why he had been dragged in.

'What do you need me for?'

'We need to know where we can find the boat. We're hoping you'll be able to trace it for us. Find out when Vinnie bought it and a name and description if you can. Best of all, if you can find out where he keeps it.'

'Ok, let's get started. I could use a hand, though. Is Constable Townsend around?'

Riley smiled at him.

'I've called him in too. He should be waiting in the office for you. Let me know as soon as you have anything, ok?'

After Shaun had left, Riley turned to Carla. She had started weeping, her eyeliner streaking down the side of her face. He felt the greatest pity for her at that moment. He was gratified, however, that Cassie and Rachel sat with her doing their best to comfort her. He had forgotten that today was supposed to be their day off and sitting in their civilian clothes, they could have been members of a grieving family.

Rachel squeezed Carla's hand before looking up at Riley.

'Cassie and I thought we might call it a day, Riley. I don't think we can do much here right now and I think Carla could use some company while Shaun's busy.'

'Yes, of course. I'll let you know if anything comes up but, yes, go. And thanks. Both of you. I'll see you tomorrow.'

They had been gone only a few minutes. Riley had just begun to write up his reports on the day's activities when he looked up to see a monster of a man blocking the front doorway.

'Senior Sergeant, O'Brien?' the man asked. 'Detective Sergeant Mick Martin.'

Without waiting for a reply, he bounded forward and clasped Riley's hand. He shook it vigorously while he continued.

'DI Smith talks very highly of you, young man. I'm sure you appreciate that's not something he does lightly.'

Riley appraised the detective. His physical presence could not be understated; he seemed to take up every available cubic centimetre that was around him. He came across as a man who would more than capably handle a recalcitrant offender but he also exuded a congeniality that was equally disarming. In every way, he was a contemporary of Paul Smith.

'DS Martin. Good to meet you in person. What's the latest on the DI?'

'Induced coma. He's taken a belting and, to be frank, I want to be the first to be introduced to the blokes who did it to him. I have a feeling they are the type that will resist arrest and I'd be delighted to help restrain them.'

Riley sensed he was deadly serious and was in no doubt that Fantis and Hargreaves would regret the day they took on DS Martin.

'Anyway,' continued the big detective, 'I believe we have a meeting with one Graham Cole and a magistrate in a few minutes. We should be making a move.'

Riley looked at his watch. His day had got away from him again.

The voice of Constable Phil Reid carried from the room next door.

'Sorry, Riley, we couldn't get a magistrate today – ANZAC Day. We managed to get Mr Wilkinson booked for nine-thirty am tomorrow.'

Mick Martin clapped his hands. 'That's actually good news. I need to update you on the bigger picture taking into account what's happened at Loxton. Where can we grab a beer and talk?'

'Why don't you come back to my house? It will be a lot more private and we can still have a beer.'

29

2016

After Jeremy's death, Debbie shrank into a solitary existence. She rarely socialised with anyone; Carla included. She could have gone back to work but that would have involved telling people her story and she couldn't cope with that. It wasn't that she was in denial; she was grief-stricken beyond comprehension. She had lost her son; the only son, only child, she would ever have. She could never be a mother again.

She blamed Vinnie, of course. She couldn't tolerate being in his presence; it just reminded her of the son he'd given her and then taken away. She could never forgive him.

For his part, Vinnie was frustrated. He still adored Debbie and knew he could never replace Jeremy. He wanted her affection but she'd become distant to him; he didn't fail to notice that when he tried to hug or kiss her, she shrank back. Sex was entirely out of the question.

Unexpected visitors to the boatshed in April complicated the situation. Vinnie was working on the deck of a boat when he noticed a woman tentatively enter the shed, accompanied by a teenage boy.

'You there, Vinnie?' the woman called.

'Who's asking?' Vinnie kept working, looking down at his work rather than facing the visitors.

'Don't you remember me? That'd be right. Fuckin' one night stand and you're done.'

Vinnie stood on the deck and looked down.

'What do you want, Louise? And put that fucking cigarette out. There are flammable materials in here.'

She ground the cigarette under her foot and smiled at Vinnie.

'I thought it was time you met your son. Vinnie, this is Loklan. Loklan, this heap of shit is your old man.' The boy stood looking at the ground, clearly embarrassed.

'What are you talking about? Are you telling me this kid is the result of our one-night stand?'

'Yes. This kid, Loklan's his name if you've forgotten, is your son.'

'So, what do you want from me?' Vinnie climbed down from the boat and extended his hand to Loklan. He looked into his eyes and saw brown, same as his; *meant nothing*. The boy took his hand and shook it feebly.

Louise smiled. 'That's nice. Father and son. Very touching. See the thing is, Vinnie, I'm a bit short on money and I figure it's about time you paid your dues.'

'Why now?'

'My old man looked after me and Lokkie but he's gone now, so it's your turn to make it up. Get it?'

'How can I be sure he's my kid?'

'Oh, he's yours, sunshine. Have a look at him.'

Vinnie studied the boy closely. There was no doubt he had the same build Vinnie had as a kid, a bit on the short side, stocky, same little freckles around his nose.

'How old are you, Loklan?'

'I'm fourteen,' the boy said shyly, 'My birthday was September 29.'

Vinnie did some quick arithmetic. The date fitted; could be his kid.

'I'm not sure. You could be scamming me, Louise. Easy way for a quick buck.'

She kicked at a paper cup on the floor. 'Well, we could always do a paternity test, if that's what you want, Vinnie. I mean, that would probably mean that your wife will find out. You know, full disclosure. It's only fair she knows what's going on.'

Vinnie shook his head vigorously. 'Nah, that's not happening. She can never know. And, sorry kid, but I don't want to see you again. I can't.'

'That's ok,' Louise said, 'Lokkie doesn't need a father, especially an arsehole like you. But you need to make good, Vinnie.'

Vinnie was defeated. He knew the boy was probably his. He knew it would destroy Debbie if she found out; knowing Vinnie still had a child while she had lost the only one she could ever have.

'How much?' he asked resignedly.

'I reckon five hundred a week is fair.'

'What the fuck?'

'Well now, Damien says your business is going alright and I've seen where you live, Vinnie. You can afford it.'

Vinnie recoiled at the mention of Damien Hargreaves. When Louise said that she knew where he lived, he saw he no longer had a choice.

'Alright, alright. But that's it, right? And don't go expecting me to be there for his birthday and Christmas and all that shit. This is a purely financial transaction.'

'Deal!' Louise fished a piece of paper from her pocket and handed it to Vinnie. 'Here are my bank details. I'll expect to see deposits each week starting next Thursday. C'mon, Lokkie. Let's go.'

And so, the payments started. Vinnie was careful to make the payments from an account other than the household account. He knew it was a hit to his income but he also knew he could afford it, for now. What he couldn't afford was to get offside with Damien Hargreaves.

A small falling out with the Anarchists did develop, however, completely unrelated to Vinnie's new relationship with the Hargreaves family.

Riley O'Brien had been promoted to Sergeant at the Goolwa Police Station. He was more perceptive than his predecessor and followed a tip that led to the arrest of Nick 'Sully' Sullivan for drug dealing. The Anarchists were furious. They tried to keep a low profile in their markets, not just to avoid attention from the police but also to keep under the radar of their larger and more influential competitors.

If Sully talked, named names, it would lead all the way through Vinnie Waters to the upstream distributors and ultimately the Anarchists.

For the first time in his life, Vinnie was depressed. Jeremy's death, the loss of connection with Debbie, Louise's demands and now this had put him into unfamiliar territory. He could feel the walls closing in. What he didn't know at the time of Sully's arrest was that things would only go downhill and mainly due to his own carelessness and lack of sensitivity.

Still reeling from a blistering phone call from Gavin Trower concerning Sully, Vinnie arrived home to find Debbie waiting for him with a piece of paper in her hand.

'What's this, Vincent?' She waved the paper in front of his face. He could make out that it was a bank statement.

He looked blankly at her. 'I don't know, Deb. Why don't you tell me or at least let me see what you're waving around?'

She flung the paper at him.

'Who the fuck is Louise Hargreaves, Vinnie? Five hundred every week. Is she your mistress, a prostitute, or what?'

Vinnie cursed himself. How could he have been so stupid to leave one of *those* statements laying around?'

Vinnie led her to the lounge room and invited her to sit. He told her about the one-night stand fifteen years earlier and Louise's visit to the boatshed. In a sense, he was relieved and even wondered why he hadn't opened up to her from the start. After all, it had all happened before they'd got together so he had no reason to feel guilty.

He was mistaken if he thought Debbie would see it so clearly. She sank further into misery, resenting that Vinnie had allowed her son to die and yet, as it now turned out, he had one in reserve. It didn't help that Vinnie told her that he would have nothing to do with Loklan. That wasn't the point in her eyes. He had a son; it was his choice not to see him, but he still had a son.

A couple of months of stony silence drove Vinnie to despair. The Sully arrest had largely resolved itself. Sully hadn't talked and, for his silence, had earned a hefty sentence. Louise had left him alone and although the weekly payment and the risk of further "extortion" still bothered him, he'd accepted the way it had worked out.

In the end, Vinnie tried to solve the problem the best way he knew how; with money. He still loved Debbie and pined for his affection to be returned. The best way to win her attention was to use his tried-and-true method; to buy her something so extravagant she couldn't ignore him.

She had a new car and all the jewellery and clothes she could possibly need. Eventually, he had a revelation. He bought her a river boat; she could make herself busy refitting it to what she wanted and they could take themselves up the river and rekindle their fondness for each other. The icing on the cake was that he would dedicate it to their son by re-naming the boat *Jeremy*.

She was beautiful and Vinnie couldn't see how Debbie wouldn't fall in love with her. Built in 1934, there were two berths below the forward deck and while the saloon could be converted to take an additional two guests, Vinnie had no intention of anyone other than he and Debbie sleeping on her.

The *Jeremy* arrived in Goolwa on a bright autumn day, perfect for a motor upriver. The skipper who'd brought her down ran through the handover with Vinnie and wished him happy times on his new purchase. Vinnie had planned ahead; he'd had a picnic basket prepared with an assortment of delicious cheeses and crackers, fruits, pates and dips. He put two bottles of Pol Roger in the onboard fridge. He had no idea if it was any good, but based on the price, he figured it was up there with the best.

He raced home to find Debbie up and about. She had been out for coffee with Carla; a good sign. She was dressed smartly, not in the track-suit she become accustomed to wearing while she moped on the couch.

Vinnie was rapt; maybe this was the turning of the corner.

'Deb, love. I've got something to show you.'

Carla had convinced Debbie that she should accept that Vinnie had a child from a previous relationship; everyone knew that he'd been a player in his early days so it was no surprise he had a child turn up out of the blue. Debbie was shocked by Carla's position on it but she realised it was true. Who knew how many others there could be? She didn't like it, but what could she do about it?

She looked at Vinnie and saw excitement written all over his face. *Still like a child.*

'Vinnie, please. Not another car. I know I've been down but, seriously, the car I have is fine.'

'Nope, better. Come on, we're taking a drive.'

They arrived at the marina and Vinnie made her cover her eyes as he guided her down the ramp. When she uncovered them, the bright sun-light made her squint.

'What do you think? She's yours,' Vinnie exclaimed.

Debbie stood gaping as she read the newly painted name on the stern. 'What the fuck is this?' she screamed.

'It's a boat, Deb. A beautiful boat. I had her renamed *Jeremy* - after our son.'

Debbie released a flood of tears.

'You think this makes it all right, do you? You think our son can be replaced by a boat just because you've given it his name. You are fucking stupid, Vinnie. And insensitive, too. Give me the fucking keys.'

'It's unlocked, love. You just have to step on board.'

'Not the fucking boat. The car. Give me the car keys.'

She grabbed them from his hand and ran to the top of the ramp. Vinnie stared after her. *What had he done wrong?*

He heard the car screech as it left the car park and watched as it sped away from the river.

Oh. Fuck, fuck, fuck.

He started to walk up the ramp, not certain what to do next. By the time he reached the top, he'd broken into a run. He ran as long as he could toward home, but eventually, his fitness gave way and he had to walk the rest.

Vinnie arrived home clutching his side, gripped by a stitch. He was relieved to see his car parked in the driveway. As he approached, he saw that Debbie was still sitting in the driver's seat, hunched over and motionless.

He ran to the car door and jerked it open violently. Debbie was shaking. Her hands gripped the steering wheel so tightly that her knuckles were white. Tears streamed down her face as she stared into the distance.

'What are you doing, Deb?' No response.

'Come on, love. Come inside and we can talk.'

Without moving her head, Debbie replied in a harsh, unhuman voice. 'Leave me alone.'

Vinnie tried to free her hands from the steering wheel.

'I said leave me alone,' she whispered menacingly.

An hour later, Debbie sat in the car in the same position. Vinnie was at his wit's end and, uncertain what he could do on his own, rang the doctor. Two hours later, an ambulance arrived and took Debbie to the hospital. After Vinnie related the events leading to her breakdown, the paramedics suggested it might be best for Vinnie not to accompany her at this stage.

With that, their marriage was over. Debbie was taken to Adelaide for assessment and shortly after was admitted to a psychiatric facility. Vinnie made sure she got the best care available. Debbie refused to see him and after four months, Vinnie gave up. He stopped paying the bills after six and within twelve filed divorce papers.

Infatuated by Debbie for years, even he was surprised at how quickly he fell out of love. It was peculiar that, if affection was not returned, the effort became wearisome and, like a bad investment, best abandoned when the time came.

30

Friday 26 April 2019 (Day 9)

Riley woke with a sore head. He had expected Mick to want to de-brief over a drink, just as Paul Smith would have. What he hadn't expected was that Mick took alcohol consumption to a new level, one that was far more than Riley was capable of dealing with. At the end of the night, he opened the front door and watched Mick stagger back toward the motel before he stumbled back inside.

Tired and drunk, he put himself straight to bed as Kate laughed at him. Asleep within moments he didn't wake until 7:30, greeted by a punishing head and a stomach that still felt like heaving. Kate tip-toed into the room until she noted that he was awake. He was grateful to see a fizzing glass of Berocca drink in her hand and he reached for it thirstily. She followed up by handing him two paracetamol capsules.

'I'm off to work, Riley. I think you should wait a little while before heading out. I'm pretty sure you might still be over the limit.'

Riley groaned. 'I know and I should be at work doing things, especially today.'

Kate kissed him tenderly before grabbing her keys and leaving.

The pounding in Riley's head was still like a bass drum echoing in his skull and, while he wasn't religious, he found he was praying, or perhaps begging, for some relief. The day ahead should be one where they made significant progress on the case, especially with the information that Mick Martin had passed on the night before.

Mick had brought Riley up to date with developments on the Loxton murders and the drug-running business based there. The team were convinced that they had uncovered the motive for the murders of Greg and Pat Satchin. A forensic examination of their accounts had highlighted that Greg had been siphoning funds from the Anarchist's business for a few months, accumulating over three hundred thousand dollars in an off-shore bank account. It was unclear whether Pat had been involved in the fraud, but because she was with Greg, she became part of the Anarchists' brutal statement. Police were convinced that had Emma been in the workshop, she would also have been eliminated.

Further investigation of Greg Satchin's workshop had resulted in a drug squad raid on a property near Taplan, about thirty kilometres southeast of Loxton. The wheat farm was marginally productive. The thousand-hectare crop yielded next to nothing compared to the sheds, once used to store seeding and harvesting equipment, now utilised for the hydroponic production of cannabis. The house, once the residence of hardworking farmers, was now set up for the chemical production of methamphetamine products and the storage of imported drugs.

Police had made four arrests; the farmer who operated a legitimate grain-growing enterprise but supplemented his income by renting the house and sheds to the Anarchists and three "chemists" working the lab. In the shed storing the imported drugs, they seized a locked storage box containing a sizeable amount of cash and a cache of arms presumably intended to protect the property and its operations.

What the Loxton investigation had failed to establish was a link between Greg Satchin's fraudulent activities and Vinnie Waters. There was no evidence to suggest that Vinnie's transactions had been anything other than on a strictly business basis, albeit an illegal business.

The point that Riley and Mick had pondered at length was why the Anarchists had decided to take out Vinnie Waters and why they had abducted or murdered Aiden Chambers. They had then debated the appropriateness of using Shaun Chambers to undertake the forensic audit of Vinnie's books. Mick was surprised that the DI had agreed to it but accepted that in the absence of an alternative resource, it was true that Shaun had a lot of skin in the game and an overwhelming cause to assist constructively.

After accepting Shaun's involvement, Mick wanted him to focus on building more links between Vinnie's business, the Satchins and the Anarchists. Eventually, Riley had persuaded Mick that finding Vinnie's boat was the best chance to track down Tony Fantis and Damien Hargreaves.

Although replaying the previous night's conversation in his mind, Riley's headache started to ease. With a jolt, he remembered the appointment with the magistrate scheduled for the morning. He looked at his watch – 8.15. He had just over an hour to get organised and to the Magistrates Court in Christies Beach. How did these old-time detectives do it?

He shaved and jumped into the shower, still bewildered by the ability of DI Smith and DS Martin to effectively investigate crime and organise for the justice processes while living the old-time lifestyle. As he left the bathroom, he heard his phone ringing. He bounded down the hall and grabbed it before it went to voicemail, nearly tripping over his towel.

'So, you live, Senior Sergeant O'Brien.' DS Martin sounded as bright as a magpie on a spring morning. 'On the assumption you are almost ready, I've asked your constable to pick me up in five minutes. We'll be there in ten to pick you up. That should get us to Christies Beach just in time.'

Riley ended the call and hastily dressed, exiting the front door just as Phil Reid rounded the corner in the patrol car.

'You're looking a little dusty, Sir,' Phil called to him through his open window. Riley simply waved.

Mick Martin leant across. 'I hope you don't mind. I don't think either of us should be driving this morning and the constable here was at a loose end, so ... here we are.'

Although he was annoyed at allowing himself to be in this position, Riley was also privately thankful that the arrangement had been made.

***

The hearing with the magistrate had gone as expected. A subdued Graham Cole listened as the charges were read.

The police were only required to explain the charges to the court and to provide reasons why they opposed bail, should it be sought. Those reasons were that the charges were serious; that investigations were still ongoing into the vicious assault of a police officer, in which Graham Cole was possibly implicated; that they believed that he presented a flight risk; and, finally that he was at risk of harm or influence from the outlawed Anarchist motorcycle gang.

The defendant's lawyer was an elderly, balding man who based his practice in Christies Beach. He had met with his client only an hour before the hearing and it was clear that his role was solely to apply the instructions that his client had given him; those instructions were simple - not to seek bail and to ensure that wherever he was to be remanded, Graham was provided the best security available to keep him safe from other inmates.

Mr Wilkinson, the magistrate, required less than ten minutes to rule. He committed Graham Cole for trial on the charges in mid-June and determined that he be remanded in custody at the Adelaide Remand Centre until that date. As to the security arrangements, he commented that these were the responsibility of the custodial authorities and that, while he would pass on the concerns of the defendant to those authorities, he would not be providing any direction to them.

With that, it was done and Graham Cole shuffled out of the courtroom, head down and shoulders hunched.

***

The police station was abuzz when they returned. Cassie and Rachel were hunched over the desk where Shaun and Oliver were working. They were poring over a list of transactions that Shaun had printed.

'Hey, boss,' called Rachel, 'you need to come and look at this.'

'Have you found Vinnie's boat, Shaun?'

'Not yet. I found nothing in the business books, so I thought I'd try his personal bank account. No boat but there is something of interest.'

Riley and Mick joined the group as Shaun pointed at the list of transactions.

'Look at this. There have been regular payments each month. They seem to be the same amount for a while and then now and again the standard amount increases. The payments were being made every month for at least three years and then about three months ago, they stopped.'

Riley stood waiting for more information but Mick was impatient.

'So, do we know who he has paid? It could be a loan payment of something.'

Shaun looked up at him excitedly.

'Well, that's the thing. The account number the payment goes to belongs to Louise Hargreaves.'

Riley looked at Mick. 'Damien Hargreaves' sister. Vinnie once told us that he'd had a fling with her. She was his half-sister.'

Mick burst into laughter. 'What the fuck? Are you joking? No, you're not, are you?' He saw the serious look on Riley's face. 'Then, why is he paying her money?'

'It's a long story, Mick and I'll tell you the whole thing some other time. The thing is that Vinnie told us that he was worried that if he told his "other" family he'd had sex with their sister, his half-sister, they would kill him. We thought he was kidding, but who knows?'

'You think this was hush money? So that Louise wouldn't spill the beans?'

Shaun chimed in. 'I reckon it's more likely she got pregnant to him at the time and the payments are for child support.'

'That makes some sense. In any event, Vinnie wouldn't have wanted Damien to find out,' Riley said. 'I think we need to go and have a talk to Louise. So, no success with the boat, Shaun?'

'No. We got sidetracked with this little development. I still have a heap more transactions to go through so there's still a chance it will show up.'

31

Friday April 26 2019 (Day 9)

The sun shone brightly as Riley eased the patrol car out of the station car park. With the onset of the Wooden Boat Festival, there was increased activity in the town and the drive down the main street was painstakingly slow. It reminded Riley that he had paid little regard to the police requirement for the festival, having left the arrangements in the capable hands of Phil Reid; at least, he hoped they were capable. He turned to Mick Martin.

'Mick, do you mind if we drop by the wharf? I just want to get a sense of where we are at for this weekend?'

'No worries at all, mate. Let's see what all the fuss is about. Hey, are we going to see any of those Halvorsen boats down here today? I'd like to see what we're looking for.'

They reached the entry point to the wharf area and found Phil talking with one of the organisers. Riley wound down his window.

'How's it all going, Phil? Under control?'

'Yes, sir,' Phil replied with an appropriately formal tone. "We're just going over the final arrangements one more time. Are you here to have a look around? It's pretty busy down there.'

'Yeah. We just want to have a quick look at some of the wooden boats quickly.'

Phil quickly caught on exactly which wooden boats Riley was referring to and pointed to an area to the side of the main wharf. Riley nodded his thanks and drove on.

They pulled up adjacent to the gin distillery building and walked down to the waterfront. A sign labelled moorings as "Hector's Jetty", named after the old man of the lake. Behind them, they could hear the sounds of business; marquees being erected, trucks arriving and unloading their goods and a plethora of food vans setting up. The town's mayor strolled past and gave Riley a polite wave.

Riley and Mick walked onto Hector's Jetty. People were scurrying along the various fingers of the jetty, ferrying supplies onto their boats for the weekend. Antipasto plates and wine would be the fare for the boat owners and their friends as they watched an endless stream of onlookers meander past their craft. The calm that the onlookers would see belied the flurry of activity that was taking place in preparation for the next two days.

Passing a few smaller craft, the two policemen came upon a row of bigger boats, designed for life on the river. These were the Halvorsens that they were looking for.

'So, this is them,' Mick said.

'Well, we think this is what we're looking for. If Emma's description was correct.'

A boat owner waved to the two men. 'Would you like to have a look on board, gentlemen?' The man was clearly proud of his boat and keen to show it off.

Riley and Mick stepped aboard. The boat had been lovingly restored with polished teak and chrome sparkling on the aft deck and into the cabin. Cushioned bench seats nestled around a table on the deck where the owner sat, enjoying his first beer of the day.

'Would you care for one, officers? Or are you on duty and I shouldn't ask?'

'No, we're good thanks, mate.' Mick motioned to the cabin interior. 'Mind if we have a gander inside?'

'Knock yourself out,' the man replied with a tip of his bottle.

The inside was compact but comfortable, featuring a tiny, but functional kitchenette, a toilet and a bed positioned in a 'v' shape at the front end.

'Not a lot of space in here for storage,' Mick said to Riley, who was also trying to establish how a boat like this would be used for hiding drugs and cash.

'Well, mate,' said the owner, 'this is just a twenty-one-footer. The bigger the boat the more storage you get. A thirty-footer will give you maybe three times as much. But this little baby, she'll do me; only eleven of these built, you know. I couldn't afford a bigger one anyway.'

'So, how much are we talking for one of these?' Riley asked.

'Oh, depends on the condition and the size. But this one's probably worth forty-five to fifty thousand. A big one of the same style that's in mint condition could be two or three hundred thousand. Out of my league.'

They left the man to his boat, his beer and his nirvana, and walked back to the car.

Finding Louise Hargreaves' address had been simple. She still lived under her birth name and was one of the ever-decreasing number of people who had retained a landline. The White Pages revealed that she now lived in Victor Harbor and a quick phone call had ensured that she would be home for the afternoon.

Driving through the township of Middleton, Martin's phone rang. He looked at it and mouthed 'Kathy Smith' to Riley as he answered. The call was brief and the detective sergeant let out a long, deep breath as he disconnected.

'I don't know how much of that you heard, Riley, but Paul Smith has regained consciousness. He's going to be ok. Looks like he's got a lot of rehab to go through but he will be all right.'

'That's great news.'

'It is, but the DI would still be pretty pissed. Apparently, the doctors have told him he should be desk-bound for the rest of his career; the risk of a compounding injury if he went back into the field is too high. What's worse is that Kathy's saying she wants him to retire now.'

'I can't imagine he would take well to that. Maybe, he should be counting his blessings and settle into an easier life.'

Martin roared with laughter. 'The day Paul Smith willingly leaves the force forever will be the day that Elvis Presley announces his come-back tour.'

They pulled up outside Louise's house in a tidy street in the Victor Harbor suburb of Hayborough. A small tree supported by two stakes sat in a dry, brown grass area on the verge. Looking south, the ocean was visible and Riley could imagine the winds that would tear up the hill and bend young trees away from the sea. The front yard was also in desperate need of water, small patches of green punctuating otherwise bare earth. A gravel driveway led down the side of the dwelling, a flat-roofed, cream brick house with white tatty curtains pulled across the front windows.

Riley knocked on the front door and was greeted by a woman who looked to be around forty years old. She had dark hair pulled back into an untidy ponytail, strands falling across her forehead and cheeks. She was thin-framed but Riley's first impression was that it was not the result of a healthy diet or attention to fitness, but rather from a life battling to make ends meet. He tried to visualise her as a young woman; a time when Vinnie would have been with her and left her with child. Removing the crows' feet around her eyes and the dark lines around her mouth, adding a few kilograms and fixing her hair, he could see that Louise was once attractive in appearance – and that was all Vinnie would have been concerned about.

He was conscious that he had been standing at the door looking at her without talking and Louise's voice jolted him back to attention.

'You're the coppers, are you?' She realised that she had stated the obvious, Riley's uniform the biggest clue. 'Yeah, of course you are. You'd better come in, then.'

Inside, the house was furnished sparsely but was neat and clean. Louise waved them to a sofa that was old but still in good condition. She sat on a footstool next to the television.

'Are you here about, Damien? He's a fucking idiot, that brother of mine.'

'How did you know we were interested in Damien?' Mick leaned forward as he spoke to her.

'Do you think I'm stupid? I know you raided his place in Yank. What's he done now?'

'Have you seen him lately?'

'Not for weeks. We don't get on that well.'

'Why is that?'

Louise let out an exasperated sigh.

'I told you, he's a fucking idiot. There must be some reason you're on his arse and I bet it's something to do with that bikie gang he's mixed up with. What is it, drugs?'

'That's the start of it,' Riley said. "What do you know about Tony Fantis?'

She laughed. 'That fucking gorilla. I won't have him in my house. Damien neither if he's with him.'

'So, you know that Damien is involved with the drug trade?'

'Nah, I don't know. But I have my suspicions, right? I got a boy, Loklan, and I don't want him gettin' involved with shit like Damien and Tony. The kid's got enough to deal with without those two having their tuppence worth.'

Riley looked across to Mick who nodded.

'Loklan's father, Louise, is he in his life?'

'Not any more. He was another piece of shit. Lokkie's an adult now. As soon as he turned eighteen, his father didn't want anything more to do with him. The child support turned off straight away.'

'So,' said Riley, 'can you tell us who the father is?'

'I reckon you already know.' Louise smirked at them both before taking a cigarette from a packet and lighting it. 'The father was Vinnie Waters and good riddance to him, I say. He never gave his son anything he didn't have to by law. Now he's stopped payments for Lokkie, I couldn't care less that he's dead.'

'What about Lokkie?' Mick asked.

'What about him? He doesn't care. He hardly even knew the man.'

'Why do you think Vinnie didn't want anything to do with you and Loklan?'

Louise shrugged and exhaled a lungful of smoke.

'Because he's a shit. I didn't care at first, I didn't want anything from him. Lokkie was the result of a one-night stand and Vinnie moved on; eventually married Debbie McLean. When I fell on hard times, I decided the least Vinnie could do was to pay towards the keeping of his kid. He didn't like it much, but stiff shit.'

'Why do you think he was upset? He's a wealthy man and could afford the payments.'

'Yeah, but I have to admit my timing was a bit off. It was just after he lost his kid in that accident. I think he was still dealing with that when I came along looking for money. But, hey, the fact that he had his own personal tragedy wasn't my problem, was it?'

This was getting into new territory for Riley. He knew about the death of Vinnie's son, of course, but it now seemed like there was a bigger story to be told.

'Louise, tell us what happened next. Obviously, Vinnie started making payments to you.'

'Yeah, he had to. I'd threatened to take him to court. That didn't ruffle him but then I said I'd tell Debbie. That got him off his arse, but she found out anyway.'

'How?'

'Dunno. Maybe she went through his bank statements or something. Anyway, the shit really hit the fan then.'

Mick had stood and walked to the window. He was looking out vacantly but turned around sharply.

'What do you mean?'

Louise laughed. 'Well, when she found out she was hysterical, on top of the kid's death and all. It spooked Vinnie so much he bought her a boat to try and get back in her good books.'

'A boat?' Mick asked.

'Yeah, some fancy thing. Imagine that! The prick complains about paying a pittance for his own son and then forks out a fortune to keep his missus happy. What an arsehole.'

'What do you know about the boat?'

Louise looked perplexed. 'What the fuck do you care about the boat? I don't know anything about it, just that Vinnie said he had to do it to save his marriage.' She laughed. 'Didn't help the silly prick anyway. Deb had a breakdown and pissed off.'

'Do you know where she is now?'

'Nah, couldn't care less. Last I heard she was in Mount Barker. Probably happy to be rid of Vinnie fucking Waters too.'

Mick asked, 'are you seeing anyone now, Louise?'

'Only the Yellow Pages, mate.'

Mick frowned. 'Yellow Pages?'

'Yeah, I let my fingers do the walking.' Louise burst into hysterical laughter until a coughing fit possessed her.

She was red-faced and gasping as Mick headed toward the door. Riley stood.

'Did Damien find out that Loklan was Vinnie's son?'

'Yeah, he's known for years but he couldn't give a shit. Why?'

Mick replied. 'Well, we think Vinnie and Damien were in a business relationship and we wondered how that might have affected it.'

'No idea,' Louise said, stubbing her cigarette into the ashtray.

'Sorry, one more question, Louise,' Mick said as he turned at the door, 'Do you know who Vinnie's father was?'

'No. Didn't he live with his sister and her hubby, Colin wasn't it?'

'He did but his sister was actually his mother, did you know that?'

'Nup, so what?'

'Well, it turns out his biological dad wasn't Colin. His father was a bloke called Wayne Hargreaves.'

The look on Louise's face told them that she hadn't known. The implications were sinking into her as she closed the door behind them.

Back in the car, the police officers were silent until they reached the main road.

'What did you make of that?' Mick asked.

Riley didn't answer immediately. He was still processing the implications of what Louise had told them ... and not told them.

'Well, for starters, I don't think Louise was aware that Vinnie was her half-brother. Whether Damien Hargreaves knew isn't any clearer but based on what Louise said, I don't think it mattered. Maybe it didn't make any difference that he knew Vinnie was Loklan's father either. Was it a motive for him to kill Vinnie; who knows? I still think it was drug-related, especially when connected with the Satchin murders.'

'Agree. How about this? Louise had no love for Vinnie and clearly resented that he shared his wealth with his wife but didn't look after her and Loklan. Could she have had a motive to do him in or at least help? Don't forget the small hand-prints at the shed.'

Riley pondered for a moment.

'No, I don't buy that. Remember, we have Tony Fantis' prints at the boatshed. It makes sense that Damien was there too and he wouldn't be any bigger than Louise, the little weasel. One thing, at least. We do have further confirmation that the boat exists, or at least existed. Oh shit, Mick, that's why we haven't been able to find the boat registered in Vinnie's name. I bet he put it in Debbie's name.'

Mick pulled his phone from his coat pocket and punched in the number for Cassie Callaghan.

'Cassie, tell Shaun and Oliver to look for a boat registered in the name of Debbie Waters or Debbie McLean. Look under Deborah as well.'

Disconnecting, he turned to Riley. 'So, Debbie doesn't know about Vinnie's death, yet; is that right?'

'Yes. We haven't been able to track her down. After her breakdown, she spent a long time in a mental health facility. Vinnie divorced her before she even got well again and, as far as I know, they haven't been in contact again. If we had found her, she could have put us on the right track with the boat straight away.'

They arrived back at the station as the evening shadows started to envelop the town. Phil Reid stood at the front counter, wolfing down a slice of pizza.

'Early dinner tonight, Reid?' Mick asked as he patted him on the shoulder. Riley couldn't help but imagine it was Paul Smith talking. Smith and Martin were two peas from the same pod, alright.

'Err, yes sir. No time for lunch today,' Phil replied, turning crimson.

They entered to find the team sharing the rest of the pizza at one of the spare desks. Shaun Chambers and Oliver Townsend were looking over a list of transactions on a printout.

'The boys have found the boat,' Cassie announced proudly.

Oliver glanced over.

'Yep, it's a thirty-foot Halvorsen that Vinnie bought in 2015. And registered under the name of Deborah Waters. Here are the rego details.' He handed over a slip of paper.

'Ok,' said Riley, 'we have the registration number and description of the boat. Now, we just have to find it.'

'That's what we're onto now,' Shaun called across. 'He must have stored the boat somewhere but it wasn't in his boatshed. I've driven past plenty of times and never seen a boat that size berthed there on a regular basis. So, we're going through Vinnie's personal records looking for payments to a marina for berthing fees.'

'Good, keep on it.'

'Riley, come on!' Shaun spat with a hint of venom. 'Do you think I need any encouragement to look for this boat? My son could be on board if you remember.'

Riley stepped across and laid a hand on his old friend's shoulder.

'Sorry, mate. I didn't mean to suggest you weren't doing your most. I appreciate all you're doing and I understand how hard it's been for you and Carla.'

'Do you? Oh, sorry. Just forget it, alright. I'm tired, I'm stressed and I just want my boy back. Let me get on with this.'

Riley left Shaun and Oliver to it and called Cassie and Rachel into a meeting room to de-brief on their discussion with Louise before calling it a day. Shaun and Oliver were still busy comparing payment transactions as they left.

Mick Martin and Cassie crossed the road to their motel. Riley was grateful that he didn't have to follow up the previous night's effort and drove home feeling exhausted. He sat on the couch looking vacantly at the television while Kate prepared their dinner. She returned with two plates in her hand.

'You ok to eat in front of the telly tonight, Riley?'

Riley didn't answer. She turned and put their plates in the oven. She'd wake him a bit later on.

32

2018

Carla sat at the vanity unit, doing her make-up with more care than she had for years. Strokes of mascara and brushes of contour were applied as if she was an artist, a studying glance after each to ensure there was enough but not too much. This was her first night out alone in years.

Motherhood had already constrained her social life and, when a baby-sitter was available, her nights out were almost always a hastily grabbed dinner or a movie with Shaun. She hadn't been out with her girlfriends since Debbie had left. At first, she couldn't bear the idea of going out and having fun when she knew what Debbie was going through. After, it just seemed too hard to organise.

It had got her down. Sometimes, she felt like she was the only person who realised that Debbie was gone. Debbie's family, like hers, had moved to Adelaide and her friends had all adjusted. As for Vinnie, he had grieved for a few months but even he eventually moved on, returning to a bachelor's life, seemingly having forgotten he ever had a wife; or a son. Even Debbie had moved on, refusing visitors and on her release from hospital, breaking all contact with her previous world.

It was Shaun who convinced her to go out with the girls. He had bought tickets to a fundraiser but was now unable to go due to the pressures of work. He insisted she take one of her friends, Rebecca, in his place; many of her other friends would be there too.

To her surprise, she felt liberated. From motherhood, from marriage, from Debbie. She wasn't unhappy with her life but tonight she was single.

Dancing and alcohol were the keys that unlocked the chains that had bound her. She flicked her hair as she gyrated on the dance floor and laughed continually. At the end of a particularly energetic song, she returned to her table and downed a glass of sparkling wine. *God, it was going down well.*

She went back on the dance floor and started swaying to a slower piece. Lost in a mesmerising trance, she felt calm and at peace with everything.

'You look like you're having a fun night, Carla.'

The spell broken, she spun around, arms still waving, eyes still closed. She dropped her hands and opened her eyes. Vinnie smiled at her.

'Vinnie, I, er ... yeah, I guess I am.'

'I haven't seen you dance like that since we were teenagers.'

'Well, a lot's changed since then, Vinnie.' She felt her lightness falling away, Instead, in front of her was a reminder of the friend she missed so desperately.

'Come, sit down for a bit. I feel like we have a lot to catch up on.'

Vinnie led Carla to a couch in a corner of the room. Away from the output of the speakers, it was quiet enough to talk without yelling. At first, Carla was angry. She hadn't wanted to be taken from her escape and certainly not by a man she felt was largely responsible for her despair.

As time went by, she found herself sharing her feelings with Vinnie. That she missed Debbie, the good times they shared and, God, she missed being single. Talking to Vinnie was surprisingly and alarmingly easy. She was aware that she needed to release her feelings but why with him? Vinnie, who'd always been cocksure, narcissistic and arrogant. Yet, now she saw vulnerability. He'd been hurt by Debbie's absence, just as she had. He explained how she'd refused to see him, leaving him no choice in the end but to dissolve the marriage. She saw that he'd had no choice but to move on, something she'd not been able to do. She also saw that if she was to move on, she had to be like Vinnie. She had to force herself to get back to her happy, outgoing self. More nights like tonight.

Before she realised, the music stopped and the room was almost empty. She'd been talking with Vinnie for ages and had been completely absorbed in sharing all her frustrations with him ... and hearing his. Tonight, they were soul mates.

'Can I give you a ride home, Carla? It might be hard to get a taxi for a while.'

'Thanks, Vinnie. I'd like that.'

Vinnie opened the door of his Land Rover for Carla. He headed down Beach Road toward Carla and Shaun's house. Before turning onto Underwood Avenue, Carla put a hand on Vinnie's knee and whispered.

'Keep going.'

Vinnie pulled the car into the beach car park and cut the engine. It was a cold, moonless night and they were alone. He turned to look at her. She pulled his face to hers and kissed him long and hard.

Fifteen minutes later, the engine kicked over and Vinnie drove back along Beach Road, this time turning left onto Underwood Avenue.

Carla crept into the house, checking on Aiden before taking off her shoes and moving silently into her bedroom. Shaun was sleeping soundly. She went into the ensuite and started removing her makeup. She splashed her face with cold water and looked into the mirror, instantly realising the enormity of what she had done. *What was I thinking? What the fuck have I done? Oh, Christ.*

She wept for ten minutes before quietly lifting the sheet and slipping next to Shaun. It took an hour before sleep caught her.

Carla woke in the morning to the sound of the television playing downstairs. She walked down to find Shaun cooking toast for Aiden.

'Ah, here she is. Good night?' It hurt her that Shaun was so nice.

She waited until Shaun had passed Aiden his toast, spread with butter and vegemite.

'Can you come upstairs for a minute? We need to talk.'

Bemused, Shaun followed her.

That afternoon, Shaun packed a bag and moved into the Goolwa Motel. Over the coming days, he tried to find a way to forgive Carla. He knew he still loved her, the mother of his son. But, Vinnie! He could not comprehend how it was possible. Worse, he knew that Carla had been discontented and he feared that she could not evade the temptation of escaping the stable, secure, predictable, humdrum life that he offered her.

He avoided her, even when he picked Aiden up. He rented a house in Brooking Street. It was a dump but he hoped it was temporary. He hoped he could reconcile with Carla and they could return to their previous happiness. But the doubt was too great.

It was in the office one afternoon a couple of months later when he heard the most disturbing news. Walking past the staff kitchen, he'd over-heard two of his employees chatting furtively. They had both blushed as he entered and his heart sank knowing that it involved him.

'What's up?' he asked apprehensively.

Their hesitancy alarmed him and he blurted in a tone harsher than he intended, 'If you have something to share, say it. Otherwise, maybe save it for outside the workplace.'

'I'm sorry, Shaun.' Heather was a few years older than Shaun and not usually given to gossip. 'We just didn't want things to be awkward for you. We thought if we all knew, we could be conscious of how you're feeling.'

'Knew what?' he demanded. The women looked at each other.

'Oh, God. You don't know.' Heather lifted her hands to her face.' I'm so sorry, Shaun, but I feel like now we have to be the ones to tell you. Carla is seeing Vinnie Waters.'

Shaun stormed out of the kitchen and returned to his office, slamming the door on the way in. He grabbed his mobile and called Carla's number.

She answered and confirmed what Heather had told him.

Carla found it hard to explain. She felt enormous guilt over what she had done to Shaun but the first person to call her and offer support had been Vinnie. He'd been wonderful; listening and comforting her in the dark days after Shaun left. He continued to show his own vulnerability as he helped her.

Of course, she'd heard the stories about Vinnie and his work ethics but she was convinced that he was mostly misunderstood and that the rumours were from malicious people who envied his success. The latest story was that he'd turfed Chad from the house he rented from Vinnie without giving him any notice. She couldn't believe that Vinnie would be so callous as to make a disabled person homeless so she asked him about it. His explanation was simple.

'Carla, I can see why people might think it was harsh, but the truth is a bit different to how it's being put out there. The thing is that Chad's lease was coming to an end. I told him I wanted to refurbish the house but he chose not to look for something else. I've got builders booked for next week, so what am I supposed to do?'

She saw his point.

33

Saturday April 27 2019 (Day 10)

Riley woke to a fresh, sunny morning. He would leave Kate to sleep in this morning. They'd not spent much time together since the murder of Vinnie Waters but he promised himself he would make it up to her as soon as he could. He hadn't been much company the night before and despite all that was on his mind, he'd slept soundly. Kate had left him to sleep on the couch for a couple of hours before rousing him for dinner. He'd gone to bed early so that he would be re-invigorated for what might unfold over the weekend.

As he got out of bed, he felt fully charged. He slipped on his running clothes and headed out the front door just as dawn was breaking. He decided to run along the river to the wharf so that he could check on the Wooden Boat Festival preparations. Not that he expected to see too many people at this time of day but he was sure he could get a sense of how prepared they were.

A smoky mist hung over the river. Dew on the grass sparkled in the morning sun. One of those days it felt good to be there right at the start. The moisture that enveloped him cooled him as he ran. Birdsong filled the air as the gravel underfoot crunched with each step, his percussion accompanying the avian orchestra.

His musings on the artistic interpretation of a morning jog were broken by the sudden shrill of his phone. He stopped in the middle of an intersection and fished his phone from his pocket.

'Shaun, you're up early,' he muttered.

'Don't tell me you're not up, Riley, even if it is Saturday. I just wanted to give you an update on what we found last night. Or rather, what we didn't find.' The flatness in Shaun's voice was unmissable.

'Ok, let's have it.' Riley started walking as he talked, keen not to cool down.

'Well, Oliver and I were going over Vinnie's books until the early hours this morning. We've been over his bank statements for the boatshed and his personal statements as well. We've even gone over those for the café businesses. We found not one payment to a marina or any other boat yard for berthing fees. There have been irregular payments for parts and even for labour on occasion but nothing for berthing. The only thing I am wondering is whether he kept the boat at a mate's jetty, maybe even over on Hindmarsh Island.'

'I suppose that's possible, but I have the feeling that if this boat is what he's using as his secret storage location for drugs, money or anything else, then he'd want to keep it well away from his acquaintances, especially the criminal ones.'

Shaun sighed into the phone. 'I'm not sure where to go next, although there is one thing that is bothering me.'

'Oh yeah, what's that?'

'On the last Friday of every month, as far back as I can go, Vinnie drew the same amount out of his bank, in cash from an ATM on the main street. I ask myself why. His maintenance payments to Louise are shown on the bank statement, so it's not them. It's possible it's his spending money but wouldn't you do that weekly rather than monthly? It just seems odd, but I can't say why.'

'I agree that it seems peculiar. There could be a simple explanation, but maybe not. We shouldn't ignore it. Listen, how much was he withdrawing? Could he have been paying the berthing fees in cash? If he was trying to keep the boat in the background, he may have been taking that extra precaution.'

Shaun paused for a moment, contemplating the feasibility of Riley's suggestion.

'I guess the amount that he was drawing out, a touch over three hundred dollars a month, would be something like what you'd pay for a berth but I don't really know. You know what I am wondering now?'

'What's that?'

'You still have Vinnie's phone, right?'

Riley wondered where this was going and stopped walking. He got the sense that Shaun was onto something that could escalate quickly.

'Of course. Why?'

'Well, we now suspect that Vinnie had a pattern of movement after he went to the ATM on those Fridays. Google Maps has a function where you can review your movements going back over time, as long as you have your phone with you and you have location services switched on. I doubt that Vinnie would have been tech-savvy enough to have disabled that function so, with any luck, we might see where Vinnie's been going and, with a bit more luck, it might be a boat marina with a Halvorsen boat called *Jeremy*.'

Riley was running again now, toward his house.

'Shaun, can you meet me at the station in fifteen minutes? Let's see if this has legs.'

While his run wasn't as far as he'd intended, the pace at which he ran compensated. He burst through the front door, allowing the screen door to slam shut behind him. He cursed silently as he realised Kate was still asleep. He peeked through the door and, seeing her unmoved, he headed to the bathroom.

Ten minutes later, he was driving to the station. Before he started the car, he'd called Mick Martin and briefed him. He left it to Mick to get Cassie mobilised and then put in a call to Rachel.

He was pleased to see Shaun waiting at the front door of the station, which wasn't open yet. Riley signalled to Shaun to meet him around the back in the car park. They entered the station and headed straight to the evidence safe.

Riley extracted Vinnie's phone, which had already been forensically cleared so he didn't need to worry about gloves. He pressed the power button but the screen remained blank.

'Damn, the battery's dead. I wonder if we have a spare Samsung charger somewhere here.'

'Bottom drawer in that desk over there, Sergeant.' Phil Reid's head appeared around the corner. 'I just dropped in on the way to the festival. You two are in here early.'

'Phil, you are a legend, mate. Yes, we're just following up on a lead. We might need to call on you a bit later if you can get free from your duties down on the wharf.'

'Shouldn't be a problem, all going well. We have enough blokes coming up from the city to look after that.'

Phil left as Riley plugged the charger into the phone and the electricity socket. He and Shaun were still waiting for the phone to charge when Mick and Cassie burst into the station. Rachel followed seconds later, still pulling her ponytail into an elastic band behind her head.

'Let's hope this isn't a wild goose chase,' Riley said, as they all made themselves comfortable.

Suddenly, the screen came to life. Riley picked up the phone and handed it to Shaun without unplugging it.

'Password?' he asked.

'Let's try the same as his computer.' Shaun grinned as the home screen came to life.

'Let's see.' He opened up Google Maps and pressed the "Saved" icon. Halfway down the screen was a blue link, "Explore Timeline".

'Ok,' Shaun continued, 'what was the date on the last Friday of March?'

Rachel raced to a calendar posted on the wall and called back, 'the twenty-ninth.'

Shaun flicked back through the days until he got to the right date. He studied the map and read the timeline showing the times that Vinnie had been to various places on that day. He double-checked before turning to the group.

'He went straight back to the boatshed after the ATM, then the pub, then home. He didn't go to any marina. Fuck!'

Riley put an arm on his shoulder.

'Let's not give up yet, mate. Maybe he took the money out on Friday but paid it on the weekend. Check Saturday, to be sure.'

Shaun flicked the screen across to Saturday the thirtieth. He looked up at Riley and then around the room.

'It's here,' he whispered hoarsely, 'it's bloody here. At ten o'clock, Vinnie went to Riverside Marina up on Barrage Road. Let me check the month before.'

Five minutes later, they had checked the previous four months and, on the Saturday following the last Friday in each month, Vinnie had gone to the Riverside Marina.

'Does anyone know who runs this show?' Mick asked. He was met by blank faces. 'Ok, let's get down there, then.'

'Do we need a search warrant?' Cassie asked.

It was Riley who responded.

'Let's see what we find first. If the boat is there but there's no activity, we will undertake surveillance while we get a search warrant. If it's there and we sense that someone is in danger, like Aiden, we won't need a search warrant to board it. If it's not there, well, that would be a bummer.'

They left in two cars and drove through town and out toward the barrages. A few hundred metres before the barrier that stretched across the river, they turned onto a dirt track leading down to the river. Cut into the bank was a small marina that comprised about a dozen berths.

'You would hardly know this place was here,' Mick exclaimed, waving at the reeds that stretched to the height of the car. 'This is your territory. I think you should manage the operation,' he nodded to Riley.

They pulled up a short distance from the water's edge and the occupants of the two cars gathered. In front of them lay the marina to the left and a small prefabricated building set back to the right.

'Mick and Rachel, can you go around the back of the building, just in case we have someone make a break for it? Cassie, you come with me. We're going straight down the guts. Shaun, you'll have to stay here, mate, but if we find Aiden, I guarantee you'll be the first to know.'

The teams dispersed, walking calmly in the two directions Riley had specified. Shaun leant against one of the cars, peering nervously toward the marina.

The four police officers reunited at the far end of the building in front of the marina.

'It's not here, is it?' Riley took off his cap and wiped his brow. He wasn't sure if his sweat was due to the anticipation of the major breakthrough they had been looking for or the unseasonably warm April day.

'No, it's not, boss,' said Rachel. 'Where to from here?'

'Excuse me. Can I help you?' The voice came from a man stepping out of the prefabricated building. He was a big man, overweight and sweating profusely. He wore a red check flannelette shirt which no doubt contributed to his perspiration, baggy blue jeans and a baseball cap emblazoned with the logo of the Chicago Bulls. By the time he reached the police officers, he was breathing heavily.

'Can I help you, officers?' he repeated.

'Yes,' Riley stepped forward. 'We're looking for a boat that we believe was moored here. A Halvorsen.' Riley pulled out his notepad and read the registration number.

'Yeah, well there's only one Halvorsen kept here. The *Jeremy*.'

'Vinnie Waters' boat?'

'That's the one. But she's not here now.'

'We gathered that, Einstein,' said Mick Martin, deflating the man. 'When did it leave?'

'Must've been last night or this morning. I only got here meself half hour ago and she was gone then but I know she was there yesterdee.'

'Do you know who took the boat out?'

'Nah. Probably one of those two blokes who boarded her yesterdee afternoon. Or it could've been the woman.'

'What woman?' Riley asked sharply.

The man looked at Mick smugly. 'You didn't know about the woman. Who's the Einstein now, genius?'

'Just answer the question, please?' Riley was firm but polite.

'She came on board 'bout a week ago. I asked her what she was doin' getting' on Vinnie's boat. She just waved a key at me and said she had permission. Who was I to question? She said she had to get her kid to bed so I just left her to it?'

'She had a child?'

'Yeah. Ten or eleven-year-old, I s'pose. He was asleep and she was struggling to carry him and open the door but she went in and closed the door and I haven't seen her since.'

'Do you know where they were taking the boat?'

'No idea, mate. I don't ask people them questions and, to be honest, them two blokes looked pretty nasty so I wasn't about to upset them.'

Riley turned to Cassie and Rachel.

'Stay with this gentleman and get all his particulars. Also, get detailed descriptions of the men and the child. We probably know who they are, but we don't know about the woman, so make sure you get as much on her as possible.' He turned to the man.

'Sir, we need to do this interview urgently and we will need you to come down to the station, say on Monday morning, to sign a statement. Your name is?'

'Billy, William that is. William Prince. Like Prince William but in reverse.' He laughed at his joke.

'Ok, thank you Mr. Prince. We appreciate your help.' Riley and Mick turned and strode back to a nervously waiting Shaun Chambers.

Shaun was beside himself.

'What happened? Where's the boat?'

Riley leaned against the car and waited for Shaun to join him.

'Ok, mate. The boat's not here. It was taken out yesterday; looks like Fantis and Hargreaves. More than likely Aiden is on board as well but we don't know whether he's in good shape or not.'

'The guy. Did he say how he looked?'

'He hasn't seen Aiden since he was taken on board by a woman. She must be an accomplice of Hargreaves. The witness says when she took Aiden aboard, he was asleep.' He rested his hand on Shaun's shoulder. 'The thing is though, Shaun, he may have looked asleep. In reality, he may have been unconscious, or worse.'

Shaun looked at him through widened, frightened eyes.

'We have to find the boat.'

'Yes, we do. C'mon, let's go.'

They jumped back into the patrol car, where Mick Martin was already waiting. He disconnected his phone call.

'Riley, I've teed up a chopper to help with the search. It should be here by early afternoon. How far do you think they could have got?'

'I'm no expert but let's say, worst case scenario, they travel at eight kilometres per hour without drawing attention to themselves for, say twelve hours. That's nearly a hundred kilometres in either direction. Shit, that's scary.'

Instead of turning back toward the town, Riley turned left from the dirt road.

'Where are we going?' Mick asked.

'Well, we can narrow it down a bit. If they've gone through the barrages, they'd be heading for the Coorong. I suspect that's unlikely because there's no way out; unless they get someone to meet them by land quite a bit further on. If they haven't gone through the barrage, it means they can only have gone away from the sea. Instead of a two-hundred-kilometre length of water, it will be only one hundred.'

'Only one hundred kilometres,' Shaun spat bitterly.

It took nearly an hour to contact all the barrage supervisors who had been on duty since the previous afternoon. They confirmed that no boat that matched the description of the *Jeremy* had gone through the barrages.

Effectively they had determined that the boat had headed inland, reducing the potential search area by half. Taking that direction, it was possible that they could have headed into one of the nearby tributaries such as Currency Creek or Finniss River. From there, or at various other points on the Murray River, the criminals could disembark and disappear by land transport.

34

Thursday 18 April 2019 (Day 1)

Carla poured boiling water into two mugs. Aiden sat at the table eating his breakfast.

'Did Vinnie stay over last night, Mum?' Aiden didn't mind that Vinnie slept at their house a couple of nights every week. He would rather his dad was still home but Vinnie was good to him and spoiled him. Just last week he'd turned up with a PlayStation and a selection of games. They'd played until late, so late that his mum got cranky with both of them.

'Yes, love. He's going to drop you at school this morning and he'll bring you home tonight. But Dad will pick you up from school, ok?'

'Whatever.'

Vinnie waltzed down the stairs and ruffled Aiden's hair as he walked past him. His phone rang and he looked at it quizzically before walking through the front door.

'Gotta take this,' he called over his shoulder to Carla, 'I'll be back in a minute.' The call was via an app called Chatterley. The only person who called him on Chatterley was his contact in the Anarchists motorcycle gang. The only time they called was if something was wrong or they wanted something that was hard to deliver.

'Vincent, good to see you're up and about early. Are you in Goolwa today?'

'Yes, Damien. All day. What's up?'

'We need to talk. This afternoon. 4.30 or thereabouts.'

Vinnie wasn't surprised by the short notice. The Anarchists expected 24/7 availability and it was worth his while to give it.

'Can you give me a heads-up? What are we talking about?'

'Check the news. There have been developments in Loxton.' The call was terminated.

Vinnie brought up his news app on his phone. His blood ran cold as he read the headline for the lead article.

"LOXTON COUPLE EXECUTED IN DRUG WAR"

Reading on, he saw that his supplier in Loxton, Greg Satchin, and his wife had been killed execution-style overnight. Their teenage daughter was missing. He remembered the girl as a lively, even feisty, kid. The article speculated that the couple had been killed because of their involvement in drug distribution but it was unclear who was responsible and why. A spokesman for Police was reported as saying that a major investigation was now underway to find the killers and to break open the drug operation based in Loxton.

For Vinnie, it meant bad news. Firstly, he wondered who had killed the Satchins. It could have even been the Anarchists if Greg had fallen foul of them and, if that was the case, was he next on their hit list? Why else did they want to meet with him today? Even if he wasn't in danger from them, his supplier had been taken out. That meant he had no product to distribute which would cause him issues with his dealers and users. It left it wide open for a competitor to come into town.

He walked inside and found Carla loading the dishwasher.

'You want some breakfast, Vinnie?'

'Nah, I have to go. Listen, can you change your plans this afternoon so Aiden doesn't have to come to the shed? I've had a meeting come up.'

'Oh, Vinnie. Remember I've got this specialist appointment I've been waiting months for. I can't cancel it now. I'll call Shaun and see if he can keep Aiden after school. I'm sure he won't mind.'

'Great, thanks. Alright, I have to go.' He called up the stairs. 'Aiden, come on. I haven't got all day.'

Carla shot him a look and he realised the call had disturbed him more than he thought. 'Sorry,' he said.

Vinnie was on edge all day. He questioned whether he should cut his losses and bolt; lose himself up north or overseas somewhere. Realistically, there was no way to escape the bikies; wherever he went, they'd track him down. He'd have to leave everything behind as well. His hidden cash, his business, even Carla.

He tried to convince himself he was worrying over nothing. All the same, he was glad he'd made other plans for Aiden. Meeting senior bikie members was not part of his plan for an eleven-year-old. He threw himself into work, fixing the keel on a Tartan yacht.

As the time got nearer to the expected arrival of Damien Hargreaves and, he expected, his henchman, Tony Fantis, he became more uneasy. He was sweating profusely, even though the day was cool. He heard the side door to the shed open. *Fuck, they're early.*

Instead of the bikies, however, it was Shaun and Aiden who had entered the shed.

'What are you doing here, Shaun? Didn't Carla ring you?'

'Yes, she did,' Shaun answered tersely. 'Didn't she let you know it didn't suit?'

Vinnie checked his phone and saw he'd had a voice message left by Carla earlier in the day that he had missed.

'Just tell me, Shaun. What's going on?'

'Carla said it wasn't convenient for you to look after Aiden, even though we'd planned it last week. Well, I can't either. I have a meeting with Council that I can't put off. Surely, you can let Aiden sit in your office for a while.'

'Nah, not a good idea. I ...'

'Yeah, you. It's always about you isn't it, Vinnie? You need to grow up and take some responsibility for your actions. You wanted Carla. You got her but you have to take all that comes with her, not just when it suits you. You work it out.'

Shaun gave Aiden a hug. 'See you later, buddy. Be good for Vinnie and keep out of his way, ok?'

After Shaun left, Vinnie led Aiden into the office on the side of the shed.

'Ok, mate. I have some really important people coming to see me. So, let's say I set up Minecraft on the computer and you can play that until they've gone. But, listen, keep the door shut until I let you know they've left and make sure you leave your headphones on. I don't want the sound of your game interfering with my meeting.'

He waited until Aiden was set up and engrossed in the game. Then he left the office, closing the door firmly behind him. He felt like everything was getting away from him.

35

Saturday April 27 2019 (Day 10)

The team arrived back at the station, confident that they now knew exactly what they were looking for – a thirty-foot Halvorsen named *Jeremy* with at least four people on board; two dangerous criminals, a mystery woman and a young boy whose condition was unknown.

A plan was hastily developed to attempt to box in the *Jeremy*, or at least to find where its occupants had disembarked. They arranged for the POLAIR helicopter to commence its search upriver, starting at Mannum and working downstream toward the mouth. Meanwhile, the team in Goolwa would commence searching by boat from the barrages travelling upstream, searching the marinas and tributaries as they went. Traffic alerts would be maintained along all points where people could have disembarked.

The river around Goolwa was chaotic as the Wooden Boat Festival got into full swing. There were boats everywhere in the vicinity of the wharf. Most were moored, their owners basking in the sunshine with cheese and wine as festival attendees streamed by. However, when a scheduled event began or finished, dozens of boats would move off their moorings into the middle of the river, then return at the end of the event. The last thing

Riley wanted was a confrontation with Damien Hargreaves and Tony Fantis in the midst of a crowd so he decided that they would keep their boats away from the wharf area until necessary. Instead, a ground crew in plain clothes would monitor boats in and around the festival, watching for the *Jeremy*.

It was mid-afternoon by the time the operation started. They received confirmation that the helicopter was in the air and two boats were borrowed, with skippers, from the Goolwa Aquatic Club. Shaun had begged Riley to allow him to be on board one of the boats. Reluctantly, and on strict instructions he was not to interfere with the operation, Riley agreed that Shaun could accompany Rachel, Cassie and Craig, while he, Mick and Phil would take the other boat. Oliver was to provide the shore-based observations and would brief the Adelaide-based officers there for the Wooden Boat Festival to look out for the *Jeremy*.

The skipper of Riley's boat was Duncan James, a long-time member of the GAC. Riley instructed him to start from the barrages and to work down the eastern side of the river, while the other boat took the western side. That meant that Duncan would have to work through all of the marina berths on Hindmarsh Island. By the time they had done that, Riley figured the other boat would have worked down past the festival activities and into Currency Creek.

Duncan maintained a steady pace, allowing his guests to scan the shores and particularly the reedy sections through their binoculars.

'There's a lot of places for them to hide along here, you realise, Riley?' Duncan was a no-nonsense boatie. He called a spade a spade and was both revered and feared by the younger generation. They relied on his knowledge and experience but knew he would give them a tongue-lashing if they stepped out of line, particularly where safety was concerned.

'Yeah, I know, Duncan, but I don't see what choice we have but to look. I don't know how experienced these guys are on the water either.'

'Well, it's a dangerous scenario if they don't know what they're doing especially with all the traffic on the river at the moment.'

Mick piped in. 'I've only ever been involved with one recovery from the river. When I was a young copper, a bloke fell out of his kayak in the middle of the night near the river mouth. We had to use an old local fisherman to find his body. It seemed like dangerous work.'

Riley looked blankly at Mick. *Surely, he wasn't there that morning.*

'Okay, nothing so far,' said Duncan. 'Let's head into the marina. Do you want to let the other boat know, Riley?'

Riley radioed and spoke to Cassie on the other boat. She waved as they weaved their way past the wharf traffic and toward the bridge that had replaced the ferry nearly twenty years earlier. The scars of the divisiveness caused by the bridge's construction had almost healed. Developers on the island and some residents had welcomed the bridge that reduced their crossing time by a few minutes most days and potentially hours during holidays. Others resented that the islandness had been taken away from them and that it had violated the secret women's business known only to the local Ngarrindjeri people.

The waterways of the Hindmarsh Island Marina complex were quieter and calmer than the mainstream river. The canals twisted and turned as they revealed new groups of houses, most with piers out front. Many of the piers were empty or had canoes, kayaks or other small watercraft stored on them. A number had boats of varying configurations berthed at them – jet boats, speedboats, yachts, river cruisers and dinghies.

The *Jeremy* would stand out. She would be larger than most and of course, she'd have her name adorned on the stern. It was painstaking work and Riley felt as though they would never finish. They came out of the marina and entered the river.

'Ok, we'll head upstream, Riley?'

'Yes, Duncan. Mick, can you check whether the shore team has seen anything?'

'I spoke with Oliver five minutes ago. They haven't seen anything but he says it's chocker block over there. Boats are double ranked at berths. He's not confident they have them all covered.'

'Ok, never mind. If they're over there, they won't be going far without someone seeing them. Look it's 5.15 now and it will be dark within half an hour. Let's get down as far as Currency Creek and meet up with the other boat.'

Riley confirmed with POLAIR that the helicopter hadn't made any sightings but that it was still working toward Goolwa. It was currently working its way around Lake Alexandrina and Lake Albert. The pilot anticipated reaching Goolwa at around 7.30, allowing for a re-fuel.

Shortly after 5.30, Duncan slowed the boat opposite the mouth of Currency Creek. The other boat was just exiting the creek and Duncan motored over next to it.

'Nothing this side, Riley,' Rachel called.

'No, it's getting too dark to continue. I'm just a bit worried about the Finniss River. If they've gone down there, they could come out at night and we'll miss them. There are also a few places where they could disembark.'

The Finniss River was just a few hundred metres along the main river, painstakingly close yet possibly out of reach for them.

The skipper from the other boat was Duncan's brother, Hamish, and he called across the water.

'Senior Sergeant, I have a floodlight on board so I can light the Finniss up like a Christmas tree if I want. Why don't we keep going so at least we can cross it off?'

It was Shaun, who'd been quiet so far, who called out next.

'For Christ's sake, let's do it. We can't stop now.'

'Ok, Hamish. I'm happy for you to continue but please, everyone, be careful. All we want to do is find the boat without creating havoc. If you do see it, don't try to apprehend them. Just move on, keep an eye on them and call for backup. We'll head back to the station and see where we go to next. Let us know when you're done.'

'Roger that.'

Riley and Mick watched as Hamish's boat sped toward the mouth of the Finniss. They saw the floodlight spread a beam across the river and both felt a small twinge that they weren't still actively in the hunt.

Duncan eased his boat in at the aquatic club to allow Riley, Mick and Phil to disembark.

'Thanks, Duncan,' Riley called. 'Mate, I don't want to mess you around, but is it possible for you to be on standby in case something comes up? Probably only for an hour or two. After that, we'll probably be done for the night.'

'No problems, Riley. I need to re-fuel but I'll be available whenever you need me.'

Phil drove them back to the station.

'Why don't I go grab us some takeaway for dinner?' he offered. 'Looks like we'll be here for a while and I'm famished.'

'Good idea, Constable,' Mick said. 'I get the impression that you're always hungry, young man.'

The team posted a map of the district on the wall and started highlighting the parts of the river and its tributaries that they had covered. They wanted to ensure that there were no hidden offshoots they could have missed. Knowing that the *Jeremy* had not passed through the barrages gave them confidence that they only had to search upstream from that point, but it was still a lot of river to cover.

Riley knew too, that while POLAIR was working downstream and they should trap the *Jeremy* between them, the area of Lakes Alexandrina and Albert was in excess of eight hundred square kilometres, far too much for one helicopter to cover thoroughly. On the positive side, if they knew the *Jeremy* wasn't downstream or upstream of the lakes, they had it isolated in that area, unless they disembarked.

Through headquarters they put out alerts around the perimeter of the lakes, hoping to learn as soon as possible if the *Jeremy* or its occupants were sighted.

It was after 7 pm when Cassie called to say that the second search boat had reached the end of the navigable part of the Finniss River. They hadn't sighted the *Jeremy* and were on their way back to Goolwa.

It was now 7.30 and the team needed rest before resuming early in the morning. Frustrated at narrowly missing the Anarchists again, Riley decided to let Duncan know that he could stand down for the night. About to make the call, he was distracted by the waving hand of Mick Martin.

'Riley, it's POLAIR. We have a possible sighting of the *Jeremy*.'

'Where?'

'Right here, in Goolwa. Apparently, there's some sort of boat parade on the river tonight.'

'Yeah, that would be the Fairy Boat Parade at the Wooden Boat Festival.'

'Well, according to POLAIR, one boat has turned off its lights and broken away from the group heading upstream.'

Mick chattered away to POLAIR before terminating the call. He turned to Riley.

'Bastards were hiding in plain sight at the wharf waiting for the chance to make a break. POLAIR is going to try to maintain a visual until we get there. Let's go.'

Phil drove to the wharf, siren blaring and lights flashing while Riley organised Duncan to have his boat ready and Mick contacted Cassie.

'Hopefully, we now have these pricks,' said Mick. 'I can't wait to touch up the bastards that did the DI over.'

The set on his face told Riley that Mick was deadly serious.

36

Thursday 18 April 2019 (Day 1)

Vinnie waited, checking Aiden every few minutes making sure he was fully absorbed in his game. Each time, he quietly opened the door, peeped in and closed the door silently behind him.

When Hargreaves and Fantis arrived, they entered quietly. Tony Fantis slid the bolt of the door to ensure they weren't disturbed unexpectedly.

'Hello, Vinnie.' Hargreaves extended his hand. Vinnie felt like he held the handshake too long for comfort. Something was definitely going down.

'Damien, Tony. This is an unexpected visit.'

'Yes, well, it is a bit ad hoc. Is that what they call it, Vince? You're a good man with words. "Ad hoc", yeah that's what it is.'

Vinnie couldn't speak. He watched as Tony Fantis walked around the shed, looking for who knew what. Just like he had in the car showroom all those years ago. His eyes followed Fantis as he opened the office door and looked in.

'Damien, there's a kid in here.'

'Good to know, Tony. Just make sure he doesn't interrupt us. So, Vincent, you've turned this into a family business, eh? Showing the kid the ropes?'

'No, Damien. He's my partner's kid. Just leave him be please.'

'You seem a bit nervous, old son. We're just here for a bit of a chat, aren't we, Tony? So, let's chat. You know that Greg Satchin and his wife had a bit of bad luck, I presume.'

'I read it.' Vinnie was almost shaking.

'Well, it seemed Greg liked our money a lot and thought he should keep some of it for himself. That's not how we play the game, is it, Tony?' The big man made no effort to respond.

'Fraud is not sustainable in our business model, so we had to make some changes, if you follow. We've been watching Gregory very closely for a while now, to see who might be part of his alternative business model. You'll be pleased to know we can't see where you have any involvement. That said, we just want to hear it straight from the horse's mouth. You aren't getting greedy are you, Vince?'

'No, mate, No way. It's all above board and everything I did with Greg was by the rules.'

'I'm pleased to hear that, Vinnie. But, now as an act of good faith, I think we need to see some evidence; call it an audit, if you like.'

'What do you want?'

Hargreaves scratched his chin as if contemplating. Vinnie knew that Hargreaves had come into the shed with a clear plan as to what he wanted.

'By my reckoning, Vincent, you have around half a mill of our money that you're processing. We'd like to make sure you still have it.'

Vinnie felt sweat run down his back. He knew he'd done the right thing by the Anarchists and kept a tight rein on managing their money. The fact that they wanted to see the money concerned him. It showed that they no longer trusted him without question. Just as worrying was that by keeping the cash in a secret, secure location he had some insurance. The cost of getting rid of him was half a million dollars and the Anarchists wouldn't give that up easily. By revealing his safe place, his insurance policy was of little use.

'Obviously, I don't keep the money here, Damien. If this place was raided, the money would be lost and it would be incriminating. Don't worry. I have it all and it's safe.'

Damien walked up to Vinnie. His small stature prevented him from getting right into Vinnie's face but he stood so close their toes were touching. Vinnie felt just as intimidated as if Tony Fantis was eyeballing him. The small man spoke quietly.

'Now, Vince. We are almost family, right? Your boy, Loklan, is my nephew so we're pretty much brothers-in-law. But firstly, that counts for nothin' if you don't run your business the way we want. Second, Louise is pretty pissed that you've cut off payments to support the boy. So, see my loyalties are sort of divided right now.

'You think we can't do without you? You're very wrong, son. In fact, your good mate, Sully, was released a month ago. He's been working with us in the city but he's keen to get back to managing a rural operation. He likes what you've done here but he's got ideas too.

'So, here's the drum, Vincent. You show me our half a million dollars by midday tomorrow – here or at your safe place, I don't care – or there will be consequences. Your kid is very well-behaved, by the way.'

Vinnie didn't miss the meaning. He knew he was shaking and took a step back.

'I'll have the money here tomorrow, midday. But leave my family alone.' His mind was racing. Could he grab the money and disappear before tomorrow? Before he'd convinced himself of the impossibility, Damien spoke.

'Ah, if you're thinking of splitting on us, Vinnie, don't bother. We're going to be very close. See you later, pal.' He motioned to Fantis and they ambled through the side door.

37

Saturday April 27 2019 (Day 10)

It took only a few minutes to get onto the water. The crowd on the wharf was several people deep and they could see hundreds of others on top of the bridge streaming back toward town after the parade.

Riley contacted Oliver and instructed him to have patrol vehicles on the mainland and on Hindmarsh Island in case the Anarchists beached the *Jeremy* and made a run.

Duncan had to weave through the boats that were returning to the wharf from the Fairy Boat Parade. The joviality of those on board the myriad of boats did nothing to help his concentration. Once past them, he pushed his boat at top speed, under the Hindmarsh Island bridge toward the searchlight beaming down from the POLAIR helicopter.

The wind had sprung up from the south and the water became choppy, slapping the bow harshly and forcing them to hold tightly onto anything stable.

Riley called Cassie. 'Where are you?'

Cassie yelled back 'We have a visual on them. I think they're only a couple of hundred metres away. We're slowing to wait for your approach.'

'Good. I think we're still about five hundred metres, judging by the searchlight. We'll be there soon.' Riley noticed the search beam suddenly change direction. 'What's going on, Cass? Is POLAIR breaking off or has the *Jeremy* changed direction?'

'The *Jeremy* has turned toward the island. They must know we're onto them. Oh, Christ, they've thrown something overboard. I think it's a person. Riley, we should save whoever it is.'

'Yes, go. We'll chase down the *Jeremy*.'

Cassie nodded to Hamish and he accelerated his boat toward the figure flailing in the water.

'Fuck, it's Aiden,' screamed Shaun as they got nearer.

The *Jeremy* pulled away at its top speed, which was no match for the boats pursuing, but the diversion they created would buy them more time.

Craig kept his eyes on the *Jeremy* and suddenly called 'they've just chucked someone else off.'

They slowed as they approached Aiden.

Shaun pulled off his shoes and jumped into the water. He grabbed Aiden and settled him before calling back to the boat.

'Throw me a couple of lifejackets. I'll stay with Aiden while you get the other person.'

Rachel had already got them and threw them to him. Hamish pulled away and called to Cassie. 'Where to? I can't see anyone.'

'Over there,' she pointed. In the dim light, they could see a person waving frantically, at times hidden by the waves whipped up by the wind so that they now had white caps. Hamish pointed his searchlight at the figure and headed toward it. It was only a couple of minutes but by the time they arrived at the spot, the person was gone. Hamish swivelled the light, trying to pick up anything on the surface, circling the boat around the spot where the figure had last been seen.

Cassie called Riley and updated him.

'Ok Cassie, we're approaching Shaun now. You stay there and keep searching. We'll resume pursuit of the *Jeremy* in a couple of minutes.'

Duncan eased the boat next to Shaun and Aiden. Phil and Riley leaned over the boat and dragged them aboard, blue and shivering. Mick covered them with blankets.

'Just sit down here and get warm. Riley, I think we need to get these two back to shore for some proper medical attention.'

'To hell with that,' Shaun retorted, 'you can't let them get away now. We'll be fine, won't we, mate?' Aiden nodded in a way that convinced no one.

'There's a flask of tea inside, Mick. That should help.' Duncan looked to Riley who nodded. He pushed the boat forward.

They passed the other boat still circling looking for someone struggling to stay afloat, although it was now looking more like it would be a body.

The beam from POLAIR was now a few hundred metres away, so Mick radioed the chopper to let it know what had happened and to maintain its vigilance.

The *Jeremy* hugged the island side of the river. It was clear it couldn't outrun its pursuers, so the Anarchists searched for a place they could pull in and make a dash on land.

Riley could see headlights on Narnu Bay Road on Hindmarsh Island near where the *Jeremy* was heading. He hoped that the car was a police vehicle watching in case the boat did try to berth and not accomplices of Hargreaves and Fantis there to pick them up.

His question was answered when, into view, a patrol car with lights flashing rounded the corner and boxed in the vehicle. The Anarchists must have noticed too as the *Jeremy* suddenly swung about heading back toward the middle of the river. They were within fifty metres now and closing.

Duncan roared his boat toward the *Jeremy* and had to ease off suddenly when it was obvious it had stopped.

'Why have they stopped?' he called across to Riley.

'Beats me,' he replied.

'They want a fight,' Mick offered. 'They can't fight and drive at the same time so they've decided not to drive. Let's hope it's only the two of them and they're not armed, Riley.'

'Duncan, as we pull alongside, we'll jump on board. Then I want you to pull away and watch. At least fifty metres. I don't want you getting caught in any crossfire. Phil, you're armed?'

Phil nodded grimly.

'Ok,' Riley said. 'No heroics. Let's talk to them first but, Phil, make sure you keep us covered. Ready, Mick?'

'Let's go. I'll take the big bastard if it gets ugly.'

As they broadsided the *Jeremy*, they could see no one on deck. Riley boarded first, followed by Mick, with Phil covering the cabin door with his service gun. He jumped on behind them and they regrouped on the deck on either side of the cabin door. After the roar of Duncan pulling away had faded, Riley shouted through the door.

'Police here, Hargreaves. It's over, mate. Open the door slowly and come out with your hands above your head, one at a time.'

'Fuck off, pigs. You want us, you're going to have to come in.'

Mick laughed. 'We can wait as long as you want, dickhead. You're not going anywhere. In fact, you've just locked yourself away like you're already in the paddy wagon so we can just drive you back to the wharf nice and simple.'

They could hear Fantis and Hargreaves arguing inside. Obviously, one wanted to come out, the other did not. After about thirty seconds, they heard Fantis.

'I'm coming out.'

'Alright, Tony. Come out unarmed and keep your hands where we can see them.'

The cabin door swung open and the huge frame of Tony Fantis filled the doorway. Riley could see that the cabin was in darkness and pulled out his torch. Fantis stepped forward, arms stretched out in front of him. His hands were empty.

'Down on the floor, Tony. Now!' yelled Mick. Tony moved forward another step to allow Riley into the cabin and then with a thunderous yell dropped his shoulder and ran straight at Mick. The policeman felt all the air driven from his lungs as the big man forced him to the back of the *Jeremy* and almost over the side.

Phil Reid still had his gun drawn but couldn't get a clear shot at Fantis. Not that he wanted to fire; he'd never fired a shot in anger before. The cabin door had slammed behind Riley and that meant that he was the only backup that the Detective Sergeant had. He kept his gun aimed at as much of Fantis as he could cover without risking hitting Mick and screamed.

'Get off, Fantis, or I'll shoot. I'll shoot if you don't get off him now.'

Fantis pinned Mick against the stern of the *Jeremy* and gripped his hands tightly around his neck. Mick was trying to get some purchase through his legs but was unable to budge the bikie.

Phil realised he had to do something but he didn't want to shoot. He put his gun away, stepped forward and delivered the strongest punch he could muster to Tony Fantis' kidneys. It was enough to force the big man to stretch out and that gave Mick space to deliver a punch to his throat.

Mick shoved Fantis onto the floor. He knelt on his head and pinned his arms behind his back.

'Cuffs,' he yelled at Phil. The young policeman had already pulled them from his belt and sat on Fantis' legs as he fastened them around his wrists.

'Thanks for your help, Phil,' Mick puffed. 'I would have got him, myself, you know. Eventually.' He stood and delivered a sharp kick to Fantis' ribs. 'That one is from my boss, you prick.'

Riley had entered the cabin and was startled when the door slammed shut behind him. He felt an arm close around his neck and a stabbing pain in his back. Damien Hargreaves was standing on the bunk, the only way he could have reached his arm around Riley's neck.

'Don't move, copper, or I'll have to slice you. I don't know what's going on out there, but whoever's in control doesn't matter because you're going to call off your mates and let us go.'

Through the door, they could hear the scuffling outside and it wasn't clear who was in control. Riley looked around the cabin. On the bed were two large rubbish bin bags filled; he expected with cash, or drugs, or both.

Mick's booming voice suddenly came through.

'We're sorted out here, Riley. Is it good for us to come in?'

Hargreaves leant closer to the door, keeping his grip and the knife, on Riley.

'No, it's not good, pig. I've got a knife in your man's back here and if you try to come in, I'm going to poke it right through him, got it.'

'Alright, Damien, calm down. I'm sure we can work this out.'

'Too right, we can. Here's what's going to happen if you want your mate to live. You two pigs are going to jump off the boat and swim well away, alright? After I've heard two big splashes and Tony tells me it's all clear, then we're going to come out and be on our way. If you all behave nicely, we'll drop this bloke off somewhere nice and safe once we're off. Can you hear me, Tony?'

'Yeah,' the muffled voice came back.

'Sounds like you stuffed up.'

'Yeah, well I had two of them, didn't I? Hey, you,' Fantis yelled at Phil, 'make sure you leave the keys to them cuffs behind.'

'Good one, mate. Alright, coppers, let's hear some splashing.'

Riley knew that if Mick and Phil left the boat, his chances of getting off alive were significantly reduced. His torch was still pointed at the two bags on the bed. Clearly, the contents were significant enough for the two Anarchists to play for high stakes. He decided he would have to at least match them. In a single fluid movement, he raised his arm flashing the torch into Damien Hargreaves' face, at the same time spinning his body away from him and his threatening blade.

Riley's momentum and the sudden flash of blindness were enough to throw Hargreaves toward the bow of the boat, stumbling as he fell onto the floor. He jumped to his feet and flashed the knife toward Riley.

Keeping his focus on Hargreaves, Riley felt behind his back and unlatched the cabin door. Phil and Mick looked in expectantly, Phil with his eye looking along the barrel of his firearm, held steadily in both hands. Riley stole a glance at him before turning back to Hargreaves.

'So, how's this going to end, Damien? You can come at me with that knife but by the time you take a step, the constable here will shoot you. Isn't that right, Phil?'

'Certainly is, sir', Phil replied with an assurance he didn't really feel.

Hargreaves looked at the men in front of him. He smirked before dropping the knife to the ground and raising his arms. Riley stepped forward and pinned his arms behind him while Phil fastened cuffs to his wrists. They pushed him out of the cabin onto the deck.

'Looks like you stuffed up too, Damo,' a prostate Fantis mumbled.

Mick waved to Duncan's boat and moments later it pulled alongside.

'If someone can drive that thing, I think I should get these guys back for some first aid before they die of hypothermia,' Duncan called out.

Phil was at the helm. 'No worries. I've got it.'

Duncan sped off and left them to make their way back to where Rachel, Cassie and Craig were still searching for the woman thrown from the *Jeremy*. Three other boats were also working an expanded area, searchlights sweeping across the angry waves.

The POLAIR helicopter had left the site, needing to refuel. Its search had been called off for the night and it was clear that it was now a search and recover mission, not a search and rescue.

Riley left instructions for the boats to continue their search for no more than an hour. If needed they would resume in the morning. The *Jeremy* made its way steadily back to shore, choosing to berth at the Goolwa Regatta Yacht Club, rather than close to the wharf. Even though most of the Wooden Boat Festival crowd had dispersed, apart from a few curious bystanders, the *Jeremy* was now a crime scene and needed to be secured.

Oliver was there to meet them and, shortly after, a second patrol car arrived.

'What happened on the island, Oliver?' Mick asked.

'We found a couple of chaps waiting for some mates to arrive by boat. Funny, that. They're on their way to Christies Beach for processing.'

'That's good. It'll take the load off us for a while. We can talk with them tomorrow. Let's get these two back to the station here. Can't wait to have a chat with them.'

Riley joined them. 'Mick, can I get you and Phil to start interviewing Hargreaves and Fantis? I want to check on Shaun and Aiden. I won't be long.'

Riley walked to the ambulance he saw parked near the ramp at the aquatic club. Shaun and Aiden sat in the back. Colour was returning to their faces but they still had the full attention of the paramedics.

'Will you talk some sense into this bloke, officer?' one of the ambos called to Riley. 'We want them to go to the hospital for treatment but he doesn't seem to understand that their body temperatures are around thirty-four degrees and that's still dangerously low.'

Riley climbed into the back of the ambulance. Shaun was reasonably well composed but Aiden looked drowsy and confused.

'Mate, you need to do what the ambos are telling you. There's no more you can do here right now other than to make sure Aiden gets the care he needs ... and you need, too.'

'But, Riley, I want to confront the bastards that took my son.'

'Well, firstly, we can't let that happen. You have to leave them to us now. Secondly, you don't want to have gone through everything you have so far to put Aiden at risk now. So just go to the hospital. I'll make sure Carla is updated and that she gets there as soon as possible. Alright?'

'Yeah, You're right. Thanks, Riley.'

Riley turned to Aiden.

'You ok, mate?' he asked. Aiden nodded weakly.

Riley rested his hand on Aiden's hand. It felt frozen.

'Aiden, I just need to ask you one question. Did you know who the lady was that was on the boat with you?'

Aiden shook his head. 'No,' was all he could get out.

Riley patted him gently. 'That's ok, buddy. We'll sort that out later.'

He climbed out and watched the ambulance head off, lights flashing.

To his surprise, a patrol car arrived to pick him up.

He arrived back at the station to a flurry of activity. Hargreaves and Fantis had been separated and Oliver was at the front desk preparing paperwork. The officers from Adelaide were de-briefing in the meeting room, an excited buzz emanating from a group that had seen a lot more action than they had anticipated.

Riley tapped Oliver on the shoulder.

'Good work today, Oliver. Picking up those two on the island was the icing on the cake.'

'Thanks, Riley. Biggest day of my career so far, that's for sure. Anything else I can do for you?'

Well, I'm just about to call Carla Waters and let her know what's happened if she doesn't already know. Do you reckon you could organise for one of the blokes to run her to the hospital at Victor Harbor?'

'Done. The DS and Phil are in with Damien Hargreaves. Will you be joining them after you call Carla?'

'I will. I'm sure Phil will be looking for a break. Or something to eat.'

Riley went to one of the small rooms and called Carla. She had been trying to call Shaun for over an hour but had been unable to get through. Riley explained that his phone had taken an unexpected fall into the river but that he was fine. He also told her, to her relief, that they had rescued Aiden and Shaun's heroics had saved him from drowning in the river. She was in tears by the time he explained that they were in hospital and that he had arranged a car to take her there.

He knocked on the door to the interview room. Mick Martin came out, leaving Phil to watch Hargreaves. He had a grim expression on his face.

'Bastard's not talking until his lawyer arrives. I suggest we leave the smug prick in a cell for a few hours. His lawyer won't be able to help him too much on this one.'

'I agree. We can try Fantis but I reckon he'll keep his mouth shut as well. Before we return him to the cell, I just want to talk to Damien for a minute.'

They returned to the interview room. Phil excused himself and Riley and Mick took seats opposite the little man. Riley laid his hands flat on the table.

'So, Damien, I understand you don't wish to talk to us until your lawyer arrives. That's ok. We think we have enough to charge you with the murders of Greg and Patricia Satchin, the murder of Vinnie Waters, the assault of a police officer, various drug and money laundering offences, the abduction of Aiden Waters and probably the attempted murder of that boy and an unnamed woman.'

'Mate, I don't know what you're talking about. I'm admitting nothin' but I can tell you right now, I don't know anything about half the shit you're putting on us. Honest. Where's my fucking lawyer?'

They took the dejected Damien Hargreaves to his cell to await the arrival of Gavin Trower, the Anarchists' lawyer. They had pulled him away from a basketball game at which he was hosting a corporate box. It wasn't the first time his respectable persona had been hijacked by his shady dealings and he had perfected the art of leaving important events with a smile on his face while he was fuming inside.

Riley and Mick tried their hand at persuading Tony Fantis to admit something. They thought he lacked the intelligence and sheer cunning of Hargreaves; but he, too, kept his mouth shut.

They waited for Cassie, Rachel and Craig to return from the river. They were all tired and frustrated at not finding the body of the woman the Anarchists had thrown into the river. Riley called the team into the big meeting room for a de-brief before sending them home for the night. He and Mick would need to stay behind until Gavin Trower arrived and they could formally interview Hargreaves and Fantis.

Riley opened the discussion.

'Good job today, everyone. I know it's been disappointing not to have saved the woman who was thrown off the *Jeremy*, but on the positive side, we did save a little boy and we apprehended two vicious murderers and two of their accomplices. So, let's keep a focus on the positives.

'Tomorrow we can launch a better search for the woman and we'll bring in more resources to deal with that. I want you all to have some well-deserved rest before returning to duty. Is that clear?'

There were appreciative nods around the table.

'So, where we are at right now, is that we have Hargreaves and Fantis here waiting for their lawyer to arrive. We expect that we'll be able to charge them and get them in front of a magistrate tomorrow. The team in Adelaide is confident they have enough to get a conviction on the Loxton murders, so that will get the process started. Most of us were also witnesses to them throwing two people off the *Jeremy* so we'll add charges for attempted murder on those two counts as soon as we can get the paperwork completed. Likewise, we'll have them on the assault of DI Smith.'

'What about the murder of Vinnie Waters and Aiden's abduction?' Rachel asked.

Mick intervened. 'Much as I think they're guilty, we haven't yet got all the evidence together to make a watertight case. They certainly are not admitting to anything yet. There are also going to be charges on drug-related offences and money laundering but we need Shaun and Oliver to compile all the transactional data they have. We'll also get forensics onto the *Jeremy*, including two very interesting bags we found on board.'

'Sir,' Cassie offered, 'is there a risk that those two didn't kill Waters and abduct the boy? I mean, if they took the kid, the woman must have been an accomplice, but then why would they chuck her in the water? If they didn't abduct Aiden, how can we be sure they killed Vinnie?'

'It's a good point, Cassie,' Riley said. 'We know they were at the shed; we know they killed the Satchins and we know they had a business relationship with Vinnie. Agreed, it's all circumstantial but if we can match their fingerprints to the wrench Vinnie was knocked out with or to the winch control, it's a lot more convincing.'

'Then how does the woman fit in?'

'I don't know. I think we need to find out who she was to answer that.'

A rapping on the front door of the station distracted them. Rachel jumped involuntarily at the sound.

Phil went to the door and returned a few moments later.

'Riley, there's a guy out front that wants to talk to you.'

'If that's the lawyer, he got here quick smart.'

'He's not dressed like a lawyer. He says he knows you. A guy called Chad Grey.'

38

Thursday 18 April 2019 (Day 1)

The woman sat in her car on a side street facing the boatshed. She wasn't sure whether Vinnie would be here and had taken a chance that he was. She'd intended to drive right up to the shed, where she saw the Land Rover parked. She assumed it was Vinnie's. She decided against turning into the lane when she saw two men get out of a blue Commodore and start walking toward the shed. Looked like Vinnie had a business meeting, she thought. She decided to wait and watch, pulling into the side street where she could have a good view.

She almost laughed, watching them walk side by side. They had the swagger of tough guys but looked more like Danny DeVito and Arnold Schwarzenegger in Twins. DeVito had a bit more padding, though.

She waited for them to leave. It didn't worry her; it was important that she talk to Vinnie alone. After fifteen minutes, she saw the shed door open and the two emerged. They walked out the same way that they walked in and, not wanting to be seen by them, she ducked below the level of the dash. Once she was sure they were in the car, she lifted her head and watched as they drove away.

She started the engine and drove slowly toward the shed, parking next to Vinnie's car only a few metres from the side door. She looked in the rear vision mirror and tidied a few strands of wayward hair.

The shed door opened easily and she took a moment to allow her eyes to adjust to the relative darkness compared to the bright sun outside. She saw Vinnie working under a large boat, unaware of her entry. His movements did not seem as relaxed and easy as she remembered. He looked clumsy and swore as a wrench slipped.

'What's wrong, Vinnie? Things not going the way you want,' she said.

'What the fuck? Who's that?' He slipped from under the boat and blinked as he looked at her silhouette against the open door.

'Hello, Vinnie.'

'Shit, Debbie. What are you doing here?'

'Do you remember how you let our son die? Remember destroying our family?'

'That was a long time ago, Debbie. And, if I recall, it was you that moved away.'

'Because you sent me,' she screamed. 'You ruined everything. And now you're destroying another family.'

'What the fuck are you talking about?'

'Carla. That's what I'm talking about. My replacement. All complete with a replacement for *Jeremy* thrown in. It's all worked out pretty well for you, hasn't it Vinnie.' Tears streamed down her face and she wiped them with the sleeve of her shirt.

'Debbie, you're being irrational. Me being with Carla has nothing to do with you or *Jeremy*.'

'Fuck you, Vinnie. Here's something rational. I want my boat.'

'What?'

'You heard me. I want the *Jeremy*. Where are the keys?'

'Go, Debbie, just go. You need help, you're a lunatic.' He threw the wrench to the floor.

Vinnie turned away. There was no way he could let Debbie anywhere near the *Jeremy*. It wasn't the boat he was concerned about; it was still registered in her name. It was the five hundred thousand dollars and stocks of various drugs stashed inside the boat.

He walked to the side of the boat and knelt to check where he'd been working. He hoped that if he ignored Debbie, she'd just walk out and leave him alone.

Debbie didn't leave. She stood for a moment, stung by his words. She followed him around the boat, bent and picked up the wrench. As Vinnie raised from his knelt position, she swung it with all her might, catching him on the side of the head. He dropped to the floor rolling onto his back.

Debbie recoiled in horror. This wasn't what she had intended. She just wanted to ball him out and get her boat. The doctors had said she needed to keep up her medication and keep building her new life. She wanted her new life to be as an independent woman living on a river-boat; travelling up and down the Murray, earning some money when she needed it by working in veterinary practises along the way.

She would still do that. She just needed to find the keys to the *Jeremy*. They'd be on the hook in the office.

Fearing the office door was locked she tentatively turned the handle. To her surprise, a young boy sat at a computer. With earphones on and distracted by the game he was playing, he was oblivious to her presence.

Debbie stepped back out of the office and closed the door. *Jeremy? It couldn't be.* She shook her head. *No, this wasn't Jeremy; this was the boy Vinnie had replaced Jeremy with.*

She tried to process it. She wanted her boat for her future but what she really wanted was her old life with a son who lived and breathed. She could have both. She ran to her car and pulled open the glove box.

Inside was a plastic bag containing a syringe and a small vial. The label on the front identified the vial as containing 'Ketamine'. Debbie had stolen it from the veterinarian practice in Mount Barker where she worked. There it was used as an anaesthetic or analgesic on various animals but she had learned that it was commonly used as a recreational drug and was also being tested for use in treating depression. The first time she had stolen some, she had a high that she'd never experienced before, dissociated but happy. Then, when she came off the high, she felt uncoordinated and clumsy. With practice, she'd refined the dosage so that most times she had a good time.

She had it in her glovebox for that reason but now she wanted it for something else. She'd assisted the vet anaesthetise several animals and was confident she could work out the right dosage. She prepared the syringe and walked back into the shed.

Inside the office, the boy was still playing Minecraft. She crept behind him and inserted the needle, restraining him until the full dosage was injected. It took thirty seconds for the boy to slump in the chair. Debbie released him gently and started to search for the keys to the *Jeremy*. As she had expected, the key was on a hook with several others. The keyring identified the boat but also where it was stored; the Riverside Marina.

She had the boat. She could have the boy too. The dilemma played on her mind. The boy was about the age that Jeremy would have been. She deserved another chance at motherhood.

He was lighter than she expected. Using a fireman's lift, she easily carried him out to her car and she laid him across the back seat.

Returning to the shed, she noticed that Vinnie hadn't moved; she wanted to feel for a pulse but couldn't bring herself to do it. Instead, she twisted his body so that his legs and lower torso were under the boat.

Satisfied that the position was right, she went to the control for the electric winch. Anyone would think it was a horrible accident. *Bastard's got what he deserved.*

Debbie ran to the shed door, suddenly fearing the boy might be starting to stir. Relieved that he was still out cold, she returned to the shed and picked up the wrench. She closed the door behind her and latched the padlock. With all the strength she could summon, she tossed the wrench into the water, returned to her car and drove off.

39

Saturday 27 April 2019 (Day 10)

It had been nine days and Debbie was at her wit's end. When she'd got to the boat with the boy, the guy who looked like he managed the marina had startled her but she'd got past that and she hadn't seen him since.

When the boy woke, he was disoriented and confused. He didn't seem to remember his name was Jeremy and that she was his mother. He kept crying and saying his name was Aiden, which made no sense. She found she had to keep him sedated just to stop him from bawling all the time. Surely after a week, he would realise who he was.

She'd been cautious, leaving the boat only at night, when the manager had gone for the day, and when she had ensured that the boy was sufficiently drugged. That had allowed her to do shopping at the local supermarket. She'd bought a newspaper early on and read about Vinnie's death and the disappearance of an eleven-year-old boy. It was hard for her to process. They called the boy Aiden and said he was the son of Vinnie's partner. Debbie was Vinnie's ex-wife, not partner and their son was Jeremy, not Aiden. And he wasn't missing; she was protecting him.

After a week, she'd started to doubt herself. She knew she hadn't been well but that was ages ago. Her doctors had cleared her and she'd been released from hospital so she must be better. She felt so well, she stopped her medication, apart from the self-prescribed ketamine when she needed it. The conflict between what she believed and what the boy and the papers were saying confused her. She needed time to process it.

An option she'd considered was to take the boy to the police and explain what had happened. That would have cleared it all up; but then there was Vinnie's death. How could she have explained that?

It was not an option any more. That all changed the day before. The boy was laying exhausted on a bunk. The drugs had made him become disoriented and he seemed to have lost his memory of everything that had happened in the last few days. Debbie took the other bunk and dropped into a deep sleep. Late in the afternoon, she was woken by the sound of the cabin door opening; she'd forgotten to lock it.

Debbie jumped up to the vision of two men in the cabin; the same two she'd seen at Vinnie's shed a week before.

'What do we have here, Tony?'

'Isn't she Vinnie's ex?' the big man said.

'I reckon. Who's the kid, lady? He's not the one the cops are going mental over, is he?'

'What do you want?' Debbie asked with a tremble in her voice. 'Just leave me and my boy, please.'

Damien Hargreaves walked and stood over the boy, still out to it on the bunk. He spotted a vial on the counter and picked it up.

He laughed. 'She's been giving the kid KitKat, Tony. Ketamine. No wonder he's a zombie. Alright, lady, here's what's going to happen. There's some of our property on this boat and that's all we're here for. I'd like to say that once we find it, we'll be on our way but unfortunately, our car's broken down so we're going to have to borrow Vincent's boat. Don't worry, we'll drop you off somewhere out of town and if you and the kid really behave yourselves, it won't be in the river.'

Debbie made for the door but was restrained by the brute hands of Tony Fantis.

'Not a good start, lady. Better tie them both up, Tony. We can't have them running around while we look for our stuff. Must be some rope on a boat, you'd think.'

An hour later, they'd uncovered a number of hidden cavities. Panels lay strewn across the cabin floor and the bunk that Debbie had been sleeping on was covered with bundles of banknotes and bags of various drugs. Debbie sat wide-eyed and aghast.

That night, Hargreaves and Fantis sat at the galley table to plan their next move. They decided to leave the marina in the morning. That gave them time to become familiar with the *Jeremy* and its operation. They would take the boat downstream and hide out near Hindmarsh Island until evening - enough time to arrange for associates to come down from Adelaide to pick them up.

In the evening, they would slip the boat amongst the boats in the Wooden Boat Fairy Boat Parade, where the *Jeremy* would not look out of place. At the end of a loop, they would slip quietly under the Hindmarsh Island bridge and pull into the upriver side of the bridge to be picked up by their associates.

40

Saturday 27 April 2019 (Day 10)

It was late. The team had been at it all day and the guys from Goolwa and Victor Harbor were not accustomed to that intensity. The adrenalin that had driven them all through the day was starting to wane. They had successfully apprehended the murderers of the Satchins and Vinnie Waters. More importantly, they had saved Aiden Waters; privately, Riley knew that they had all, even Shaun, feared he was dead. The exhilaration of the day's success was ebbing with the realisation that there was a woman still somewhere out in the water, probably drowned. Now they were all filled with the dread of resuming the search the next day, almost certainly a search and recover operation.

Riley sent everyone home. Mick Martin wanted a private chat with him after he had attended to Chad Grey but Riley was exhausted and he convinced Mick they could do it in the morning. The question on Riley's mind was what Chad could possibly want on a Saturday night when the station was not supposed to be open. He assumed that Chad knew about the events of the night and perhaps thought he could get a heads-up to pass on to the good citizens of Goolwa.

Chad had a drinking problem. *Who could blame him?* The best years of his life confined in a wheelchair, no real job, no permanent place to live and no female companionship that lasted more than a couple of months. Sure, he'd brought a lot of it onto himself, but Riley still felt genuine empathy for his old schoolmate.

Riley opened the door to the front reception area. Chad was drinking from a vodka bottle that was now only one-third full.

'Hi, Chad. It's late, mate. Shouldn't you be heading home? I can give you a lift if you want.'

Chad looked up at him through foggy eyes. He slurred when he spoke.

'I don't need a ride, Riley. Got my own wheels ... in case you didn't notice. I saw your lights were on so I thought I'd just drop in. I know, if you'd known I was coming, you'd have baked a cake.' He erupted into laughter until he caught his breath and started coughing harshly.

'Chad, I've had a big day. Did you have a reason to come in now, this late?'

'Yeah, you've been busy. I hear you dragged in a couple of blokes. Did they kill Vinnie?'

'Well, we believe so. Why?'

'Why? That's the question, Senior Sergeant.' Chad mocked. 'Personally, I'd give those blokes a medal for fixing up Vinnie fucking Waters. Anyway, I digress, don't I? The thing is, Riley, I don't give a flying fuck about Vinnie. That prick has always made my life miserable. I don't think much of Shaun either, but I guess he never really did me any wrong. He's just piss poor.'

'Are you heading somewhere with this, Chad?'

'Yeah, yeah, sorry. I've had a bit to drink, but you know that don't you? I'm in here because of Shaun's kid.'

'What about him? Do you know something?'

'It's not the kid's fault, is it?' Chad started weeping. 'I should have come here before but, you know, I didn't work it out.'

Riley sat on the bench next to Chad and laid a hand on his shoulder.

'It's ok, mate. Better late than never,' Riley said without meaning it. If Chad had had a lead on Aiden's whereabouts, they could potentially have solved his disappearance days ago. 'What do you have?'

'They said there was a woman missing in the river. I reckon I know who it could be. I think it's Debbie McLean, Vinnie's ex.'

Riley's shock was obvious. He looked queryingly into Chad's eyes. They were moist and opaque; the eyes of a broken man whose life was hallmarked by a sequence of tragedies, followed by periods of self-pity and remorse. Riley's tone was gentler.

'What makes you think it's her?'

'I saw her in Mount Barker a couple of weeks ago. She's been trying to get back on her feet. She'd been in and out of mental institutions for a few years after her breakdown.'

'After Jeremy? I know. What did she say?'

'Nothing much at first. It didn't seem like she even knew me for a while. Then she might have figured we had a bit in common. We've both been screwed over by Vinnie. Anyway, she was telling me how she was working as a vet nurse in Mount Barker and how she was coming good but still seeing a shrink and all that stuff.

'Then she started asking about Vinnie and it got a bit weird. I told her that Vinnie had kicked me out of my flat, put me on the street. And then I told her how he'd screwed Shaun over too; you know, pinching his wife and all. I said that him and Carla were all happy families now, living together and how he even had Aiden to replace Jeremy. Not the best way to put it, I know, but it felt good to share my bitterness with someone that knew what Vinnie was really like.'

Riley knew he had to be patient but still wasn't sure where this was heading. The fact that they had an unknown woman lost in the river meant that he needed to take every lead that was presented.

'So, Chad. What did Debbie say to you that makes you think she's involved in this?'

'Like I said, it got weird. Up until then, she'd been like her old self but then she started getting really excited and not making much sense, to be honest. She said that she blamed Vinnie for Jeremy's death. Can't blame her for that; he should have been more careful. But she said stuff like "Vinnie's ruined my life. Well, I can ruin his too." She was really pissed that she'd lost everything, especially her son, and now Vinnie had basically got back to normal with a new partner and son. She also thought that Vinnie had always wanted a piece of Carla.

'The last thing she said to me was that she was going to confront Vinnie and get what was rightfully hers back, starting with Jeremy. I thought "Fuck, she's really lost it now." You know what I mean?'

Riley was silent and pensive. Chad took a swig from his bottle. Riley turned to him.

'Chad, I need you to think carefully. Did Debbie say she was going to get Jeremy back or *the Jeremy*? Vinnie bought a boat for Debbie called *Jeremy*.'

'Shit, look at me, man. Do I look like I could tell the difference? I don't know. Sorry.'

'It's ok, mate. You could have filled in a few gaps for us. What say we get you home?'

41

Epilogue – One Month Later

Paul Smith sat on a recliner seat surrounded by a small group of well-wishers scattered on sofas and dining chairs. His wife, Kathy, emerged from the kitchen with a tray of teas, coffees and biscuits that she put on a table in the centre of the room.

'It's so good to have him home, Mick. I mean the hospital gave him the best care medically but I can make him much more comfortable at home, can't I, love?'

Paul shot a glance at Mick Martin, lifting his eyebrows.

'You're doing a great job, Kath, but I have to say that I'm busting to get back to work.'

Riley and Kate sat on a lounge while Rachel and Cassie sat on dining chairs.

'So, when do you think you'll be cleared to return, sir?' Riley asked.

Smith looked to Kate. He'd liked her from the moment they were introduced.

'Kate, will you tell this clown that he doesn't need to call me "sir" in casual conversation? I've tried so many times I can't count but maybe he'll listen to you.'

Kate laughed and said, 'He's still in training but I'll do my best, Paul.' She nudged Riley in the ribs.

Cassie interjected. 'Have you noticed he's avoided the question, Riley? So, when will you be back at work?'

Smith grimaced as he shifted position. 'That's still under negotiation. I want to return to full duties but the powers that be want me to take a desk role.'

'And, so you should,' Kathy scolded, 'you're not getting any younger, Paul.'

'And I reckon we have enough good people to cover you in the field,' added Mick.

Smith cast a glance at Riley. 'Which brings me to a question for you. Let's say I do agree to a desk-based role, and I'm not saying I will. In my mind, we'll need to add more resources to my team for fieldwork. It would be great if you could join us; I agree with Mick that we have some good people already but I reckon you're ready to join the detective ranks.'

Mick nodded and Cassie clapped her hands excitedly. Rachel had been sitting on a dining chair and was the one person who seemed off-put by the proposal.

Riley looked at Kate. He knew she would go along with whatever he decided but the fact was that he wasn't sure what he wanted. He enjoyed the challenge of a major investigation but he also loved working in his community.

'I don't know, sir. I'd need to think on it.'

'Alright, you do that.' Smith winked at Riley. 'Anyway, bring me up to date. What's been the wash-up in Goolwa town after this latest drama?'

Riley was relieved at the change of topic.

'Well, Shaun and Carla are working on their relationship. I think, or at least I hope, they'll make it. Young Aiden is doing remarkably well after his ordeal and it doesn't look like he'll suffer any long-term ill effects.'

'And Emma Satchin?'

'Obviously, her relatives are pleased to know she's ok. I don't think she'll be returning to Loxton anytime soon. She's still staying with Sally and Callum and they seem to be happy to let that run for as long as she wants.

'One surprise has come out of Vinnie's death. He'd appointed Shaun as his executor; not even Shaun knew that. But anyway, it seems that Vinnie left the whole of his estate to Loklan, the son he never really knew. Of course, the trick will be working out what of Vinnie's assets are legitimate and what are the proceeds of crime.'

'I don't envy Shaun on that one,' Smith said. 'What's the latest with Hargreaves and Fantis?'

Mick responded. 'We've charged them with the murders of Greg and Pat Satchin and with the manslaughter of Debbie McLean. We could charge them with the attempted murder of Aiden Chambers but whether that sticks will depend on whether Aiden will testify. Oh, we also have them for aggravated assault on a police officer, namely you. That was downgraded from attempted murder, but they'll still get up to five years for that on top of everything else. It looks like they'll plead guilty to all those charges so they'll be away for quite a while and we're still processing the drug-related charges.'

'What about that other sleaze-ball, Graham Cole?'

'Well, he's just a bit player. We got him on drug-related charges but we didn't pursue him on your assault. There wasn't enough to prove he was an active participant and he did cooperate in nailing the other two. Of course, we'd been planning on using his cooperation to get Fantis and Hargreaves for the murder of Vinnie Waters but that didn't pan out.'

Smith smirked. 'A woman scorned. Who'd have seen Debbie McLean coming into the picture?'

'Very sad,' Riley said. 'You know, along with Carla, Vinnie and Shaun, Debbie was one of my closest friends at high school.'

'You certainly have a knack for personal involvement in cases down there, Riley.'

'I know, sir, Goolwa's a small town and I guess I've known most of the long-term residents for much of my life. It's what I love about my job.'

With that, Smith knew he had an uphill battle to convince Riley to join his team in Adelaide.

ACKNOWLEDGEMENTS: ▌

Firstly, I want to thank all those readers of my first novel, *The Grave At The Top Of The Hill*. The positive feedback and continued interest provided the spur that allowed *Still Waters* to be born. It's one thing to have an idea for a second story – it's something else entirely persevering to make it happen and hopefully be as well received as the first.

Again, I relied heavily on Wendy and Judy to provide honest and meaningful feedback on the initial draft(s) of the manuscript. The characters, in particular, are better for your input.

My good friend, Phill Jones, with whom I have shared the odd red wine and dozens of stories, thought the book would benefit from the inclusion of extra challenges. Vinnie's liaison with his half-sister arose from one of Phill's "truth is stranger than fiction" stories (apologies to Yvonne and her family). Also, I would never have known what a shaduf was had it not been for Phill's challenge to include the word in this book.

It is always helpful having someone that can sense-check a writer's interpretation of facts obtained through research. I am grateful to Ally Gosling who, as a paramedic, provided guidance on some of the medical-related sections in the book – the impact of crush injuries; the effects of certain drugs and the ways that ambos might respond to an incident. If there are errors in the book in these areas, I am confident it was the result of my failure to correctly interpret Ally's advice.

Still Waters does not have the same historical context as *The Grave At The Top Of The Hill*. However, I had always been keen to recognise a Goolwa identity in one of my books. Hector Semaschko was a person I never met, but I heard a lot about from our former Goolwa neighbours Mary and Eldon Zimmermann. Hector was known as the Old Man of the Lake and his life is commemorated by a street name on Hindmarsh Island, a jetty near the Goolwa Wharf and at a couple of private enterprises. Mary Zimmermann was very generous in filling in many gaps in my knowledge of Hector, particularly in terms of his personality and habits. Thank you, Mary. I hope I have done this fascinating man justice through his cameo in *Still Waters*.

ACKNOWLEDGEMENTS:

Geoff Malpas is another friend who always has a story to tell. As a retired copper, he was able to give me some good insight into the police cadet program in place during the 1990s. It's also fair to say that there could be a little bit of Geoff in some of the senior police characters in this book.

Raechel was born and bred in Goolwa and she, in fact, went through her own adolescence during the era that my young characters did. Raechel gave me great understanding of what life was like for young people during the 90s, what they did in their free time and where they hung out.

Peter and Meredith Young were the test audience for the rough drafts of Still Waters. You each provided feedback on the plot and whether the story stuck together. It was also most helpful to know what readers have analysed at various stages of a novel. As the drafts evolved there became an opportunity to develop some side stories, incorporate false leads and assess the whodunit rating.

In completing the final versions of the book, I am immensely grateful to Heather England for her proofreading and other constructive feedback.

I want to thank Yvonne Jones who created the cover art for Still Waters. A fabulous artist and Goolwa resident, she was able to translate my concept image into a piece of work that reflects exactly the mood I was looking for – three mates on the cusp of adolescence, treading their way gently through still waters; not knowing the challenges that lay beneath the surface; not knowing what the future held for them individually and together. Beautifully done, Yvonne.

Finally, it's worth acknowledging that nearly all characters in this book (and in "The Grave" as well) are an amalgam of people I have met throughout life. If any of my friends or relatives, or past or present acquaintances, think that they can see a little bit of themselves in any of my characters, you never know; perhaps there is. I will neither confirm nor deny it, but I thank you for the impression you have made on me through our journey.

The Grave At The Top Of The Hill
Goolwa Murders #1

In 1854, the barque Mozambique runs aground off the coast of South Australia. Among its unremarkable cargo, one item stands out as a once-in-a-lifetime opportunity for a mariner who has taken the hard road to the town of Goolwa. But his decision comes at a cost, one that will haunt him and his descendants for over 150 years.

Fast forward to the present day, where a robber is caught digging up a Scotsman's gravesite. As the investigation unfolds, a web of intrigue stretching back to the wreck of the Mozambique begins to emerge. With his guilt weighing heavy on his conscience, the robber must delve into the dark secrets of the past to uncover the uncanny links between the crimes of 1854 and the present day. But as he confronts his own demons, he realizes that absolution may come at a price he's not willing to pay.

In this gripping tale of mystery and redemption, the past and present collide, revealing a haunting tale that will keep you on the edge of your seat until the very end.

Testimonials (by real readers)

What a GREAT read. Well done
I was hooked until the end.
Tania J

...... really enjoyed it. Loved that I knew all the locations and how the story intertwined between past and present. Have recommended it to many.
Wendy C

I bought a copy of this book ...... about 11:00 am Friday ..., I reluctantly put it down to make myself some lunch (about 2:00 pm), had to put it down again when my dog demanded his dinner and again to cook some dinner for myself (8:00 pm), finished it just now at 12:30 am. It's been a long time since I found a book down hard to put down but this one really had me glued to my seat. ......Great story. Highly recommended.
Jan M

My Hubby soo enjoyed this book, we're off to buy another to send to family in U.K.
Margaret B

Just finished reading .... loved it, can't wait for the next one
Yvonne J

Great read the plot keeps you glued to the book.
Phillip J

Just finished reading this book. Brilliant, couldn't put it down, house-work suffered!!
Pamela S

I've never read such a great story before, the research you must have done, whoooo, unbelievable & yes I could almost think I knew some of the Goolwa folk we have already posted your book to U.K. But I'm buying yet another for our son who lives in NSW
Marg B

I loved it.... couldn't put it down.
Jan McM

Great book I enjoyed reading it
Jennifer N

Once picked up again could not put it down until finished. Abso-lutely loved it. Can't wait for your next book.
Brigitte S

Just finished it...unfortunately!! A great read
Lynne J

Just finished reading ..... The idea was clever - the crossover in time & characters was different yet how it all came together. I found myself trying to solve the crimes as I read, but the twists & turns kept the mystery.
Jane J